"A commanding voice in the historical fiction genre . . .
Holland consistently satisfies her readers."
—*Publishers Weekly*

ACCLAIM FOR THE NOVELS OF CECELIA HOLLAND

"[Holland] is at all times a superb storyteller, and her talents have never been better displayed. She not only re-creates a prehistoric people with every aspect of their life opened up for us; she also makes us share that life." —*The Cleveland Plain Dealer*

"[An] intelligently and lushly developed saga . . . moves with great energy but without neglecting rich detail; the dim past springs to buoyant and believable life." —*Booklist*

"Lively and entertaining . . . a rousing good read." —*Kirkus Reviews*

"Engrossing narrative . . . excellent descriptions." —*Los Angeles Herald Examiner*

"Miss Holland's style is simple, almost stark. She belongs to that small band of writers who can still show us what distinction the historical novel can attain." —*The Times Literary Supplement*

"Full of action and imaginative twists of plot. A considerable achievement." —*The New York Times Book Review*

"A fast-paced, action-driven, and highly satisfying saga . . . a wonderful story." —*Library Journal*

D0167100

The Secret Eleanor

A Novel of Eleanor of Aquitaine

CECELIA HOLLAND

BERKLEY BOOKS, NEW YORK

THE BERKLEY PUBLISHING GROUP
Published by the Penguin Group
Penguin Group (USA) Inc.
375 Hudson Street, New York, New York 10014, USA
Penguin Group (Canada), 90 Eglinton Avenue East, Suite 700, Toronto, Ontario M4P 2Y3, Canada
(a division of Pearson Penguin Canada Inc.)
Penguin Books Ltd., 80 Strand, London WC2R 0RL, England
Penguin Group Ireland, 25 St. Stephen's Green, Dublin 2, Ireland (a division of Penguin Books Ltd.)
Penguin Group (Australia), 250 Camberwell Road, Camberwell, Victoria 3124, Australia
(a division of Pearson Australia Group Pty. Ltd.)
Penguin Books India Pvt. Ltd., 11 Community Centre, Panchsheel Park, New Delhi—110 017, India
Penguin Group (NZ), 67 Apollo Drive, Rosedale, North Shore 0632, New Zealand
(a division of Pearson New Zealand Ltd.)
Penguin Books (South Africa) (Pty.) Ltd., 24 Sturdee Avenue, Rosebank, Johannesburg 2196,
South Africa

Penguin Books Ltd., Registered Offices: 80 Strand, London WC2R 0RL, England

This book is an original publication of The Berkley Publishing Group.

This is a work of fiction. Names, characters, places, and incidents either are the product of the author's imagination or are used fictitiously, and any resemblance to actual persons, living or dead, business establishments, events, or locales is entirely coincidental. The publisher does not have any control over and does not assume any responsibility for author or third-party websites or their content.

Copyright © 2010 by Cecelia Holland.
"Readers Guide" copyright © 2010 by Penguin Group (USA) Inc.
Cover illustration by Alan Ayers. Cover design by Judith Lagerman.
Interior text design by Laura K. Corless.

All rights reserved.
No part of this book may be reproduced, scanned, or distributed in any printed or electronic form without permission. Please do not participate in or encourage piracy of copyrighted materials in violation of the author's rights. Purchase only authorized editions.
BERKLEY® is a registered trademark of Penguin Group (USA) Inc.
The "B" design is a trademark of Penguin Group (USA) Inc.

PRINTING HISTORY
Berkley trade paperback edition / August 2010

Library of Congress Cataloging-in-Publication Data

Holland, Cecelia, 1943–
    The secret Eleanor / Cecelia Holland.
        p. cm.
    ISBN 978-0-425-23450-1
    1. Eleanor, of Aquitaine, Queen, consort of Henry II King of England, 1122?–1204—Fiction.
2. Louis VII, King of France, ca. 1120–1180—Fiction. 3. Queens—France—Fiction.
4. France—Fiction. 5. Courtly love—Fiction. I. Title.
    PS3558.O348S43 2010
    813'.54—dc22

                                                                2010011392

PRINTED IN THE UNITED STATES OF AMERICA

10   9   8   7   6   5   4   3   2   1

To Ralph V and Chris S,
for all their help.

One

Louis, King of France, seventh of that name, kept his court in his great hall in Paris, on its low sandy island in the River Seine. The hall was a low cave of stone at the center of the palace, dim and shadowy, with loops of filthy cobweb hanging from its upper reaches, and banners and pennants too dusty to distinguish drooping on the walls. Two tall double doors, now yawning wide, led in from the wide porch; the roar of the crowd beyond gusted out like a hot breath, a hundred struggling voices, the stamp and rustle of feet. Petronilla led the little parade of the Queen's women up onto the porch and stopped, looking around for Eleanor.

Her sister came up beside her. In the magnificent long gown, the golden crown on her head, Eleanor was already drawing every eye to her. She turned to Petronilla and nodded.

Petronilla set forth to lead them into the hall. She dreaded this; she hated calling attention to herself. Nonetheless, as she always did, she obeyed Eleanor. She brought the edge of her widow's veil over her face and pinned it above her ear and marched toward the throne.

The King's court always drew a crowd, hangers-on, monks and

churchmen, people with petitions, gawkers, Louis's men, the few faithful Poitevin knights who had followed Eleanor to Paris when she married. The hall was stifling hot, the damp air heavy, stinking of the close-packed people; when Petronilla went in through the door, it was like walking into the sea.

Of course no one really heeded her. At first, just entering the hall, she saw nothing but the backs of the court, a wall of bodies facing toward the throne; but as the pages called for room, in among the packed bodies, heads began to turn, one after another. For an instant, their eyes probed at Petronilla, striding through their midst, her hands lifting the hem of her skirt up out of the mucky rushes on the floor, her eyes aimed straight ahead of her. Then, all together, they looked beyond her, and saw Eleanor.

Her name went up, and all around the hall everybody was turning, in a rustle and stamping like a herd of restless horses. They moved out of Petronilla's way, doubling over in bows that swept the floor, but they hardly noticed her: they all yearned toward Eleanor. A momentary hush fell over them. Petronilla reached the dais at the far end of the hall, bowed down to the dim man on the throne there, and then stood off to one side to watch her sister approach.

Eleanor moved through the crowd like a swan over a lake, looking neither left nor right, while the courtiers surged around her, bent and bobbed and jostled each other and waved their hands and spoke her name, begging for a glance. Her name sounded constantly. Among this homage she walked as if she were utterly alone, her attention fixed on the throne, and the whole crowd turned after her as if she held their eyes on leading strings. Coming up to the foot of the dais, she dropped into a bow down to the floor and bent her head until the tender nape showed.

"My lord," she said, and lifted her head up and looked him in the face. "God give all grace and honor to the King of France."

King Louis was leaning forward a little, his face pale and puffy, his eyes soft. He had limp, stringy hair. His long hands were knobby, his fingernails bitten. He said, "Eleanor. My Queen and wife, come sit."

Eleanor straightened. The King's secretary, Thierry Galeran, stood beside the throne, as always, his chubby beardless cheeks creased with his humorless smile; he came forward to help her and she ignored his outstretched hand. On the dais, she turned deliberately around toward the crowd. She gave them a long, heavy look, as if she saw each one separately; spoke to him alone; and beneath the pressure of her gaze, they bowed again, all together as if in a dance, a ripple of flexing bodies across the great shadowy room.

Petronilla clasped her hands before her, warm with pride. *She is true Queen*, she thought, *and everybody knows it.* The other women had come up around her, and now they bustled around Eleanor, settling her on the stool beside Louis, straightening her skirts and smoothing her sleeves, and then drew back behind her. Petronilla sat on the dais beside her stool, drew her feet up under her skirt, and sat there quietly and waited.

Louis had turned toward Eleanor, as longing as the rest of them, soft-eyed, moist. "You look more beautiful every day, dear Eleanor."

Eleanor's hand, resting on her thigh, tightened almost to a fist. Petronilla was glad of the veil to hide her smile. She looked quickly through the side of her eye at Louis, whom she could see well enough beyond Eleanor on his lofty throne; his face was drawn, lined, still fish-belly pale from the recent fever. Gray strands glinted in through his yellow hair. She remembered her onetime husband, Ralph, saying the King had been born old. She crossed herself, burying the familiar ache of loss.

Eleanor said, "Sir, I hope you are feeling better."

"Much better, in fact, my dear. You are kind to ask."

So close beside her sister, Petronilla could sense every move; she felt Eleanor recoil slightly, and guessed he had tried to touch her. He loved her still, Petronilla realized. Like everybody else, he loved her.

Eleanor said, "What do we have here today, sir? Has the Count of Anjou come yet?"

On his far side, Thierry Galeran said, "Oh, don't bother yourself with that, Your Grace." He had a greasy voice. "Such is kings' work." He rocked back and forth as he stood. It was rumored he had suffered an injury to his male parts, making a gelding of him, and his looks confirmed this.

Petronilla turned away from them all. She disliked Louis, although she knew he didn't deserve it; he wasn't wicked, merely weak.

She wondered if being weak in this world were not worse than sin.

Louis always reminded her of the first time she had seen him, and thus of the calamities that had brought her there: her father's death off on pilgrimage, the sudden news, the horrible sinking awareness that he would never come back again, that she would never see him again, who had been more wonderful than a god, and who had given her everything.

Worse, that she might always be an exile, all the rest of her life.

Eleanor was talking to the King. "When the Count of Anjou comes, my lord, you must insist on our rights. He settled Normandy on his son, and the boy has to give us the proper homage. You are his overlord and you can't let that slip out of your hands."

On the far side of the dais, out of Petronilla's sight, Thierry said, in a chiding voice, "Your Grace, we are masters of this; this is no matter for a woman."

Louis rocked in his throne, looking unhappy. He smelled bad, and he looked feeble. Petronilla could tell that Eleanor was losing her temper, not at him, but at Thierry; she sat rigid, canted a little forward, scowling at him, and her hand was fisted in her lap.

Then Louis turned his eyes toward the hall, and his voice lightened, relieved. "God be thanked. Here is the blessed Bernard." He stood up, his hands out, speaking out.

"My lord Abbot, you are most welcome here. Come grace us with your presence."

Petronilla hunched her shoulders, her hands together, and ran her tongue over her lips. The Abbot of Clairvaux frightened her. She hoped he would not notice her, even to look at her. He had led the Pope to condemn her marriage; he wished ill to her sister. From the shelter of her veil, she watched him approach, tall and gaunt as a stork, moving up through the crowd like something on stilts. Eleanor had turned to cast an arrow of a glare at Thierry, but now she sat back, her hands in her lap.

Bernard of Clairvaux was as thin as the walking stick in his hand. His face hung from his skull like a sheet over scaffolding, the sunken cheeks stiffly pleated above his narrow jaw, his eyelids draping his eyes in their hollowed pits. His hands were bony claws. The heavy white habit of the Cistercian order covered him like a husk. Rumor said that he ate as seldom as most men fasted. He seemed worn down to his truest, most essential self, hard as adamantine, and pure as a flame. He made the rest of them seem like gross fleshmongers, and he loved to tell them so.

"My lord King," Bernard said. His voice was cavernous. He leaned on his staff like a vine on an elm tree. His gaze flicked toward Eleanor and steadied on the King. "I am pleased to see you, since I had been told you were sick." There was a faint scolding tone to his voice, as if being sick were Louis's fault. He spoke to Louis as though the man were one of his monks, and not the King of France.

"I was," Louis said, tremulous, reminded of his trials. "I burned with fever, like the pains of hell; when I woke from it, I was so glad to find myself alive that I wept."

Petronilla felt a sudden stab of contempt for him, as much that he would admit it as that he would weep at all, and under her breath, Eleanor muttered something of the same sentiment. Tilted up against his staff before them, Bernard gave the Queen another sharp look. He paid no heed to Petronilla.

Turning back to the King, the saint made the sign of the cross and said, "God has spared you for a purpose, Sire." His voice sounded like thunder out of the cavern of his chest. "Listen to God, Sire, and to His purpose for you, and no other."

Eleanor said, "And what is your purpose, my lord Abbot?"

His head swiveled toward her, his deep-set eyes half hidden behind the curtains of his lids. "I have no purpose of my own, woman. I serve only God."

She said, "And are you proud of that humility, my lord Abbot?"

Petronilla covered her mouth with her hand, alarmed; only Eleanor dared to provoke the saint. But Bernard was looking toward the King again and ignored her.

"Sire, I come here this day to make peace between France and Anjou, and I will have your word that you will take my peace as I have made it."

At that Eleanor recoiled back on the stool, and Petronilla herself gave a startled little twitch. Not even Bernard, a mere abbot, should speak so to the King, however close he was to God. Eleanor clamped her lips together and shot Louis a hard look. But Louis said, "My lord Abbot, you have done great service to me and my kingdom, bringing the Count of Anjou to be reconciled to me. I will take your peace as you have made it, if he only do the same."

Bernard said, "I have his word on it."

"Bah," Eleanor said, furious. Petronilla reached out and took hold of her hand again, afraid of what she might say next, of what she might draw down on them. Then suddenly there was a crash at the far end of the hall, and the main door slammed open.

A harsh roar of voices sprang up around the vast crowded hall. Through the open doors a gust of wind made all the hangings flutter up off the walls. Everybody turned to look as in through the open door a crowd of men tramped, mailed and helmed, their spurs jingling, as if they had just gotten off their horses. There were some ten or twelve of them, and in their midst they dragged someone all loaded down with chains. Shoving and pushing through the crowd, they marched straight through the hall up to the foot of the throne, and there stopped, and from their midst they cast the chained man forward to lie on the ground at the King's feet.

The King hunched down onto his throne. Thierry Galeran rushed out before him, shrilling, "What is this? My lord Count, what do you, coming into the King's hall like this?"

Count Geoffrey of Anjou stood forward, his face still masked behind the cheek pieces of his helmet. His men all shifted back, save for two who prowled after him like wolves in metal pelts. Before Louis's throne, the Count pulled off his helmet and stood there, at his ease, one knee bent, the helmet in the crook of his arm.

As a boy he had been named Le Bel, the Handsome, and for good reason: He was a splendid beast, a manly lion, with bold, strong features in a high-colored face. When he was only fifteen, his father had gone to be King of Jerusalem and left Anjou itself to him; he had commanded men for twenty years and he knew the art. Stuck in the crest of his helmet he wore a sprig of green plant to ward off demons, from which it was rumored he was descended.

He stood there with his head thrown back and talked straight into the King's face, with no grace and no respect.

"You sent for me, Abbot, so don't bother to ask me what I'm doing here. Out of respect for Mother Church!" Anjou stuck his chest out, grinning. "Not anything I owe you, Louis Capet. I am lord of Anjou, and we were masters there since before your family ever heard of Paris."

He swung his foot back and kicked the captive on the ground before him; the chains clicked, and the man in them groaned. "This dog dared hold a castle against me, and this is what happens to those who stand against me."

So Bernard had not made the peace as firmly as he thought. Petronilla glanced up at Eleanor and saw her sitting rigid and fierce with her hands in her lap and her gaze intent as a hawk's on Anjou, while her husband sat stoop-shouldered there on her far side and let all this happen, passive as a mere onlooker. Petronilla turned toward Anjou again, wondering what he would do next—what he meant to win by all this bluster. The two young wolves in mail who attended him were likely his sons; one was standing still, watchful, but the other paced restlessly back and forth, as if he could not wait to get this over, or to find some new victim to pounce on.

On Louis's far side, Bernard in his long white cassock had remained completely still, his lanky shape craned slightly forward, his jaw set. Now abruptly he stepped in between the King and the Count, and his voice rang out.

"Anjou! Did I not command you to set this man free? What do you mean, coming in here like this, like a pack of dogs dragging along a lamb? Unchain him, now, or this goes no further, and the ban of excommunication stays on your head."

Geoffrey d'Anjou took a strutting step toward him. Some of the effect of this was spoiled because Bernard was much the taller, but the Angevin Count produced a fine sneer anyway, jamming his fists against his hips.

"By God's balls! I told you I would come; I told you I would bring him, although I should have hanged him when I got my castle back. And so I would have, except for the Pope's immunity decree. But now that's over." His head swiveled around toward Louis, sharp, like a snake striking, and his lips curled contemptuously. "Now that you're back from your glorious Crusade."

Bernard's face was taut; he moved a step to one side to put himself farther from the King, and in the rolling deep preacher's voice that carried without shouting throughout the wide hall, he said, "I will not accept you back into the community of the faithful unless you free him, my lord Count."

"By God's cock!" Anjou wheeled toward him, so that he was almost backward to Louis. He pulled back his foot and kicked the groaning lump of chains again. "I don't care if you absolve me of the ban or not, Abbot. Why do I need to go to church? I've got my own bread and wine. I'll hang him. God listen to me, I'll hang him today, and from this puling King's own rooftree."

Bernard jerked backward a step, as if the Count's words had struck him like stones, and his hand rose to the breast of his shabby white robe. Tall and ungainly, he swayed, seeming for a moment about to fall over. Petronilla admired his ability to command every eye. Even Anjou was motionless, staring, and the man pacing back and forth behind him was the only movement in the fascinated stillness of the hall.

Then Bernard straightened to his full height, his arms thrown out as if he himself were on the cross and his head tipped back toward heaven.

His voice was soft, so they all had to strain their ears to hear him, and yet every word was clear. "Oh, God. To Whom alone belongs all glory and all praise. Hold back Your mighty hand, although they mock You, these creatures of Yours, who imagine themselves free, these scum, who dare take even Your holy name into their mouths and defile it thus worse even than their foul oaths and foul acts defile it."

As the words rolled out, his voice rose, clear in the silence; he pressed his right arm wide, as if to summon up the divine wrath, and with his left hand pointed down at Anjou, who was for once quiet, for once listening to somebody else. Even the pacing man behind him had stopped, drawn into the transfixed hush, and pulled his helmet off.

Bernard lowered his head toward Anjou, and suddenly his eyes opened wide, his lids drawn back to uncover the startling crystalline blue blaze of his stare. Petronilla had seen this before, this stunning effect, as if God himself looked through Bernard's eyes. Then Bernard's voice cracked out like thunder in the silent hall.

"Hear this, Count of Anjou. You have gone too far. Within a month, you will be dead, gone to judgment. There will be no more time to change and to repent. Listen, and hear me, because God speaks through me. Repent. Repent now, before it is too late, and hell yawns for you!"

In the stillness the curse seemed to billow out like a poison fog. Every gaping face was aimed at Bernard and the Count. Then Petronilla felt her sister give a violent start, and she glanced at Eleanor beside her.

Surprised, she saw that her sister wasn't even heeding Bernard. Her gaze was aimed past Bernard, her eyes wide and bright and hot. Petronilla turned her head to follow her line of sight, and at the end of it found one of Anjou's sons.

The older one, the restless one, now stood stock-still, his helmet at his side. He was not heeding Bernard any more than Eleanor was. It was the sight of her that had stopped his pacing, and she who transfixed him now. He was staring back at her with such a look on his face that Petronilla caught her breath. Her gaze returned to Eleanor, who was still gazing into his eyes, and her sister smiled, as if in the whole world no one else existed save her and him.

Petronilla reached up and gripped Eleanor's arm, trying to draw her out of this; she thought everybody there must see what she saw in her sister's face. Eleanor abruptly twitched her gaze away from the young Angevin and glanced down at Petronilla, but with a vague look that meant she saw her not. Then her eyes sharpened, and she smiled at Petronilla, not the same way, and reached down and took her hand and squeezed it.

Anjou was now snarling some retort at Bernard. His voice was strident with sudden doubt. Behind him the son had begun to pace back and forth again, as if he could not bear to be still. He was not tall, but square-shouldered and barrel-chested, redheaded, with a short pale curly beard. Petronilla realized this was Henry FitzEmpress, the son who owed Louis homage for Normandy. Young in years, but not a boy. He roused a little tingle of interest in her, like a powerful animal close by. Then she thought of Ralph, and felt guilty.

She wondered why she still kept faith with Ralph, who had broken faith with her. She lowered her head, morose. On the stool beside her, Eleanor's face was flushed, and she was smiling as if she could not stop.

"You can rant all you want to your milksop French," Anjou said to Bernard. "I'm made of stronger mettle than that, you'll find. God gave me Anjou, and He gave you only words." But he nudged the pitiful chained man with his foot, rolling him over. "You can have this. I'm done with it." Turning on his heel, he strode out toward the door, and his men fell in behind him, Henry was now only a broad back in a short red Angevin cloak, walking away.

Petronilla lifted her head, startled, and glanced at Eleanor again. Her sister had stopped smiling. She sat rigid on the chair, her gaze aimed furiously at the departing men. Beside her Louis was slumped on his throne, mute and passive. Bernard still stood before them, his eyes now closed, his head bowed, his lips moving. Nobody was doing anything about this. Then Eleanor shot straight up onto her feet.

Her voice pealed out as loud and sharp as a war trumpet, cutting across a rising hum of voices. "Count of Anjou, stop where you are! We did not give you leave to go."

The murmuring crowd fell abruptly silent; everybody turned toward Eleanor. In the sudden, crackling stillness, the Count spun around, red-faced, and glared at her. "What is this? Who do you think you are to command me, you harlot?"

Around the hall people gasped, and feet shuffled and scraped on the floor, and everybody seemed to move forward a little, their eyes bright with attention. On the dais, Eleanor stood above them all, and she smiled coolly, gazing steadily at the Count. "Fine righteous piffle, indeed, from one with bastards in half the villages of Anjou. Guards, to the doors!"

On the far side of the hall, a few men moved quickly together across the yawning double doors; among them, Petronilla saw, was Joffre de Rançun, her sister's captain, who now planted himself square in the way out, his hand on the hilt of his sword. Anjou turned to fix his blazing look on Eleanor.

"I have a safe conduct!"

Eleanor pealed out a scornful laugh. "If that was a safe conduct he just gave you, I shall teach a horse to climb trees. You do not turn your back on the King of France, my lord. You come here by his leave, and you do not depart his hall without it. Come here again and await his word."

The packed audience stood open-mouthed, silent, rapt. Petronilla was warm with pride; she cast a quick glance up at Eleanor, and then turned to watch Anjou suffer. She heard Louis whisper, "Eleanor," chiding, and again, querulous, "Eleanor." Thierry Galeran leaped nimbly up onto the dais and pulled on his sleeve, drawing him away. Off to the side, Bernard stood rigid, his gaunt face like a terrible mask, his gaze moving back and forth from Eleanor to Anjou. The Count of Anjou set himself, as if he would never stir again.

"By God, I'll do nothing at the word of a mere woman!"

But his head turned and he looked at the door and the knights standing there; more of Louis's men were gathering around de Rançun, and the way was well blocked. Anjou swung forward again, his face fretful with indecision.

His son suddenly strode forward, impatient. He spoke into Anjou's ear, and the father straightened, his face red as a cock's comb, and nodded. Henry FitzEmpress walked calmly up before the King of France and bowed, not very deeply.

"My lord King. I ask your leave to go."

"I give you leave," Louis said, blinking. "All of you."

Henry wheeled and marched toward the doors. In the sudden silence the clinking of his spurs sounded loud as bells. Eleanor gathered her skirts in her hands and sat down again on her stool. Petronilla gave her another quick look and saw her watching the young lord; as he went by his father and the other Angevins, they turned around and followed him. At the doors, the wall of knights quietly broke up and moved out of their way.

"Well," Eleanor said, "that was certainly very interesting."

Bernard stepped heavily toward the dais, his eyes hooded, his jaw gripped in a frown. He spoke in a voice aimed just at her. "How shameful your name, Lady, in the dirty mouth of an Angevin."

Eleanor said, unguardedly, "I never heard him say my name."

Bernard dropped his voice softer yet. "The name of harlot, then." He turned and walked away.

Petronilla gave a start and went stiff with fury; she could sense Eleanor's rage, but Eleanor said nothing. Her head turned, though, her eyes narrow, as she watched the tall storklike abbot walk out, without anybody's leave; but he was a saint and could go where he pleased. Several of his monks followed him.

Petronilla's spirits plunged. She lowered her gaze to her hands in her lap. Bernard's absolute clarity daunted her. Everything was simple to him: God, or not. He made her feel messy, scattered, indirect, and compromised. The very definition of female. She turned and looked at the front door, where the Angevins had left. The hall was all stirring, competing voices rose like the rattling of dry reeds.

Eleanor said, under her breath, "What a muddle."

Louis was talking to her; he said, "You should leave such things to me, my dear, but I admire you nonetheless." He leaned forward, looking down at the moaning chatelain in his chains on the floor. "Somebody loose this poor fellow."

Petronilla looked away from them both. It was indeed a muddle. Nothing was as it was supposed to be—the weakness of the King left a hole in the center, which Eleanor and Thierry Galeran and Bernard de Clairvaux fought to fill in an endless indecisive sparring match. Most of the crowd had moved up much closer now, and several people were pushing forward, shouting to the King, trying to reach him with their pleas and complaints. Thierry went out to garner the most worthy of them, or, more likely, the ones with the biggest bribes. Petronilla began to long to be somewhere else. She put her fingertips together, her head down.

Beside her, suddenly, Eleanor spoke to Louis in a low, urgent voice. "Did you mark what just happened, sir? It's the son we have to deal with, this Henry; he's obviously gotten le Bel under his thumb. It's well said the Angevins don't let their fathers get old. We have to make him pay homage for Normandy, my lord, before this prince grows any greater and decides he doesn't have to."

Petronilla looked away, tired of statecraft and trouble. Louis, who clearly felt the same, was putting Eleanor off in a weary voice— "I've been sick. I'm tired, I can't think. Leave it to Thierry. Bernard will do something." His secretary was leading forward a petitioner already babbling of his cause, a stout old nobleman who had doubtless just pressed a purse into Thierry's hand. Eleanor shifted on the stool, restless, and she glanced constantly toward the door, after the redheaded duke of Normandy. Petronilla lowered her head; she felt ground between the millstones, meaningless and lost.

◆   ◆   ◆

Outside, in the courtyard, while the grooms brought their horses, Henry wheeled on his father. "I told you coming here would just get us in trouble."

His father handed his helmet off to someone else. "Louis is a nothing." His eyes glittered; he combed his beard with his fingers.

Henry said, "He is not nothing in Paris. Here he is King. You should have foreseen this. You thought you could defy him to his face, but instead you had to yield; you gave up all the edge we got when he gave up the war." Henry moved off a little way. His father was more of an annoyance all the time. Nevertheless, he was glad they had come to Paris.

She was magnificent, he thought, as beautiful even as rumor had it—more beautiful. And the fire in her blazed as hot as a star. Wild and proud, Duchess of Aquitaine and Queen of France, she was the finest woman he had ever seen. His balls tightened just thinking of her.

His father said, "You bowed."

"I did what I had to do to get us out of there," Henry said. He spun toward him, his hands fisted, ready to fight. "You ass, you let that monk make a fool of you." He shot a hard look at his brother, on his father's far side.

The Count's lips were pressed together, as if he held back some blistering remark. Henry stared at him until his father lowered his eyes.

His brother cleared his throat and said, loudly, "Here are the horses."

The grooms were leading up their mounts and they rode out of the courtyard and down along the island. The Count had a house in Saint Germaine, across the river near the monastery. Henry was thinking of Eleanor again and he slowed his horse, falling farther behind his father, drifting backward out of the crowd, The other men rode up past him, and among them his own knight Robert de Courcy glanced at him; Henry nodded to him to stay with the Count. On the other side, his brother turned to scowl back at him. With a sharp word, Robert cantered on ahead, leading away the rest of Henry's knights to drive the common folk off the bridge. The river smelled bad here.

Henry said, "I'll see you all later."

His brother said, "Hey." His father glared at him, twisting in his saddle.

"Where are you going?"

Henry made no answer. The whole stream of horsemen had passed him now, the other Angevins riding on without him, although the Count watched, over his shoulder, until he was on the bridge. Henry trotted his horse back toward the royal palace, on the southern end of the island.

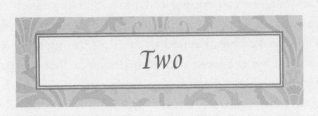

Two

The midday August sun was broiling the city. Back in the stifling-hot tower room Eleanor quickly shed the layers of her gown, shook her hair loose, and let her ladies slip her into a plain linen dress. Marie-Jeanne took the court clothes away to brush and air out. Petronilla seemed in a better mood than before; she sat on the floor laughing with Alys and had sent for wine and fruit and cakes. Alys had a piece of sewing in her hands, and the other women gathered around them with their own handiwork.

Their voices rose in a henhouse cackle of gossip, all thrilled with the clash with the Angevins; chiefly they were interested in Bernard's curse.

"Do you think it will work?" little Claire said. Eleanor's gaze passed briefly over her; she suspected the girl was a spy, and it annoyed her that she had to watch her tongue around her—watch more than her tongue. She turned to the window, putting her back to the other women.

"Anjou is evil enough," Petronilla said, behind her. "It's a foul curse that sticks without some evil on the receiving end."

Alys retold the popular story that a long-ago Angevin count had

married a demoness, who had flown out the window of the church
at the Elevation of the Host, and that they all had tails, and perhaps
cloven feet. Eleanor had not noticed a tail. She longed for the occa-
sion to make sure of the feet. She climbed into the deep sill of the
window and looked out. Beyond the wall of the garden below, the
river ran close by; she loved to watch the birds that lived along it,
swooping and diving over the slow-moving water.

Bernard's curse didn't interest her. He pronounced such anath-
emas often, but nobody noticed unless one came true. If he could
curse at will, she would be a withered crone by now. Then, maybe she
was and didn't know it yet.

Yet she admired the white monk. He made a harsh contrast with
Louis. The King was spineless. Sometimes the urge filled her to slide
her arms into his sleeves and actually move his hands for him, but
even that would do no good. He listened to her, but he listened to
everybody, and he had no weight of his own; he floated on the air like
a dandelion seed, driven by any fickle wind.

The men around him wished her nothing good, wanted of her
only an heir and her duchy Aquitaine. If by some amazing pass she
bore a son, a prince of France, she would be a prisoner here the rest
of her life. She saw herself disappearing, replaced by a sort of jug in
human form: mother of the next king. They would likely send her
into a convent, her duty done.

Even if she stayed at court, barren, there was no such merry exciting life as she remembered her father's court in Poitiers, forever happy,
always thrilling to something new: a jongleur with torches, a preacher
full of God, songs and stories never heard before, and gallant young
men and beautiful clever women, brilliant wits, gardens and music
and tournaments. In Paris there was only the plotting, the planning,
the web of power, the game of kings, and they forbade her that.

She sat there staring out toward the water, trying not to hear the other women's chatter and laughing behind her, and in the corner of her eye she glimpsed something moving in the garden below.

Her gaze sharpened. She leaned out a little, looking down, and saw there, among the clumps of blue rosemary and herbs, a blotch of red. Her eyes grew keen. It was a man, looking back at her. A shiver of delight went up her spine. It was Henry FitzEmpress, in his short red cloak.

"Eleanor?" Petronilla said.

Eleanor did not answer. She leaned against the warm stone of the window and looked out at him. He stood there with his head thrown back, staring up at her, making no sign to her, no sound, only looking. In her mind suddenly she imagined she might fly out the window and soar into his arms. She caught herself straining forward, about to take wing.

He wheeled suddenly and vanished up over the wall, and a moment later two kitchen women came into the garden and began to cut the rosemary.

"Eleanor," her sister said. "What are you doing?"

She drew back into the tower, her heart banging in her chest. She longed to run down there to the garden, to find him, now, at once, perhaps tearing off her clothes as she went. She dared not move. Behind the smooth round faces of the women now staring at her, at least one busy head was already thinking whom she would tell about this, as she told about every little thing she saw.

Eleanor said, "Nothing. The heat is unbearable. I feel like a boiled capon." She paced around the room, outside the circle of the women, her hands locked together.

Once she would have gone. She knew that; in her youth she had defied them all, followed her own will, and loved where she wanted, in spite of the churchmen's tongues and the stories they all told about her. Now she could not bring herself to go out the door.

She wanted him. She wanted his youth, his strength, his admiration. More than anything, she wanted to be free to do as she pleased.

She began to think how to satisfy this, her mind flickering from idea to idea—where to meet, how to send him a message—these were easy enough. How to distract the others so she could get away for a few hours, that was the hard part.

As she thought it over, her heart began to beat faster with excitement. *The passion of the chase*, she thought, and gave a low laugh.

"Eleanor." Petra came up beside her, one arm around her waist. Behind her all the women were watching, intent. "What is it? You look very strange."

Eleanor turned and smiled at her. "Dear Petronilla." She took her sister's hands and kissed her cheek. Already she saw how Petronilla could fit into her schemes. She told herself that it would be something to amuse her sister, lift her out of her doldrums. "Let's go out for a walk in the garden, and talk about old times."

• • •

Petronilla said, "My life is over, Eleanor. I don't think I shall ever smile again." Her voice was heavy and toneless. They were walking up the garden, toward the far end, where the little gate was. Eleanor took hold of her hand and wound their arms together.

"What you need, my dear, is a lover."

Her sister gasped. "Eleanor! Oh, oh—" She tried to pull away, her face flushed. A wisp of her dark red hair had come loose over her temple. "You don't understand." The tears spilled down her cheeks in streams. "My husband cast me off. No one wants me, I'm worthless." She tried to pull her arm away from Eleanor's, but Eleanor held tight to her; with her free hand, Petronilla wiped away the tears.

"Well," Eleanor said, "what *I* need is a lover, and you can help me."

Petronilla ground at her eyes with her fist. "You've never needed anybody's help for that." She sounded grouchy now, rather than grieving.

"But you will, won't you?" Eleanor glanced around; they were far from any listening ears, although in the high window of the castle tower she saw against the light along the sill the lumps of heads still watching them.

"You have always protected me," Petronilla said. "Although I don't know what I can do. I swear, Eleanor. I will do whatever I can, whatever you need me to do."

"Good." Eleanor took her hand and kissed it.

Petronilla's mouth twitched, trying against her will to smile. She looked much prettier when she smiled. Her green eyes gleamed, narrowing. "And this lover. I'm sure you have him already picked out, haven't you?"

"Yes. But as I said, I need your help. Now listen."

◆ ◆ ◆

Petronilla went back to the tower, leaving Eleanor behind in the garden, strolling back and forth, vainly trying to quiet her nervous energy. The Poitevin knight Joffre de Rançun stood at the door into the stairway and gave her a quick smile when she passed him. She fought off the usual urge to tarry with him; he was Eleanor's, and so he had always been beyond her reach. She went on into the stairwell.

When she entered the room, the other women were all busy at their work, as they had been when she left. Alys sat by the window, her hands full of her needlework, the broad green band of silk spilling down over her knees to the floor. Marie-Jeanne was plumping the cushions on the Queen's bed. The girl Claire was fussing with the clothes in the wardrobe.

Suddenly Alys said sharply, "Claire, what have you got on your hands? You've made that all dirty." She sprang up from the stool; there was the sound of a slap, and Claire yelped. "Go wash your hands."

Claire fled. Petronilla went to the window and leaned on the sill. Out there, Eleanor was pacing up and down among the rosemary like a caged lioness.

What her sister had told her still turned over and over in her thoughts. She knew Eleanor well enough to guess that her sister had not spoken her whole mind to her; this was only the beginning of one of Eleanor's long schemes, risky, probably sinful, certainly dangerous for both of them. Her eyes followed Eleanor's restless course around the garden. She crossed herself. She would do anything for her sister.

Some small thought nagged at the back of her mind: that perhaps sometime she should do something for Petronilla, or there would be no Petronilla. But she thrust that away, unworthy of a good, loyal sister.

While she stood there, battling her jittery misgivings, Alys reached out and plucked her sleeve. Petronilla turned. The older woman's mild blue eyes met hers.

Under her breath, she said, "The little one, Claire, left us, was gone awhile, and came back all red-cheeked and happy, and with sticky fingers, as if someone had given her sweetmeats."

Petronilla's stomach turned. She kept her gaze away from Claire, who was washing her hands in a basin, her eyes downcast and her cheeks blazing red. She carried the basinful of water away. Petronilla's heart sank. So they were already caught. Their schemes traded for honeyed walnuts. She met Alys's gaze again, dear Alys, who loved them both.

"Thank you." Only her lips moved.

Alys responded in the same wise, her mouth forming words without breath. "Be careful."

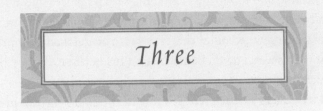

Three

In the morning they were back in court again. In spite of his defiance, Anjou had not left Paris; he came in to talk about the homage Henry owed for the duchy of Normandy. Thierry Galeran was carrying on this negotiation, over on the far side of the dais, head to head with the Count. Eleanor would have liked to join this talk, even with Thierry there, but they would not allow her to say a word. Petronilla sat beside her, as always, and she reached down and took her hand a moment.

Meek and mild little Petra, she thought; *this is what they want me to be like.*

She was trying not to look at Henry FitzEmpress, who was shifting impatiently from foot to foot while his father argued with Thierry. The rest of the meager crowd was all busy, broken up in little knots of men, talking, making bargains, telling jokes, paying off debts, and collecting favors. By the door her knight Joffre de Rançun smiled at her, square-shouldered, tawny-haired, handsome in his red coat; like Alys and Marie-Jeanne and Petronilla herself, he had come with her from Aquitaine, when she was married, and never left her, faithful as a brother. He knew all her secrets and kept them like a mute. She could depend on him.

The Count of Champagne came in, with some ceremony, so that everybody else stopped what he was doing and watched him. Still a young man, he seemed older than he was, broad, jovial, sumptuously dressed, with several gold chains around his neck and a medal in his cap, which he swept off splendidly when he bowed.

A dozen lackeys pattered around him, enlarging his presence. Eleanor was glad to see him, as he spoke well and cared about gaiety. He might have brought a lute player: The whole family was fond of music. Louis broke off listening to the talk between Anjou and Thierry. His gaze swiveled around toward Champagne, and his fingers tapped nervously on his knee.

"Peace, sir," Eleanor said to him. "It's the son, not the father. Send for the princess Marie."

He blew out his breath, his eyes hollow. Champagne's most puissant and high-tempered father had been the hero of Louis's youth, until they quarreled, and came to blows; Louis still ached over this. He and Champagne had finally, formally reconciled, but never in their deepest hearts. The father had died in the previous winter, and Louis had wept for days.

This son was more genial. To mend the rift between them, he was to marry Louis's and Eleanor's older daughter. Yet the King still shied, like a horse that had seen a snake once and now flinched every time he passed the place.

Eleanor murmured again, and in a high voice Louis said, "My lord, we are glad to see you." He sent a page to bring the little princess. The child, who was six, appeared with her nurse and her own court of women, and in front of everybody she and the Count of Champagne exchanged kisses and rings. The Count had to kneel down to put his kiss gently on her lips.

Eleanor sat with her hands in her lap, watching her daughter:

another bride without a choice. It was hard to see anything of herself in the little girl. There seemed nothing familiar in the shape of her face, the color of her hair and eyes, the way she stood. They were strangers. As soon as she was born, while Eleanor still groaned in the straw, the cause of her pain had been whisked off to a wet nurse; the first time Eleanor actually saw her, Marie was just a little round hairless head, snugly tucked against another woman's breast.

Then Eleanor and Louis had gone on the Crusade, and when she came back, the bundled infant she only vaguely remembered was a pale girl in a long dress, who had to be told, "This is your mother."

And who bowed, her slim white hands folded before her, graceful and compliant, already shaped into her womanly fate. "God's blessing on Your Grace the Queen."

Now, the child held her hand out for Champagne's ring, smiling, her eyes bright; when he had slipped on the token, one of her women brought out her ring for him, and she took it and fit it on his hand. She had to reach out with her free hand and hold his finger to put the ring on, and Eleanor saw in his face how touched he was at this.

She took heart; he would be a kind and gentle husband, perhaps. Marie might be safe with him.

She wondered if the girl would want that for herself, merely to be safe, with a kind and gentle husband, and hoped not.

The betrothed pair drew apart. Standing in the midst of her waiting women, her own set of spies, Marie turned her head suddenly, her face quickening with curiosity, and looked toward her mother. When she saw Eleanor watching her, she gazed shyly back. Eleanor smiled at her, and a little uncertain smile formed on the child's lips. Then somebody spoke to her, calling her attention away.

Keep her away from that whore her mother, Eleanor thought. She wondered whose words she heard in her head, and looked around for Bernard.

"My lady Aquitaine."

The gravelly voice sounded on her left. She knew it immediately; her body stirred, luxuriant, coming awake. She turned to face him, standing by the side of the dais, only the empty air between them. The pale eyes were gray as stone. In the short, wiry red beard his mouth twisted into a smile that broadened when their gazes met. She smiled into his hard gray eyes, delighted.

Hundreds of people watched them; every word fell on dozens of ears. She said, "Good morning, my lord." She would not call him Normandy yet, not until he gave homage. "I hope you are enjoying your stay in Paris."

"Well, well," he said. He stood on the stone floor below the dais, so that his eyes were still slightly lower than hers, although she was sitting. He had something of Anjou's look about him, but rougher, harsh, and fierce. He folded his arms across the muscular barrel of his chest and was twitching his weight from foot to foot, as if he could not bear to be quiet. His fine red coat was figured in gold thread with lions passant and gardant, but he wore no gold rings or jewels or other fancy work. Although he was younger than she was by several years, he gave off an expansive certainty—not Champagne's assured ease, but more a wolfish appetite. He said, "This is as fine a city as there is in Christendom, I think." His smile kinked; his eyes were intent. "But somewhat overcrowded."

She held herself calm, aware she was leaning toward him, sensing on her skin the attention of the people around them. She said, "I find it so. Have you been outside the city, to Saint Denis? The new church there is quite fine."

He said, "Do you go to Mass there?"

"Sometimes," she said. She was looking unblinking into his pale eyes, as if through them she could inscribe her meanings into his understanding. "Usually we pray in the palace chapel, here, as we will at Vespers, but it's so dark and old, I cannot brag about it. Especially in the Queen's stall and the ambulatory. Saint Denis is much finer."

"Perhaps when my father has concluded his business we will go out to see the new church, then," Henry said.

"I'd like to show it to you." Her cheeks felt stiff from smiling. Her hands in her lap were locked together.

He said, "I will speak of it to Anjou." Backing up a step, he bowed down to her, and went off.

She sat down again, realizing only now she had been canted forward, tipped almost out of her place, her muscles tense. Petronilla was watching her with a frown between her eyebrows and gave her a little warning shake of her head; back behind the dais, whey-faced Claire held her hand up to her mouth, her gaze steady on the Queen. Eleanor lowered her gaze. She thought back over what he and she had said, in her mind, and decided their words had gone sideways enough that she could deny anything if she had to. And it served her that they might suspect her, as long as they didn't catch her at it.

Surely he had meant what she had meant. Her skin tingled; she ran her hand down over the sleek stuff of her gown, impatient for the evening Mass.

* * *

The afternoon crept by. Long before Vespers Eleanor was sure that she had misunderstood, that he had meant nothing, that he was only passing idle talk with her. He was so young. He was so forward and eager. She was short with all the women; when little Claire was sent for water and brought a jug of wine instead, Eleanor slapped her and pushed her away.

"Go, you brainless brat!"

Claire gave her a look of horror and stormed off sobbing. The other ladies barely heeded her. They were cleaning the floor, carrying out the old broken rushes and bringing in new. Eleanor went to the window, to stay out of their way, and her sister came up beside her. In the bustle, for once, nobody was paying much attention to them.

Petronilla said, "You are jumpy as a cricket in the heat."

"Bah," Eleanor said, "that's it, the heat." *Some heat, anyway,* she thought wryly. And having to speak of something, she said, "Did you see Marie—how prettily she behaved?"

"Yes. They say she is very strong-minded, though, and not always so demure," Petra said. She lowered her voice to a murmur. "I think that it was not Marie who lit your fire at court, my sister."

"I never hear any word of her," Eleanor said. "When you hear anything, you should tell me."

"What did he say?"

Eleanor said nothing, turned her head, and stared out the window. Petronilla glanced over her shoulder, where Claire was gathering an armful of old rosemary from the floor. The girl went out the door, and Petronilla swung back to her sister.

"Be careful, my dear one. Bernard has worse means even than curses."

Eleanor turned to her, and hugged her, and spoke into her sister's ear. "When we go to Mass. Then will I need your help, as we spoke." Alys was coming in, faithful and competent Alys, who set about at once strewing out the firm new sweet-smelling herbs, too busy to be eavesdropping on them.

Petronilla leaned her head on her shoulder. "I'm afraid. What if—"

"Sssh!" Eleanor drew back. "Marie, though—she looked so timid, at court, but she's not?"

"No, they have their hands full with her." Petra gave an uncertain laugh, drawing back, her eyes wary, fixed on Eleanor. "She will not listen to anyone; she does as she pleases. This to me sounds very familiar."

"Good," Eleanor said. "She fights for herself. That's good."

Petronilla made a rueful face. She said, quietly, "When you win, fighting is well enough. When you lose . . ."

Eleanor coiled an arm through hers. "I won't lose."

Petronilla leaned against her, her voice barely audible. "Then sometimes, too, winning brings its own kind of curse, Eleanor. Think of that. Maybe—"

Eleanor snorted at her, turning back to the window. "Don't argue with me, Petra."

"Do I ever argue?" Petronilla gave her another soft caress and left her alone. She would manage the other women when Eleanor needed them out of the way. Eleanor turned her back on them. The gray eyes of the Angevin looked out of her memory, smoky with desire. She turned her gaze blindly out the window, willing the Vespers bell to ring.

When at last the bell did sound, they all went down to Mass, and that seemed to last forever also, the priest speaking as if each word were a stone to be lifted and put into place, the constant racket in the low dark church numbing her ears, the women around her whispering. She did not try to pray. The thing was too complicated already, without trying to sort it out for God. God was a man, anyway, and would not understand. When at last the service was over and they all started out of the stall, she said to Petronilla, beside her, "Take them all home again, now," and left the stall in the midst of the crowd of women. But in the ambulatory, when they kept on toward the door, she went the other way, into the darkness at the back of the church.

Petronilla's voice sounded once, hollow in the stony vault, and the women's footsteps faded. In the pitch-dark silence of the back of the Queen's choir, Eleanor stood, her fingers picking at each other.

She was alone. She had misread him. Or he only played with her. Then, behind her, she heard, or sensed, someone move.

"I am here," the harsh voice said.

She turned toward him, in the dark, and reached out blindly; her hands brushed over the rough cloth of his coat, and then his arms were around her, strong and fierce. She lifted her face and his lips brushed her forehead, her cheek. He gave off a heat of passion, like an oven in her arms. She stroked her hands up over embroidered cloth, up over the broad, muscular chest, clasped her arms behind his neck, and kissed him.

His arms tightened around her. His lips parted; she touched the tip of his tongue with hers, her eyes shut, her body tingling in a dizzy reel of lust.

He said, in her ear, "You're the most beautiful woman I've ever seen. I thought so from the first, but when you stood up against my father like that— Where can we go?" His hands slid inside her clothes and his thigh rose between hers. "I could not take my eyes off you." His hands were plunging in through the folds of her gown. "Where can we go?"

She caught herself. Fast in his arms, she made herself see that this could not happen, not here, like this. She said, "Not now. They'll come for me soon."

He groaned, and his arms tightened around her, sure and strong. He moved against her, and she felt on her thigh the prod between his legs. "Then when?"

"Tomorrow," she said. She pressed herself against him, soaking up his heat. "There is a house called The Sunrise, in Saint Germaine, on the Left Bank. Be there at midafternoon." She laid her cheek against his shoulder. "I want you."

"Oh, I want you, too," he said. "When I saw you today, it was like a sign. I'm meant to have you. We belong together. Someone's coming." His grip slackened.

She straightened, forcing herself away from him. "They watch me every moment."

"You're the greatest treasure in this kingdom, and so they guard you well." He drew back, in the dark, his hands on her arms. "You're sure you can get away?"

"Tomorrow," she said, again. "I will not disappoint you." Behind her, back near the door, she heard footsteps on the rough stone floor.

"Nor I you," he said. "I swear it."

"Go. Hurry. If they catch you here, all is lost." She turned away from him into the cold, empty darkness.

Behind her, he said, "Tomorrow." And was gone.

She stood shaking in the darkness, feeling the imprint of him over her body, as if he had branded her with her own lust. Turning, she composed herself as well as she could. Down near the door the half-lit space was full of people now, calling for her. She clasped her hands together and walked up out of the darkness, in among them, and through them, past Petronilla, whom Thierry Galeran had by the elbow.

"I was praying," Eleanor said, without stopping, and went on toward the tower.

＊　＊　＊

At night, when they had put Eleanor to bed, the other women all went out to the room next door, but the guards on the landing were Thierry's men, and often listened, even easing open the door to do it. Petronilla drew the thick bedhangings tightly closed and in the darkness whispered, "What happened? Did you meet him?"

Eleanor was lying on her stomach, propped on her elbows. She leaned closer, speaking into her sister's ear, lest anyone outside even know they talked. "Long enough to make arrangements."

Petra snuggled closer to her. In spite of her misgivings, she was beginning to enjoy this. "That sounds like a handshake. Was that all?"

"He kissed me." Eleanor laughed, exultant, remembering. "God's love, he is a bull, and I cannot wait to have him mount me, Petra."

Petronilla murmured in her throat. The widow's lot: She'd been chaste for months now, when the blood began to heat, the skin to yearn, the dreams to seem better than waking. "He's much younger than you," she said.

Eleanor laughed. "Yes, but he's so well-grown for his age." She had spoken too loudly; they both stiffened and went still a moment, holding their breath, listening for any sign someone else was listening. Finally Petronilla felt her sister relax in the darkness, drawing closer again.

"Ah. Who cares. All the better. I said I would meet him again tomorrow."

"How can you? They follow you everywhere!"

"I have a plan," Eleanor said. "With your help, I shall have plenty of time." She stretched out along her side, her arms over her head. "Ah, he is perfect, so far."

Petronilla folded her arms under her chin. "What's so perfect about him? He's not even that handsome. Have you ever seen him before?"

Eleanor laughed. "Oh, his father is much more lovely. But Henry is . . . better endowed. Henry has Normandy, and he will have Anjou."

Petronilla snorted in the dark. "Cold and stony."

"Yes, but—" Eleanor hitched up closer to her. "His mother was the Empress Matilda, the daughter of Henry Schoolboy, the King of England before they started fighting over it. So that way this present Henry has an excellent claim to the crown of England."

"Cold and stony and far away."

"God in heaven." Eleanor moved, crunching the mattress in the dark. "Is Paris so sweet and gay?" She turned her back.

There was a long silence between them.

A trickle of sweat ran down Petronilla's side. In the breathless space within the bedhangings she felt lightly cooked in her own skin. She realized Eleanor had more to her plans than just an afternoon playing Phaedra to Henry's bull. "Well, Paris is what we have. And Henry FitzEmpress doesn't even have England yet."

"I'll help him," Eleanor said, over her shoulder. "We'll do it together."

"And England has a king already." FitzEmpress's mother, Matilda, had failed in her efforts to take the crown; she was old now. "As in fact, you do, too. Have a king."

"Yes," Eleanor said. "That's a sticking point."

"And the King of England is Stephen of Blois, whose son—whose son and heir, this is—is married to your husband's sister."

"How like Louis to choose the wrong man," Eleanor said.

"Every thing you do, Eleanor, turns upon some crown or another. What do you want of me tomorrow?"

"I need to meet Henry in the afternoon. I thought—I've noticed, from time to time, you go off, and no one follows you."

Petronilla was damp all over with sweat; she longed to throw the bedhangings back and let in a cool rush of air, but she dared not. "Nobody cares about me, Eleanor. I could leap off the New Bridge into the Seine and nobody would care."

"That's not true; I love you best of all. Especially, though, speaking of the New Bridge, you could go over to the Left Bank."

"Ah." Petronilla licked her lips, trying to suppress the feeling that she was getting into far more than she knew. "That's so, I could go to the Studium and hear the masters there. I've done that often enough." She liked to practice her Latin, listening to the magistri dispute, and they played with ideas there the way carefree boys played with balls in the street.

"That's good," Eleanor said. "And if I took your place in your widow's white and veil, and rode your old mare, I could do as I please, and once I got anyway from the palace nobody would look very closely. But that won't be enough."

"What?" Petronilla said, alarmed.

"We need to lay down a false scent. Otherwise they'll notice I'm missing."

"What are you suggesting?"

Eleanor said, "Well, there's this." And she leaned so close that her lips brushed Petronilla's ear, and whispered it.

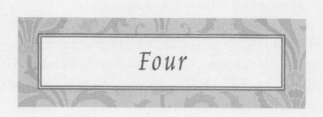

Four

During the night, rain fell in a crash and roil of wind. Petronilla woke from a fitful, sweaty sleep and lay in the dark beside her sister, listening to the storm.

Eleanor slept on, sprawled across the bed, her arms flung wide. The bed hangings ruffled in the wind. Petronilla burrowed her head into the pillow, longing for sleep. Ralph's face came into her mind, and she saw the words again: "We must not be together. We have never been married." She gritted her teeth together, angry.

Discarded. Worth nothing. Her eyes stung with tears. Outside, the wind howled like a demon, and she pulled the covers up over her head.

Beside her, Eleanor called out in her sleep. Dreaming again of escape.

It was too hot to breathe under the covers. She pulled the bed-clothes down again.

She longed to go home, back to live in Poitiers, where she had grown up. She wanted, more than anything, to start over.

The darkness all around made the memory vivid in her mind. She saw the gardens of the palace there, the red roses blooming against the gray stone, the Maubergeon Tower, and nearby music, and the sway of skirts and the tap of silken shoes in a rousing dance. The calling of the vendors in the streets and the women in their coifs talking from window to window. A fruit-stuffed pastry popped into her mouth. The crisp skin of a pullet cooked with lemons, her favorite dish in her childhood, and the crusty bread, the creamy cheese, whose taste lasted forever on the tongue.

The Occitan people themselves had seemed different to her than those in Paris: loud, but not harsh; forceful, but not judging; proud, but not contemptuous. She ached to go back; she longed to be a girl again, in Poitiers. But they kept Eleanor here, in Paris, under key, under watch, and that meant Petronilla stayed here, too.

She would never be a girl again. And perhaps Poitiers was out of reach also, a fairy kingdom, lost in spells. Her spirits sank. She saw disaster ahead for them. Eleanor, in her heedless rush to have everything she wanted, was falling in love with her husband's worst enemy.

Eleanor had not asked for help. Eleanor had commanded it. She was gritting her teeth again, tears in her eyes again. Eleanor always got her way. She dashed at her eyes, angry at herself for this weakness.

Maybe they could just run away. Maybe, in Poitiers, she could forget about Ralph, and be happy.

She wanted to forget Ralph. She felt now that everything between them had been a sham.

She wiped her eyes on the damp bedclothes. She couldn't just run away. Eleanor's marriage was like an iron cage all around them, and she could see no gate through it. She had to trust Eleanor. She had to have faith that whatever Eleanor was scheming would make both of them happy somehow. She knew she would do what Eleanor wanted, anyway. Everybody, in the end, did whatever Eleanor wanted. And she was only Eleanor's little sister, not even a wife anymore; what choice had she? She squeezed her eyes shut, aching for the oblivion of sleep.

✦ ✦ ✦

It rained all night, but the morning, fortunately, was fine, and not so hot. The women bustled in, carrying the tray, the cups, the warming pan, the little jars of spice. They gathered in the middle of the room. Petronilla looked drowsy. "I didn't sleep well," she said. "You dreamed, again." As if this were some new crime of Eleanor's, to dream.

Eleanor leaned toward her, keen with conspiracy. Under her breath she whispered, "Are you ready?" She ignored the little hesitancy in her sister's manner. Petronilla would warm to this; they had always loved to play tricks on people, even when they were children.

Petronilla's head bobbed. She reached for the cup of wine and announced, as if she were some kind of herald, that she would go out after Mass and cross the river to the Studium, to hear the masters speak of Aristotle.

"Fetch a page for Joffre de Rançun. He can escort me."

Alys said, "My lady, you said you were tired—"

"I'm fine now," Petronilla said. "I can't stay cooped up in here all day long." She seemed almost angry, and Alys backed away, her hands up, placating.

Eleanor said, "Be careful, Petra. Perhaps Alys is right."

Her sister gave her a quick, fretful, warning look. "I will be fine. I love the Studium." Her voice had a knife edge to it. *Do you want me to go along with this or not?*

"Very well," Eleanor said hastily. "You know I can deny you nothing."

Alys said, "My lady, should not one of us go with you?"

Eleanor stiffened, alarmed, but Petronilla laughed. "Which of you would not fall asleep before the masters and disgrace me? Joffre will be there." She waved her hand to end the conversation. "I am going; say no more. No one else will care anyway."

They went to Mass and then ate bread and cheese. Afterward, Petronilla sent a page down to make sure that Joffre de Rançun had brought her little mare.

She turned, and Alys swung her white cloak around her. Petronilla pinned the veil up over her face. Over the top edge, her sister's eyes found Eleanor's. "Good day, Eleanor."

Eleanor smiled, and the understanding passed between them. Petronilla swept out the door. Eleanor paced around the room, unable to be still, while the women watched her owlishly and jumped at her every turn. Claire stuck herself with a needle and wailed, which made the rest all laugh.

After what seemed half the day, the bells began to clang for Nones, which was the signal. She wore only a plain dark gown, and now she went herself to the wardrobe and took out her red hooded cloak.

"Where are you going?" the women all said at once.

She whirled the cloak around her. "I am going out into the garden for a while. And no one is to go with me, or follow me. You will stay here, or I will wring all your necks, one by one." She glared at them, even Marie-Jeanne and Alys, whom she loved, whom she trusted. "And if any of you watch at the window, I shall know." She raked them with a scowl and went to the door.

The guard there, as usual, was half-asleep; she got past him before he could stir and ran down the stairs. There on the first landing, in the dark angle between the stair and the wall, Petronilla was waiting. They needed no words but acted together as if they were one; Petronilla seized the red cloak from Eleanor, and Eleanor flung the white cloak on and tugged the veil over her face, and was on down the next flight of steps almost without pausing, and into the bright sunlight.

De Rançun, faithful and good, was there as he had promised,

with Petronilla's small brown mare. Eleanor rode astride, but Petronilla always rode aside, so now she let de Rançun lift her up to sit sideways on the saddle, knees demurely together, and de Rançun led her off toward the little bridge, which crossed onto the Left Bank of the Seine.

She lowered her head and kept her hands on the saddle pommel, to look meek, like Petronilla, but in her heart she laughed and danced for her freedom like a bacchant.

* * *

Petronilla, swathed in the red cloak, kept her head down under the hood as she walked out by the guard. From there a short turn took her out through the door into the garden. She squared her shoulders, trying to carry herself with Eleanor's pride and grandeur, her head high; it felt very unnatural, as if some iron bar ran down her back, and her toes barely touched the ground. But she strode off down between the rows of rosemary bushes toward the far wall.

Her anger at Eleanor faded. To her surprise she was enjoying this, after the long boring summer brooding over Ralph. If Ralph knew she was doing something so bold, anyway, he would be amazed, maybe even admiring. He had always admired Eleanor for daring what she did. She wondered what Eleanor did now.

She went a long way down the garden without turning around, but then almost to the little postern gate, she whirled around and looked back.

Up in the top of the tower, in the chamber window, several faces popped quickly down out of sight. Before they could vanish, she saw that there were only two of them, and she gave a crow of laughter. Without waiting for further signs that she was being followed, she went on the length of the garden to the postern and let herself out the narrow wooden gate.

She walked along more slowly, wanting to let whoever was

coming after her keep on the track. This western tip of the city island narrowed down to a flat yellow spit, ending in three tiny shoals whose sandy banks barely rose above the surface of the river. The ground above the spit was sloping and covered with grass and yellow flowers; here some early king had built a wall of earth, which since had crumbled under a thousand rains to grassy lumpy mounds. She went along the curve of this relic, never looking back, toward the gardens and houses of the city.

At her approach a flock of little birds flew up in a busy whir of wings. Turning east again, almost at the water's edge, she went up the bank, past a man with a hoe, to his knees in onion greens, who bobbed toward her and pulled his forelock without ever stopping in his toil. In the first cluster of houses, a goat browsing on one of the thatched roofs gave her a long look, its jaws munching. Between two of the little mud-daubed houses she could see down to the river, where women were washing their laundry.

The bustle and racket of the city rose around her. She could hear the thunder of the mill by the big bridge, and ahead of her a shrill voice was hawking meat pies. The path was wide and dusty here. A white chicken scratched industriously at the ground as if to summon worms by sheer desire.

The air smelled of smoke and garlic and baking bread. A stream of half-naked children ran past, shrieking. She started to turn to watch them, remembering when she had been such a carefree child, but thought of her duty, and kept her eyes forward. She went along a crumbling wall of yellow stones meshed in a rose vine, pink petals fallen like warm snow on the ground.

Behind that was a little stable connected to the monastery beyond; the monks, she knew of old, used it seldom. Bright orange lichens like round badges grew on the stone wall, and half the slates of the roof were missing. The door was balky, and she needed all her strength to push it open.

Inside the air was still and dusty and dark. Something scuttled away from her into the shelter of the stone wall. A great musty heap of hay stood in the middle of the space. She circled that, going to one side, where a broken shutter covered a little window. The shutter's missing slats let in thin fingers of light, filmy with suspended dust. She took the red cloak off and hung it over the shutter, so that someone peeping in from outside could see it.

Then she went nimbly out through the back, climbing like a child over a manger and squeezing through another little window, and circled through the monastery's neglected orchard toward the old rose-covered wall, and hid there, crouching behind the stones, where she could watch the stable door.

For a while nothing happened, and she fretted that the game had failed, that they were even now pulling Eleanor from her wicked bed. But then along came the pasty-faced Claire, and she had Thierry Galeran with her.

Petronilla clasped her hands together, her heart merry. She watched them notice the red cloak; Claire pointed, and the King's secretary grabbed the girl roughly and put his hand over her mouth. Hot-eyed, eager, he tore the grating door aside and plunged on into the stable, with Claire now on his heels.

Petronilla held her breath, waiting, her eyes on the bit of red showing through the shutter; then she heard a roar of rage, and the red cloak was snatched away. She covered her mouth with her hand, to keep from laughing out loud. Something crashed in there. He was stamping around searching for her among the mangers and the musty hay.

There was a yelp of pain inside the stable, and a volley of curses, and a thump. Out the yawning door came Claire, shrieking, her coif torn and dangling, her hands stretched out before her as she tried to run away, and from behind Thierry pounced on her and punched his fist into her and knocked her down and kicked her.

Petronilla froze, horrified. She could not protest this, could not intervene, which would betray the whole trick prematurely, and likely she could not stop him anyway, and would only get some of the same for herself. Anyway, Claire was escaping. With surprising strength, the girl squirmed away from Thierry and leaped up and ran. The secretary howled vile words after her. He had the red cloak in his hand, and now he looked down at it and gave another volley of awful words, and stamped away.

When they were surely gone, Petronilla stole out of her hiding place. Her mirth had vanished like a mist into the sun. She could not get the sight and sound of Thierry beating the girl out of her mind. That was her fault. She had brought that on the child, just a child, after all, however evilly she did.

She crossed herself, asked God's forgiveness, and promised to do penance. That would do no good for poor Claire, would not erase her bruises or her fear. She felt again that she was slipping into something deeper and more dangerous than she had thought at first. There were two sides to everything, and the evil side of this frightened her. She had done it for Eleanor's sake. That, of course, made no difference. Heavy of heart, she went back around the western edge of the island again, back toward the royal garden, to wait for Eleanor to return.

Five

Eleanor lay on her side in the rucked and tousled bed, her head on her arm, and reached out and laid her hand on his chest, sprinkled with curly red hair. He smiled at her. His young, muscular body was smoothly shaped and strong; she had held that square hard chest against her own, and she looked on it now possessively. Her fingers traveled softly down the line of hair that led past his navel to his manly stalk, and he caught her wrist and pressed her palm against it, still sticky with his seed.

"That was brave, my red leopard," she said. She curled her fingers around him. "That was very passing brave."

"That milk-blooded Louis doesn't deserve you," Henry said. "I would carry you off now, if you'd let me." Still holding her hand against him, he massaged himself with her.

"Come away with me," he said. "Be my Eleanor, in spite of him."

She leaned on him, her head on his shoulder. "No—not like that. Don't you see? There's so much more than that. If I were free—if we could marry—"

"I would marry you tomorrow if you were free. But—"

"Then heed me." On the enseamed linen between them she traced a circle with her finger. "The Land of the Franks—it seems like a great kingdom, and it was great in older times, but over the years they've lost great pieces of it, either outright, like Anjou, or giving them away as fiefs, like your Normandy. France is shrinking away; it's hardly more than the lands around Paris now. If you and I married, I would have Aquitaine, and you would have Normandy and Anjou—"

"And England," he said, his voice crackling. "I will have England, if I must hack Stephen to pieces to get it."

"Ah," she said, "it gives me heart to hear you say that. Because then, mark, we would have such a kingdom that would swallow up poor Louis and his little France." Her eyes on his, she traced a circle around the mattress between them. "France is dying, and something new could now be born."

She saw his eyes widen as he took this in. "We would hold the greatest kingdom in Christendom," he said. "Greater even than the Empire, and rich as the powers of the east."

Drawn to that lust in his voice, she reached out to him and they joined again, fierce as leopards, scratching and clawing and roaring at the peak, as if they crushed worlds between them. Afterward, his weight still pressing her down, his lance still deep inside her, he said, "Come with me now. We can get Aquitaine back from him, he's a milksop. Come away with me, be with me always."

She laughed, loving this in him, how he knew no boundary. "No, no. We must play this one properly. There is a lot to win here. I must get rid of my husband, first, and then I will marry you. That way no one can challenge us."

"Women can't break their marriage vows. He'd have to give you up, and he'd be mad to. Just come with me, my Eleanor. I'll make you the greatest queen in Christendom, and be damned to marriage."

"Oh, don't let a priest hear you say that."

"I hate priests."

She laughed, and kissed his mouth again, long and tenderly, and then drew away. His manhood slid slowly from her crevice. "You throw yourself over the river before you even reach it. I will do what I must, and then we can be together, and all right with God and man." She sat up on the edge of the bed and used her shift to wipe his jism from her thighs. "I must go. They'll know by now I am gone, even with my sister to lead them astray." She hardly cared if they knew she was gone, if they couldn't stop her or catch her. It was even better if they knew, as long as they could prove nothing; it would sour Louis against her, so he would more willingly let her go.

"I'll see you again? You promise?" He gripped her wrist, as if to hold her there. "I'll die every day I don't see you again."

"I promise," she said, and made the sign of the cross on her breast. Her clothes lay scattered around the little room; she gathered them up, pulled the gown down over her head, cast the underclothes aside. He was sitting up; he caught her discarded shift in his hands and buried his face in the sheer silk, drawing in a deep breath as if he could inhale her. When he looked up, a wicked smile adorned his face.

"I'll keep this."

She gave a little laugh, warmed in his young ardor. "As you wish, my red darling. I will send for you, when I'm free."

"I'll be waiting, every moment," he said.

She felt, suddenly, the age between them, as if he looked in through one side of the window of the years, and she through the other. She knew such a fire as this would not last forever. But meanwhile she meant to burn with him and set the world ablaze. She bent and kissed him again, and he tried to draw her down again, and she laughed and got herself loose.

"What, you want more?"

He laughed up at her. "Of you, always," he said, and caught her hand again and kissed it. She pulled his hand up and kissed him back, and went out of the house.

De Rançun was leaning up against the wall in the lane, one foot cocked up behind him, while the horses cropped blades of grass along the side of the house. Eleanor had swathed herself again in the widow's cloak, the veil over her face, and without a word de Rançun lifted her back up onto the horse.

He had a sour look on his fair, honest face, and he said nothing, all the way back. She knew he disapproved of this. They had grown up together, and he had always loved her, an older brother, a fellow Occitan, her favorite knight. He was loyal. That meant she did not have to mind his feelings, much; he would resign himself, as he always did.

Her body still hummed with the secret thrills of love. She remembered the crisp red hair on his chest, the hard muscled horseman's legs. She remembered him in the king's hall, his quickness of thought and decision. He was determined to take England. She was determined to get out of her marriage. They were a match in everything. Whatever she did not have with Louis she would have with him.

The only problem was her husband.

At the palace, de Rançun lifted her down at the tower door, and she cast off the white cloak and hung it on the saddle, to recover it later. Then she went lightly up the steps, toward the hubbub of noise at the top, where she could hear Thierry Galeran's ragged oily voice, and Petronilla's, arguing; the sentry was standing there rigidly by the door and reached out to open it for her.

When she went in, they all wheeled toward her, agape. Thierry had her red cloak in his hands, and a rush of words in his throat.

"Your Grace, this is an outrage—"

"Ah," she said. "You found it. I wondered where that was, I lost it somehow." She took the cloak from him and swathed herself in it, in case anyone noticed she was naked under the gown. "Thank you. Now go, I have been praying, hard work as you know, and I want to rest."

"Where have you been, Your Grace?" Thierry planted himself before her. Behind him the waiting women were clustered together, like a bundle of sticks propping each other up. Claire was not among them. Petronilla had drawn away toward the window.

"I was in the chapel," Eleanor said, lifting her eyebrows at him. "Did you not look there?"

He said a raw oath and flung himself out of the room; his feet sounded loud on the stair beyond, just before the door slammed.

He would find out she had come in on the brown mare, but too late to stop her, too late even to find out where she had gone. She relished the idea of his helpless rage.

By the window, Petronilla turned away, her head down, morose, but the women crept up around Eleanor like eager fish to a bait. "He was so angry," Alys said, round-eyed. "And where is Claire?" Her eyes roamed over Eleanor. "You look—gilded, Your Grace. All glowing."

"Ah," Eleanor said, "the power of prayer." And smiling, she went to the wardrobe to shed the cloak.

◆   ◆   ◆

Claire had crept away into a corner of the wall by the river and wept until she couldn't cry anymore. Her face hurt, her wrist, where he had gripped her, but what would happen to her now seemed likely to be even worse.

She could not go back to Eleanor, not now; they knew she had betrayed them, she saw they had used her to delude Thierry. They cared no more for her than he did. Even as she blinked the last tears out, she was gloating over how they had deluded Thierry.

But she could not go to him, obviously. Nor home, where her father had made it clear she should make a marriage at court and stay there, no matter anymore of his.

She rubbed her hand over her nose. There was a hard painful

lump on her chest. Her mind was blank with fear. Dark was coming. After a while she trudged away down the island, to the last refuge of the sick and homeless, to the Hotel-Dieu, where the hopeless and unwanted went to die.

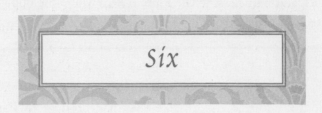

Six

Henry had never even dreamed before of having Aquitaine. Duke of Normandy, someday Count of Anjou, yes, and he had been pushing his claim to the crown of England since he was nine, but until now Aquitaine had not entered his mind.

Everything he had ever heard of the place flooded back to him: the old cities, the beautiful women, the wine and the troubadours. Hard to rule, they said. But rich.

He wondered if she could break the marriage vow. He did not see how that would happen. Yet now that the notion had been ignited in him, he burned to have Aquitaine. He began to scheme to carry her off somehow. His father would make problems for that, to say nothing of the King.

After he left the house where they had met, he went around the city for a while. He had heard of the Studium, on the Left Bank of the river, and he walked up and down the rows of ramshackle halls, then went into a tavern full of men in the black hooded gowns of priests, drinking and talking in Latin and grabbing at the women. He listened to them, but said nothing, knowing better than to risk his churchboy Latin against their quick and merciless tongues.

At nightfall he went back to his father's house, in the village of Saint Germaine, west of the Studium. In the courtyard Robert de Courcy was waiting for him, and another of his knights, Reynard.

"My lord, the Count's been sending for you constantly."

"It's a big city," Henry said. "There's a lot to look at. Where is everybody?" Most of the knights they had brought to Paris with them were his father's household guards. Some of his own men, like these, had come along, too, but he saw none of the others.

"My lord." Reynard was shorter than Robert and stood straighter as a consequence. "They will be back, I promise."

"You promise," Henry said sharply. "Where the hell are they?"

"They will be back. I have sentries on all night."

"Good. I don't trust this place." Henry went up the step past him and into the hall, Robert on his heels.

The hall was stuffy and smelled bad. One end was full of lumber. Around the other end the servants had arranged a hasty elegance for his father, an arras, a table covered in silk and some chairs. His father stood before the table, facing three or four men who bowed and nodded continually, their hats dragging the ground. Men from the city. Anjou's spies in the city. Henry went around to the end of the table, as if he were not listening, and busied himself shrugging off his cloak.

His brother Geoffrey sat on the far side of the table, his back to the huge brazier warming the room, a cup of wine in his hand. The light of the fire shone behind them, so that to Henry he was only a dark lump.

One of the Parisian men said, "The King was so sick he could not eat, 'tis said."

Another voice cut in. "Not so sick. Any time the King of France falls sick, he takes a fear of dying, because he has no heir."

Father of sons, Anjou grunted, amused at that, and the other men obediently laughed. Henry lowered his gaze to the tabletop. A servant put a cup of wine by his hand. The spies were talking again, vying with each other for the choicest, best-paid news.

"Thierry Galeran is his closest man, but the monks always have their way with him."

"No, 'tis the Queen, in the end, he listens to."

"She heeds him little. Thierry Galeran is always with him; the Queen avoids him."

"The monks—"

"She is wicked, she is lusty; he should put her in a convent, all say it."

"Then he would have no heir," Anjou said, the amusement still trembling in his voice. They jabbered at him, several opinions at once, and he turned to Henry.

"Where in the devil's name were you?" Anjou waved off the spies and turned to sit down by the table. He slumped on the bench, one arm sprawled across the silk table cover, and took a cup of wine in the other hand. The spies retreated, bowing.

"I went to the Studium," Henry said. "You know, they have people there who think. It's an interesting experience." He put his hands on his hips, looking from his father to his brother and back again. "What are you going to do now, anyway? Now that you've walked us in here like this and there's no way out."

His brother said, "You were all day at the Studium?" He raised his cup and slurped at it.

"Did anything happen?" Henry said.

His father tossed his empty cup aside. He was getting drunk, if not already there. "I'm minded to go on home and forget the whole thing." He said this so slurred he repeated it, more clearly. "Forget the whole thing."

Henry turned toward the middle of the hall. His knight Robert stood there, waiting for orders, and he crooked a finger at him. "Go find those other men and get them here."

"Yes, my lord."

On his far side his brother Geoffrey spoke out of the gloom. "Gisors castle. Did you hear that? He wants us to give up the castle of Gisors in exchange for accepting your homage. Does that make sense? We should not show them homage for Normandy and also give up something, especially a position that important."

Henry wheeled on his father. "What's this?"

Anjou leaned heavily on his forearm on the table. There was a litter of gear on it: crossbow bolts, a broken spur. Anjou's fingers padded aimlessly over the rucked silk. "They sent a messenger while you were gone." He sneered, as if Henry's being gone had made this happen. "They want you to swear homage for Normandy, as promised, in two days, and we're to give up the fortress at Gisors in return."

Henry did not speak for a moment. Into his mind came the image of the big tower that dominated the border there at Gisors. His belly tightened. Giving up anything was like having a piece cut out of his flesh.

His father said, "We can just go back to Angers. The devil take the excommunication. The devil take us. Just not Gisors."

Henry struggled with the two things: giving up a corner of his realm, and getting his hands on Eleanor and her duchy. He said, "There are certain—advantages—to doing what they want. I have to give homage for Normandy; that duty goes back a hundred years or more, to the first dukes. But if I do, Louis as my overlord has to defend that border. Even against King Stephen. It breaks any chance of an alliance between him and King Stephen. I can turn my back on France and go after England." It was England, and the crown, that made him worthy of her.

His father grunted. His cheeks were flushed. "England. I don't think we'll ever get England. Even your mother gave up trying."

Geoffrey sneered at Henry. "You've had your chances, and I didn't notice you did all that well either."

"I haven't stopped," Henry said.

"You're making us the laughingstock of Christendom."

The Count sprawled on the bench. "Shut up, both of you. We could spit in Louis's face. I go back to Angers, Henry, you to Rouen, and fortify the whole country. Geoffrey could go down to Mirebeau, Chinon, and those other castles." His head swayed to the other side, the other son. "Those will be yours, Geoffrey." He nodded toward his namesake. "Then dare this wetnose king to come get us. Dare them all."

Henry stiffened. Lately his father had been implying that he intended to give Geoffrey some land out of Anjou; his temper rose. Geoffrey was no good at anything, and a sneaking little liar on top of it. There was no sense giving him a crumb.

"I have every intention of taking England," he said. "The old King wrote me into the list of succession." He began to walk around before them, his anger flaring that they wanted to think about anything else. He leaned toward his father, firing his words into his face. "You were wrong about dragging around that Frenchman, see. Getting Bernard on us like that, and then you come here and have to give in just to get out of the hall; that was stupid. You let that woman back you down. Pay heed to me. A peace with Louis means I can put every man I can raise into England."

On the far side of the brazier his brother's face jutted out into the light, his eyes gleaming. "When you have England, surely, you can just then leave me heir to Anjou." He nodded at the Count. "That's what Father wants."

Henry said, "I'll give you my fist." He lunged at his father. "You swore Anjou to me."

He had to have England, but he needed Anjou, more than ever, the bridge in his empire, linking Normandy and England with

Aquitaine. He saw the lands closing together as he closed with her, possessing her. He walked restlessly in a circle. What she had said still gripped his mind, the huge possibilities open before him. He would be the greatest king in Christendom, in liege to no one but God. For that he needed Anjou. And England, and for England he needed Normandy secured, as the ritual of the homage would secure it. He turned on his father again.

"You agreed to this. You hung us up on the whims of this monk. Do what we have to do now and we can call it done. Give him Gisors. This is still Louis, who can't make anything really happen, anyway."

Geoffrey said, "But I get Anjou."

"You don't get anything but a mouthful of fist."

"Shut up," the Count of Anjou said. He waved his arms between them. "Stop arguing. We have to get out of here anyway. And he'll lift the ban." For all his big talk, the excommunication obviously made him nervous. He found his cup and held it out, and a servant came for it. "We'll give him Gisors." He barely lifted his gaze toward Henry. Once again, he had given in to him; Henry was pleased with this. His father said, looking elsewhere, "As you said, it's only Louis, anyway." The servant came back with the filled cup, and he took it.

"One more thing," Henry said, remembering. "Tell him we want to have the rite celebrated in the new church, out at Saint Denis." He thought, *Let her take that for a message.*

His brother frowned. "Why there? Isn't that off in the country somewhere?"

"I've heard this church is interesting," Henry said. She would know what he meant. Robert had come in, was waiting to talk to him. He went off toward the door to make sure all the knights were back.

Seven

A few days later they went out to Saint Denis for the rite. The day was fine, sunny and hot. They rode out from the palace to cross the river over the Old Bridge; Joffre de Rançun and some knights of Louis's led the way, and then Eleanor and Louis themselves, riding side by side. Anjou and his sons and retainers came after. Petronilla did not go, disliking crowds.

They went out the palace gate into the city. Eleanor looked around her. When she and Louis were first married, the mere opening of the palace gate would have brought a crowd of people to watch. Now nobody seemed to notice.

If she had been Louis, she would have made it all merry, brought out baskets of nuts and fruit to distribute, and started the parade with pipers and a drum. She would have had them glad to see their king. Louis made no display of himself, looked so unlike a king, in fact, with his plain gown and hood, that sometimes his own people didn't recognize him.

They went along the street past houses made of old stone, grown mossy and green in the shade, their thatches overgrown with flowers and squeaking with mice. Doves fluttered and cooed in the linden trees. The little market square beyond was already busy, and a cry went up at the sight of the procession, and a crowd rushed over to watch them ride by. Someone sent up a cheer, and several others joined in a single voice, "God love King Louis!" Market wives in black gowns with their aprons stained and creased, dirty-faced children, and burly half-naked porters pressed up against the side of the street to watch the King pass and stretched their hands out, as if they could draw off some of his royalty.

On impulse Eleanor reached her hand out toward them, to give them something back. They clutched at her, and their voices rose in a chorus of her name. She laughed, holding out her arm, brushing her fingers over the steady succession of outflung longing hands.

The square fell away, and she straightened in her saddle, aware suddenly that the people riding with her were annoyed. Louis was saying her name, over and over, chiding. On his far side, Thierry Galeran glared at her. She bit her tongue; no use getting in a fight now. But her eyes turned nonetheless to look all around, to see everything.

They went on down through the huts of the poor, where women carrying buckets of water stopped and stepped aside to let them pass, their sun-browned faces uptilted to watch. In their fists they held their skirts out of the muck of the street, showing their bare legs and bare muddy feet. Ahead, the bridge swarmed with wagons coming in from the country, heaped with onions and cabbages, and the street stank of crushed rotted fruit and trampled dung. The knights pushed on ahead to clear a space on the bridge. As they approached the stone rise of the bridge, the thunder of the mill wheel under the first arch drowned out every other sound, an invisible wall of noise.

Either side of the long Old Bridge was packed with shops no bigger than cupboards: small treasuries, goldsmiths and jewel shops, arrays of spices that spiked the air with their scents; Jews in gabardine, standing with their hands idle, their money waiting. The bridge humped up and over to the far bank of the river, where women in white coifs hawked flowers and caged birds, and the streets of the city gave way to lanes between houses farther and farther apart, past strips of garden, to the fields and orchards of the monastery.

They rode through the monastery gate and left their horses under the trees on the far side of the great courtyard. The Abbot came to greet them and went along with them toward the broad porch, flanked on either side by figures of the saints. Behind her and Louis came Anjou and his sons, and she wanted to turn and watch, to see his face change, when he saw.

The new church from the outside probably seemed little different from any other, in spite of the statues, although the front doors were magnificent, and she knew of no other church that had a big round window filling the high front wall. The Angevins would not know from this what to expect. It was when they passed through the door, as if through a veil, that they would know. Henry would see. She wanted to watch him see. But she walked along ahead of him, her eyes forward. They entered through the massive doors, like walking into the side of a mountain.

Inside, as always, she had the sudden feeling of tremendous height, of a space that rushed on up toward heaven. She heard, behind her, even through the clump of so many feet, a sharp, harsh intake of breath, a gasp of amazement.

She walked steadily forward into the center of the light-filled space, where the sunlight seemed more substantial than the stone of the walls. Ahead lay the main altar, while on either side, high as clouds, one by one the great windows shone forth like visions, streaming color into the dim vault. She felt the now-familiar rising of her spirit, lifted up, called to glory; for all the strutting of priests and the high words of abbots, she knew the real church was this space, this light, the stonework serving only to shape it.

As she walked, she felt herself reaching out across the empty stillness, struggling toward the center, the place of peace. The high altar climbed up like a ladder to heaven; hung above it, the standard of the King floated in the mysterious currents of the air like a silken hand.

She came into the center of the space, then stopped and turned. Around her, all the men also stopped, turned, and lifted their eyes, and from the Angevins came a collective low gasp. She understood how they felt. She still felt its impact, after seeing it a hundred times. The great round window above them in the darkness shone pure as the sunlight, blue and red and green. In the center Christ was smiling down on her, blessing her with His hand. Every time she saw it a surge of pleasure turned her almost dizzy, strong as sex.

This is God, she thought, exultant. *This beauty, this delight, this is God, no matter what Bernard says.* He was a saint, but he was walled around with old belief, and he could not see the power in this.

They held the ceremony in one of the chapels along the ambulatory. Everything was very carefully done. Henry came bareheaded, unarmed and alone before the King, who sat in front of the altar with his crown on. They spoke the ritual words, solemn as prayers and probably older, and Henry knelt down and put his hands into Louis's hands, and commended himself and his duchy unto the King.

Louis at this point was supposed to clench his hands hard around Henry's, to hurt him a little, reminding him of the King's power. Eleanor, sitting behind and to the left, saw Louis's pale white hands tighten, and she saw Henry's eyes widen in surprise, and then flatten with contempt. Louis had no strength to humble him. When Louis leaned down to give him the kiss of peace, Henry shut his eyes.

Afterward they went into the garden of the monastery, under the pear trees, and there feasted, with the young Duke on the King's right hand. The sun shone softly through the leaves of the trees and cast dappled shadows all around; at the edge of the orchard the monastery wall rose, its limestones overrun with ivy. The air smelled dusty.

Eleanor sat on the King's left, the only woman at the feast. Bernard had come to see the ceremony and was there at the table, a darker shadow in the mottled shadows of the pear trees, sitting among his followers on Anjou's far side. The Angevins' own pages served them, which privately she thought was wise; there were those who might try to help Bernard's curse along.

The monks had a good array of meats for them, and some choice breads, all done up in odd shapes and unnatural colors. Eleanor was to share the King's cup and so she drank nothing, not caring to touch her lips to something Louis's lips would touch. She took only a few bites of a roasted duck's breast, dipped in its cherry sauce. She laid her hands in her lap and studied the men around her, watching them through the corners of her eyes, through her lashes, so that they could not say she stared.

Bernard as usual ate nothing, but sat hunched, his head down, his eyes closed, his lips moving. He shrank from every pleasure, every carnal thing, as if it were a weight of earth that kept his soul from God. His skin looked dry as paper, his hair like straw. She thought, suddenly, *His faith consumes him.* Her old cold doubts began to waken. Surely one who gave himself so utterly to God got something in return; maybe he was right. Maybe she should submit to the will of God.

She choked that down, tearing her attention away from him, to the other men up and down the table from her. Everybody else was champing away like a horse at a manger: Louis picking the meat off a capon with his fingers, Le Bel Anjou soaking up bloody meat juice with a chunk of bread, no sound but the contented moving of their jaws. Watching them reminded her of cattle munching. Just beyond Louis, Henry FitzEmpress sat back, planting one elbow on the table, brushed a litter of small bones off the board in front of him, and reached for his wine cup.

His eyes turned toward the spire of Saint Denis, rising above the thatched roof of the refectory. Raising the cup, he made a little homage to it and drank.

Eleanor said, "What do you think of my church, then, my lord Normandy?"

Beyond him, in the shadow of the pear trees, she saw Bernard twitch abruptly and turn toward her, and wondered what she had said this time.

Henry said, "I think it a great marvel. In all the world surely there is nothing so splendid. Some of it reminds me of a church in England, although that is not so great—Durham, it is."

Bernard leaned forward into the light of the sun, grim-lipped, his half-hidden eyes darting from Henry to Eleanor and back. "Many of the masons came from Durham."

"Yet it is not the same," Henry said. "Durham is excellent, but this church is something new; it seems so much larger, the vault, the way the columns are set so far apart, the windows, all united in one work, one idea about space, about light. And a new idea."

His eyes flashed; he stirred on the bench, eager with enthusiasm, and his voice quickened, higher pitched, questing after his thoughts. "There are so many new ideas. In your Studium here, in the new books, in the very air, it seems—our time is full of change. It's as if some great wind, blowing through the world, sweeps away the cobwebs. My grandfather was called the Schoolboy, because he was so learned, and yet he knew nothing of such things as this church, any more than he knew of Alhazen and the order of the stars."

Eleanor cast a warm look on him, smiling. Beyond him, over his shoulder, Bernard stood watching her, but his voice was a scythe to mow down Henry's new ideas. "God ordered the stars before He made Adam. There is nothing new under the sun."

Louis began to whisper, leaning toward Henry, trying to restrain him; Eleanor, pleased, saw the young man shake the King off. He had turned to face Bernard, and his voice had no respect in it. "Yes, the stars have always been there, the first great Book, but nobody understood them before." His back was to her; she faced Bernard over his shoulder.

The saintly monk recoiled, sliding back into the shadows, his hands rising before him like a barrier. "This is dangerous false knowledge, full of delusion and pride."

Henry shrugged. "What's a danger to one is a weapon to his enemy."

Eleanor set her hands on the table. "Is that all it is, then?" She kept her voice quiet; she knew they would all listen. "Is it always a war? Abbot Suger's ideas led to the sublime beauty of this church, not to a battlefield."

Henry wheeled around toward her, his face shining; she saw how he loved to argue. Before he could speak, Bernard's voice rolled forth again. "A church that draws the soul away from God."

Between him and Eleanor, Henry swiveled his head around toward the monk again. "Or leads the mind to Him."

Eleanor put her elbows on the table and set her chin in her hands. She sensed every move he made, every breath, as if they were her own. She said, still quiet, making them listen, "Why did God give us the power to think, if we are only to do as we're told?"

The monk's voice cracked like a door slamming. "God tempts us, to test our faith. God sets seeming choices before us. But there is no real choice."

Henry said, "All your syllogisms have only one term."

On the heels of this, the bell for Nones began to ring. Bernard stood up, going to his prayers. He looked down at Henry, still seated on the bench, and said, "When the term is God, I need no other."

"Oh," said Henry, with a snort, "that puts you beyond the reach of reason, surely."

Bernard stood like a withered tree, staring at him. His head hung slightly forward of his body, as if a wire into the top of his spine connected him straight to heaven. "Reason will not serve you if faith fails you, boy. If faith guides you, reason will tag along behind."

"That's bread and water," Henry said. "I'll let logic and ideas lead me; there's more meat in them. Do you condemn me for that?"

Bernard looked down his long nose at him. "I have no need to condemn you." His gaze flicked toward Eleanor. For an instant, his eyes opened wide, blue as stars. "You've chosen your own fate." He turned and walked slowly away, trailed by his acolytes.

Eleanor stared in another direction, fighting a rising pitch of anger. She thought, *To him, I was damned when I was born with a keyhole where he has a key.* She wanted to look at Henry, but could not; she thought, *What if he shrinks?* If Bernard intimidated him, she didn't want him.

On her right side, between her and Henry, Louis said, "What did he mean by that?"

Eleanor sighed; she had been perched rigid in her place, and now she subsided a little, calmer. Through the corner of her eye, over beyond Louis, she saw the Count of Anjou turn toward his son, who was sitting still for once, his hands raised before him and his head down. The father's face twisted with suspicion.

"Let's get out of here." His gaze slid from Henry toward Eleanor and back. "My lord," he said to Louis, "we'll take our leave—we've been here too long—our work here's done, and it's a long road back to Angers."

Eleanor turned to look at him, puzzled; under the pear tree, the mottled shadows and sunlight blurred his face, so she couldn't quite make him out, as if he were disappearing away in front of her eyes. Bernard's curse, already working. She shook that folly off. Henry was trading some parting words with Louis. She lowered her eyes from him, trying not to seem too interested.

It didn't matter, because somehow everyone around them knew anyway, some mystic cord already binding them. She was almost bursting with the will to speak to him again. That rasping, growling voice declaiming of Alhazen, quick with passion for newness and ideas, ready for anything. Wanting everything. And yet he had let Bernard shut him up. She found herself with her arms crossed, as if she warded something off. She could not raise her eyes to see him leave. If she found him looking back at her, she would throw herself into his arms. And once he was gone, the space between them would grow cold. She felt as if some huge stone door were shutting on her, sealing off the world. Maybe this was done before it started. She lifted her eyes toward his disappearing back, bereft.

Eight

The Queen's chief lady, Alys, was of the highest blood in Aquitaine, but she had been born on the wrong side of the blanket. So she served Eleanor, and did her needlework, and seemed content at it. Petronilla envied her this repose, this way of belonging. She leaned over and poked into the tangle of colored silks in Alys's basket. Against the pale purple the green suddenly seemed much merrier. "Those are pretty, and prettier together. You have such an eye for those things."

Alys made soft disparaging noises, smiling. Her modesty became her because she so obviously knew her praises were earned. She changed the subject. "Why didn't you go to the feast? Isn't the cathedral beautiful? The light there is so wonderful. The first time I saw it I wept." She crossed herself. She had long, fine-boned hands, with perfect oval nails.

"Yes," Petronilla said. "But it's a long ride for monk's meat." They were walking up the street from the Little Bridge, where Alys had gotten the silken ribbons in the basket. The day was hot again, dry, with billowing big clouds gathering up out of the haze in the distance. Two pages followed them and Marie-Jeanne. "Besides, soon enough we'll be riding every day."

"We're going on another progress?"

"We're supposed to go to Poitiers," Petronilla said.

"Poitiers!" Alys turned and beamed at her.

Petronilla felt that same excitement, just to say the name. In the course of the King's progress they would spend the whole fall riding down to Limoges for Christmas, stopping along the way, for a while, at Poitiers. She had not been there in some years, and the ride to reach it seemed over the world. Yet she would see Poitiers again, and Eleanor was hinting now that they would not leave it. Whatever Eleanor was plotting, it centered on Aquitaine as much as Henry FitzEmpress.

Then, as they were coming up to the pavement before the palace, a horse jogged toward them, and the rider dismounted; even before she saw his face she knew by his long legs and easy grace it was Joffre de Rançun, her sister's knight. She caught herself smiling to see him, glad of the veil to hide it. He took off his hat and came up, leading his horse.

"My lady." He gave her a little bow, since they were among others. "You sent me to find the girl Claire. I did. She's in the Hotel-Dieu."

Behind her Alys let out a gasp. Petronilla licked her lips, her gaze meeting de Rançun's. Impatiently she reached up and unhooked the veil. "What's she doing there?"

"Afraid to go anywhere else, maybe."

Alys said, "The poor child."

Petronilla wheeled on her. "Go back to the tower. Marie-Jeanne, you also. Joffre, come with me." She stepped to the side, so the other women could walk past her.

Alys hung back. "My lady, such an ugly place—"

"Go," Petronilla said. De Rançun stood beside her, silently drawing the leathers of his reins through his fingers.

When they were gone, he turned to her. "What are you doing?" He was not bowing now. Since they had been children together he had treated both her and her sister with an easy, courtly informality when they were alone.

She turned and started off down the narrow street that led east along the island. "Well, someone's got to do it."

He walked beside her, the horse clomping along just behind. They followed the rutted, stony road down between rows of stalls and houses, past a donkey teetering under a mountain of firewood, past market wives carrying their bags of onions and nuts, their half-plucked chickens.

He said, "I'm sorry about Vermandois." He meant Ralph, the husband who had cast her off, who had been Count of Vermandois.

She bit her lips. "I should have known," she said. From the beginning, she had ignored a certain oiliness in his voice. What he stood to gain, marrying the Queen's sister. She began to think she had loved him because he seemed to love her so much. Her gaze slid toward Joffre de Rançun. She wished— What she wished didn't matter. On the left, past a graveyard, was a patch of meadow where a cow was tethered to graze. The long low barn of the Hotel-Dieu stood on the opposite side of the road.

"Well," the man beside her said, "he is a swine, and I'll tell him so if I see him again."

"Good old Joffre." She gave him a grateful smile.

They were coming up to the ramshackle almshouse. Grass grew on its roof and out of its rotting walls. In the yard a half dozen people in rags sat around waiting for the evening bread to arrive. She felt their eyes poke her as she came in, with the knight beside her, and was ashamed of having shoes and clothes. The big double door was ajar. She went in, then stopped, blinking in the dimness. The stink roiled her stomach. A moment later, de Rançun came up beside her.

Before her, as her eyes learned to see it, was a long, dark room, divided by two rows of posts that held up the roof beams. All around were people, many all but naked, hunched over, rocking back and forth, lying curled asleep: a man pacing back and forth along a wall, a baby wailing in the corner, a nun carrying a basin of water, people sighing and singing and calling out. So full the air of names, of pleas and curses, as a forest was full of birdsong.

She took a step forward, reaching to put up her veil again, and de Rançun went past her a little and nodded, and she saw Claire.

The girl sat with her back to the wall, her shoulders rounded, her head down, dozing. Petronilla's hand rose to her mouth. Unwillingly she remembered that she had led Claire to this. She was guilty of this as much as Thierry. The girl was filthy and her face was bruised; she clutched a cloak around her as she sat, so Petronilla could not see her clothes, but her feet were bare.

Petronilla went forward, before she had even seen all this, went to the girl, and knelt down beside her. "Claire." She put her hand on the dirty little shoulder. "Claire, wake up."

The girl startled and tossed her head back, her eyes popping open, and turned toward Petronilla. Her face was bruised and filthy. She wore no coif, and her hair was matted. She shrank away, but Petronilla caught her hands and laughed.

"Where are you going? I've come to take you home, girl. Come along." She rose up, lifting Claire by the hand. "Come along home."

◆   ◆   ◆

After the feast at Saint Denis was over, Eleanor went back into the church a moment, to glory in it again, but at once they were calling her out. Her horse was already brought to the steps. She mounted, and therefore had to join her husband.

With the afternoon sun on her left, they went back to the city through the meadows and gardens, past the markets of flowers and birds, toward the Seine, but just before they would have gone over the bridge, Henry of Normandy galloped up to them.

Eleanor and the King were riding side by side, not speaking; Thierry was on the King's right, and behind them. Ahead were only a few pages and squires. When Henry cantered up they scattered, and he rode through them and stopped before the King's face, right before the Queen.

She could not keep from smiling; her eyes met his for an instant, and a spark leaped.

"I have come to say good-bye," Henry said, looking first at Louis, and then again at Eleanor.

She lowered her eyes, but she could not hide her smile.

The King said, puzzled, "Well, then, good-bye, my lord."

For an instant the young Norman held there, blocking the way; she wondered wildly if he contemplated seizing her away, right then, and her whole body rippled, although she knew it would be folly. But then he wheeled and galloped off.

"What did that mean?" Louis asked, blankly.

Beyond him, Thierry shot her a black look. "What did that mean?"

Eleanor kept her eyes down and her smile wide. She knew what that meant. She nudged her horse on, up over the bridge to the royal island.

•   •   •

"You've brought her back here?" Eleanor said. Barefoot, in her shift, she flung herself down on the window stool and stared at her sister. "You're so softhearted."

"Eleanor." Petronilla sank down beside her. "She's just a girl. Let her come back." She reached up and raked her hand through her hair, damp with sweat. The ugly stink of the almshouse remained with her.

"She'll just spy on us again," Eleanor said. The other women had taken Claire off to clean her up. Eleanor had caught only a glimpse of her, but certainly she had no courtly look about her anymore.

"I saw what Thierry did to her," Petronilla said. "She will not spy for him, of that I'm sure." She did not say, *I saw it, and I did not stop it.* She took Eleanor's hand. "We shall need her, anyway—Alys and Marie-Jeanne can't do everything, and the progress is coming."

Eleanor squeezed her fingers. "They'd just send somebody else, I suppose." With her free hand she wiped her face. Her eyes had an inward, dreamy look.

"Did the Angevins like the church?" Petronilla said.

"Oh, yes. Ah, it was magnificent. And then afterward, for amusement, I had my own little disputation of scholars." Her mouth quirked. She lifted Petronilla's hand to her lips. "Send the child in; I'll talk to her."

◆   ◆   ◆

Alys and Marie-Jeanne had done what they could for Claire: washed her face and hands, combed her hair, put her in her best clothes, given her some shoes, but Claire could not stop crying. She was terrified of Eleanor; and when she came into the midst of the other women, she could not lift her gaze from the floor.

Instead she sank down on her knees, her hands together as if she prayed and, sobbing and blubbering, confessed everything, that from the beginning she had run to tell Eleanor's secrets to Thierry, who had given her sweets and money in exchange for gossip about Eleanor's dreams, what she ate, what jokes she heard, and how she lost at tables.

The women of the Queen's chamber made a circle around her. Petronilla went to stand beside her sister, who sat by the window, her hands in her lap. When Claire, panting, came to the end of her speech, Eleanor gave a little shake of her head.

Petronilla felt a start of alarm and put out her hand, but her sister waved her off. Alys and Marie-Jeanne stood behind Claire, their hands folded together.

Claire began to cry again, crumpling down over her knees, her hair tousled and damp. Alys had put some disguise over the great livid bruise on her cheek, but the swelling still marred her face.

Abruptly Eleanor said, "Well, my girl, have you learned your lesson? Will you go off again to Thierry with spying reports?"

Huddled at Eleanor's feet, the child groaned, her teeth clenched. "No, my lady, I swear it. I promise." Fresh sobs shook her. "I hate him. I hate him." She lifted her head and spat vehemently, like a stable boy.

Eleanor laughed. "Well, I hope you will come to love me instead. I forgive you. You may stay with us."

Petronilla swelled, pleased, reached out her hand, and touched Eleanor's shoulder. Both of the other waiting women were beaming in an easy, sentimental joy. Claire looked up, her puffy, discolored face wide with surprise, suddenly hopeful. She lunged at Eleanor and caught her hand and began to kiss it.

"Your Grace—Your Grace—"

Eleanor snatched her hand away and, with her hand on Claire's shoulder, held her firmly off. "Don't blubber on me. You're wetting my gown. Keep your pride, girl. Or get some, whichever it is."

Claire said, "Yes, Your Grace, yes, Your Grace," backing away on her knees. Eleanor lifted her gaze to the other waiting women, her eyes wide, her face grave. "And now we have the progress to come. With only three, and the two of us, here, your work shall be hard. Do we need to find another?"

"No, my lady," Alys said. "We, who love you both, can do anything you require." Marie-Jeanne came to Eleanor and kissed her on both cheeks, and Eleanor took these kisses gladly, raising her face to her old nurse, smiling. Claire had drawn back, tears on her face again, her gaze on Eleanor.

Then her eyes shifted, and she was looking at Petronilla, and she smiled.

*   *   *

Later, after prayers, when the women were readying the room for sleep, Eleanor said, "I hope you have been wise as ever in this, Petronilla."

Petronilla said nothing. Claire was helping Alys shake out the bedclothes. Now that the girl was back among them, her suspicions came swarming in, against her will, her doubts twining around her good intentions, sprouting thorns. "I don't know," she said. "I never know what's going on anyway, Eleanor."

"Ah," Eleanor said. "Leave it to me, then."

Petronilla said nothing. All she knew now was that everything was changing. "What will become of us, Eleanor?"

Her sister said, "I don't know. But I'm not going to sit here and rot away. I'm going to get back to Poitiers, somehow, and be free."

"Poitiers!" Petronilla felt her heart leap. "Oh, let it be so, and soon."

Eleanor put her arm around her waist and leaned her cheek against her sister's. "I promise you, my dear one." Her voice dropped to a luxuriant whisper. "We'll be home again. And there, my darling, we'll have our own court. With music, and stories, jongleurs and troubadours—" She laughed, exultant, as if it were already happening. "There's a new age before us. I heard it, when the masters from the Studium talked at court—what Duke Henry said at our feasting. And we will rule over it. I'll open up my palace to every new idea, every wonderful gift, you'll see. I mean to make Poitiers the garden of the world." She pecked a kiss onto Petronilla's cheek. "I promise you."

Petronilla heaved up a sigh. In her mind she saw the narrow hill-climbing streets of Poitiers; her imagination leaped past her sister's words to the promise in them, a new life in a joyous place, where men and women moved happily and freely, where she no longer had to watch every word, or worry who ran with what tale to which enemy.

Then Claire came in again, carrying the dog-faced ewer.

A cold foreboding washed over her. She wondered if she had made a mistake. She stiffened on the stool, drawing a little away from Eleanor. "That makes me worry even more. Now that there's so much to lose."

Petronilla glanced toward the center of the room, where Alys sat sewing; Marie-Jeanne had the wardrobe open and was hanging the gown inside, tucking dried flowers into the folds of cloth. Claire was pouring the wine into cups. That at least she had learned to do gracefully. Eleanor reached out and smoothed back the sleeve of Petronilla's gown where it had been rumpled. "Sometimes, my dear one, you have to risk something. Otherwise, there's nothing gained." Her eyes were merry, green in the sunlight, fearless. Petronilla turned to her, wanting that clarity, and laid her head on her sister's shoulder.

◆ ◆ ◆

Claire helped Alys shake out the Queen's dress, trying to imitate the older woman's grace. It had come to her, as she settled down into the relief of knowing she was back where she belonged, that she really didn't know as much as she thought she did. It wasn't that she wasn't good, so much as she did not know how to be good.

Alys knew something, she carried herself well, and she had a way with face powders and the colors of clothes. But there was more than that. She kept thinking of the Hotel-Dieu, so cold, and then Petronilla's voice saying, "Come home," and how that had made her feel; she thought she wanted to be the person who could say that, and make someone else feel that way. Safe again. Wanted.

Eleanor was magnificent, too high above her to make pretend with; that would seem like mockery. Petronilla, gentle Petronilla, was within her reach. She would try to be like Petronilla. Carefully she laid the Queen's shift down into the chest.

Nine

From Paris the Count of Anjou and his sons rode westward toward Angers. The sun beat on them, the heat of the summer. In the middle of the second day, they drew rein at an inn, where they took over the back room, and the innkeeper brought them a keg of ale and a dish of eels and some bread. The Count hung on his younger son, trading empty compliments with him, and both looking sideways at Henry.

Henry could hardly bear even to sit down. He went out and supervised the changes of horses, but he had to go in again to eat. Everything his father did seemed intended to cross him up, keep him in knots, break his charge, and this sudden love for the younger brother was no different. The low, dusty room was so hot they were sitting around in their shirts and still sweating. He sat at the door, where the draft was, and remembered her magnificent green eyes.

He saw no way she could escape her husband. It amazed him such a man had her, that white-livered sickling. To think of them in bed together made him want to laugh, or puke. She would ride Louis, he thought, she would take the lead, and the picture of this flashed

into his mind. He caught himself smiling, replacing the King in the
bed with himself, on top.

His brother watched him narrowly. Geoffrey was tousled, his long
hair matted from the windy ride. He was drinking too much and his
face was flushed. He said, "Oh, my lord of Normandy, is it now." He
lifted his cup to his lips.

Henry grunted at him, contemptuous. With his knife he stabbed
at the stringy meat in front of him. He ignored his brother, but he
kept a careful eye on his father, slumped on the bench. The Count
was eating the grilled eels. He shot a look at Henry.

"What did that damned Bernard mean, anyway?"

The eel tasted bad. Henry spat it out. He reached for the loaf
of bread; a squire came to fill his cup again. "Where's Robert?" He
knew the sun was falling into the west and he longed to get back on
the road.

"You'd better not dally with that slut from—"

Henry wheeled off the bench and grabbed his father's shirtfront,
dragging him up onto his feet. The bench crashed down. Anjou staggered back, his eyes white. Henry let him go at once. His hands were
shaking. He flicked his fingertips at his father's chest, as if getting rid
of the last of his touch.

Sweat spangled his father's forehead. Anjou shuffled backward
out of reach. Breathless, he said, "I've had her myself. There's something in the Bible about going in where your father's been."

Henry clenched his fists. "There's something else in there about
the devil's crooked tongue." He felt as if he were about to explode. "I
am going." Anjou lied all the time about women. If he'd had all the
women he claimed, he would have no time to get in Henry's way. A
squire had come up with his hat and Henry took it. "I have things to
do in Rouen and I don't need to listen to you two drivel. I'll meet you
in Lisieux on Saint John's Day to talk about how we're going to attack

England. Or I'll do it without you." He should have seized Eleanor at once, back on the road, when he was thinking of it, and to hell with everybody else. He glared at them both and went out, shouting for Robert to get his men to horse.

◆ ◆ ◆

They rode north toward Rouen, the land baking in the summer heat. Henry said, "What did you think of Paris? It's much bigger than London."

"I don't think it's bigger," Robert said. He was middle-aged, of English birth, exiled under King Stephen from his lands there; Henry had met him on his own first disastrous campaign to England, and Robert had not left him since. "But there's more—" Robert made a cupping gesture with his hand. "Money. Things to buy with it."

"Certainly bigger than Rouen." Henry steered his horse around a herd of pigs tippling along the muddy road. If it had been sheep or cows he would have ridden right through them, but pigs could do damage to a horse. "I wish I had some place near Rouen like that Studium." There was the Yeshiva, where he heard they argued meanings, but it was all in some other language.

Robert said, "The Studium is full of heresies, they say."

"Heresies. All the better. Salt for the meat, if you ask me. How can you ask questions when you already know what the answers are?"

He was trying to forget what his father had said about Eleanor. They followed the road where it forked to the north. He remembered her in his arms, sinuous and sweet, the arch of her body, her legs coiling around his. Thought of her in his father's arms, the same. He wanted to pound his father to mush. He was lying, he always lied. But she was loose; she'd proved that with him.

She was Duchess of Aquitaine, too. And long a wife. He'd already lost the virgin part. When they were married he'd keep her constant, if he had to chain her to the bed.

If they ever married. A daydream, surely, bed talk, gone when the scum dried. Yet he despaired now that he might lose Aquitaine, which he had never had.

They rode on. Toward the end of the day's ride, with no village in sight, they were thinking of pulling to under a tree, but then a man appeared on the highway behind them, galloping after them. This turned out to be a messenger from his father.

"You've got to come." The messenger was hollow-eyed. His horse was sagging, froth crusted on its nostrils. His horse would die within the hour. "The Count is sick, and likely he will not live."

"What?" The other men crowded up around Henry.

"What?" Henry said, breathless.

"We stopped at the river. The Count went swimming, and he came out shaking, and they took him to a house nearby and laid him down, and an evil fever took him, hot and dry, and he's gushing at both ends, my lord; no man can endure such very long."

Henry turned back to his horse and looked across the saddle at Robert, whose wide blank face was wrinkling, starting to take this in. Henry said, "Go to Rouen. Guard the treasure there, and my mother. This will not be good."

"Yes, my lord," Robert said, and turned at once to his horse.

The messenger from Anjou had sat down abruptly on the ground, and someone handed him a wine flask. Henry bent over him; Robert was riding off.

"Where is my father now?"

"At the castle of the Loire, that old tower, there by the river."

Henry turned, looking among the few men left to him for Reynard, the shorter of his two most trusted seconds. He found him with his eyes. "Go to Caen and get the rest of my guards, and hire some more, if you can. Get me forty men, two horses and a squire each. Men-at-arms if you can. Meet me at Lisieux on Saint John's Day." He thrust out of his mind the memory of the fiery blue eyes

of Bernard of Clairvaux, predicting this. He took his reins, bounded
into his saddle, and started back down the road.

.   .   .

He rode that horse until it dropped and found another and rode that
one staggering into the gateyard of the tower where his father lay.
Long before they led him into the room with the Count of Anjou, he
could smell him. The messenger was right. No man lived long with
his insides coming out of him like that.

In spite of the stench, a dozen men, including his brother, Geoffrey, stood around the room. The Count lay on the bed, a blackened
stick with wild eyes, candles all around him, a cross above him, as
if he barricaded himself against devils. The light was bright around
him but turned yellow and smoky above, on the ceiling, billowing in
the draft.

"The will." The old Count's head rolled on the mattress. His hand
moved, and Henry saw there on the bed a crumple of paper. "Agree
to the will."

Henry looked around him at the other men and saw among them
the same men who would challenge him as Count of Anjou anyway:
the Bishop of Lisieux, his uncle Elias. His brother, smirking at him,
triumphant over the horrible bed. Henry said, "Let me read it."

"No! Agree!"

"How can I agree to something I have not read?" He lifted his
gaze to the witnesses ringing the deathbed. Their eyes shone back at
him, a wall of stones.

He shouted, "It's all to Geoffrey, isn't it? All to Geoffrey." He
stormed out and walked around the courtyard, beating his hands
together.

Lisieux came padding after him, a bluff little man with gold in
his robe enough to buy bread for a hundred poor men. Puffing as he

ran, trailing his clerks, he caught up with Henry on the down ramp. "Wait now, my son."

Henry wheeled toward him. *"My son.* My father is up there trying to give my inheritance away."

"Now, son, listen." Lisieux faced him, smiling. He had bright little eyes like a bird's above his rosy cheeks. He put his hand on Henry's shoulder and patted him. "Not all. He wants only to give to Geoffrey a few castles, along the eastern border—so he has land. You are the eldest son. You receive almost all."

Henry gritted his teeth together. He wanted all. He looked stonily over the bishop's shoulder. The churchman patted his arm again. "You must see how this is. He is going to die. He has made us all swear not to see him buried before the will is opened and obeyed."

Henry saw this like an abyss yawning before him. The burial threat was serious. If his father lay unburied, he could not properly be Count of Anjou no matter what the will said.

Most of it was his, at least. Count of Anjou. "Has he been shriven and anointed?"

"Yes. He is ready for God."

"I doubt that," Henry said. They stood in the dark on the sloping pavement of the tower; off over the wall he could see down onto the river valley, the water gleaming in the moonlight, and the faint fire of a hall in the distance beyond. Out there, somewhere, the edge of Aquitaine. He thought again of Bernard's curse. The saint had brought this on, or somehow at least foreseen it. He shook that off. The old man had caught some luck. It was just fate. Chance. It didn't seem to matter much. If Bernard was right, then they were all doomed. They were all doomed in the end anyway. He wondered, briefly, if his brother had done something.

"My lord." A page came trotting down the slope. "My lord, the Count wants you there again."

"Jesus," Henry said. He walked up the uneven pavement, and the Bishop went along beside him.

"My lord, he must be buried when he dies. It's an affront to God to leave him above the ground. We'll take him to Le Mans, it's closest."

"Le Mans," he said. He was not ready for this: his father young and strong, who had always been there, who would be there forever. He had hated his father, but he had relied on him. This was traditional in his family. His father had hated him, also traditionally. Out of spite he could have given half the domain to his brother. Even if the will did name Henry the Count, on the news many of his vassals would rebel; he would have to call up whoever stayed faithful, go from stronghold to stronghold, forcing them open, demand that each baron in his turn submit. And in Normandy, too, they would turn on him. The whole of his realm could go up like a pile of tinder. He had enemies all around, and in spite of the peace, the French would meddle and England might attack him.

First he had to find out what was in the will, and the only way to do that was to agree to it. Grimly he marched up to the door and into the room with the rotting, dying Count, and biting his sleeve in his rage he accepted the will as it was.

Ten

PARIS

AUGUST 1151

"David played the lute," Eleanor said. "The beloved of God. The ancestor of Jesus."

Louis hardly looked at her; he laid his hands on his knees and pressed his gaze down on them. He said, "If they played but psalms, I would welcome them." His hands moved, pushing together palm against palm. "I must do right, Eleanor. For this I am King." He glanced toward her, his eyes bright, almost wistful. "You should not come to court, as Thierry says. This is man's work here, and you only disturb matters. It is unfit for your delicacy. Yet I am glad of it, just to see you. Is this not suffering? Why have you no care for me?"

She turned away from him and looked out over the noisy, busy hall. The quiver in his voice repulsed her; she thought, *You have too much care for yourself, sir, to need any from me*, but she did not say it. Instead she fed her senses on the color and bustle of the court. If she could not have a lute player here, and jongleurs, and merriment, she could at least enjoy the raw steamy rush of real life.

Beneath the cobwebs and old banners festooning the high ceiling, the cave of the hall thronged with people, all talking in little knots and swirls around the room, some moving here and there from group to group. She thought she could detect the news traveling among them, the currents of gossip, jokes, threats, and offers. Thierry Galeran sat on the King's left hand and said nothing, but people came up to him and spoke into his ear and went to other people in the hall and spoke to them, in widening ripples of influence and interest. Eleanor wanted to bring Louis to talk of their marriage but could find no subtle entrance to it. She sat idly twining her fingers together, considering how to get her way.

In through the crowd came a flock of blackbirds: four men in long black gowns like Benedictines, hooded and capped, carrying rolls of paper in their wide capacious sleeves. She recognized them at once for teaching masters from the Studium on the river's Left Bank. They lectured on Aristotle there, Alhazen, the wonderful thinking of ancient men. Petronilla loved to tease her wits with theirs, and Eleanor herself had recently made good use of that. These blackbirds came up before the King and immediately one began to declaim their case, without even waiting for Thierry.

"Sire! We are here to beg your protection!"

Intrigued by this boldness, Eleanor sat listening to the harsh langue d'oeil, untempered by any humility or indirection. From the other side of the room, Bernard was coming, his acolytes trailing after.

Thierry sprang forward into the gap between the King and the blackbird, who then turned and began to argue with him. The King said, "What is this?"

"Let them speak," Eleanor said. "You see that Bernard means to hear it."

Louis's head swiveled, his eyes seeking the angular figure of the white monk, now drawing near the dais. Apparently Bernard gave him some sign of assent, because the King turned back toward Thierry then and said, in the high-edged voice he used when he tried to be commanding, "Let them come forward. What is your issue, fellow? Why do you come before your King?"

The master, a little hot from his disputation with Thierry, drew his attention from the knight, collected himself with a tug on his sleeves, and approached the King with his head thrown back.

"Sire, we have come to ask that you protect our students from the Provost of Paris. Yesterday as I stood before my class discoursing on the Analytics, a gang of his men burst in and hauled away some of my scholars, and there was much fighting and many fled away for fear. Yet he should have no power over us, since we are clerks, and we beg your intervention, for justice's sake, as you are the King."

Bernard spoke out, in his true commanding voice. "What is this but foolishness? You teach quarreling. You reap the very harvest that you sow. You let men espouse dangerous novelties and encourage them in disputation. Your students are arguers and doubters, when they should be humble believers, and corrupt in their thinking they are corrupt also in their deeds, and so the base policemen come for them like the common criminals they are."

The white monk had drawn closer as he spoke and now stood nearer to the throne than the blackbird. To Louis he said, "Let the Provost clean out the Left Bank. It has been rotten from the beginning, when the unsteady Abelard first discoursed there. They still read there by the witchfire of his false brilliance."

Eleanor said, "On the contrary, sir, you should protect them. Who will write your charters, who will keep your records, if not people who learn their letters in these schools?" She thought, also, the more part the King took, the stronger he was in it.

Thierry had drawn back out of the confrontation. The master from the Studium faced Bernard without awe. His voice carried clearly, as effortless as Bernard's: a schooled voice, in an easy Latin clear and everyday as French. "With respect and honor to the holy Abbot of Clairvaux, may God exalt him, let him consider that God did not give men the faculty of reason, nor the whole great cosmos to explore, to stop us from wondering and learning. We feed our faith with understanding of the Creation. It was by books that Augustine himself found his way to God."

Bernard did not face him, but spoke almost over his shoulder, his eyes heavy-lidded. "God gave you faith to discipline your reason, but like heedless cattle you break out of your proper pastures and go grazing on thorns."

The master stood, unperturbed. "Yet the essence of a man is his free will, as Erigena has said. And among thorns often grow the finest flowers, so the flowers of thought among the thorns of disputation."

Bernard was turning toward him, drawn unwillingly into the combat of words. His voice lashed out. "You tread on dangerous ground, brother. You mentioned Augustine, father of us all, who wrote that men are so corrupted by the fall of Adam that if we act freely we can do nothing but sin. And Erigena is proscribed."

"Yet," the master said, "we should come to God freely, and of our own will, as Jesus Himself has told us. And if it be sin to come to God, my lord Abbot, how sweet to God that we sin?"

Eleanor burst out laughing and put her hand over her mouth; Louis reached out and gripped her sleeve. Bernard wheeled toward her for an instant and turned back to the master.

"You make a mockery of everything you touch, even your own false idol reason. Go out, get away; you don't belong here."

Louis was pulling on Eleanor's sleeve. "Don't try to deal with this; this is between the priests, don't you see?" He waved his hands at the masters, who were already moving off. Thierry had circled quietly around behind the dais. In front of the King, Bernard wheeled toward the throne, his gaunt face like a plowshare behind his thrusting jaw.

He said to Eleanor, "You laugh at sin, lady."

"Make a joyful noise unto the Lord," she said.

"Yes. Birds can imitate sounds also, without knowing what they mean. And they too are beautiful, and they too are utterly of this world."

Eleanor raised her brows at him. "Do you compliment me, my lord Abbot? I accept."

Then, from behind her, Thierry's voice poured over her good spirits like a sluice of icy water.

"Sire, listen to the revered abbot—send her to a convent, shut her away from the temptations of the world, that she might be saved for God."

Eleanor stiffened, cold to the bone; she had forgotten about him, her worst enemy. They were closing in around her, Thierry behind her, Bernard in front, and at the mention of the convent, for an instant a vision of that life opened before her: she felt the stone beneath her knees, the constant prayer, the dirty habit full of lice, the airless, sunless days.

Louis said, "The Holy Father himself charged us to remain together."

Bernard's bony head swung toward him. "You have done all that God could wish of you, Sire, and yet He withholds the blessing of a son." His eyes flickered at her like darts. "Two children in fifteen years, and both girls. God speaks in such wise. The vessel is impure, can cast only impurity. Perhaps a convent might—indeed—"

Eleanor sat straight, her hands twisting in her lap. His voice was edged with malice, and she dreaded the convent but she saw the opening before her. She could not seem too eager. She had to seem reluctant. She said, "It's true, we have no prince." She lowered her head, as if this were a very great grief to her.

Through the corner of her eye she saw Louis's face working, fretful, and his fingers stroked the robe over his knees. He spoke to his knees. "I cannot—this cannot be the will of God, to immure her. Then there would be no prince ever."

Eleanor lifted her face, solemn, earnest with hard thought. She let her voice come slowly, the words unwilling. "Sire, perhaps the blessed Abbot is right—another wife, another woman would be more favorable to God, and bear a son to France. That may be the only solution."

Bernard gave an unsaintly, throaty growl. She turned to look at him. "It's true—we should not be married anymore."

Bernard's eyes widened in a blue fury. Thierry said, "Sire—if the marriage ends—we lose Aquitaine."

She ignored him. She kept her whole attention on the tall, lanky Abbot of Clairvaux, her quarry. He half-turned away, the hoods of his eyelids shuttering down. His white robes hung around him like dirty wings; his sparse white hair clung to his scalp like softest wool. *Lamb of God*, she thought, *take away my sinful marriage*. She said, "My lord Abbot? What say you on this?"

His voice grated like broken teeth. "She is right in that, twisted though it be, as everything she does is twisted. Your marriage is a curse upon you."

Eleanor felt suddenly huge, and light, and on the wing, as if she had burst up out of a narrow little box. She stifled a smile. In a voice she could not keep entirely steady, she said to Louis, "Pray, sir. God will show you what to do."

Bernard faced her, crooked, his hands clawing at each other. She realized he had seen, too late, how she managed him to her own use. His voice flew at her like a volley of arrows. "Foolish woman! You think to be free—as those schoolmen think they are free, and then fly here to be defended from their follies. Who will protect you, if the King gives you up? You go from a kind heart into a wilderness of wolves. You will be a hind fleeing the hunt. Trust no one, I warn you—even those you have never doubted will turn on you now."

A hush had fallen over the whole hall, as everybody strained to witness; as always he commanded every listener, held the crowd utterly in his sway. Everyone else, she thought, heard his words as another curse. Only she saw the door he opened for her.

She plunged through it. "We must have an annulment, Sire. For the sake of France. You see even the blessed Bernard agrees."

Thierry cried, "Sire—Aquitaine—"

She said, "What use is Aquitaine, if no prince is born to rule it when you die?" She stabbed a look at Thierry. "Not that such a thing as inheritance matters to him, of course."

Thierry jerked his head back. Louis gawked at her, his dazed eyes white, his mouth half-open. Bernard's clutching fingers rose, as if he could rend her apart. He reeled up his eyelids and fixed her with his fierce blue gaze. "How dare you," he said. "How dare you."

She sat back, enjoying his temper, triumphant, and folded her hands in her lap. She knew she needed say no more; Louis would heed Bernard as no other, and here was the saint, agreeing with her, even against his will, but agreeing they ought not to be married.

Bernard raked his gaze away from her and turned to the King. For an instant, she feared he would take back what he had said.

The shrouds of his eyelids lowered. He seemed suddenly pale. He spoke in a heavy, weary voice. "Sire, I think I have come here for the last time. I am growing sorely tired here of dealing with the same matters over and over, and I have done what I wanted and brought peace between you and Anjou, although at an unforeseen cost."

Louis broke in on him, his voice keen, for once, with real feeling; he said, "My lord Abbot, I would keep you by me. Let me know what I might do to make you welcome in my court again."

Bernard shook his head slowly. "I feel my age upon me. Since old Suger died I have thought much of death, and I know my time approaches when I shall emigrate this world, and I would come to that beginning in my own abbey, in my own cell."

Louis said, "Without you, I cannot tell what God wants of me. Think of me. Think of my kingdom."

The saint shrugged his shoulders. He never looked again at Eleanor. He had just given her everything she wanted, but against the King's pleading he was unmoved as a stone. He said, "Sire, I go."

Louis said, "Ah, I beg of you—"

But the Abbot was already moving. On stiff legs he teetered toward the door. His acolytes fell in around him and he swayed away across the hall, his head bowed.

"Then he will not stay?" Louis said, in a childish voice.

Eleanor glanced at him. He had outwardly agreed to nothing, and yet something had happened, something surely irrevocable. Thierry knew it and was bent over him, plucking on his sleeve, whispering in his ear; she heard the word *Aquitaine*, over and over. Louis's eyes blinked at her, damp in the corners. She came to her feet.

"By your leave, my lord."

She dropped into the slightest of bows, and her women got up around her with a great general whispering of their skirts and followed her away, but it seemed to her, in her lightness and triumph, that she flew rather than walked.

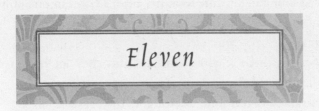

Eleven

"The King will allow an annulment, and we'll go back to Poitiers."

Petronilla clutched Eleanor's hand. "Poitiers!"

Eleanor put her arm around Petronilla's waist and leaned her cheek against her sister's. "I told you. The King is going to see that our marriage is dissolved. Aquitaine is mine, by my own right, so that goes with me." Her voice dropped to a luxuriant whisper. "We'll be home again. And we shall command it all. I will bring every great troubadour, every poet, every man who thinks for himself to Poitiers." She leaned back, her eyes merry, green in the sunlight, fearless.

"Now—I have a longing to celebrate my victory. We'll dance!" She leaped to her feet and kicked her shoes away. "Marie-Jeanne, lock the door. No one will stop us, not the King himself. Alys, sing a roundel for us. And all—come dance with me!"

For a moment, no one moved, but then as if the sun rose before them their faces brimmed with excitement. Marie-Jeanne pulled the latch closed. Alys, who had a good voice, cleared her throat and began an old melody. Petronilla's hair prickled up. A thrill passed through her, as if somehow in this little room she were free as a bird in the sky.

She began to sing with Alys; she remembered this song from her childhood, and thought perhaps her grandfather, the great troubadour, had first sung it. She took her sister's hand in one of hers, and Alys's in the other, and Marie-Jeanne joined the ring. Now they were all singing.

Uncertain, little Claire came up, and they let her in between Marie-Jeanne and Alys.

Alys sang, "White and radiant goes the bride—"

Eleanor cried, "One, two, three, kick!"

They whirled in a circle around the room, knocking stools and cushions out of the way; they were making a lot of noise. Petronilla bubbled up with laughter. She dipped and swung her arms as they all sang along with Alys.

"The signs rise of a new love, sacred on the altar—"

Leaping into their midst, Eleanor drew back her skirts, pointed one toe forward, then the other, and spun around, her arms over her head, her hips swaying. The others clapped and whooped; even Claire looked happy now, and suddenly she also began to sing—not the words, which she could not know, but the sprightly tune. She had a fine, high, clear voice, sheer behind Alys's. Eleanor swung back into the circle.

Someone banged on the door and gave a muffled shout of indignation. The women ignored this. Hands joined, they all rushed into the center, their arms lifted.

"Love! Love! Glorious is the new love—"

Then back out again, bowing, and wheeled around the room. Surely everybody in the tower heard this. Surely even Louis heard this boisterous joy. Petronilla leaped into the center of the circle, stepped and stepped, and whirled, and joined hands again.

"Claire," Eleanor cried. "Claire, you do it next!"

The girl's pocky, bruised face was flushed. As they circled around, her tongue ran over her lips, and she looked shyly from one face to the next. Then the other women dropped back and began to clap, and Claire sprang into their midst.

She did not know the steps; awkwardly she kicked out one foot, and then the other. Eleanor bounded in to join her. Taking her by one hand, drawing her skirts aside with the other, she showed her how to point her toes, how to hop from foot to foot. Claire laughed. She lifted her face to the Queen, unafraid, her cheeks glowing. Eleanor leaned forward and kissed her on the lips. They spun apart, and back into the circle, and all the women whooped. The door thundered under a rage of banging, but no one went to let them in.

"Kiss the cross, and cast off weeping—"

Petronilla saw that Claire had been seduced; her sister had won her over. She clasped Alys's hands and whirled around, amazed.

"Glory, glory to the new love, the one that I have waited for!"

Oh, Petronilla thought fervently. *Let it be so. Let it be so.*

◆   ◆   ◆

The day following, after morning Mass, the King sent his chamberlain to summon Eleanor to him.

Petronilla started to accompany her, but the chamberlain, with many bows, forbade it; the King wanted to see the Queen alone.

Her sister gave her a frightened look. Eleanor smiled, to reassure her, but she felt a start of warning in all her nerves. A little queasy ripple went through her stomach. Maybe they had uncovered something, Thierry and Louis; maybe they knew about Henry d'Anjou. Somehow, maybe they knew what she herself was only now coming reluctantly to suspect.

If they found out anything, there was no telling what Louis might do; she had no control over what might happen next. She wondered if she had celebrated too soon.

She set off after the chamberlain, collecting her arguments as she went. The old man led her up into the North Tower, to the King's private room, and announced her, and held the door for her, and she went in.

She expected to find Thierry there, and to hear reproaches, and possibly proofs of her adultery and other sins, and as she went along she prepared her defenses, thought of quick, hot words for Thierry, and how to nullify whatever suspicions they might have. But when she came into the chamber, the King was alone.

He had been kneeling at his prayers, on a prie-dieu below the floor below the cross on his wall, and he got to his feet when she entered. He wore the plainest of robes and his feet were bare. His chamber was stark as a monk's cell, save for the crucifix of vermeil and jewels, the silver basin where he washed, and the splendid furs on the great bed. No hangings covered the stone walls, and the rushes on the floor were plain and filthy as in a peasant's hut. The only furniture besides the bed and a few stools was the kneeling board, uncushioned, worn into hollows from the King's obeisances.

In the center of the room Louis stood with his head bowed and his hands together, like a monk. Eleanor dipped down into a salute to him, wondering, with even more alarm than before, what he intended.

"My lord," she said. "Good day to you, sir, I hope you are well."

Louis was wan as paper, his eyes red-rimmed. He said, "Eleanor. My Eleanor. Thank you for coming to me."

She gave an angry laugh, taut, unreassured. "Sir, you command me utterly."

"Oh, would that I did," Louis said. He went to a stool by the wall, sank down on it, and passed one hand over his face. "But you are your own lord, my Eleanor, and you heed only your own commands. Come sit by me, and share your mind with me, as you did when we were first married."

With dragging feet, she approached him. The other stool was on the far side of the room, and she spread her skirts out on the dirty rushes and sat on the floor next to him. Thus she had done when they were so much younger, newly crowned and fresh as flowers; then they had talked like angels over great plans and schemes, which she realized now had been all *her* plans and schemes, which he only longed to inhabit.

He seemed so heavy now, and old. He ran his hand over his face again, as if he could push his features into shape. For a moment he did not speak, and she did not hurry him, edgy as she was over what he meant to tell her.

At last, he said, "The Holy Father himself said we were fit to be married. He led us to the chamber with his own hand. I cannot believe—"

"You heard Bernard," she said; her belly tightened. Everything she had thought settled seemed about to come undone. "Sir, we cannot stay together. God Himself has unmade our marriage, by keeping from us the seal of it, our son, the prince of France. I know this is God's judgment. I will obey it; I shall never come to you again as a wife."

"But what will happen to you?" he cried. "You know—" He bent toward her, took her hand between his; in spite of the heat, his palms were clammy and cold. "If you heard what they say of you. Of what may befall you, if I withdraw my protection from you. I can't bear it." He let go of her and raised his hands up to his face; his fingers wound in his hair. "God gave you to me, and now I am giving up my charge; I am failing, again."

"Sir," she said, looking up at him, "calm yourself. Remember, you are King of France."

"I can never forget," Louis said. He lowered his hands to his lap. Perched on the stool, he straightened a little, as if with a great effort, his lips pressed together, and gave her a long look.

He said, "What I have of kingship I have learned from other people: Suger, and Father, and you. But you were born royal."

"Bah," she said.

"I never know what to do," he said. "And yet everything I do shakes the world."

She said, "Without me here, you will find it easier. You could marry a German princess. I understand the cold weather gives them iron wombs, where you may cast a prince."

His pale eyes searched over her face. "Then you want this, in spite of all?"

"Yes," she said, "for both of us. Louis, it's the only way."

He put out his hand, and she took it, trying to be patient, waiting for him to agree, as he must agree, but before he spoke, there came a thunderous knock on the door.

Eleanor got up to her feet, knowing that imperious clamor, and Louis spoke. Thierry Galeran came in, his face shining with sweat, drawing after him a man in a dirty coat. The eunuch secretary went up before the King, who was still sitting on the stool, holding her by the hand. She backed away, letting go of Louis. She expected some barrage of accusations from Thierry, but he spoke straight to the King.

"Anjou's dead."

Eleanor said, stupidly, "What?" She thought, at first, he meant Henry, and her heart shrank. Louis only blinked, his lips parting. Thierry looked from Louis to Eleanor and back again to the King.

"The Count of Anjou, Geoffrey le Bel, is dead. They were riding back to Anjou when they left here, and they stopped at the river to swim, it being so hot, you remember, this was a week ago, how hot— anyway, he came out of the water and took a chill and he lay down in a strange bed and he died."

Eleanor turned slightly away, hiding her chaotic thoughts from them. In her mind, Bernard's voice rang out, telling Anjou he would be dead inside the month, and now he was. She shivered. Louis's voice creaked; she knew he remembered that also. "Who is this with you? The messenger? You, tell me your news."

Eleanor looked over her shoulder. The messenger stepped forward; the dust of the road lay in a gritty film on his skin. He said, "I saw the Count lying there, cold as cheese."

Eleanor pressed her hands together, not praying. She forced her mind away from Bernard's curse, toward something else about this: With his father dead, Henry was Count of Anjou, as well as Duke of Normandy, all the better to promote himself to the English crown. She remembered his impatience, his fierce lovemaking, and she began to feel better; a thrill of delight went through her, a lusty throe, that he who wanted her grew greater by the day.

She laid one hand on her belly. Something there, she feared, grew greater day by day, and that could ruin everything.

The messenger was saying, "They dragged him on up to Le Mans, and he's buried there. There's a council called, they say, but it's a wonder who will come; they're already fighting over his leavings."

Thierry said, "So. Now that there's all this uncertainty, we could stir up some of the old rivalries." He rubbed his hands together, smiling like a merchant over his scales. "Half the barons will rebel, and in Normandy, too. We'll see how well this new lord manages that."

Louis waved that off. "They'll do what they usually do." He turned his head away, looking down. Anjou's death itself still held him. "So sudden. He was a man in the fullness of his strength, not much older than I am." He would not put his mind to policy, was still thinking of Geoffrey the Handsome, now worm meat, Bernard's curse come to pass. He rose from the stool, which grated on the floor, and Eleanor twisted toward him, looking up. He was watching her. He said, "Bernard knew."

"Yes," she said, harsh, following the path through this to her own desires. "Bernard knows what must be, sir. Heed what he said about our marriage."

"Still," Louis said heavily. "Anjou dead, and he was only here a little while ago, full of life as a kitten." He turned to Thierry. "Go. Await me outside."

"My lord—"

"Go."

Thierry went out, with his dusty messenger. Louis faced her, his shoulders hunched, his face drawn. Now, with the prospect before her of escape, she looked across the widening space between them and saw how he struggled to be good, and her impatient, resentful heart woke to him, who could never be good enough.

He said, "See how it is. We think we have time, and if we did as God willed, we would have time, God would give us time, but then the blade comes down." He nodded to her. "My dear Eleanor. You will ever have what you want, God willing or no, but maybe God wills this. I will see to it."

"Sir," she said, excited.

"It will take some while," he said. "There will have to be a council, something, I don't know. We are to go soon on a progress to Aquitaine, anyway, and I suppose we can summon a council there. Perhaps in Poitiers. We must have the priests at it, the bishops, who know the laws. Be patient."

Bishops, and priests. She knew how such men twisted laws into their own designs. A new urgency prickled in her veins. Something might yet happen. She said, "Patience is not my virtue, sir." She had not given much thought to how they would actually accomplish this.

"We have to do something in law, in keeping with holy law, and well announced and proclaimed. We aren't villagers; we can't just stand on the threshold and tell the passersby." He laughed and passed a hand over his face. "Let me do this, Eleanor. It shall come to pass."

"Thank you," she said, and bowed, to hide the look on her face from him.

On the landing, Thierry still stood with his messenger and some other men, talking. By the abrupt way their voices stopped when she came out, she knew their subject. They all bent in courtly bows, but they watched her, their eyes gleaming in the dim light, like a pack of wolves. They would dare do nothing now, she thought. But in the time to come, they might try. When she was free of Louis, they might do anything. She would be like a hind, Bernard had said, pursued by packs of hunters. Without a man to protect her. She went on down the stairs; at a word from Thierry a page attended her, who was never allowed to be alone. Behind her, up on the landing, the men's voices rose in a crackle of excitement.

She was not afraid of them, or of any man. She would protect herself, if need be. They had no understanding of this.

She walked along toward her own rooms, and as she went, she thought unwillingly of Anjou, alive, that handsome lion, that splendid body, all heedless in his prancing and strutting, who as Louis had said must have thought death comfortably far away. And then suddenly it was on him; there was no escaping, no bargains, no calling it something else.

She realized also that the new Count Henry would have his hands full. He might fail; her new love might vanish into another twist of fate. As the fabric of her life here came undone she had to weave another, and that from unknown threads, and full of dangers. Petronilla had already foreseen this, whose cares Eleanor had so airily dismissed. She strode firm-footed back toward her tower. Her stomach was still uncertain. Maybe it was nothing. Maybe she had eaten something. But she had been pregnant before, and she knew how it felt. She climbed the stair up to her chamber, to tell her sister what had happened.

Twelve

"Anjou, dead!" Petronilla said. They had come out into the garden to talk; Eleanor had set de Rançun at the gate to make sure no one crept near enough to hear them. Petronilla wondered a little that she was so cautious, this of Anjou being likely common news.

Yet it was startling, and frightening. She thought, *It's true, Bernard has the gift of sight.* With a wrench of the heart she turned toward Eleanor, remembering what he had said about her.

Her sister was watching her pensively. "And I think I may be pregnant."

"Oh." Petronilla clapped her hands to her mouth.

Now she understood the secrecy. She lowered her hands, her mind racing over this, which could ruin all their plans. "Oh. That's terrible. Eleanor. Just when everything was going so well."

"Yes," Eleanor said. "And I mean to keep on going, just as well. We can do this. No one must find out."

"Alys and Marie-Jeanne are good—but there are so many other eyes—" She felt them teetering on the blade of a knife, poised above disaster.

"I trust them," Eleanor said. "Even Claire, now. They will learn, soon enough, but maybe not until we're on the progress, when we'll all be together all the time anyway, and have little to do with anybody else. And they'll never betray me." Eleanor licked her lips, the only sign of uncertainty, even fear in her. Petronilla thought, *If the King finds out—*

She turned on her heel and walked down farther into the garden, where the strip of grass shrank down between the rosemary bushes. She sensed rather than saw Eleanor come after her. She said, "It would be adultery, wouldn't it?"

"They'd put me in a convent. Or, you know," Eleanor said, trailing along at her side, her palms sliding over the little blue flowers. "In the Bible they stone adulteresses. That way Louis would be a widower, and could marry again."

"Eleanor, stop." Petronilla faced her and took her hands.

"No one can find out," Eleanor said. "Not even, oh, my God, not even Henry."

"It's his." Petronilla squeezed her sister's hands.

"Yes." Eleanor dragged in a deep breath. "It could be no one else." Petronilla glanced up the garden, making sure they were still alone. Her sister's voice murmured in her ear.

"I know that certainly. But he cannot—how would he be sure he was the father? It's all over I'm inconstant, and I was inconstant with him. In his mind, it could be anybody's child, cuckoo cuckoo." Her voice went ragged. Petronilla turned her gaze back to her and their eyes met. "My God, it ruins everything. By law anyhow, it would be Louis's baby, and if a son, then—even if Henry claims it, a royal bastard's only in the way. We need legal heirs, true princes, not gotten under a bush."

Petronilla said, "But it's a baby, still."

"Yes. Maybe, who knows, a sign: We are to be together." Eleanor raised their clasped hands between them, swung her hands down, and let go. She turned away, her shoulders high and square. "A sign of something, anyway. Maybe, if we get the annulment and go back to Poitiers, I can go into seclusion. I could say I was sick. Have it in hiding."

Petronilla was counting in her head. "When will it be born?"

"Sometime at the end of the winter. Around Easter, likely." Eleanor was still turned away. Petronilla thought she was trimming this very fine. They had to get quickly out of the marriage with Louis, and away from Thierry and his malice.

She said, "When is this council?"

"In Poitiers. Before Christmas. We're to spend Christmas in Limoges."

They could hide a pregnancy that long, Petronilla thought. If not much longer. She put aside her annoyance with her sister. She said, "How are you feeling?"

"I nearly threw up this morning."

"Oh, well, that would—"

"I'm going to ask the others to sleep next door. Because of the heat."

"That room's so small." Petronilla shrugged. "They'll all believe that." Her hands were wringing together without her even noticing. She made herself grip her skirts, to keep still. "What about Claire?"

"You trust her."

"That was before. One wrong gossip—"

"I think she will keep faith with me."

"I hope so." Petronilla thought of the girl's pasty face and awkward ways. "We're risking everything on an unsteady child's whims."

"I told her she could stay," Eleanor said. "You have championed her. And we need them all, with the progress coming on. There's the packing and the sewing, and then on the progress all that work."

"Yes," Petronilla said. She caught herself looking at Eleanor's waist. Her sister had borne two other children. She would very

quickly show the one to come. She went to Eleanor and put her arm
through hers.

"I'll help you. Tell me what you want me to do, and I'll help."

"I knew you would," Eleanor said, and kissed her.

◆ ◆ ◆

Alys sent Claire off to the market to get some apples, and on her
way back, as she went by the corner of the chapel, suddenly a hand
gripped her skirt and dragged her into the shadows.

She gasped, ready to scream, and then froze. It was Thierry Galeran, the King's secretary, staring at her. He let go of her skirt. She
put her hand to her mouth, her heart pounding.

"So," the fat secretary said. "You've made your way back into favor.
You have more wit than I believed."

"No," Claire said into her hand, and shook her head.

He fixed her with an unblinking stare. He had pale eyes, shiny,
like glass. He said, "But you have. Clever girl. You know I will take
care of you, either way, if you serve me, or you don't."

She put her hand down and lowered her eyes. She had thought
herself finished with him. Now he lowered over her, and she trembled, remembering the blows of his fist, and she hated him.

His voice droned on, soft and cruel. "I will know everything she
does, especially now, when we are to go on progress. There is this folly
of an annulment—I will hear everything she says on that subject.
Everyone she talks to. Do you understand me?"

She swallowed. She knew what he wanted. She made herself think
of the other, stranger thing, that he was coming back to her to find it
out. Maybe he was right, and she was cleverer than she thought. She
had thought herself done, after he beat her, but then Petronilla had
come to rescue her. She had vowed to follow Petronilla, out of gratitude and the warm feeling it gave her. But now he too still wanted her
for something. That gave her another feeling, cooler, harder. She had

some worth, if she could figure out what it was. She glanced sideways at him, not afraid anymore.

His lip curled. He looked her up and down as if from some height far above her, and his eyebrows arched, expecting some answer.

"Yes, sir," she said, having to say something. She dipped him a little bow, to make that look good.

He said, "Excellent. You will tell me everything, or she will hear that you've betrayed her. She won't forgive you twice, Claire. Do you understand that?"

She gave the barest nod. She gripped the basket of apples. It seemed not to occur to him that he was arguing both sides of his question. She had to get away from him before someone saw them together. "Let me go, she will be waiting."

"Yes," he said, "like wicked Eve, she craves apples. She is full of sin, Claire. Think of that. It's from her own sins we will save her. I will see you soon. Have some news." He turned and walked away.

Claire clutched the basket, her heart shaking in her chest. She hated Thierry; her face still bore the marks of his blows. It was horrible of him even to think she would help him. She vowed she would never help him, no matter what he did. She would give him no news.

He was right, Eleanor was full of sin, proud, and boisterous; she delighted in defying the King, and she had gone behind his back with Duke Henry. She was full of joy, too, and she drew Claire toward her irresistibly.

And there was Petronilla. Petronilla would tell no tales. Petronilla would not lie. Claire started up the steps toward the Queen's rooms. She liked them both as they were, sin or no.

Then it came to her, like a cold dash of water, that it was easier for them.

They had crowns and gowns, and she had only crumbs. Somehow, because she was so clever, she had to find a way to get more.

But not for Thierry's sake. And with honor, as Petronilla did. On the landing, she gathered herself and lifted the basket of apples in her two hands. The guard reached out to open the door for her and she went into the room, among the other women, safe.

Thirteen

Eleanor slept restlessly, and dreamed of things she remembered only for an instant, and when she woke, her stomach rolled and heaved. She was barely able to scramble out of the bed and reach the chamber pot by the wall before she gave up the bitter remnants of her supper in a stream. Petronilla sat up in the bed behind her. Eleanor hung there a moment, scraping her hair back with her hand, until she was sure it was over, and then rose and went to the window, gulping the fresh morning air.

Petronilla said, "It's true, then."

Eleanor turned toward her. "Yes, I think so."

She put her hand on her belly. Petronilla would protect her. She felt a sudden grateful pulse of love for Petronilla's tact.

At the same time they both looked toward the chamber door. The waiting women were outside, coming in with the morning wine, their voices sounding. Petronilla swallowed; she gave Eleanor a dark look. Maybe she had not guessed until now what helping her could mean. Eleanor knew better than to say anything.

There was a gentle rapping on the door.

"Call them," Eleanor said, steadily. If Petronilla gave her up, she was finished. "They'll think something is wrong." She turned out the window again, and Petronilla spoke and the door burst open.

Alys and Marie-Jeanne came in first, leading the cook's boys with the trays of morning bread, and after them Claire, and then two more men with braziers, in spite of the heat, to warm the wine. The aroma of spices and of the fruity wine filled the room. Petronilla said in her high herald's voice, "Will you come clean this up, please—the wine last night did not sit well with me."

Her voice rang through the room. The whole room fell suddenly hushed. By the door the cook's boys stood, their eyes big as biscuits. Eleanor sat down at the window and looked out and said nothing. At a word from Alys, Claire took the chamber pot hastily away. Everybody was staring at Petronilla, who flung herself back into the bed and buried her face in the covers.

Alys brought Eleanor a cup of the wine, warmed and spiced. The waiting woman's face was flushed with interest. Under her breath, she whispered, "Is the lady Petronilla with child?"

Eleanor frowned at her. "It was the wine last night. Don't spread rumors." She took the cup and sipped a little of it, but she dared not swallow it. Alys went off across the room, and Eleanor made sure no one looked, spat the mouthful back into the cup, and emptied the cup out the window.

◆ ◆ ◆

The weather was breaking, and at last there was a cool breeze in the afternoon and mild evenings. With only three waiting women to help, they all had to work making ready for the progress. Along the way Eleanor meant to see again the places that were part of her patrimony. After the council at Poitiers that would free her from Louis, presumably, they would spend Christmas together at Limoges, where the singing was the best in Christendom, and where they would proclaim the annulment. Then she would go a little way north to Poitiers again, and Louis would go a great way north into France.

Petronilla felt an itch of impatience along every nerve, a hunger for this to be finished and done without any more trouble.

She stood back, looking over the four gowns she had spread out on the bed, Eleanor's best gowns; for a while at least their plentiful folds would disguise the changes in her sister's figure. She turned to Marie-Jeanne. "Take all these, then. Alys will know which jewels and shoes." She glanced toward the window, where Eleanor stood in a shaft of sunlight, her arms folded over her chest, looking out. Even to her knowledgeable eye, her sister looked no different—and she had stopped throwing up in the mornings.

She turned back to Marie-Jeanne. The older woman was kneeling by a chest, folding underclothes into it. By the wardrobe, Alys was taking out more shifts and giving them to Claire to air out and bring away.

At Petronilla's feet, Marie-Jeanne made a little soft sound.

Petronilla glanced down, surprised; the older woman was so quiet they often wondered if she had gone mute. She was still kneeling by the chest, her gnarled hands full of cloth, but she had stopped folding. Petronilla looked closer, wondering what had startled her.

In her soft pale hands the older woman was holding rags, ordinary rags. With a start of understanding, Petronilla realized they were the cloths saved for Eleanor to use when the curse of Eve came on her, and standing there stiff as a pike she watched Marie-Jeanne move mentally through some calculation, and then the waiting woman looked up toward Eleanor, and Petronilla saw she knew.

She made no sound; Marie-Jeanne lifted her head and raised her eyes to her, shining with astonishment and worry. Petronilla said nothing, and did nothing, but only looked into the woman's soft, kind old face. Marie-Jeanne met her gaze a moment, and then she looked down with some effort, quietly folded up the rags, and stuffed them down into a corner of the chest, far down, burying them.

She rose, then, and crossed the room to Eleanor, whom she had tended since childhood. She put her arms around her and hugged her like a mother with her child. Eleanor, surprised, looked down at the soft gray head and held her close against her for a moment. No one else seemed to notice. Finally Marie-Jeanne came back to the chest and to her work, but now her face was seamed with worry, and her customary smile was gone.

· · ·

The week before they were to leave on the progress, a page came to Petronilla as she walked alone in the garden and bid her attend the King.

Her belly tightened. She said, "Go fetch my sister, please, to accompany me." The end of her veil hung down by her shoulder, and she lifted it up over her face.

The page flexed up and down in a jerky bow. "No, my lady—they want to see you alone."

"It's unseemly," she said, frightened.

"My lady, I am to tell you, the King—"

"Ah," she said. She turned, looking toward the tower behind her, hoping Eleanor saw—Eleanor would rescue her. The tall stone column stood unhelpfully blank and solid in the sun. Reluctant, but afraid to refuse, she followed the page around through the busy courtyard and up the stair to the door into the King's chamber.

She imagined they knew everything; she imagined their judgments on her, and by the time she reached the door her hands were clammy and her heart was doing a mad gallop in her chest and she was cursing Eleanor for ever getting her into this.

When she entered the room and saw Thierry Galeran standing there behind the King's chair, her knees almost gave way.

She had always hated him and feared him, who wished her nothing but evil, when he noticed her at all. She remembered how gleefully she had enjoyed tricking him and wished she knew how much he understood. On wobbling legs she advanced into the middle of the room. There, she collected herself; she clasped her hands before her and dipped her head to Louis, who was of no higher house and rank than hers, a mere Capet against the ancient House of Aquitaine. She said, "God keep you, Sire."

The King mouthed some greeting. Thierry came around the throne toward her, his head up and his chest thrown out, as if he were a real man.

He said, without any gentling, "My lady. We have had several offers for your hand, and mean to dispose of you soon. But an ill gossip has been whispered lately of you, and before we can assign you to a new husband, we wish a midwife to attend you."

Petronilla jerked her head up, hot with sudden rage and shame, both at what he said and how he said it; she wanted to melt into the floor. She said, "What is this?"

On his throne behind Thierry, Louis looked apologetic and made some gestures. Thierry strutted back and forth before her.

"I need not be more specific, my lady. You must know to what I refer. A midwife—"

"I will not," she burst out. "This is an insult—this is humiliating."

Tears trickled from her eyes; she felt already groped and poked and inspected, some piece of merchandise offered for sale. She stretched out her hands to Louis.

"You cannot wish this for me, sir. I have done you no harm, ever. How can you subject me to such base, cruel usage?"

Louis leaned forward, reaching out to take hold of Thierry's arm, and drew him back a step. Thierry ignored him, looking at her down his nose. "So it is true, then, what they say."

"Your Grace!" She spoke still to the King, her only hope. "Please, protect me—Oh, God, my Holy Savior—" She folded forward, her hands to her face, sobbing with fear and anger into the crumpled cloth of her veil. "If my husband were here, he would strike you down like a dog for this."

"If you still had a husband, my lady, your condition would be a joy to all," Thierry said.

The King said, "Let her go, sir. She will not comply, and I will not suffer her to be forced."

Thierry said, "Sire, we cannot very well marry her off if she is heavy with someone else's bastard."

Petronilla let out a gasp, lowered her hands, and stabbed at him with her eyes; for the first time in her life, her temper soared beyond her prudence, and she took a step forward and slapped his face as hard as she could swing her arm. Thierry flinched back, his cheek bright red. Louis let out a yelp that might have been a smothered laugh. Petronilla turned on her heel and marched out of the room, streaming tears, her hand stinging, her head held high.

She expected them to chase her, to drag her back. To force her into the midwife's arms. To submit her to this rape. Nothing happened. With each wobbling step, she grew more surprised, and secretly, buoyantly triumphant. She had won. She had defied them. She was stronger than she had thought.

. . .

Later, when she told Eleanor, her sister gave a whoop of a laugh.

"My darling. You are a valiant knight—if they had found out it wasn't you, they would have suspected me at once, and then it would all be over. I wish I'd been there! You won the joust against him, sure enough, I'd have given you the rose."

Petronilla flushed, angry. For her sister's sake she had endured humiliation, and Eleanor was treating it like a playful game.

She said, "Someone told them. That I was sick, in the morning, that time. Do you think it was Claire?" She glanced around to see if anybody could overhear. "Someone told him."

Eleanor had a piece of paper in her hand and was reading it; she laid it down and said, with great patience, "You can't blame Claire. Half the tower heard you own the prize. It's worked out so far. Now, help me do this; there are so many people coming along on the progress, and I have to arrange the order for each one."

Petronilla bit her lips together and bent obediently over the list on her sister's knee. She was angry again, and this time it touched on her sister. Everything, she thought, was not just something to do with Eleanor. Thierry had wanted to abuse her, Petronilla herself, and in some way, with mere words, he had, and Eleanor had hardly even noticed what was done to her. Eleanor had even tricked her into this. As soon as she could, she slipped away to the garden and walked awhile by herself, until she had herself calm again.

There was another Petronilla, deep inside, that Eleanor did not know. It came to her that Eleanor would not be so pleased if she did know of this secret person. That gave her a grim satisfaction, as much as defying Thierry had. Or maybe, even more.

She went on down the sunlit garden. Near the gate, a shadow moved on the grass, and she looked sharply up. There sitting on the wall was Joffre de Rançun, her sister's knight; he smiled at her. Guarding them, as he always did. She waved back at him, glad to see him there, and her mood rose. She went over to tease him into walking back with her.

*   *   *

Amazed, Claire said, "What did she do?" They had all heard vague tales of the Lady Petronilla's confrontation with the King's secretary.

Alys shook a linen shift vigorously in the sunlight. It smelled of old roses, and a dried petal went flying across the room. "She slapped Thierry's face for him. One of our pages heard it from one of the King's pages. He said the King laughed."

Claire drew in a breath and held it, delighted. She turned to look through the window, where Petronilla was walking. Her satisfaction in this unnerved her; she wanted to run out there and throw her arms around the Queen's sister. She turned back to Alys.

"But that is so . . . unwomanly, isn't it?"

Alys handed her a little pile of silken shifts. "Everything Petronilla does befits a woman."

Claire blurted, "But she is with child, mysteriously."

Alys glanced beyond her, at Marie-Jeanne, and wordlessly put her hands into the wardrobe for another gown. Claire lowered her eyes and said no more. She busied herself laying the shifts as neatly as she could into the chest. From the bowl beside the chest she took dried rose petals and sprinkled them over the sleek cloth. She thought about what Alys had said, and not said, and her understanding leaped the gap. She licked her lips, excited, watching Alys shake out another shift.

Eleanor it was who was pregnant, she thought.

This made her a little dizzy to think. This was a secret worth a kingdom. She had sworn off telling tales, but now here was the greatest of tales. Perhaps she had turned virtuous too soon. To hide her galloping thoughts, she said, "What then else is there that befits a woman?"

Alys smoothed the lavender silk beneath her fingers. She glanced at Marie-Jeanne and said, "I have never heard it spoken outright— perhaps it befits a woman that no one speaks her virtues outright." She laughed. "But for me, it is like to what makes a perfect knight, who is mighty at arms, loyal to his lord, frank and open in his manner, and great of heart. A woman cannot be mighty in arms, but she can be pious."

Claire thought, uneasily, *I am not very pious.* Nor, she thought, was Eleanor, the highest woman she knew. But Eleanor was brave, and that, she thought, was more like the man's virtue.

She said, "And loyal, and honest, and . . . and kind."

She remembered Petronilla's smile, when she found her in the Hotel-Dieu. That still to her was the first goal, to make someone feel as she had felt then, when Petronilla drew her back from hell.

"Yes," Alys said. "I think so." Her eyes were bright with amusement, and she glanced at Marie-Jeanne again, as if they knew something.

They did know something, and now Claire knew it, too. The little homily on the virtues of women was only froth, but the secret they had inadvertently given up to her was something of incalculable worth.

For that knowledge Thierry, for one, would give anything. But Thierry would never get it. She bit her lips shut, pleased, that she had what he wanted, and would keep it from him, her revenge. To keep a Queen's deep secret was an honor in itself, perhaps, far more valuable to keep than to pass on.

Alys's words of virtue sounded in her mind again. None of it had to do with her. She was not pious. She had already proven she was not loyal, or honest. She wondered if she was kind, and could not say that either.

She wished she had not asked. Her heart felt shrunken. She felt like nothing, again, somehow. She reminded herself that all those words were only puffs of wind. Only deeds and consequences made the difference. That moment when she had heard, "Come home." She had to learn how to do that. She held out her arms for the dress, to help Alys fold it for the progress.

◆   ◆   ◆

Some days later, they left Paris, for what Eleanor hoped would be her last departure from it.

It took the whole day for the progress to start. The court moved in batches out of the city in a vast train: people great and little, many riding but most on foot, and wagons piled with their baggage, horses and mules in harness, braces of greyhounds and alaunts, running hounds in packs, the silent dewlapped lymers with their long dangling ears, hawks in baskets and on the fist, the cooks and the grooms, the laundry women and the kitchen girls, and all kinds of hangers-on.

The King rode first, with his great men and knights, leaving the city in a fuss of his banners and heralds and trumpeters. Eleanor followed well behind, to stay out of the dust of his passage.

She intended to be in his presence as little as possible. Under the loose gown, her belly was beginning to swell, and that morning, for the first time, she thought she had felt something inside there squirming around. She wanted no chance of inspiring the slightest suspicion.

De Rançun and his men ranged along around her, their horses dancing and tossing their heads. Her own horse wore skirts of fringed silk that rippled with every stride. One knight carried her banner, green and gold, and pages and servants and the people of her court followed after her in a great drove. In the fields of the Beauce, just south of the Seine, women out gleaning the last of the wheat crop straightened to watch her go by, shading their eyes from the sun, and their half-naked children came running to the side of the road.

Most of her waiting women sat tamely in a wagon, chattering and passing a cup, but Petronilla rode with her, and de Rançun carried Eleanor's hooded falcon on his fist. They watched the stubbled fields for quarry for it, but there was none. Likely Louis's passage earlier had frightened everything off. In a basket on the back of a mule, the sparrow hawk screeched indignantly at the jostling.

The season had turned toward winter, and even the sunlight had a cool edge to it. Yet the day was clear and brilliant, and Eleanor exhilarated at being out of the city, out of the close tower room, and going somewhere, anywhere, else.

As they passed down through the broad wheatlands south of Paris, the Queen looked ahead and saw the great winding stream of the progress and, twisting in her saddle, could look back and see it stretching far behind her, a river carrying her away to her home.

At that thought her spirit soared, and she lingered in the notion, the river taking her home again. It might be a long, crooked stream, but in the end she would be where she wanted.

Of course, everybody at the beginning was in high spirits. When they first set off, people joked and sang, wandered off to make water or just sit down for a while, ran up and down the road carrying messages and calling to their friends. Later, she knew, they would trudge along like whipped slaves, wanting only to stop. But now everybody was eager, even the horses and the hunting dogs, straining at their leashes.

Her horse snorted and pushed against the bit, and she let him break into a little jog trot, frisking off his excitement. She had just received him as a gift from a Spanish count. A splendid Barbary horse with a mane like silk, his hide all dappled gray, he was too mettlesome to ride aside, which suited her very well. Petronilla trotted along after her on her mild little brown mare, both legs neatly tucked together on the left front of the saddle, but Eleanor held her horse between her knees, and bent him to her will.

Late in the day they let the fierce little sparrow hawk fly at hares, in the meadows along the road. Almost at once the hawk took a great fat buck twice her size. It seemed to Eleanor a perfect omen. Soon, she thought, she would be safe in Poitiers, where she alone ruled. There in dark and quiet she would bear the little worm inside, and then she would send for Duke Henry and come into her great new kingdom.

When she thought of him her body grew warm and taut, and she remembered his passionate mouth, his muscular chest with its mat of thick curly red hair, his thighs like columns, the sword between them that fit her scabbard so well. His passion for her. She loved being loved. She caught Petronilla watching her with a little smirk on her face, and realized her sister knew exactly what was in her mind. When she met Petronilla's eyes, though, her sister looked quickly away.

Lately Petronilla had been fretful, sometimes, perhaps brooding over Thierry's harsh treatment of her. Eleanor wished she would put it aside; she liked her sister blithe.

The road swung west, toward Anjou. The King, half a day's ride ahead of them, would make a show of strength along the border with his fractious vassals there. Eleanor hung back, to have the excuse of staying somewhere else, and sent Joffre de Rançun on ahead to find a suitable place. Briefly, she wondered what Duke Henry was doing. His lands bordered theirs; he could be only a few days away.

Fourteen

NORMANDY
SEPTEMBER 1151

After their father was dead, and the will read, and the old man buried in Le Mans, Geoffrey d'Anjou went south to his new castle at Chinon. Henry rode up to Lisieux to meet the council of his loyal barons.

On Saint John's Day, he stood in the hall, and the room stretched away from him in a wide and empty swath of space. Not a single one of his barons had answered his summons.

After a moment the door opened and his knight Robert walked in, with Reynard just behind him. Robert crossed the empty room toward him while Reynard stood by the door, waiting.

Henry said, "Well." He was so angry he could not force out any more words.

"My lord," Robert said, "We have forty knights and thirty sergeants."

"That will have to do," Henry said, and ground his teeth together. He took his cap, and went to meet Robert, and took them right away back down toward southern Anjou.

* * *

His father had given his brother three castles: Chinon, Loudon, and Mirebeau, along the southern march of Anjou. He came to Chinon first.

The position was magnificent, a broad flat-topped rock high above a river winding to the Loire. The green country around it was just yielding up its harvest: the fields full of wagons, horses tethered in the wasteland, people with scythes moving through the standing corn. In the middle of it stood Chinon.

Henry loved the rock at once. Its stacked heights commanded the whole river valley and, recognizing this in ancient times, the Romans had built walls on it. Those walls were long crumbled, and such fortifications as the old ones had made were gone, but Henry's father had raised a wooden tower on the peak that overlooked the whole valley.

Chinon was too beautiful and too well-placed therefore to leave in Geoffrey's hands. Henry studied the tower a moment; if he burned that tower, Geoffrey would have nowhere to hide. He turned to Robert.

"Get them making torches," he said. "We'll attack at sundown."

So he burned his brother out and chased him down the river south. As Geoffrey escaped, many of his men surrendered, as the custom was, and became Henry's men instead, which got them fed and led well and, most important, on the winning side. In the morning, Henry stood on the smoldering peak of the rock above the river as these men came before him and swore themselves into his service.

The wind blew hard up the river, rolling the thick smoke ahead of it; he looked around at the steep white descents of the rock, terraced and buttressed here and there with Roman work. The flat land sprawled below him like a vast skirt, striped with stands of trees, clumps of buildings, ordinary men struggling to reap and shock their harvests.

Although it was still morning, the sun was fierce and hot. The river swept to the south side of the rock, almost under this peak. A wooded island protected that bank. He thought, *I would build a curtain wall around the whole rock here, enclose it all.* In his mind he saw this place as the heart of his new kingdom, stretching from the mountains south of Aquitaine to the hills of Scotland.

Another of the prisoners knelt before him, and reluctant to spare any attention from his dream, Henry struck him impatiently on the shoulder before he even finished his vow. Henry straightened, looking south and east, where the rich tree-studded land rolled into the hazy, uncertain distance. That was Aquitaine, down there somewhere. This castle would command it all. The castle that would be raised here when he had brought the whole country under him, curtain walls and towers and great gates. When he brought Aquitaine under him.

He thought of bringing her under him, as if he ditched her with a sword, and his body tingled with passion.

Robert came up, his hands behind him. "Are we staying here the night, my lord? I can give the order to make camp."

Henry barked a laugh. "It's hardly midday." He judged there were two or three hours of daylight left. "I can't let my brother get so far ahead of us. He went on toward Loudon. We ride in an hour."

"Yes, my lord." Robert's voice wavered only a little, but Henry could tell he did not like this.

"Make sure everybody eats. We need a garrison here," Henry said. He watched his cousin narrowly. "Pick out ten, fifteen men for a garrison."

Robert said, "There's no castle left."

"They can build one. You can take command."

At that Robert's eyes bulged. He had not anticipated this either. Hauling rocks was worse than riding. He said in a crooked voice, "My lord, we have ridden a long way together; I—"

"I'd rather have you with me," Henry said. He clapped Robert on the shoulder. "Pick out a commander."

Robert said briskly, "Yes, my lord," happier now about going on, and stalked off. His voice rose sharply. Henry turned back to the row of the prisoners and nodded, and the next came up and fell to his knees, mumbling his submission.

*   *   *

By dawn, with Geoffrey still well ahead of him, Henry rode into a village and found an open innyard.

"Here. We'll stop here and rest the horses." He dismounted. His vanguard spilled out the inn gate and filled the narrow street beyond. The village was only a straggle of huts along the road and the inn was the largest building in it, a rambling shack. The smell of food came deliciously from a back building. Robert came up, gray-faced. He did not bear up well on long rides without sleep.

"Yes, my lord."

Henry said, "We can't fit all the men into this village." Several more of Geoffrey's men had joined them on the ride down. More than a hundred men followed his banners now, even though he had left behind garrisons at the strong places to hold the ground they had taken. With so many, he could not move as fast as he wanted, and they all needed orders, which made things more complicated. "We'll get them camped outside the town. Reynard—"

The other knight led his horse up. The innkeeper himself came bustling out, a fat man in a filthy apron, with cups and a jug. Behind him came a girl with wheat-colored hair, younger than Henry, her arms cradling a basket of bread. Henry said, "We have to make sure everybody gets fed. Put the horses on pasture." He reached out for a loaf.

The girl's eyes were lowered, but then suddenly she glanced up at him, and then down again.

His interest leaped. He knew that look, what girls meant by that look. He thought of Eleanor, who was far away. The girl's bodice curved over pretty little breasts. She was a kitchen wench, young and clean. But later.

He turned to Reynard. "Come along, let's do this. Robert, see to things here. Find me a place to sleep. Fresh horses." Without another look at the girl, he mounted his horse and rode out of town to stop the rest of his army before they reached the village and get them bedded down along the road, their horses staked out, their sentries posted. Reynard followed doggedly after him.

When he was done, the little camps of his army stretched back on both sides of the road for nearly a mile. Their fires bloomed in the dusk. Besides the bread and wine Robert managed to find for them, they had been foraging as they rode and the smells rose of cooking meat, among the sounds of men laughing and gossiping. When Henry went back to the innyard, trailing squires, his horse stumbling with fatigue, the moon was rising.

The yard was almost empty. His squires trudged off with the horses. The hall was shut, quiet, and he would sleep in there, eventually, but first he went toward the kitchen, behind the hall. Just as he reached the door, it opened. The thin glow of a rushlight spread out over the threshold and shone on him. Behind it, holding the lamp high, was the girl with the wheat-colored hair. Her eyes burned. The thought of Eleanor touched his mind again, and he pushed it out of the way. Aquitaine was all over the hill. This one was here before him. He reached his hands out and drew her toward him.

◆   ◆   ◆

In the morning he was chasing Geoffrey south through the hills. Having lost Chinon, his brother was predictably making toward Loudon, the second of his castles. His dwindling army left a trail any fool could follow, through trees and meadows and fields where sullen men stood in the middle of their trampled crops and glared at Henry as he rode by.

Almost to the high ground, in the crease between two rolling hills, Geoffrey ambushed Henry's vanguard. Henry sent Robert and a few men up to fight off the attack and keep his brother busy, and with the rest of his army galloped around the back of the hill to Loudon itself, stormed the gate, and overran the little town. At this, cut off from his base, Geoffrey fled, and more of his men submitted to Henry, so many of them that he took their vows all at once.

He did this in the street inside the gate, just before sundown, and afterward a villager in a broad hat came up and bowed and begged him to keep Loudon, to protect the houses and farms. The villager was an old man, his face the color of dirt. He swept off his hat and rolled the brim unceasingly in his hands. "My lord, give us peace. We have the harvest. I pray God, my lord—the lord Geoffrey took everything, but now, we have the harvest to bring in, I pray you—"

"Harvest your crops," Henry said. "I am lord here. I will keep the peace. Let any man with a grievance come to me." The long slanting light of the late sun flooded the place with pink. The guards at the gate called out, and Robert rode up with a half dozen other men of the vanguard and a stranger.

He wore the colors of the Empress, so Henry knew he was a messenger from his mother in Rouen, head city of Normandy. Henry held him aside. Robert swung down from his horse.

"I lost some men. There are a lot of wounded."

"Bring them in and lay them in the church," Henry said. "Get Reynard to help you. Camp the rest outside the wall. No looting, no rape." He would have to arrange to bury the dead. Robert went briskly off. The villager in the broad hat was trying to talk to him. Henry shut him up with a glare and turned to the messenger.

"My lord—" The messenger was filthy. "Her Imperial Majesty bids you God's greeting—" Henry plucked the note out of his hands and turned aside to read it.

The villager followed him. "My lord, thank God for you, I swear, we are loyal, we will—"

Henry looked over his shoulder. "Is there a surgeon here? A midwife? I have wounded men."

"There's an herbswoman, my lord. And the priest, of course."

"Naturally. Go get them." He read quickly through his mother's uncluttered Latin. There was nothing new, only the old woman getting nervous, as she always did, throwing off a spray of advice and orders. Half of the Norman barons had thrown out his chatelains and were proclaiming themselves free, and she expected him back in Rouen at once.

He had to get the south under control first. With Anjou solid, he would deal with the Norman lords. They hated each other more than they hated him, and he could take each one down separately. He walked back and forth a few moments, thinking about that, trying to see everything whole.

Robert reappeared, and so did the villager, who had a priest with him. Henry sent Robert off with the priest to settle the wounded but held the villager back by the arm.

"You say Geoffrey was here for a while?"

"Yes, my lord." The villager clutched his hat in his fists. "He took everything. They drove us out of our own houses. No woman could go anywhere." He drew in a deep breath. "There were Bretons here."

"Ah," Henry said.

This was interesting to know. Wild Brittany, to the west, was his enemy; the reigning Duchess's husband was a stirrup friend of King Stephen of England, whom Henry was trying to dislodge. Who then would have an interest in dislodging Henry. "How many? Soldiers, merchants?"

"A high one, my lord, with knights, and a banner."

Henry grunted. All the more reason, he thought, to uproot Geoffrey. He had been right to come here first. Leave this here to fester and he would never get to England. He said, "Anybody else?"

The villager blinked at him. Henry said, "The French, for instance?" The palms of his hands prickled up. If his brother brought together the French, the English, and the Bretons, they would have him almost encircled.

The old man licked his lips. He said, "The French King and Queen are on a progress, just up the river. Very like, from here, he could have sent to the King."

"A progress. Both of them?" Henry said.

"Yes, my lord."

He struggled a moment to remember exactly what Eleanor looked like. Magnificent eyes. All that coppery hair. Yet he could not visualize her face. He thought, *She's probably forgotten me, too,* and his gut ached.

The villager said in a whisper, as if the softer he spoke the more it was worth, "It's said they're quarreling. The King and the Queen, wild thing that she is. They say they're traveling days apart sometimes. He is to come tomorrow to Saint Jean to hold court, but she is far behind him, way up above the river."

Henry made a sound in his chest. Suddenly he wanted to see her, more than anything else, hold her, make her remember him.

He hardened himself against this. The Breton lord, the nearness of the French King—he had to keep after his brother. If he slackened now, even for a moment, Geoffrey might get a foothold, some backing, some money to turn and defy him.

She was so close, so close.

He walked over to the church, where they were laying wounded men out on the floor, and went among them, but he thought of her. She could be within a day's ride. Even nearer. He began to think how to reach her. He thought suddenly of the note from his mother and pulled it out of his purse. Now all he needed was something to write with. He went looking for ink.

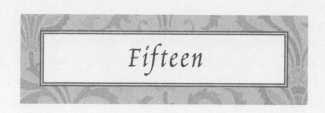

Fifteen

By now Eleanor was traveling a good two days behind the King, and avoiding the places he had stayed even after he had left them. During the day they wandered along the road, and in every tiny village the streets were full of wretched-looking, road-worn people. The knights worked to keep the common folk from her, but she saw women with children huddled on the porch of a church, and seeing an old woman begging on the side of the road, she stopped and made de Rançun bring her up beside the Queen's horse.

The old woman smelled, and the hand she held up was filthy. Eleanor sent hastily for some bread and a purse to give her. "Where have you come from, mother?"

"Anjou—they are fighting—burning everything—"

She gave the bread and purse into the old woman's hands, then sent for the village's head man.

He was old like the beggarwoman, but cleaner, and he bowed properly to her. She said, "What is going on now?"

"The Count is harrying his brother south," the old man said. "These people have fled—unwisely, I think; things will settle down quickly." But when she gave him another purse to care for the people, he babbled with thanks and bobbed up and down and kissed the hem of her gown.

"Thank you, lady—you are the most gracious of queens—"

At that the crowd pushed around her again, all of them bubbling with thanks, surrounding her horse. She leaned out of the saddle, reaching out her hand to them, as she often did, letting them touch her; some girls held out flowers to her, and one thrust a wad of paper into her grasp.

She closed her hand on it. Her skin tingled in a sudden racing excitement. De Rançun and the other knights were shooing the crowd off. She let the Barb carry her on ahead of everybody else, then swiftly opened the bit of paper in her hand and read it.

Petronilla jogged her mare up beside her. "What is it? What is that?"

"Nothing," she said. "One of them gave me a flower." She opened her hand to show the crumpled petals. The paper lay buried underneath, and she would burn it later. She could not keep from smiling, and she looked up the road, eager.

＊　＊　＊

In the afternoon she called de Rançun to her, and said, "Isn't there a little monastery up ahead somewhere? We could spend the night there."

He gave her a sharp look. "I don't know. I'll find out." And he came back a little while later, saying, "There is Saint Pierre, but it's considerably off the road. We could go on to—"

"Saint Pierre will do," she said. "Go bid them know we are coming." Petronilla was watching her intently. It was hard to keep anything from her sister. But part of the thrill of this was its secrecy. She gigged the Barb into a trot down the road.

* * *

The monastery of Saint Pierre was old and small, its abbot overjoyed to have a royal visitor; he led Eleanor to the best room in the cloister, with the best bed, a mattress stuffed with straw, and the linens patched. It was too small for all of the women, and the three waiting women went into another room. De Rançun took the men and the baggage and attendants down into the village.

The monks brought Eleanor and her little court their finest fare: a ripe cheese and decent bread, a rough fruit wine. Eleanor's hawk had killed that day, and so they dined well enough. They heard Vespers in the monastery chapel, and then, going back along the cloister, Eleanor said, "I think I shall go for a walk. The rest of you all go in and get ready for bed; don't wait for me."

Petronilla frowned at her. They were going side by side along the arcade of the cloister toward their rooms. "I'll go with you."

"No—I want to be alone—I have to think. I'll just walk in the cloister. Unless you fear some lecherous monk lies in wait?"

The women behind her laughed. Petronilla gave her a long sideways look, suspicious, but all she said was, "Go on, then, but don't be long. I'm going straight to bed, you'll wake me up."

"I won't."

The women all turned to go in; she walked on alone down the arcade. Her heart was thudding in her chest.

Her hand slid down her belly, where the baby lay like a rock in her dreams. She held herself straight, pulling her stomach in. He would not notice. She was hardly showing. He could not know; that could ruin everything. Because she was still married to Louis, it was by law Louis's baby, and to everybody who knew better it was more proof of her wicked, lascivious female nature. To Henry himself, it could be a reason to call everything off.

She could not have ignored his call; she burned to see him again. He would not notice. She pulled off her coif and shook her hair loose. She did not care who saw her now, but she was alone in the dark.

The square of grass in the middle of the cloister was pale with moonlight, the arcade deep in shadows. She walked along to the corner, where the two walls did not meet. The opening between them led into a little crooked passage through to the outside. Beyond the cloister's outer wall was a row of gardens, bounded by a thorn hedge, and behind the cabbages she found a little gate and let herself out.

She stood at the top of a long grassy slope running down to the tree-lined river. The moonlight turned the long grass silver. The wind swept up from the west, moist and sweet, like a cool kiss that set the grass rippling. She stood a moment in the swirl of it, the wind's long fingers in her hair. The road led away down the hillside, toward the village. She looked carefully all around for sentries but saw no one. The grass sang in the windy dark. Then through the susurrus of the wind she heard a long, drawn-out whistle: a falconer calling his hawk.

All her hair stood on end; she went toward him like a hawk swooping through the air, running through the moonlight, until near the foot of the slope he stood up suddenly out of the grass and she ran into his arms.

"I had to see you," he said. "I had to see you." She clung to him, her arms around his neck, said his name. They kissed. "Come on." He led her into the shelter of the trees. In the dark she could hardly make out his face. His hands were urgent on her body, his mouth demanding. She helped him gather up her skirts and leaned against an old tree and they joined, his hands on her hips, his lips against her throat. She wrapped her arms around him. She whispered his name again.

"Come with me," he said. "Forget about Louis. Come with me now."

She laughed; it felt as if she could never leave him, as if they were permanently connected. She said, "This must be done well, I have told you. Be patient." She kissed him. He leaned on her a moment more, gasping, and then they were sliding apart. The cool breeze chilled her thighs.

He backed away, pulling his clothes together. "I'll curse every day until I see you again." His arms slid around her again; she was doing up her shoulder brooch. His hand moved over her body. He said, in a different voice, "Are you pregnant?"

Her body went cold down to her heels. But she had thought of this. She was ready for this. She laughed. "No, 'tis only the fat bird I dined on. But soon, my darling. We shall have an army of princes."

He kissed her, his lips apart. He believed her. "Soon."

"I need to get back." She had to get away from him, before the suspicion returned. She nuzzled his cheek, her arm around his waist. "We will be together before summer. I swear it." She turned and went quickly up the slope toward the monastery.

◆　◆　◆

Henry went down through the trees to the bank of the stream, where he had left his horse. His body still thrilled, keen at her touch; he was sweating even in the gentle cool of the night. He led his horse a little way down the stream and swung into the saddle. It was a long ride back to his camp. Yet just thinking of her sent him high again, like a leaf on a storm wind, reeling with excitement.

Up there on the ridge someone shouted. He twisted to look over his shoulder; a horseman was riding into sight past the west end of the monastery wall—a sentry, maybe. The rider shouted again to him to halt, to stand. He touched his spurs to his horse and galloped off down the stream. He was over the next ridge, almost to the old road, before it occurred to him that after all he had never really seen her face.

◆   ◆   ◆

In the morning, Alys brought her a new gown, plain dark russet, with a subdued gold trim; Eleanor said, "What of that old green thing—it is so comfortable for riding."

Alys leaned slightly toward her, laying the new gown down for her, and murmured, "My lady, I have let this one out a little at the sides. It will be better, I think. I will work next on the green one." She smiled and touched Eleanor's shoulder, and Eleanor understood this was her way of saying that she knew, and would protect her.

But it cooled her excitement a little. She realized that the secret, like the baby, was growing, that more and more people were finding out. That this road might not be leading her home at all, but to the failure of all her hopes, to the dark convent, the penitent's straw, or worse.

She throttled that away. With a sudden fierce desire, she willed the days ahead of her to go as she wished, and quickly crossed herself and said a prayer for God's help. But the annoying doubt remained, that maybe the unknowable, unbiddable God intended something else for her, and that which lay ahead for her was an ordeal she, even she, could lose.

◆   ◆   ◆

They traveled slowly along the river. Eleanor held her train back from the King's, so that they never met, even when some delay brought them close enough that they stayed overnight in the same area.

The broad wheatlands of the Beauce yielded to softly rolling tree-covered hills, cut through with little streams, all running, as the royal progress ran, to the Loire. During the day they stopped to eat wherever the noon sun found them, sometimes in an open field, where the household spread linens on the ground, and ate from baskets of bread and cheese, and sometimes at an inn, where they took over the whole place and drained the local cellars dry.

They followed west along the river, flowing sleek and brown between woodlands now leafless for the winter. On the low hillsides, the thick stocks of little vineyards traveled in rows up toward the sky like crooked old men with outstretched arms. The cut heaps of last year's vines were piled up at the ends of each row, and the smell of dead leaves flavored the air. In the stands of trees, globes of mistletoe clustered in the bare branches, with here and there the messy nests of magpies, like bowls of twigs. The birds circled overhead, crying in their hoarse, mocking voices.

They stayed one night at Blois, the ancient city on the Loire. Stephen, who was now King of England, had been born there, his mother the daughter of the Conqueror, William the Bastard. Eleanor thought a curse against King Stephen, for the sake of her lover Henry. She clasped that thought to her, luxuriating in it: her lover Henry.

But now the city and its famous old castle and rich lands belonged to the younger son of the Count of Champagne, Count Theobald, hardly older than her lover Henry himself. He gave a great feast for her and Louis, at which Eleanor stayed as far from Louis as possible. Count Theobald was a lanky young man with pimples and a raucous laugh. His court was rough; he had no wife or sisters to give it polish, and she was glad to leave. In the morning they crossed over the river on the arched Roman bridge and followed the old road, the pilgrimage road, down into the south.

West of here and north was Anjou, she knew, where he was.

There had been no rain for a while, and the brown water coursed slowly along between banks of dry crackling reeds, where the narrow boats of the local fishermen were drawn up in the shallows, and the women washed their linen and spread it to dry on the bushes. The weather was turning gray and grim, and a cold wind met them, sweeping up the river valley from the distant sea. Eleanor sent Claire to the baggage to unpack their fur cloaks, and she and her sister rode with their hands drawn up into the warmth of the sleeves.

Day after day passed. At last, ahead of them, in a twist of the valley, they saw the black slate rooftops of the great abbey of Fontevraud, sprawled along the gentle skirt of the hillside. The people around Eleanor sent up cheers at the sight, and even the horses quickened their steps, their heads bobbing; she turned toward her sister and saw Petronilla already smiling at her, and the old shared love rushed back over her. Whatever had come between them was surely gone. She urged her horse closer and reached out her hand to her sister, and so, holding hands together, they rode into the abbey.

Hereafter, on this side of the river, they were in their own country, and foolishly enough, they thought everything would be well.

◆ ◆ ◆

Fontevraud was a double house, containing both men and women, ruled over, as all such houses were, by an abbess. The dukes of Aquitaine had supported the place from its beginnings, endowing it with wealth and lands, and the current Abbess, who met them at the gate, was a cousin of Eleanor's. Louis had already arrived and gotten the great welcome, and so there was little ceremony in their greeting.

Petronilla and Eleanor left their horses and train in the gateyard and followed the Abbess down into the central courtyard of the dormitory, where the shadowy recesses of the galleries rustled with people sneaking away from their prayers or chores to watch. Petronilla was glad to be out of the saddle and longed to take off her dusty clothes; she followed at Eleanor's side as they went down to the rooms kept for them during such visits as these.

The Abbess was an older woman, short and round of face, who looked out of her wimple like a baby from swaddlings. Petronilla at once sensed some coldness and aloofness in her manner. Eleanor spoke to her once, familiarly, as a cousin, and the woman only gave a little bow, not meeting her eyes. Petronilla thought perhaps it was a mistake to let Louis arrive so long before them, so that Thierry

Galeran and his minions had the chance to set people's minds in his mold.

The corner rooms on the ground floor of the cloister were kept always ready for the Duchess of Aquitaine, and the Abbess led them there now. The other women trailed after in a disorderly straggle, behind them some of the monastery's porters with the baggage, loud and awkward. Flocks of nuns stuffed the corners, the doorways, watching them pass, giving off muffled gasps and giggles like penned-up geese.

"Who else is here?" Eleanor asked. Her voice was a little too loud; Petronilla guessed she had also noticed the Abbess's cool restraint. "I thought I saw the Archbishop's colors."

"Bordeaux is here," the abbess said. "And Geoffrey d'Anjou."

"He's dead," Eleanor blurted out, stopping at the door.

The Abbess stood back so that a servant could open the door into the cell. "This is the son, the younger son, who has been robbed of his inheritance and seeks the King's help." She stood with her hands clasped over her rosary, letting Eleanor go by her, and as Petronilla passed her, the black gimlet eyes poked at her, clearly assessing the size of her waist. Petronilla flushed at this and went on deep into the room, toward the window.

Across the room, she looked at Eleanor, and between them there flashed an understanding: If little Anjou was with the King, then Henry had driven him out and won the war.

The Abbess pursued them into the cell, which was twice as large as most, and well furnished with bed, stools, and a clothes chest more suitable for a duchess than a nun. She said, "My lord Archbishop is here to meet the King, of course, but will come to you soon, Your Grace. And when he does—"

In the center of the room, Eleanor swung around toward her; Petronilla marked the set of her shoulders and the loft of her chin, and knew her sister was angry. The Abbess went on, "When he does,

I hope you will submit yourself to his wisdom. This is mad and wicked, what you propose, to separate from our good King Louis, and we all beg you to resign yourself to the fate proper for you."

Eleanor fixed her with a stare. Her back was stiff, her shoulders square, as if she made herself a wall against enemies, and her voice rang hard with anger. She did not pretend to misunderstand. She said, "God alone decides my fate, not the Archbishop of Bordeaux. Or you, my lady Abbess."

She fairly spat the final words, and the Abbess shrank a little; her slender hands rose, blue-veined, to smooth her stainless coif. Her knuckles were the color of ivory.

"It is our duty as brides of Christ to pray for you," she said. "And to counsel you in the right way. The King is your lord, as the Son of God is ours; your marriage to him is what must be, as ours must be. This is gravest sin, what you propose, and cannot happen."

"No," Eleanor said. "I accept your prayers, mother, but I do not accept your view of this. For the King's sake, as well as mine."

"It is God's will you should heed," the Abbess said, but she was already backing toward the door. Her mouth twisted like a wound. "God made you a woman, Eleanor of Aquitaine, and you must conduct yourself as a woman of honor." Her gaze flitted toward Petronilla. "As others may not."

At the hurt and injustice of this look, Petronilla took a step backward. Eleanor said, "Get out."

The Abbess's eyes, wide with shock, twitched toward Eleanor, and her mouth fell open; already almost on the threshold, she said, more protesting than defiant, "This is my place; I am Abbess here."

"This is my duchy," Eleanor said. "And you will obey me, lady. Now."

The rest of them were still and silent as hunted rabbits, every gaze fixed on Eleanor. The Abbess hesitated only a moment, bowed her head, and went tamely out the door. Petronilla sighed and relaxed, pleased. She laid her hand on her flat belly. Alys rushed to shut the door behind the fleeing Abbess, and in the center of the room, Eleanor wheeled around, her hands flying up.

"Damn them!"

Behind Petronilla, she heard a little gasp; it was Claire, still not used to Eleanor's temper. Petronilla said, "They have changed his mind."

Eleanor turned in a circle in the center of the room, her skirts swaying out, as if her rage drove her into motion. "I will not be treated like this—a mere woman! Ah! Damn their souls to some deep, hot hell where only men can be—a hole dug with penises! Ah!"

The other women went into a flurry of action: opening chests, and laying out the great bed, and seeing to the fire and to the ewers of water and wine, while Eleanor paced up and down and swore. The room was larger than any monk's cell, but it had only a small window to let in light and let out the smoke of the braziers. Petronilla stood by the window, where the air was clearest; she watched her sister steadily, seeing the cold fear that fed her rage. She was carrying the baby high and deep, so that her cloak and gown hid it, but as she swept her cloak off and flung it down, Petronilla could plainly see the swelling curve above her waist, and now Eleanor put one hand to her back, in the way of pregnant women everywhere.

Suddenly Eleanor turned to the door. "I will go at once to the King."

Petronilla bounded across the room and into her way. "No. Eleanor, you must not." She thought Eleanor did not realize how she looked—how obvious her pregnancy was; if she went to the King now, the game was all up, and Petronilla put her back to the door and spread her arms over it like a bar.

Eleanor flashed at her. "Get out of my way! I know how to manage Louis—I must force him to my will." She raised her hand. "Move aside, Petra!"

Petronilla had never before stood against her, but she stayed fast, her arms out. "I am not letting you go from this room, Eleanor."

Eleanor struck her on the face. The other women caught their breath in a collective gasp, and Petronilla rocked her head to one side, but she straightened and fixed her eyes on her sister's. "Strike me as you wish, Eleanor. But stay, and listen to me."

In her sister's blazing green eyes she saw the fiery anger flash. Eleanor's mouth twisted. But she lowered her hand.

"I beg your pardon. I should not have done that." As sharply as her temper had risen it was falling now, her shrewd wit coming to the fore. She reached out and laid her fingers against Petronilla's cheek, as if her touch could heal what it had wounded. "But we must act— you know this."

"Yes," Petronilla said. Her cheek stung, but she throttled down a feeling of triumph. "We must act wisely, and with effect. Think about what sways Louis—what has won him in the past? Always a churchman: Suger first, the Pope, that time in Rome, and then Bernard—he longs for God's own word in everything. Only God moves him."

Eleanor tossed her head, impatient. "Bernard and Suger both are gone. I can deal with Louis as well as they."

Petronilla said, "Yes. But you got him to agree once before, Eleanor, and he changed anyway. Thierry Galeran is always with him, and you cannot be. Thierry wants only to have Aquitaine, as long as possible, which means you, as long as possible. We have to try something else."

Abruptly Eleanor wheeled, looking around the room, and her gaze fell on Claire, in the middle of the room by a chest. "Have you seen Thierry? Has he approached you again?"

The girl bobbed up and down, her hands on her skirts, her eyes wide. "Oh, no, my lady. I have been with you always. I have not seen him."

Petronilla said, "If she had betrayed us, they would surely know it is not I with child." Yet she cast a sideways look at Claire, who was flushing. Petronilla ran her tongue over her lips. There had to be some way to get by Thierry to the King. "What about Bordeaux?"

"My lord uncle? The archbishop?" Eleanor laughed. She turned, her hands flexing, restless, and paced around the room in a circle. "He is less like Bernard and Suger than any man with a tonsure."

Petronilla also laughed; the Archbishop had bounced each of them on his knee. An Occitan to his fingertips, he was worldly and indulgent and easy. Nonetheless he was a churchman and Louis, apparently, only heeded celibates. "Who else is there?"

Eleanor circled the room again, banging her hands together, and her gaze came back to Petronilla. "Yes, perhaps. Send for him, then; bid him here, my good uncle Bordeaux."

Petronilla's taut muscles softened; she had not known until now how hard she had girded herself for this battle. She had not even known it was a battle. Amazed, she realized she had won it. She let Alys go past her out the door, to find a page.

Sixteen

FONTEVRAUD
OCTOBER 1151

Bordeaux was as large around the middle as if it were he, not Eleanor, who bore another life within; his cassock was splendidly trimmed with silk shot through with gold thread, and his rosary glittered with jewels. Eleanor met him in a secluded part of the garden, so that she could swathe herself in a cloak. Sedate as elders they walked along among the pruned vines, through a pale wintry sunlight, a couple of pages trailing behind out of earshot. The Poitevin hillside beyond the monastery wall lay dormant and brown in the first cold of winter. Somewhere nearby a magpie chattered, and from the rooftop of the monastery a second answered.

One for sorrow, she thought. *Two for joy. Let it be so.* She crossed herself, to seal the omen to her.

Eleanor had known the Archbishop of Bordeaux all of her life, and she had no awe of him; she knew he liked best to have things easy. At first he showed the signs of a recent conversation with the King, or more likely, Thierry Galeran, but she was patient; she could deal with him. After she had dipped her head for his blessing, he said, "Now, my dear, I hear very odd things of you. I had thought you past your girlish whims."

"Not so," she said. "I shall ride my girlish whims all the way to the grave, Uncle."

"Oh, my," he said, mildly. "That's unhappy to hear." He patted her arm; he was speaking in the langue d'oc, which she always used, their common tongue. They went along a line of cropped shaggy stalks, barren for the winter. He said, "Lady Eleanor, think of your duty to God. You can resign yourself to being Queen of France, surely, and fussed over and adored all the days of your life; what is so ill about this?"

"Rather I were merely Duchess of Aquitaine," she said. She rounded on him, nearly as tall as he was, and gripped his hand in hers. In spite of the cold, his hand was warmer than hers. "Think on it, Uncle. You are a true Occitan; do you want these cold northerners with their callused knees and their greedy fingers ruling our sweet land forever?"

That tripped up the graces of his easy manner; he pressed his lips together, his eyes flattening. She went on, pushing where he was soft.

"Think on it. They are steadily eating up our lands, our customs, taking away whatever they want, blighting everything else, and stuffing their laws down on us, telling us what to think and how to worship, and sneering at our language and our ways. How much longer before they have taken away everything that's beautiful and merry and worth living for?"

He said, "We are not such sheep as to let them do that."

"I mean to come back and rule here," she said, "without Louis. I mean to live in Poitiers, where I belong, and which belongs to me. Where the antique Romans whose children we are came for the sun and the wine and the pleasures and made the old life live on when

Rome itself was weary unto death. Poitiers, where we all can best remember and honor the glories of the past, where my own grand-fathers ruled in splendor that the North is too dull even to dream of. There people can think as they want and learn what they choose. I will give justice and bring peace, so that everything prospers, and I will have a court that every other court in Christendom will long to be, which will call to it every art and every pleasure, and which will send its glories out to all the corners of the world. But I must be free of Louis, whose mind is too small. Especially I will be free of Thierry Galeran, who means to destroy me."

His round face flushed, but he made no immediate answer. His gaze drifted away toward the bare-branched orchard that began at the edge of the garden. His mouth curled down at the corners, and she guessed he remembered some slight against himself. She said, "How do they keep my duchy, sir? Is it fair, and rich, and lively as always? Or are they sucking the blood from it, and chilling even the sunlight?"

He said, "Perhaps it is God's will."

"I cannot believe that the gentle Jesus who called children unto him and walked among the humble artisans willed that we who are the true heirs of Rome should be subject to the furry, snorting north-erners of Clovis the bloody Frank. You must help me."

"I?" he said.

"Go to the King. Remind him that Bernard himself decreed we should part." She leaned toward him, her hand on his arm, her words in a hot rush. "The saintly monk saw clearly, sir. And you know he had no love for me—he would do nothing for my sake. He knew the truth in this. The marriage should never have happened. It will blight every-thing—Louis and France, as well as Aquitaine and me. The dynasty of Hugh Capet will die with Louis, unless he sets me free."

The Archbishop crossed himself. "Blessed be Bernard of Clair-vaux. He said this to the King himself?"

"Before everybody, sir. Even Thierry will have to admit it. I pray

you, do not let the likes of that fat, bloodless eunuch subvert the clear
vision of the saint."

Bordeaux's eyebrows performed a little bow, up and down, and
she saw his pale eyes change. She had made him see what she wanted.
A surge of triumph warmed her. She gathered the cloak around her
with her hands, watched her uncle narrowly. The trick with him was
to let him come to his decisions as if he made them himself.

His fingers went to the garnet-studded crucifix at his waist. His
lips pursed. His eyes rolled toward her.

He said, "But if you come back, you will have some new duke
over us."

She said, "Leave that to me. I alone am Aquitaine. I promise you,
I shall be your champion even before I am another's bride, and always
after."

He smiled, his eyes twinkling. "Not for nothing are you the
granddaughter of the Troubadour."

She gave him back the smile, flattered at that, and he put his hand
on his heart, and bowed to her.

"My dear uncle. God bless you for that; I shall be worthy of it."

"I shall speak to him, my dear. You have convinced me."

"Good," she said. "Then the council will sit at Poitiers, during
Advent?"

"A council. No, I fear the King has done nothing so immediate.
But that's certainly the way; there must be a council of churchmen,
to declare the marriage null. The church, you know, is very zealous
about marriages; we believe it's for the sake of the women, mostly,
foolish men that we are. Advent is too soon; we cannot all come
together so quickly." He patted her hand. "You spend Christmas in
Limoges? Perhaps after that, around Epiphany."

"Epiphany." She steadied her voice against her disappointment;
Thierry was still winning, somehow; for her, Epiphany would be too
late.

"Limoges, then. But even that may be hasty. By summer, surely, though."

She did not say, *By summer I will be ruined.* Maybe the best she could hope for was the convent. She bowed her head to him. "Thank you, my lord. I am most grateful." Her heart was galloping, and then, deep in her body, something twisted strongly and struck her in the side, as if the child himself caught her alarm.

Oblivious, Bordeaux was talking on, reviewing who should sit in the council, and she recovered at once. To her relief she realized all of the men he was mentioning were French prelates, near at hand. It would not take so long to gather them, if she could keep Louis to it. She mouthed words at Bordeaux, agreeing to everything, and leaned on him a little, to let him feel manly. He turned toward her and said, "And there is something you can do for me."

"Ah," she said, taking hold of his hand. "What is it? A tax, an estate, a city? Make me Duchess of Aquitaine and I will give you everything you desire in Bordeaux."

He chuckled, but his cheeks reddened a little, and she guessed he had such desires; there was something to work with, then, in time to come. He smiled at her. "No, this is more immediate. I have a certain lute player whom I must get rid of, because he cannot keep his hands off women."

"Aha," she said. "So you would send this lusty musician among a gaggle of women. Turn him into the street, what's so hard about that?"

"Oh, no. He is too good; I do not care to see him go out of the country and ply his considerable skills elsewhere. Any court will profit from his presence; he can make a man great with a song, and probably ruin him, too. Poitiers would be perfect for him. I merely want him off my own hands, and you will love his work."

"Provençal?" she said.

"No, from the west, over the water, some borderland to England,

I forget the name. His name is Brintomos, Brantomos, something like that." His smile broadened, irresistible. "He has a song about a knight who falls in love with his Queen that I think you'll especially enjoy."

"While he seduces all my chamberwomen?" she said. "Very well, we're stronger in defense than we seem. Send him to me."

* * *

Martinmas began, when everybody was supposed to be merry, and Eleanor wished she were merrier than she was. There was no way to avoid attending the great feast, but even the music could not amuse her. She sat at the head of the great table in the refectory, not beside Louis, but as far from him as their chairs could be placed. Still she could not escape him; she felt his gaze constantly on her, and his pages came by every few moments with little gifts of meat, a wine, a comfit.

She ignored them, keeping her gaze forward, sitting straight as an icon, and ate only a few mouthfuls. In preparation for this event, before they put on her sumptuous gown, her ladies had wrapped her up from armpits to hips in two tight layers of damp linen that had dried now to an unyielding armor, and she could barely breathe. Before her, stretched across the whole refectory, crowds of people stood watching her, and if only one wondered about her, she might be lost.

Petronilla was on her left hand; Petronilla fed on most of what the King sent, not Eleanor. Bolt upright, bored with the bad music, Eleanor lifted her gaze to the high ceiling of the refectory, where cobwebs swayed in the little breezes like dusty tapestries.

She had forgotten how pregnancy was like being made a servant of her own body, now occupied by a demanding and finicky stranger. Petronilla was right; she could not bear this very long, nor continue going before the eyes of their enemies. Between her sides the baby churned again. Around her at the high table they had eaten their fill of the fat goose and its attendants, and now the rest of the court was falling on the meats and bread and puddings heaped on the lesser tables all through the refectory.

At her knee, Petronilla sat primly in her chair, her eyes restless. Framed in the dingy white of her gown and coif, her face was a younger version of what Eleanor saw in her own looking glass; but washed of color and boldness, she looked plain as a mouse. She was deep in thought and would not be spoken to. Eleanor turned away, crushed inside the linen bands, looking for something else to distract her from her sufferings.

Behind her, she heard her steward send off someone else trying to approach her; she had given them orders to let no one through, and obeying her was keeping them busy, this the seventh or eighth supplicant for her attention. She glanced over her shoulder and saw a tall man in a green coat stalking away down the table, no one she knew.

Her wandering gaze stuck on someone down by the wall: Geoffrey of Anjou.

She gave a start, the faces similar enough there also that she thought at once of his father, Le Bel, and his brother, but this was the younger boy. Strapping, tall, he was a preening cock, with a mane of tawny curls and jewels in his ears and on his fingers. He had Le Bel's animal beauty, but sleek and spotless with the untested innocence of youth. She caught the steward's eye and nodded to him, and a page went down the rows of courtiers. She turned forward again to see another man walking up to her on the far side of the table.

"My lady, welcome to Aquitaine."

This was the Vicomte de Chatellerault, of course another cousin, an older man, with a well-kept beard and a jeweled collar. He was twice a widower and doubtless looking for a third wife to suck dry. He and Eleanor shared a grandmother, remembered by the interesting name of Dangereuse, who had been the object of one of the great

Duke William's more strenuous romantic maneuvers. Therefore she had to speak to him, and she bantered with him a little, holding herself thin as a stork's leg, and moving as well as possible when she had to. When he went away, Geoffrey of Anjou stood just behind her elbow.

She turned with stately slowness toward him, and he gave her a deep, flourishing bow. He wore a truly remarkable red and gold coat, and the bobs in his ears were carved rubies. His hair and crispy curled beard were combed to perfect smoothness, as if painted on. He straightened with practiced flattery on his lips. "My gracious Queen, pardon me my stutters and gasps; your beauty has taken all my breath away."

"You speak excellently well, for the lack," she said. "What do you here, my lord, so far from home? And still in mourning, surely." She glanced at the short-skirted red surcoat, puffed and filled, fur-trimmed and sewn with figures in gold thread; the golden links of the collar around his neck were studded with crystals. "How kind of you to come to us, in your time of sadness."

His bright blue eyes gleamed at her. He said, "Mourning does not unman me, Your Grace. How could I keep myself from seeing you, and still call myself a man?"

She glanced off into the open hall, where the first bad lute players had been replaced with two more, no better, plucking twangs and thunks rather than music from their strings. Petronilla, beside her, staring into the indefinite distance, was obviously listening to everything she said to Anjou. She leaned a little closer to the slick-tongued boy and gazed deep into his eyes, and when his eyes widened with hope and excitement, she said, "And what news of your brother, the Duke of Normandy?"

His ardor dimmed like a cloud crossing the sun. He scowled at her, insulted. "What to say of him that is not an outrage? He has stripped away all my father's gifts to me, except poor old Mirebeau.

The will said also I am to be Count of Anjou, one day—small chance he will honor that. Now he's north again, bringing all the Normans to heel—but I don't want to talk of him!" He reached out for her hand. "It's you I came to see."

She eluded his touch. "Better you should be off north, heeling Normandy."

That drove him back a step. His smooth, tanned face tightened with bad temper; his sun-bleached hair bristled. In that he was his father's son, rash and headstrong. His temper gave his voice a whining edge. He said, "My brother has driven me from my own lands! Surely, simple honor compels you to support my cause."

She laughed. Geoffrey of Anjou did not seem amused. Across his handsome, clear-eyed young face went a slow progress of thought, and his initial indignation warped into a sly smirk. He leaned closer to her, his voice silky.

"You mark that he is not here, pressing his suit with you. He'd rather stay in Normandy, cracking heads. And—Your Grace, I am loath to tell you this, lest it lower your esteem for him, but you should know he has another leman. He never sleeps alone."

She sat back. For an instant a white rage heated her. At once she knew this was what the raw youth before her wanted, and she cooled. Nonetheless the wording irked her—*another leman*. As if she had ever been his leman. She felt little Anjou's eyes greedy on her, taking in this struggle in her. She thought she would rather be a sinner than betray one. "Well," she said, "perhaps it keeps him warm." The linen clutched her like an iron girdle. With her forefinger she traced a figure eight on the arm of the chair.

In her mind, something she had thought solid cracked apart.

Her gaze never left little Anjou, whom she hated now for telling her this, the pig. "You're here, then, to get my lord the King's approval for your cause? Has he given it?"

A page was waiting with yet another tray of comfits, and she waved him off. Once the boy was gone, Anjou leaned even closer, gazed at her tenderly from his cornflower-blue eyes, and said, "I came here to see you, my Queen, and nothing else. The mere sight of you consumes me with a passion."

She smiled at him. "Such a fire in green wood," she said. "Season awhile, my lord, and you'll burn cleaner."

Geoffrey straightened up like a fighting stag, all fine indignant strut. "I'll prove to you what kind of man I am, if you let me."

Eleanor turned away, watching him through the corner of her eye, her head tilted. "Get out of here before I set the cat on you."

He flushed to the roots of his yellow hair, turned on his heel, and marched off. Eleanor straightened, her gaze on the musicians. Her whole body ached. She had to get out of the scratchy embrace of the linen, to breathe freely, to lie down and let her body alone. When the page came to fill her cup, she drank half of it in a single gulp.

Petronilla said, "What a pretty fellow that is."

Eleanor said, "A pretty little serpent."

She thought again of what he had said, his brother with another woman, and she shifted in her chair, restless, angry again. She imagined him spewing all that hot passion over someone else. She had thought—he had said—there had been some things said about *always*. She didn't remember anything about chastity. She wished a poison dart into little Anjou's back. Across the room, she noticed someone watching her.

It was her cousin the Vicomte de Chatellerault, standing alone behind some others. When she saw him, he looked away immediately, but she still felt the cold quality of his stare. She sat straight up, her hands in her lap, uneasy all over her skin. Many men watched her, she was used to that; she enjoyed that, the admiring looks, the longing, desirous looks. This attention had a greedy edge to it, a fresh hunger.

Wolfish, she thought, remembering the clever, saintly Bernard and his prophesies. A wolf on a hind.

Now she glanced around the hall and saw other faces, on all sides, watching her, who would soon become a woman alone, and Duchess of Aquitaine. Every one hoping to profit somehow thereby. This was what she had come into, a country of wolves.

Yet it was her country, hers alone. She held herself straight as a scepter. She was Duchess of Aquitaine and these were her servants, obligated by blood and duty to her. They gave themselves away with their lustful looks; they gave her power over them. They were here, after all, because of her, and not she for them.

That was why she needed Henry, even more than for his passion and his lusts. He had what was better than love; as he had proven again, now he had the gift of power. She had to remember that fore-most. She kept her hands in her lap. Avoided touching her belly, or bracing her back. Beside her, Petronilla gave her another half-smiling look.

"I hope neither of these is the lute player Uncle Bordeaux wants to give us."

"So do I, very heartily." Eleanor turned to send a page for more wine. "It should not be said of any lute player that I would rather listen to flatteries than him."

Seventeen

As soon as they were back in the Queen's chambers, the door shut, the braziers glowing hot, Eleanor almost burst out of her bonds, flinging her gown off, turning around and around as Alys unwound her. She sprawled out on the bed with a sigh. The other women hurried around, putting her discarded clothes away and setting up the room for the night. Petronilla sat down by the window, her hands in her lap, watching everything.

She had been thinking over what Eleanor had told her of the talk with Bordeaux, and she agreed with her sister: They were running out of time, and there seemed no way to force the issue. Claire went by her with a candle, shielded from the draft, to light the candles by the bed. Eleanor's hair, spread out on the pillow, picked up the light like a bed of embers. Petronilla looked away. She had begun to lust for her freedom, and now they were snatching the chance away from her.

Then, in through the window, came the first notes of a lute.

Petronilla's lips parted; in the heat of the crowded room the notes fell upon her like drops of cool clear water. The jangling of the monastery's musicians faded out of her memory. This was how the lute should be played, the tones firm and mellow at once, deep and singing. She turned her gaze toward Eleanor and saw her sitting up in the bed, looking toward the window. All of the other women had fallen utterly still.

The melody came in, two or three lines of pure music, and then the voice rose. And it was equal to the lute, strong and manly, deep and resonant, like a dark slow-flowing river of sound.

Born to sorrow was this knight—

She found herself smiling. Her gaze went again to Eleanor, who was flushed, her eyes bright, canted toward the window. The song went on, telling of the courage and honor of the knight, the beauty and passion of the Queen, the fate that exalted and destroyed them like a pure, cleansing flame. Inside the room, the candles guttered, and one by one went out. Claire huddled up, her head on her knees. The other women lay down on their blankets. Slowly, everyone else, even Eleanor, fell softly into sleep, but Petronilla stayed by the window, listening.

The song and the voice seemed only for her, and especially for her, as if the night itself wakened her from some prison of memory, called her back to life. Locked in her current frets, she had not thought for days of the treacherous Ralph, and now, in her mind, he seemed faded, thin and insufficient. The song lifted her up strongly on its sensuous wings, and she felt herself opening to that, her body yearning, as if the music were a key to some door inside that she had forgotten was there.

Even as she wakened, she felt herself hesitant, almost withdrawing, afraid of the risk. In the great bed, Eleanor murmured luxuriously in her sleep and cast one arm wide—Eleanor, who loved risk, and risked everything, at every opportunity.

Petronilla thought, *Am I going to spend the rest of my life sitting under the window listening to someone else's song?*

The last notes hung in the night like struck silver. The troubadour's voice faded. At last she got up and went to the bed, to lie by her sister and sleep.

*   *   *

In the morning, the room was icy cold, and when they brought in the braziers, full of smoke and smells. Eleanor gave a flurry of orders, and the women rushed around to clean up and try to improve things. Petronilla went out to the garden with some pages to look for rosemary to sweeten the floor.

They had to go far out into the garden to find bushes not already cropped nearly to their bare stalks. By the wall at last she found an untouched stand, and she pointed here and there, and the boys with their shears cut armfuls of the sweet blue-flowered sea dew, which would perfume the room. The boys gathered them and ran on ahead of her, and she walked back slowly through the winter-deadened garden.

The path took her around a corner, and there she came on a man sitting on the ground eating an apple.

He looked up at her, startled, a stocky, ordinary-looking man, with a shock of thick black curly hair. She shrank back, wary. He leaped to his feet, his eyes gleaming, bobbed a little bow, and smiled.

When he smiled, she felt a ripple all along her body, as if he radiated some intense interest, fixed totally on her, a wave of desire. Beside him on the ground lay a leather sack, lute-shaped. She realized at once who he was, even before he spoke.

His voice was like dark honey, roughened with a strange accent. He said, "My lady, excuse me—is this your garden? You must excuse me—I have no business being here—I hoped to go unnoticed." His black eyes glistened. "Are you the Queen?" And he smiled again.

She knew he was lying; he had intended to be found. In spite of this, his smile drew her a step toward him. "No," she said. "Only the Queen's sister. You are the lute player, though—Brintomos?"

He bowed, only with his head, not with the whole body bent as the French courtiers did it. "Well, something like that. Thomas will do, I suppose." His smile deepened, mischievous. He had dark eyes under thick black brows. "They told me of a beautiful Queen. Nothing of an even more beautiful princess."

She did not disabuse him of the idea of princess. She gathered her hands before her, her body warm with the compliments, but wary, as she always was, of being held worthy only for her sister's sake. She said, "We heard you last night—my sister is very pleased with you. You should go to her steward, Matthieu; he will give you a place in her retinue." The magic of his art laid hands on her. She wanted him to sing to her again; suddenly she wanted to sit down beside him and let him lavish all his attention on her. She could not look away from his smile, and his brilliant black eyes. Then the page came up behind her, with Alys.

"My lady—"

She turned, swirling her cloak around her, as if she had been naked before. "Alys, what is it?"

"My lady, we need more rosemary," the waiting woman said. A half smile curved her lips, and she looked from Petronilla to the lute player. "Did we disturb you, my lady?"

Petronilla felt her neck and cheeks warm, and knew she was flushed. She cast a look over her shoulder at the lute player, Thomas.

"This is the man who sang to us last night, Alys. You, Thomas, go, as I said, to the steward, Matthieu. You may say that Petronilla has sent you."

Alys said, mildly, "The Queen will want to see you also, sir." Her voice had an edge of amusement. Petronilla took her skirts in her hands and skipped away up the path, her spirits rising, but she did not look back.

◆   ◆   ◆

The lute player came that afternoon and sang for Eleanor herself, surrounded by the women; Eleanor was much pleased with him and gave him a ring and bade Matthieu provide him with a mule to ride, so that he could accompany them when they left Fontevraud. Petronilla reveled in the music, with its soft, sinuous invitations. He had the gift of seeming to sing to her alone, even in a roomful of other women. Every time his glance strayed near her, she saw a message in it. All the women made much of him, but she held back, as if going too near him might burn her.

In the evening, restless, she went again into the garden. The night was falling, cold and blue, the light gone out of the air, and yet everything still visible in the half-darkness. She held her cloak close around her and her feet were quiet on the pebble path. Then, turning that same corner, she found the lute player Thomas again, not entirely by accident.

But he was not alone. He sat on the ground, with Claire on his lap, her arms around his neck, and her lips against his. In spite of the cold, the girl had half her gown pulled down, revealing one small, perfect, virginal breast.

Petronilla's jaw dropped. She saw at once that his glamour fell equally on everyone who heard him—it was part of his craft, like playing the lute. She wondered briefly if he was a spy. Claire had spied, and now her heart turned to ice against the girl; unreasonably, she longed to scratch her eyes out, and claw the lute player's face until he bled. Quickly she went away up the pebble path.

With each step she went more easily. His spell was broken; she saw there was no truth in all his flatteries. He wanted only some advantage, like all the rest. She felt suddenly sorry for Claire, whom he had seduced, and her anger drained away. She remembered that she liked Claire, and began to hope she did not give in to him. When she reached the door, she was smiling again, relieved she had escaped.

When she went in, Eleanor said, "We are going tomorrow, are you ready?"

"Oh, yes," Petronilla said. The room was more orderly and smelled a little better, but the braziers still filled the upper air with smoke. She went to the window, where the air was good. "I'll be glad to leave. Every day takes us nearer to Poitiers."

·   ·   ·

In the morning, with the porters hauling all their baggage out, Petronilla walked in the gallery, and Claire came to her, looking guilty.

She said, with no preamble, "My lady, I saw you. In the garden."

"Oh, did you," Petronilla said. She took the girl by the elbow, and steered her into a corner. "I trust you enjoyed yourself."

Claire fumbled with her hands. "I didn't mean—I had no-he—he—" She shook her head slightly, casting off cobwebs, and said, "What should I do?"

Petronilla leaned against the wall, watching through the side of her eye for anyone listening, and said, "Well, what did you do?"

"Nothing. Only what you saw." Claire's face was crooked with worry. She looked much younger. Her voice was taut as a lute string. "I knew it was wrong, but I couldn't stop him, until I saw you there." She lifted her eyes, imploring. "Then I stopped him."

Petronilla grunted at her; she did not believe her. She said, "Give him nothing more. He can give you nothing; you are noble, and he baseborn." She doubted this advice was timely. "His heart's in his music, girl. You cannot win him to any other love. Go along, now, there's much to do."

"My lady—" Claire licked her lower lip. The creams Alys had given her had improved her complexion, her skin smooth, pink and white, but her nose was too large, her eyes too small, ever to be beautiful. She gave an unhappy laugh. "Don't tell the Queen."

"Why do you think the Queen is even interested?"

The girl looked away, her mouth drooping, and a tear coursed down her cheek. Then, abruptly, she was facing Petronilla again.

"He has talked to me. My lord Thierry."

"Ah," Petronilla said. "That will interest the Queen. What did he say?"

"He wants—" Claire swallowed. "He wants to meet with her. The Queen. Quietly, in some private place."

"Does he," Petronilla said, startled. She glanced sideways again, to see they were unnoticed. "What did you say to him?"

"Nothing, my lady, save that I would convey the message." Claire bobbed up and down in a little bow, her head down.

"He did not ask about us?"

"He did, my lady, but I didn't tell him anything. I promised my lady the Queen I would not."

Petronilla drew herself closer under her cloak. She felt the attentions of the eunuch like the snufflings of a questing hound. Thierry would not leave them alone; the combat with him was not yet over. Yet she thought there was an opportunity in this, somewhere. She made herself consider the whole matter, not just her fear, Eleanor, the baby, but everything. She said, "We are leaving Fontevraud; there will be no way to speak to him here."

"No, my lady, I think not." Claire's voice quivered with surprise. "You mean to agree? To meet with him? I thought—"

"Hmmm," Petronilla said. "Don't think, Claire, you will be the safer for it."

Claire dipped downward in another abbreviated bow, but this time she kept her eyes steady on Petronilla's face. "Yes, my lady."

"If—when he approaches you again, though, say—" Petronilla let her mind run on ahead of them, down the road toward the next stop. "Say we shall meet him. In Chatellerault. We will be in the castle, there, in the tower called Saint Catherine, by the gate—we can meet privily, as he says."

The girl's eyes widened. "Yes, my lady." Her face flickered with an intense curiosity. "You won't ask the Queen first?"

"You're thinking again," Petronilla said mildly. "Remember what I said about that."

"Yes, my lady. I shall obey you in all things."

"Good." Petronilla did not believe this. Claire seemed very devious to her. Her mind was leaping ahead, toward the little town Chatellerault, and the castle there. "Tell him . . . tell him to come to the chapel. In the early morning, the first day we are there, after Mass. Bid him come to the confessional. Nobody will be there; we can send away the priest if necessary. He should go into the confessional and wait."

This pleased her at once, a good plan; if Eleanor did not agree, then Thierry would sit all morning in the confines of the confessional, in the cold, like a fool. If Eleanor did agree, the little booth would be dark, with the screen between them, so he would see nothing. She smiled at the girl before her. "If you do as you say, all will be well between us, Claire."

"Then you aren't—angry? About Thomas?"

"No, only concerned for you." Petronilla gave her a little, condescending laugh. "You must not give him what he wants, girl. Or he won't want you anymore. Such is the way with men like that, who pluck girls like flowers, sniff them once, and cast them down dying." As she said this, she thought suddenly of Ralph, seeing him in a different way.

Claire swallowed. "I won't. Thank you, my lady."

"Keep faith with me," Petronilla said. She took the girl's hand in hers and held tight. "All will go well if you keep faith. You have my leave."

The girl went swiftly off. Petronilla folded her arms together, thinking of this—of what Thierry might want. Eleanor would know, maybe, or have some interesting guess.

But she didn't want to tell Eleanor, not right away. She wanted to think about this awhile, keep it to herself, and sort it out. She began to think she might meet him herself, without Eleanor knowing about it. At least she could find out what he wanted. She hugged her arms around herself, pleased.

◆   ◆   ◆

Claire busied herself packing up the Queen's gowns for the next move, but her heart began to burn against Petronilla. The Queen's sister only wanted Thomas for herself; that was why she had advised her so.

Whenever the chance came, she went looking for him, but the monastery was so large, and she was so busy, she could not find him. In the evening he came to the Queen's room and played for them all; then she flushed hot just from his presence, found a place in among the other women where he could see her, and waited for him to recognize her.

He played half the night. She got lost in his music. She wished she could sing like that, play like that. She was ready with a smile for him when the moment came, when he looked at her, and remembered, and smiled at her.

But he never turned his eyes to her, never seemed to see that she was there. Petronilla had been right, after all.

Eighteen

The King left Fontevraud early in the morning, with his baggage and the train of his servants and courtiers. Eleanor waited awhile, to keep from encountering him, as it always took a while anyway to get a large group out of the cramped streets and gates. Finally at mid-morning, she and Petronilla rode out of the monastery, while in the gateyard behind them de Rançun struggled the rest of their following into order, a great tangle of wagons banging together, people screaming, and drovers shouting and cracking their whips. Slightly ahead of this confusion, the two sisters rode up through the village toward the highway. The day was raw and blustery, and Eleanor was fussing with her cloak, paying little heed, when suddenly in the cramped street strange horses surged up all around them.

Petronilla gave a short, high-pitched yell of warning; Eleanor flung her head up, the hood of her cloak sliding back. Geoffrey of Anjou, his face red and his eyes shining with purpose, was riding in close beside her, with several of his men on his heels.

"My gracious Queen and Duchess," he said. He wore a mail coat under his cloak; a helmet hung at his saddlebows. "I am off to war!"

Eleanor said, "To it, then, I've heard it's fine exercise." She reined the gray Barb down; the horse was eager and pranced sideways, tossing his head at her grip. His hooves clattered impatiently on the cobblestones.

The Angevin boy craned toward her, his head bare, his wild fair hair a windblown mass of curls. "Give me a favor, I beg you—let me fight in your name! Then none can defeat me!"

Eleanor pressed her horse away from him, crowding into Petronilla, who waited behind her on her smaller, tamer mare, her eyes keen above her veil. "Go on, sir, I will give you nothing. Fight for yourself." Then abruptly de Rançun was pushing in between them on his big black horse, one arm out, thrusting Anjou away.

"Get back, baby-hair! You heard her!"

In the tight space, the Barb spun around, bouncing up half in a rear, his long silvery mane flying. Eleanor lost her balance. One foot came out of the stirrup; hanging out over the stony street, she scrambled desperately to keep her saddle. Her sister wheeled her mare closer. Anjou was shouting, de Rançun's voice roaring louder and closer; through the corner of her eye she saw Anjou lash out with his fist at de Rançun, and then the Poitevin knight struck back so hard he knocked the boy off his horse.

The gray Barb heaved under Eleanor, trying to throw her off, and Petronilla reined up alongside her. Eleanor reached out and gripped her sister and held herself steady, wrestling with the Barb's reins. She stabbed the stirrup with her foot and squirmed awkwardly back into the deep of the saddle and had him mastered again.

"Get away from her! You heard the Queen refuse you!" Anjou had landed in the road; de Rançun was reining his horse hard after him, forcing the boy to scramble away on all fours from the hooves. Neither of them had seen Eleanor nearly fall. She straightened, panting. Her body felt suddenly enormous, off-center, precarious. Petronilla's hand gripped her elbow, and Eleanor turned and gave her a quick smile, which her sister did not answer; above the white linen of her veil, Petronilla's green eyes were dark and wide with fear. She drew back away and looked around at the men. Eleanor pulled her disarranged cloak around her again. De Rançun had driven Anjou ten paces off down the lane, the two of them volleying insults at each other. Eleanor turned the Barb and rode away from them both, up onto the highway where it ran across the slope.

Petronilla kept pace with her. Behind them, shouts rose, and the clatter of hooves. The wheels thundered on the cobblestones and a drover's whip snapped, the wagons coming through, so that she saw Anjou now across a widening landscape of baggage and wheels. Out in the open road, she turned the Barb in a close circle, making him behave. In spite of the cold, there was a sheen of sweat on her forehead, and she wiped it off on a fold of her cloak. Petronilla was watching her; she pulled her veil down, her face taut.

"Are you all right?"

"Damn him," Eleanor said. She glared off down the lane, where Anjou had disappeared into the general traffic of wagons and riders and dust. De Rançun rode up toward them, leftover temper dark on his face, and she waved him on past to lead them. She followed, Petronilla at her side.

The whole train was pulling out onto the high road, the wagons loud and bulky, raising dust. Two more knights jogged past her to join de Rançun; one carried her banner on its staff. She was holding the Barb too tight, and he tossed his head, and she let the reins slide through her fingers.

"Send for the lute player," she said. "Let's hear some music." She felt unsteady still, and she looked straight ahead, her head swimming.

Petronilla turned, waved at a page, and faced her again. "That was a near thing," she said, low. "You must be more careful."

"It was that stupid boy," she said. She was feeling better now, and the world had stopped circling slowly around her. Her voice was rough. "I hope he takes a sword between the teeth." They were riding downhill, toward the river, and the cold wind met them. She pulled up the hood of her cloak. "Where is that lute player?"

Petronilla veered off; for a few steps Eleanor rode alone, trying to settle herself into the saddle, aware now how clumsy her body was becoming. *Too much*, she thought. *Too much is happening, too much I can't control.* Petronilla jogged up beside her again, alone, folded primly sideways on the saddle like a doll.

"Where's the lute player?" Eleanor cried. "Didn't you hear me?"

Her sister turned toward her, expressionless. "He's gone—he left this morning, apparently, maybe with the King."

"Ah," Eleanor cried, "everybody is against me!" Her eyes burned with a sudden, furious rush of tears, the ultimate humiliation. She clamped her mouth shut, struggling to master herself, plodding on down the road toward the next unforeseeable mess.

◆　◆　◆

They followed the road south. Even so late in the season, they came on pilgrims trudging back up the road from Compostela: ragged people in their broad-brimmed hats, jingling with bells, their faces lean with fatigue. Along the road now and then lay a broken scallop-edged shell. Eleanor thought she would go to Compostela someday, not for the sake of the saint and his absolution of sin, but because her father had died there.

The absolution seemed to her like a cheat. You sinned or you didn't, and the main restraint, she thought, was fear, not virtue. Therefore, as the master from the Studium had implied, it wasn't even really virtue not to sin. She thought of Bernard and his curses. They went by an empty pilgrims' refuge, a broken-in lean-to in the middle of a field of blackened firepits.

She would give money to build new refuges and repair the old ones. Those people who wanted the pilgrimage should have it. Petronilla rode along just behind her, deep in some talk with de Rançun; behind them, the waiting women were singing, as they had taken to doing often lately. She heard Claire's voice, pleasingly round, above all the others.

A few days later, as they were approaching Chatellerault, de Rançun rode up beside Eleanor and said, "I have some news of Henry d'Anjou, if you would hear it, Your Grace."

In his bald and formal tone, she recognized that this annoyed him; he still disliked Henry. She smiled at him to soften his mood. "Thank you, my old friend. Is it about his absurd little brother's so-called war?"

"Aye, that," he said. His square, sun-browned face was still stern, but when she caught his eye, he could not help but smile at her, and she pleased herself that she had soothed him. He said, "You know how the old Count left the younger brother some castles in the south. And Henry came down after and drove him out of Chinon and Loudon."

She made a sound in her throat, remembering how close that war had come to the progress. That was his border with France. "Yes," she said. "And I can understand why."

"Indeed. Ambition above honor. Now Henry is in Normandy, on the coast somewhere up there, and while he's out of Anjou, his brother with a tableful of local men is raising banners against him."

"Ah," she said, with a twinge of alarm. "They try to take him while his back is turned, the dirty dogs."

"I will find out what I can, as the plot goes on," he said, and raised his hand to her. "Now shall I fetch the hawk?"

"Yes," she said. With this news disquieting her, she needed some diversion. She turned toward Petronilla, riding along beside her on her placid brown mare.

"Did you hear that?"

Petronilla gave a wiggle of her head. "Nothing in this seems like news to me, Eleanor."

"Should I—" She edged the gray Barb closer to the mare, so that they could speak without being overheard. Behind them, in the wagon, the women were still singing, a good cover. "I could send him a message. Warn him. Offer him some encouragement."

Petronilla only laughed and looked away, which meant she was against it. Eleanor settled into brooding on the problem. She rejected the idea of a message. This was another test of him; if he did not master it, he would be of no use to her.

De Rançun came back with the sparrow hawk, still hooded, on his gloved fist. He had a rare hand for a hawk, and they flew beautifully for him; Eleanor gave herself over to watching his skill with the wild, dagger-beaked little bird. Like all animals, she trusted his deft, tender touch. There was no game on the cold winter roadside, but they flew the hawk anyway, baiting her with scraps of dry meat, to pass the time until they came to Chatellerault.

◆　◆　◆

The Queen's progress arrived late at night in Chatellerault, and Eleanor slept on in the morning. After all the other women had gone to their morning prayers, Petronilla eased herself out of the bed. Because the winter cold was fierce, she wrapped herself tight in her heaviest cloak, not widow's wear, but dark, with fur around the cuffs and lining the hood. Then she went to the chapel, as she had bidden Claire to tell Thierry.

The morning Mass was over and the little chapel quiet, dark, and very cold. When she slipped into the confessional, she realized with a start that he was already there, on the other side of the screen.

She sat on the priest's narrow uncushioned bench, her hands tucked into her sleeves, her heart thundering. The screen showed her only the vague outline of his head beyond.

She said, "What do you want?"

"Your Grace," he said. "Thank you for meeting me. I have hopes we can find a way through this quandary of ours, to the benefit of all."

She made the sign of the cross, mechanically, because of where she was. For a moment, startled, she could not speak; he thought she was Eleanor. She almost laughed, and mocked him for his mistake, but then she forbore. She saw some use in letting him go on in this belief, and she bit her lip, amused.

He waited only a moment, and went on. "Your Grace, there is a way for both you and the King to have your way. He could let you go to Poitiers, to live there without him, all the rest of your days. We will give Aquitaine entirely into your charge, which is what you want, isn't it?"

"What are you saying?" she said. She kept her voice a harsh whisper, for disguise.

"Let him—visit—now and then—and if—when—you have a child, then . . ." Thierry hesitated a moment; in the dim, narrow enclosure she could sense him leaning toward the screen between them, as if he might pierce through it with his look. He was only a darker shape through the mesh screen; likewise, she must be hardly more than a voice to him. "If you had a son, he might still be claimed for the King's."

She gasped, outraged. Thierry's voice tumbled on, ragged.

"Perhaps even . . . your sister's child, Your Grace. Could be passed off. Or . . . as long as the King could visit—now and then—pretend."

"God's breath," she said, low-voiced. Her amusement that he had taken her for her sister boiled up into rage. "What are you saying? This is indecent. This is monstrous." She was shivering in the cold, and with more than the cold. "You would pass off a—a nameless bastard as a prince of France—"

"The King may never have a son," Thierry said, harshly. "In many ways he is good, and worthy, but he abhors all earthly pleasures. My concern is the throne of France and the succession. The realm of France, Your Grace, of which you have been Queen. Please, consider this. It's a way for us all to get what we want."

"Bah," Petronilla said, one of Eleanor's favorite exclamations. "Go. Get away from me. You are evil. Indecent."

"Think of it," Thierry said. But he was going. "Just consider it, Your Grace. For the sake of the realm, the kingdom. Consider." The door beyond the screen opened and closed, and he was gone.

She sat shivering in the dark, the stale smell of the enclosed space in her nostrils. Dusty, like a tomb. The sheer outrage of it numbed her—to offer to accept a baseborn child for the King of France. She let herself consider the irony that within her sister's sides now there grew the child of the King's worst enemy, who might be a boy, and therefore the plausible heir Thierry was seeking; a son of Eleanor and Henry's, who could by tortuous ways become the King of France. Worth a ballad at least, she thought wryly, if not a fabliau.

And, beneath that, the other startling thing: Thierry had taken her for Eleanor. Of course he could not see her. But he had thought she was Eleanor. She sat there a long time, in the dark, thinking about that. All her life she had wondered what it was like to be Eleanor. At last, hearing someone stir outside in the chapel, she got up, pulled the hood of the cloak well over her face, and left.

•   •   •

Claire drew in behind a column while Petronilla went out of the chapel, and stayed there, in the dark, in the cold, wondering what to do.

She was sure that Petronilla had not told Eleanor of the meeting with Thierry; she had watched them carefully, after she told the Queen's sister he wanted to see her, and Petronilla had never said anything. Claire had thought then she meant to let Thierry sit in the dark and fret for hours, a laughingstock; thus she herself had gone, to laugh.

But Petronilla had kept the meeting with him. She could not believe that Petronilla would conspire with Thierry. There had to be some good reason for this. But the suspicion crept in under the edge of her thinking, that Petronilla, the woman of perfect virtue, who sternly ordered her to keep faith, Petronilla had lied.

That pleased her, somewhat, to see a high one lowered; they were no different, really, she and Petronilla. But the pleasure was cold, and a little sour. She had loved Petronilla.

She still loved Petronilla. Differently, perhaps. She went out of the chapel, toward the Queen's tower.

◆   ◆   ◆

"Where have you been?" Eleanor asked, when Petronilla finally reached their rooms in the Saint Catherine tower.

"I went for a walk," Petronilla said. She thought, *I will tell her, in a moment.* They would laugh over Thierry's indecent proposal, and especially that Thierry had mistaken who she was, and Eleanor would surely spurn the whole suggestion, and that would be the end of it all.

"At least you're out of your widow's white, for once," Eleanor said. "You look a lot better, there's color in your face. I want my wine heated up again and spiced; will you do it? Where is Alys?"

"Oh, probably still at church," Petronilla said, although she knew that was not so. She went for the warming pan. It irked her to be ordered around like a mere servant; Eleanor could do this as well as she. Eleanor always took her for granted, a sort of second self, a bid-dable shade, with no will of her own. Perhaps she would not tell her about meeting Thierry—about Thierry's base offer. Perhaps Eleanor didn't have to know everything. She knelt by the fire and poured the wine into the pan. Claire came in the door from the next room, quiet, her eyes downcast, and murmured, "I will do it, my lady." Petronilla gave her the warming pan and went to play tables with her sister.

Nineteen

The Vicomte de Chatellerault, Eleanor's cousin, was a notorious miser, and his shabby, dreary hall cradled the winter cold to
it, instead of holding it outside. So Eleanor could swath herself in
fur cloaks, and, wrapped also in the iron fist of her linen, she went
to dinner every day and strained her ears to catch the gossip at the
men's side of the table, trying to hear news of Henry.

She remembered again the brawny body, the quick, fiery action,
and thought little Anjou would get nowhere. England would be the
real test. He would bring her the crown of the richest kingdom in
Europe for her morning gift. She stirred, lively at the thought of that.

She noticed Bordeaux in the King's company, talking to him, but
Thierry, also, on Louis's left hand, looking at her often. Louis spent
a good deal of each day in the chapel, and Eleanor saw him only at
a distance, each of them surrounded by attendants, and in a hurry.
The weather was foul, all those days, and she spent them playing
tables with Petronilla, who always won, because she never chanced
anything.

◆   ◆   ◆

Claire went to the kitchen to find the Queen some sweets she craved; she had been told to say of course they were for Petronilla. While she loitered there, waiting for someone to notice her and help her get what she needed, she saw the lute player Thomas coming in through the gate.

She had not seen him since they left Fontevraud and he had gone over to the King's side. Her heart leaped at the sight of him, the old feeling wakening. He took no care with how he looked, always a little wild, unkempt, his clothes shabby, but he had a cocky strut to his walk, nonetheless, like a prince. It was the music that made him so, she thought. A flock of girls followed him, giggling and flapping like the silly geese they were. Claire felt herself blushing. She saw him suddenly in a new way. He went in their midst like a lord, his lute in its sack over his shoulder, his dark tousled head bare, and his face bright with laughter, but he never really looked at any of them.

She thought she would call out to him, would raise her hand, but some foreboding kept her frozen in her place. She would be just one of all of these girls, who clung to him, shameless, adoring. His gaze passed over her and he did not notice her; he went on by her, laughing. Claire lowered her eyes, trying to pretend she was not looking at him. The girls around him battled each other to be close to him. So it was, she thought. So it was. But now her anger at Petronilla rose a little hotter.

◆   ◆   ◆

When the weather cleared, they began on toward Poitiers, some days off, and on the first night of the journey, they stopped at a monastery near the River Creuse. Eleanor's train arrived much later than the

King's, and before she had dismounted, de Rançun came up to her on foot, his face expressionless.

"I think we'll see little Anjou back here soon."

"What?" she said, turning abruptly around, and as she did so the horse moved abruptly and she lost her balance.

She was dismounting, swinging her leg across the cantle of the saddle, and she began to fall. She caught herself, both hands on the saddle, and the horse sidestepped away from her and she did fall. De Rançun caught her almost at once, his hands on her sides. The Barbary horse, snorting, swiveled away from them, his ears pricked up. She hung one arm around the Poitevin knight's neck, her whole body in his arms. Her eyes went bleared and her head muzzy, as if the world disintegrated around her.

De Rançun set her on her feet again, holding her until she was steady. She turned toward him and looked into his stiff, drawn face, and at once she saw that he knew what was going on with her. He lowered his eyes, as if nothing had happened, his voice unnecessarily loud.

"The plot in Anjou's done. Duke Henry heard about it and rode down there from Normandy—in a single night—" He gave a little shake of his head, a grudging admiration. "That must have been quite a ride. Picking up his garrisons as he went. Caught the whole batch of schemers all at once, still cooking up their little rebellion, and stewed them together in their own pot."

"Good," she said, pleased; she told herself she had foreseen this, knew him well enough to know what he would do, questing toward his crown. She drew in a deep breath. The spell was fading, and in a moment she would be strong again. She glanced at the knight. De Rançun, she knew, would tell no one about what had just happened. She forgot about losing her saddle; that was nothing. And she would shake off the little lingering dizziness. "Give me your arm, I'll go inside. Where is my sister?"

◆ ◆ ◆

They reached Poitiers the day after the King arrived, on a bright breezy winter day, when little silver-bellied clouds scudded above the city on its rocky hill like ships across the blue sea of the sky. They rode over the bridge and up the steep narrow street toward the palace through crowds of cheering people who screamed Eleanor's name and reached their arms out to touch her.

The noise and confusion spooked even Petronilla's little mare, usually calm as a nun, and Petronilla kept a nervous eye on Eleanor, on the Barbary horse, which tiptoed along with his head bowed almost to his chest, snorting with each step. Eleanor mastered him utterly; they went through the gate into the palace with no trouble, and left the thunderous cheers behind.

The huge rambling palace covered the hilltop, the center of it old Roman work, patched and expanded with new stone halls and towers. Eleanor took one look at it and turned to the double tower on the right, under the two hats of its peaked roofs. "We will house ourselves there," she said, and so they moved into the Maubergeon.

Her grandfather had built the great double tower for his mistress Dangereuse, and so it had acquired a certain disrepute. Nobody had lived there for years. The rooms were full of dirt and trash, rats and owls and bats, terrible smells and crawling things that hissed. Eleanor got everybody to cleaning it up, carrying out masses of junk and dirt, sweeping, washing down, bringing in what suitable furniture she could find elsewhere in the palace.

She herself decided everything. Except for a brief appearance at dinner on their first day, she ignored the rest of the court; she watched over every task in the Maubergeon. She went into the rooms and found the new-style hearths, set in recesses in the outer wall, which had been plugged up by somebody who did not understand their use.

Birds had built nests and clogged the openings above them, which were supposed to let the smoke escape without coming into the room. She set a crew of men to digging them out, and made sure they did it properly, especially the smoke channels. In the meanwhile she sat with Petronilla beside her to choose new hangings for the walls.

She remembered this place from when she and Petronilla had grown up here—the hearths, the curving staircase, the sunny windows—and she meant to bring it back again, and with it, that world of poetry and music, new ideas and new dreams. Sitting with Petronilla, running her fingers over a heap of silky damasks, she said, "Was it this color? Or green? There was a dark green."

"No," Petronilla said, "it was blue, in this room, blue and gold, like this, only Grandfather's initial, not yours. Big gold Gs. Dark green upstairs, and a lighter green, what they call salamander, across the way."

"Then let it be so," Eleanor said.

She intended to live here, to make her greatest place here, when she was free. When they were all free. Yet they were no closer to that, even though they were in Poitiers. The King still had not summoned any council, although he was certainly promising. She put off the gnawing twinge of doubt. Maubergeon and the life she wanted lay within her grasp now, and she refused to let this not happen. She haggled with the merchant over the blue and gold damask, as if she could make the future by furnishing it.

Something was going on with Petronilla, she knew not what. Her sister had lost her easy openness, which once Eleanor had seen through and through like glass. Some part of her was closed away. Twice she had almost said something, but held back—as if she did not trust her, Petronilla, who had been by her side all her life. Downcast at this, she struggled to put off her doubts, thinking that being pregnant was always a mild form of madness.

That afternoon, a neatly folded, elegantly written letter appeared, laid on a cushion just inside the door of the middle room, and she did not need de Rançun to tell her that Geoffrey d'Anjou was back.

She tossed that paper into the hearth, but over the next several days there came more such in a steady stream. She sent them all after the first, without reading them. The other women happened on them, as they were tossed in through the windows or tucked into the usual gifts from the court and people in the city, and quickly the servants understood what was going on and gathered in giggling bunches to read them before they brought them to her. She refused to let them tell her what they said. She contented herself listening to de Rançun's stories of Duke Henry.

"He's tireless, they say; he rides everywhere, drives everybody, and he is fearless, and certain—you don't see him down here hanging on Louis's sleeve."

She said, "Anything you hear of him, though, bring to me." *Anything*, she thought, *save whom he takes into his bed. I will make him love me*, she thought. *Once we are married.*

"I hear he is ruthless, and cruel," de Rançun said. "And if he would do such to his own brother, Eleanor, what would he do to a wife?"

She laughed, angry. "Bah. I am not a mere wife, am I?"

He hesitated; she saw he had something he wanted to say. "What is it? There's more news? Tell me."

"No, my lady." He swallowed, his head down, and she guessed it was something else entirely, which she wanted not to hear. He started to speak, and she beckoned him off with her fingers.

"Well, then, go off to court, listen to them over there. If anyone asks of me, tell them I am far too busy here to attend their idle chatter-feasts."

He turned on his heel and left. The room was quiet, sunny even in the winter, warm from the banked hearth; she curled her arm around her belly and sat down awhile, her back hurting. *You did this to me*, she thought. She summoned up the image of Duke Henry: the gray eyes, the spiky red hair. Surely the baby would have red hair. He must never know. He would doubt her always if he even suspected that she had gulled him—so men thought evil of women, where they themselves were prone to evil. She turned into the warmth of the hearth, easing her back, and tried not to think about anything at all.

Twenty

Claire loved Poitiers, so different from anywhere else she had been; even in winter it seemed warmer and brighter than the rest of the world. The rooftops were not covered with the black slates of Paris and Fontevraud, but with rounded clay tiles, once red but now patterned gray and green with lichens and moss. The streets wound up along the hills past shops full of laughing people, pie men with their trays and hoarse cries and delicious trails of aroma, women selling fruit and fish, the clip-clop of big horses, always the chatter of this different kind of French, which she understood well enough but which still sounded so strange, rounder, sweeter than her own.

Monks paraded through the streets, and preachers stood on the corner, talking about a life nearer to God, a way of pure spirit that left the body behind. It sounded good but, she thought, for her, not yet. Her body loved this place, with its wonderful smells and sounds and sights. She loved to go out on the Queen's tasks, run to the cathedral to admire the beasts carved in its columns, beg a sweet from a baker woman with a promise to tell the Queen how good it was.

Usually, too, she made her way to the King's court, which Thomas the lute player still attended; she dared not approach him, but she loved to see him and to hear him play. If he noticed her, he didn't care. He had forgotten her. But all he played for the King seemed like dirges.

Then one day to her surprise she almost walked into him as she went one way around a corner of the tower and he came the other.

He was pulling his clothes straight; he had just made water. He saw her and began a mindless sort of bow, and started past her. She mumbled and flushed, and then suddenly he recognized her.

He faced her again. He caught her hand and gave her his beautiful, irresistible smile.

"Oh, little Claude, the Queen's girl." He pulled her toward him. "Give me a kiss."

His hand was warm and strong, but she held him off. Petronilla's words rang in her mind. *His heart's in his music. He will never love you.* She said, "Claire, it is," and could not keep the annoyance out of her voice. "But I am happy to see you, Thomas."

He turned a little to put the wall beside them, giving them a little privacy from the crowded yard; he hitched up his lute in its sack on his shoulder. "Yes. Claire," he said. "Very well. But what do you want, if I cannot kiss you?"

She said, "I wish I could sing like you. Can you—" She twisted her hands together. "Can you teach me how to sing?"

"To sing." That startled him into silence, into a shocked look that, she saw, for once reflected his real thoughts. He put one hand on his hip. "You want to sing."

"I try to sing," she said, "but when I hear you, I know I am a creaking hinge. Please. Show me how to do better."

He glanced around them. They were at the far edge of the courtyard, the kitchen around the corner behind him, and the broad paved court behind her crisscrossed with hurrying servants, grooms, a train of horses. He turned his eyes on her, not smiling. "Sing for me, then."

"What?" She gripped her fists to her chest, afraid. "Here? Now?"

"Here and now," he said. He unslung the sack and pulled his lute out. Holding it ungainly in his arms, he plucked out a few notes. "Sing that."

Her heart was slamming against her ribs. She wound her hands together. Suddenly she saw that if she failed now, he would not teach her, would think nothing of her, forever, and his judgment would be true: She would never sing again. She swallowed. She collected herself, and with the notes he had just played in her mind, she sang them out wordlessly, beat for beat.

His face did not change. Terrified, she watched for any sign she had done it well and saw none. The lute shifted in his grip; standing up, he could not hold it properly. He played another, longer, less connected string of notes.

She shut her eyes. She reminded herself that she loved to do this. She sang the notes back to him, keeping her voice strong, reaching for the joy she had found in this, all those days and nights in Eleanor's court.

After that, he lowered the lute. His eyebrows rose. He nodded to her. "Yes. I can use you. Come to me here in the evening; I will find some place where we can work."

"No—I must serve the Queen."

"When she is abed, then."

In the dark. She said, "I will only sing."

His smile spread across his face. He said, "I understand that." It was a different smile than before, his eyes dark, fixed on her, on her alone. "Come tonight." He cased the lute again and walked off without another word.

．　．　．

"Good," Thomas said. "Drink some more of the wine. Keep your throat smooth."

She reached for the cup. She was damp with sweat under her coif and her bodice; she had been singing since they came in here. She looked around the back of the stable, down the darkened aisle past the rumps of mules. Here where the lamp shone its feeble circle of light everything was yellow: the straw, the dusty air. Her throat was sore, not smooth.

Over and over, he had played streams of notes, and she had sung them; he had shown her different rhythms, playing them on the lute while she clapped and sang. He had taught her to hold her body upright, as if she were a pipe, so the notes came from the bottom, not the top of her throat. In all that while he had paid heed only to her. She had never had anyone so interested in her.

"Down here," he said, his hand under his ribs. "The note comes from down here. Not—" Patting beneath his chin. "Up here, you flutter. But mostly you are good at this. When did you sing, before?"

"The Queen's other women and I sing, to pass the time," she said. "On the progress."

"Huh," he said. "What kind of songs?"

"Just—" She struggled to put some name to them. "Country songs. Like dances. Or games. Rounds, you know, where everybody sings a piece of the song, one on top of the other."

His head rose; his eyes shone. "Really. Come, then. We can do that."

"But there are only two—"

"Here," he said, and played notes. As he had taught her, she listened to the rhythm, saw where it folded back on itself, and broke the stream of notes in her mind into matching lines, so she could remember them. When he came to the end and nodded, she began to sing.

He played along with her, the lute cradled in his arms, the quill in his fingers plucking the first line of the song from the strings, then, as she went on to the second, he began to sing also.

Different notes. Her voice wobbled. She struggled to stay in her tune, while his, rich as dark honey, climbed and twined all around like a vine. His voice was so much stronger, held the notes deep and warm, found some place in her that longed for that deep warm power; she longed to do that, to move him as his voice moved her.

Her voice broke. She could not listen to him and sing also, and her song collapsed in a welter of notes and he began to laugh and she laughed also and suddenly he leaned over and kissed her.

She gasped. She clung to his arm with one hand and felt his lips warm on hers and for an instant she would have done anything for him, anywhere.

She drew back, breathless. She could not lose this, not for a quick tumble. He was watching her, smiling.

"We'll do it again," he said, and played the song on the lute. "Later. You'll learn it. I've wanted to do this for years. I have never found any-one—it had to be a woman and there are few women troubadours. If we only could get the King to hear it—"

She said, "I have to go. They'll be wondering where I am." She lifted her gaze to him, his smile on her so true she wanted to kiss him again.

He said, "Tomorrow, then, Clariza." His hand drew a long seeking call from the lute. She went quickly out of the stable, half-skipping.

◆　◆　◆

Petronilla leaned on the wall, looking down toward the glitter of the river. The wind rose toward her, smelling of dried leaves, of moldering flowers, cold stone, and the icy river. She loved this place, the city, and this tower, and this very garden wall. Everything she saw was familiar to her, lush with memories, and she ached doubly to see it, the first with the pleasure of being back, and the second because they would soon have to leave it again.

In the years since Eleanor had been forced into the marriage with Louis, they had come to Poitiers seldom, and only as guests, to leave

it again almost at once. They had had to watch a Parisian court holding forth in the heart of Aquitaine: music, poetry and jousting and
games and dancing, all forbidden, all gaiety proscribed, a broken
stone in a garden of living blossoms.

She leaned over the wall, drinking up the flavors of the city. The
stone walls along the narrow lanes were the color of old lemons, laced
with vining roses heavy with ripe red hips. Above the red clay caps
of the walls the crooked arms of apple and plum trees held off the
emptiness of the winter sky. In the spring, she knew, the lemon trees
would shower their sweet perfume everywhere, and flowers would cascade over every wall and every bough, littering the streets with pink
and white petals like the offerings of pilgrims. The common people
would dance in the street, would sing as they went out to their fields,
throw open their churches to festivals and processions. Even the most
ancient stones, older than the Romans, would have their garlands of
new blooms, as if the people reawoke the memories of deepest time.

She knew the spring might be too late. By then, she and Eleanor
might have lost Poitiers forever.

She thought of the baby growing between her sister's sides, wondered what would happen to him after he was born. If they kept
the secret well enough, he would likely become some unimportant
fosterling, a minor courtier in a noble Poitevin household, one close
enough to Eleanor that she could trust them to keep his true identity a secret forever, from him and from the world. Bordeaux's court,
maybe, if he were lucky. Chatellerault's, if not. She imagined him a
happy little boy, loved and carefree, as princes never were.

Down below, a drone of voices sounded; she looked keenly in
among the tangled streets, and thought she saw a chain of moving people. Some procession: Advent was full of them, each church
sending out its particular relic, and gathering worshippers to chant
and pray behind them as they wound a way through the neighbor-
hood. There was such a one the next afternoon, also, that Eleanor

had promised she would ride in. Another chance for her sister to be revealed. She tapped her fingertips impatiently on the wall.

Thierry's evil offer came back to her. It had occurred to her more than once, since their meeting in the confessional, that he did know it was Eleanor who was with child—that he was bargaining in his devious scoundrel way for her baby. Did he believe it was really Louis's? Maybe that was why he hadn't simply dragged her up before the King and destroyed everything.

Louis might not allow him to humiliate the Queen, even if he did know. She recalled how the King had defended her, Petronilla, against Thierry, that time over the midwife. He was certainly a nobler man than the secretary. Maybe Louis himself had finally given up the marriage, in his heart, as Eleanor had.

That was all guesswork. The chances were that if they found out about the baby, the marriage for Eleanor would end in a penitent's cell. And, to make sure Louis could marry again, a cold cup of poison.

Poitiers was full of churches, their spires pointing up into the sky like signposts to God. From this place along the flank of the palace, she could see the back of the old church of Saint Pierre, gray with lichens, and the looming mass of Notre Dame, both more venerable than anything in Paris, being the onetime churches of the Romans, like the Baptistry down the hill. In these places the people of Poitiers had worshipped strange spirits before Saint Hilary brought the light of Christ into their lives. The music of their bells would begin soon, marking the midday hour.

The city abounded in even older shrines, the strange constructions of the pagans, mere boulders tipped together, like houses for trolls. She and Eleanor had played hide-and-seek among them as children, with the other children of their father's court. In Poitiers they had run free as colts, up and down the streets, so beloved that the common folk called their names and tossed them cakes and fruit and blessed them with laughter.

The great age of the place reassured her, the walls of countless years around her; she felt safe here as nowhere else.

Her mind kept twitching back to the problem of the procession the next day. It was to honor the Virgin, whose image they would carry. Petronilla would have chosen to ride in the procession from the Baptistry, which was her favorite of all the churches in Poitiers. Eleanor had chosen Saint Hilaire, because it stood much in need of work and she wanted to draw some interest to it. Eleanor understood those things; Petronilla would have done something sentimental and useless.

But for Eleanor to ride through crowds up and down the street was dangerous; there had to be some other way. A hint of a solution came to her, but she pushed it down, too dangerous, and presumptuous, too.

The sun was shining on her now, moving out from behind the high loom of the tower. She turned to look up at the faceted walls, each vertical plane overhung by a water channel carved into the stone, whose outlet was a shouting head. Each stone was slightly different in color or pattern from each other stone, and she often found herself lost in the subtleties, walking around and around the foot of the tower, looking up.

This tower was the heart of Poitiers—maybe the very heart of Aquitaine. Her grandfather the Troubadour had planned it himself, called on his masons to make of stone what he saw in his mind. Her grandfather had been such a man that tales of him still lingered here, how he sang and fought and loved throughout his days, a great wild spring wind in Aquitaine, the land's living spirit. Eleanor should be such a one as that, if she escaped the cold prison of the north.

Petronilla lifted her face into the sunlight, enjoying the warmth. She wanted to stay here forever, leaning on the garden wall, waiting for the spring.

"Petra. Let me come closer."

It was de Rançun. She turned toward him as he stood there with his head a little bowed, waiting to be recognized, who almost alone of the world other than her sister could call her by the silly, childhood name. "Joffre," she said, in the same wise. "Joffrillo. Why have you ever needed permission? What is it?"

He came across the little garden toward her. Near the gate, a page started up, ready to attend them, and Petronilla waved him off, and she did not veil herself. De Rançun stood beside her and took his cap in his hand.

"You must pardon me for this, but I can talk only to you." He swallowed. She straightened, warned by the look on his face what was coming. He said, "Petra, hear me, I say this for love of you and her."

"Of course," she said, taut.

"It's this procession, tomorrow, that will be all afternoon, and through huge crowds. She cannot ride so much anymore. It's too dangerous."

"Ah," she said. "Your thoughts trace my own." She turned her eyes away, alarmed at that; she was not then just being womanish. And he knew, too, of the baby. A mere man, outside the women's circle. The spreading ripples reached wider and wider, always a little less of a secret, more of an understanding in common. She gave him a sideways glance, thinking, *But he is loyal.*

He snorted at her. "What do you think? I must lift her into the saddle every time she rides. Do you think I don't notice?" He too then glanced around, making sure they were alone. "And she has almost fallen, that I've seen, at least twice."

"She could ride in a wagon," Petronilla said. "Or at least, a less mettlesome horse."

He said, "She will never consent to that, I think. She would find it humiliating."

Petronilla studied him from an angle, his square, ordinary face, his hair almost white, like sheep's wool, shagging down to his shoulders. He had always loved Eleanor best. She remembered when they were children, once, how he had run full tilt into a pond to fetch her ball back to her, only to find, when he bore it up to her in triumph, that she had lost interest and gotten into something else. He had turned and handed the ball then to Petronilla, and she had never forgotten the glum disappointment in his face. Like her, he was in second place.

She put her hand on his sleeve. "Thank you, Joffre. You are good and loyal and noble."

He said, "I have gone every step of the way with her, since she became the Duchess. I will be steadfast now. I have no love for the French."

His hand brushed hers on his sleeve. His touch was warm as the sun. At once, they realized they were too close, and both moved apart, saying nothing.

"Nor do I," she said. "We are one on that." And she flushed a little, at something too nearly said. She lowered her eyes.

Beyond him, in the shadow of the tower, the page suddenly bounded up and leaped to open the door. Eleanor was coming out into the garden. Petronilla turned, glad. "You can say this to her yourself, now, about the procession, because here she is. But I agree, and will help."

"What do you two do, here?" Eleanor said. Behind her, Claire and Alys were trailing along the path. Eleanor wore a billowing dark cloak, and the wind was quickly teasing her coif apart; she reached up suddenly and pulled it off, and her hair streamed down like a cascade of russet silk. The wind brought the high color into her face. Her eyes were a bright, golden green.

"My lady," de Rançun said, "I want to say—I have to beg—you must not ride the Barb in this procession tomorrow. It's too dangerous."

Eleanor stopped still on the path and her face settled. She did not lose her temper, which surprised Petronilla; she guessed then that her sister had already been considering how to manage this. Eleanor's eyebrows went up and down, and her gaze flicked toward Petronilla, taking in that she and de Rançun had discussed it, and then she came up beside Petronilla and stood looking out over the wall. Her hand slid down her front, and under the cloak the bulge of her belly showed round and ripening.

"I can still ride the Barb. They have put it out very widely around the city that I am to lead this procession. It will be a great event, and everybody will be watching. Everyone knows that's my horse. If I don't ride him, they'll suspect something. And once they begin to suspect, everything will fall apart."

"You can say he's come up lame," Petronilla said. "Or you like another horse. Or you could ride in the wagon with the icon."

"You think the wagon is less a jostle than a horse?"

"We can make you comfortable in the wagon," de Rançun said.

Eleanor swung to face him. "Do you think then people won't know what's going on? If I ride around Poitiers in a wagon, everybody in France will know at once there's something wrong with me. Have we come all this way for nothing? Have we gone so far, to give it all up now?" Her eyes glinted, full of anger, and then, abruptly, full of tears. "No. I won't give up, not now. I will be free of Louis, one way or another, child or not."

Petronilla said, "Or I could take your place."

They all stammered silent, and all their faces swiveled toward her. She said nothing; the words had jumped from her, all but unbidden. Eleanor said, "Sweet Jesus."

De Rançun said, his voice low, "Yes. She's done it before, my lady—from any distance, how often are you taken for each other?"

Alys stepped forward. "Oh. Oh, yes, that is the perfect way— Your Grace, don't you see?"

Eleanor's mouth was open, as if she would speak, but she said nothing; in her eyes, Petronilla saw the wild thoughts racing each other back and forth. Eleanor jerked away from them all, turning to stare at the tower.

"Can you ride my horse, Petra?"

Petronilla collected herself, excited. Eleanor was considering it, then. She imagined the Barb and could not see herself in the saddle. "I don't know. You know I don't ride astride very much."

"Then we say he's lame, and get you another," Alys said.

De Rançun said, "If she rides the Barb, they'll believe without a doubt she's Eleanor."

Now Eleanor faced Petronilla again, narrow-eyed, with a little smile. "You would have to cast off your widow's white, at least. I'd see that, anyway. In my clothes, and if you take on my manner, which I have seen you do quite well—"

As the thought matured, Petronilla's courage gave out; she went stiff as wood, a carved puppet. They would all stare at her, everybody, for miles; there would be nowhere to hide. They would laugh at her presumption. She would make a fool of herself.

Yet she could be Eleanor, in front of everybody, just for a day. She could find out at last what it meant to be the center of all attention, the glory of the world.

Alys said, "There are ways to make your faces utterly alike. My lady Petronilla, I have told you often, a little brush of color in your cheeks, and I have a trick for your eyes, that would make you the image of the Queen."

Petronilla licked her lips; she tried to tell herself that she did not really want to be Eleanor. That it was to save her sister that she did this. But in her heart a new, eager lust stirred up, a sudden ambition.

Eleanor said, "Then we will do it. Petra, you are sure of this?"

Petronilla blinked; she could not meet her sister's eyes. "I will try," she said. "I know how to do it, I suppose. And we have to do something. But—" If she was going to be brave, she would be brave all the way. She turned to de Rançun. "As you said, I have to ride the Barb, and I have to ride astride. You must help me."

"Good," de Rançun said, with a quick smile; he reached out and touched her arm. "You're a better rider than you think, Petra. You can do it." He remembered again, and said, "My lady."

Eleanor hugged her. "My sister." Petronilla hugged her back, her cheek against her cheek, and shut her eyes, fighting off her fears, her wild surmises, her awakening will.

◆ ◆ ◆

De Rançun and Petronilla left almost at once to work with the Barb somewhere; Eleanor lingered in the garden, enjoying the crisp air and the view of the river plunging along far below the wall. Alys went swiftly off to gather her brushes and paints. Only Claire remained behind.

The girl had stood back from all the excitement. She was doing nothing, her hands twining together, her eyes downcast. Eleanor turned away, looking over her shoulder, but still Claire did not leave. A tingle of suspicion went down Eleanor's spine. She said, "Do you wish something, child?"

The girl lifted her eyes and met Eleanor's, direct, although a frown dented her forehead. Eleanor faced her, now keenly attuned to her. "What is it, Claire?"

"Your Grace," Claire said, and came forward, and dipped into a bow. But still direct. Eleanor had never seen her so bold. "There is something—I have long known this, but I thought—what just happened, though—I must tell you."

Eleanor was drawn tight as a sail in the wind; she watched the girl's eyes. "Speak, then," she said.

Twenty-one

The Barb was agile as a cat, headstrong and mischievous; as soon as Petronilla mounted him, he threw her.

She landed hard on the grass, her hands under her. Her stomach seemed to bounce even after the rest of her had stopped. De Rançun was settling the gray Barb down, and he said, "We'll get another horse."

"No." She got up off the ground, shaken but whole, and went back toward him and the horse. They had come outside the city to do this, to a meadow in the woods, and there were no witnesses; here she looked like a fool only to herself. And to de Rançun, who knew anyway.

The horse snorted at her, his ears switching back and forth, and his eyes gleaming with a wicked joy, as if he had just done something wonderful. He tossed his long white mane and snorted. Now that he knew he could pitch her, he would try it again as soon as possible. She said, between her teeth, "I will ride him—help me."

She thought, *I am not worthy if I cannot ride her horse.* She did not think what she was worthy of, if she could.

De Rançun said, "Keep your heels down and your head up—I'll hold his bridle this time." He boosted her effortlessly up into the saddle, and she flung her leg across, pulling her skirts after her, sitting astride as she had not done since she had ridden her pony bareback as a child.

The horse bounced again and rocked her forward, but this time, expecting it, and with de Rançun holding his head, she stayed on, got her feet into the stirrups, and drove her heels down. De Rançun had the reins close under the horse's chin, talking in a steady, soothing stream as the animal danced and sidled around him, light on his feet as a deer. She took up the reins.

"Let him go."

"Keep him collected. Don't let him stick his nose out!" He turned toward his black horse.

Under her the Barb bounded forward, swift and soft and powerful; she gathered him up, touching her leg to his side, driving him onto the bit so that he had to flex his neck. Turning him in a circle, she held him to a mincing slow trot. De Rançun rode up beside her, and the Barb shied violently, and she went forward out of the saddle again and he bolted.

De Rançun galloped alongside a moment and then fell behind, shouting. She found her seat after only a few strides and, working the reins, was able to turn the horse in a circle, and slow him down again, and get control of him again.

"He's so fast," she said, as de Rançun caught up to her.

"He's a damn devil." He leaned out to slap the curved muscular gray neck. "You did that very well. I told you, you can ride this horse. Just keep him collected. He can't run away with his chin tucked in."

Petronilla was trying to picture how Eleanor sat in her saddle, her shoulders square. Often she held the reins overlapped in one hand, one over and one under. Often she laid her hand with the reins together on her thigh, her other hand on her hip. Petronilla's own thighs were already sore, and her backside hurt in a new place; this was much less comfortable than riding aside, she thought, but also she had more mastery of the horse. She made the Barb canter in a circle, his action smooth as cream, like riding in the crook of an angel's arm.

I can do this, she thought, with a surge of excitement. *I can do everything she can do.* With a kind of raw lust, she threw her head back and laughed out loud.

◆ ◆ ◆

That night Bordeaux came to them, as Eleanor and Petronilla were playing tables in the hall of the Maubergeon, with six candles in a sconce set high over the board. At the announcement of him, Petronilla glanced quickly at her sister to make certain that the darkness disguised her. With relief she saw that only Eleanor's face showed in the light, and her hands.

The Archbishop strolled across the room toward them, smiling, but he looked weary and worn, and Eleanor with a glance sent a page for a chair for him.

"Good evening, my dear girls," he said, in his informal, Occitan drawl. He took his place carefully on the chair the page had brought; Petronilla suspected a few untested stools had collapsed under him. He planted his hands on his widespread knees and looked over the board between them. His jowls hung around his collar in round folds; his eyes drooped a little, like little red swags, as if he were always sad in spite of his jokes. "Well," he said, "you see, playing at tables, here, your girlish impulses serve you very ill, Eleanor."

Eleanor laughed at him, annoyed. Petronilla said, "Uncle, are you going on with us to Limoges, when we set out again?"

"Ah, no," he said. "I'm for Bordeaux by myself; I must keep court there, and the quarter day is coming up." He took off his cap and swiped his hand across his shining head.

Eleanor said, "Then I should thank you now for your service."

"Now, Eleanor," he said, "listen to me first. The King agrees on the annulment, but having the council in Limoges is impossible. Now they're saying Beaugency, on Palm Sunday."

Petronilla looked away, rolling her eyes, exasperated; she thought, *We should have known this would happen. It's always just too far off. It's always out of reach.* She looked down at the board before her, the counters neatly lined up on the dagger-shaped lines, no home column left unblocked. She scooped up the dice into the little cup and shook them until they rattled. Perhaps they should find some way to get Eleanor into seclusion to have the baby in secret, and put off the council until summer; at once she knew this was impossible.

Eleanor's voice was tight as a wire. "Uncle, this is not good news. I want to stay in Poitiers, and now I will have to leave again, and until I am free of the King I cannot come back."

Petronilla gave a little murmur of agreement. Bordeaux bobbed his shoulders back and forth a little, as if he were dodging something. "It's that bastard shaven Templar, he wants to wring the last drop out of Aquitaine before he lets it go."

"Before he lets go!" Eleanor rounded on him, her face blazing in the candlelight, vivid with temper. "He will never let go, Uncle, he will keep on putting this off forever." Abruptly she gave a sigh, and sat back, and turned toward Petronilla. "What now?"

Petronilla said, "We'll think of something." She put one hand out, to keep her sister from standing up and revealing herself.

Bordeaux said, "Be patient. I'll be back with the King after Christmas; I'll go at it again with him. But—" He gave them an apologetic smile. "I have a favor to ask."

Eleanor said, "Of course. What is it this time?"

"It's Thomas again," said the Archbishop. "The lute player. He wants to come back to you and is afraid he's lost his welcome."

Eleanor gave a harrumph of angry laughter. She turned around toward him, her eyes narrow. "Well, how very clever of him to have discerned that. He found the King indifferent to his arts, did he?"

"They will hear only psalms," Bordeaux said. "Take him back, Eleanor; he is too good to let go to some German, or worse, Troyes."

"Tell him to sing tonight outside my window again," Eleanor said. "Let him be a true nightingale. And I will consider it."

"You're a generous woman." Bordeaux heaved himself upright out of the chair. "I'll deal with the King. I promise I will get you this annulment." He gave her his hand, and she took hold of it, looking up at him.

She said, "Thank you, Uncle. You've done as well as possible, perhaps." She gave him back his hand, without kissing his ring, and nodded him away.

When he was well gone, she said, "Well, that is evil news."

Petra reached out and began to lay the pieces on the board for a new game. They had come so far. There had to be some way to win still. "Be patient, Eleanor. Everything will work out."

Eleanor sat back in her chair, her head down, looking a little upward at her, beneath her heavy brows. She said, "Petra. Tell me the truth. Claire has told me you spoke to Thierry."

Petronilla went cold all over; her breath stuck in her throat. She said, "Oh, the little slut."

Eleanor was not smiling. Her eyes were unreadable. She said, "What did he say?"

Petronilla lowered her gaze to the board, where the counters stood on their pointed stations; she shook the dice and moved her men. Her hand trembled a little. When she spoke, even to herself her voice sounded off-key. "It was—it was so monstrous, Eleanor, I could not bring myself to tell you. He offered to give us Aquitaine in return for a baby."

"Then he knows." Eleanor's voice was utterly calm.

"I don't—I'm not sure." Petronilla looked up at her. "He thought

I was you. He thought he was talking to you. He made it seem as if you—might have a lover, get a child that way, and give it to the king."

Eleanor's head shot up. Her face was vivid with astonishment. "Oh, hideous. What a foul thing is a man without his manhood."

"I would have told you, I swear it. I meant to." Petronilla knew she was babbling. "But it was so absurd—I half did not believe it. I wanted only to forget it."

"Yes." Eleanor sat up straighter and took the dice cup. Her eyes went to the board, and she rolled out the dice onto it. Her voice was cool, pensive. "I certainly would want to forget it. But Thierry may have given us something. Perhaps we could see him again. In secret."

"What," Petronilla said, confused. "You would agree?"

Eleanor smiled at her, not a pleasant smile, thin-lipped and cruel, her eyes half-shut. She had rolled doubles, and she moved her men quickly down the board. She said, "But this time, it will be really me he speaks to."

Petronilla took the cup, her hand shaking. Yet Eleanor did not seem angry, and she felt easier. "Do you think that's wise?"

"How did you meet him before?"

"In the confessional—in the chapel at Chatellerault. It was dark, and the screen—"

"Ah, yes. You're very clever, Petra."

This did not seem as much of a compliment as it might have. Petronilla tipped the cup, and the dice flew out: a five and a four. She moved her men, not thinking, her mind tumbling over with guilty feelings, and a wash of relief that she had not come for one of Eleanor's tongue-lashings.

"Well," Eleanor said. "That was unlike you, Petra. You gave me such an opening." She took the cup, and rolled again, and with her next move carried two of Petronilla's pieces off the board. "I think we shall arrange this with Thierry, and see what might come of it."

✦   ✦   ✦

Claire had been studying Alys's crafts, and her face looked actually pretty, not by nature but from art. She had grown and she held herself with more grace, even pride. Petronilla went by her into the shadowy space behind the stairwell, where they could talk unnoticed. It was early morning, and the hall was still empty, everybody so far waiting down in the courtyard, but they would come quickly up.

Yet the first thing Claire said was, "Please, my lady, thank you for letting Thomas come back."

Petronilla said, "Give me no thanks. I should box your ears, for telling tales of me to my sister." Eleanor had made her promise to be kind.

The girl raised her head, her eyes direct. "I am the Queen's servant, my lady. I may not be brave, and I am indifferent honest, but I can be loyal." Her voice was prim, pleased with this righteousness. She dipped down in a little bow. "What you are doing, to protect her and save her, that is truly noble, my lady, and very brave; I admire you very much for it."

Petronilla narrowed her eyes and turned her head slightly away. "And you were annoyed with me over Thomas."

The girl went red, and her teeth chewed her lip. Petronilla laughed, facing her straight on again. "Then we are even, are we not?"

Claire's lips parted, and her eyes rose, wide with surprise. Uncertainly she began to smile. Her eyes glinted. "Yes. I suppose we are, my lady."

Petronilla said, "Good. And I suppose you were being honest, and keeping faith, which I must depend on. Because I need you to do me an honest service."

Claire's head bobbed. "I will, my lady."

"I want you to go to Thierry again."

The girl blinked, her brow furrowing, and put her head to one side. "*You* want me to?" she said, with a slight emphasis on the first word.

"Tell him it is the Queen, of course. Tell him she will meet him as before, this time in the palace chapel, here. It must be late—tonight."

Abruptly a burst of noise resounded through the hall; people were gushing up the stairs from the courtyard, the place suddenly booming. Boys with torches ran across the room to light the sconces at the far end. Petronilla reached out and rapped Claire on the shoulder, harder than necessary.

"And in spite of what I said, you are still dallying with Thomas."

The girl swallowed. "We sing. He is teaching me to sing."

"Oh," Petronilla said, and laughed. "I've never heard it called that before. Go wherever that takes you, I suppose; we're all in up to our necks." The room was full of people now; she could not linger. She poked Claire again. "Go now and do as we bid. And you are forgiven, you need not cower anymore."

Claire was watching her, her mouth open to ask something else. But there were already too many people. Laughing, clapping, they bumped in around her. Claire dropped into a quick bow to her, and went off. Petronilla drew back into the deep shadow under the stair, to pin her veil up in place.

◆　◆　◆

Claire went down to the courtyard to watch for Thierry. The meeting with Petronilla still churned in her mind. She had expected the Queen's sister to be angrier.

Honest and brave, loyal and generous, she thought. *If not always, most of the time.*

Brave as a hero, she thought. What they were proposing, that Petronilla ride in the procession in the Queen's place, moved her like something from one of Thomas's songs.

Then, across the snowy courtyard, she saw Thierry coming, and she left these thoughts and went to put herself in his way.

◆   ◆   ◆

Later, sitting in the midst of the women while they readied her for the procession, Petronilla was so frightened she thought she would throw up. She felt like a piece of wood being painted, and she wished she had never agreed to this. She fixed her gaze on Eleanor, on the bed watching, and told herself she could not fail her sister; she kept thinking this, a litany, over and over.

Eleanor wore Petronilla's own severe white mourning gown, with the veil dangling ready by her ear. Meanwhile the other women were turning Petronilla into the image of her sister.

Alys said, "Now, hold still, my dear." With her finger she tipped Petronilla's face up into the sunlight.

Petronilla shut her eyes. The magnificent clothes felt heavy, scratchy, too loose, or too tight, she wasn't sure, and she was already sweating, although it was cold. The women all around her staring at her made her feel naked. The brush stroked her cheek, and then Alys was daubing something on her eyelid, and under her eye, and smoothing with her thumb. She kept her eyes shut. The deft fingers on her chin tipped her face to the other side, and the brush caressed her skin again, seductively soft.

She straightened, and Alys stepped away from her; she opened her eyes, and all around her the women gave a sharp, collective gasp, the truest of compliments. Petronilla fixed her gaze on Eleanor, before her, and Eleanor picked up a looking glass, and came over beside her and put her head beside Petronilla's, and held the glass up before them.

Petronilla's mouth fell open. In the murmuring of the women she heard what she saw in the looking glass, that she and her sister were as like as two rosebuds on the same vine. Two copies of the same face looked out at her: the wide lush mouths, the gold-flecked green eyes, the flare of the cheekbones, the red hair swept back from the deep peak over the brows.

In spite of her fears, she felt a surge of triumph. It seemed to her she had waited all her life for this. She was as beautiful as Eleanor, at last.

More beautiful. Eleanor, going back to the bed, lumbered along, her body thick under the white drapery. "Go," she said. "This will work. No one will know. Go now. I'm very tired." She sank down on the bed; Petronilla heard the fretful edge in her sister's voice, the jealousy.

She had to work to keep from smiling. When she did, Alys said, "No, no, that ruins it—that's Petronilla, that frown—let your face relax, child. There." Petronilla smiled, obediently, and lifted her eyes, and Alys said, delighted, "There!"

Marie-Jeanne, as she always did, took the crown and set it on her head. She wound the tail of the coif over it to keep it in place and tucked the end behind Petronilla's ear. Petronilla rose, and with the other women attending her, she went out of the room and down into the courtyard.

There already a great crowd waited, and when she appeared on the steps, a roar went up: "Eleanor!" They called it in the langue d'oc, *Alienor*. She raised her hands to them, as if she were a god, blessing them. She felt the blood rush into her cheeks. She held herself perfectly straight beneath the golden circle of her crown, proud as a goddess, and walked down to where the Barb waited, his tail frisking, de Rançun holding his bridle.

She thought this was the greatest day of her life. When she rode out, the streets were packed with people, all shouting the name now hers, at least for the moment, and waving banners and boughs of mistletoe and ivy, and lifting their children up to see her. The Barb shied and sidled along, snorting at the crowds, his ears flipping back and forth. She was ready for this and knew him for a fraud anyway, with his pretended fright, knew that he was afraid of nothing, simply seeking an advantage like any other courtier.

Ahead of her, the wagon appeared, with the big ugly statue of Saint Hilary, bishop and Father of the Church, who had preached here when the Kings of France were fur-bearing savages. She followed it through the narrow hilly streets of Poitiers, beneath the overhanging signs of merchants, by the gateways of inns, past windows stuffed with cheering people. The roar of the crowds washed over her like the sea. She smiled, and waved her hand, and had her pages run around giving away sweets, and the adulation of her people washed around her like a great warm ocean.

Part of her felt small and cold and scared, inside this huge person everybody else was seeing. She crushed that part down. She let the excitement carry her up as she rode along, with her pages and knights ahead of her pushing people out of her way, more and more sure of herself.

This was what it felt like to be Eleanor, she thought. And she would feel this way for days to come. Eleanor should now keep in the wagon, out of sight with her fat belly and her weariness. Petronilla had risen up into her place, and she meant to enjoy it, now, as long as she could.

◆ ◆ ◆

In the dark, Eleanor made her way into the confessional, sat down on the priest's bench, and pushed the little shutter open. There was no one on the other side, which was as she had planned it; no sense in letting him see her approach. No one now, even in the dark, could mistake that this was a woman well along with child.

She laid her hand on her belly, thinking of the baby; in spite of his inconvenience, she loved him. She dreaded what she must do when he was born.

She dreaded bearing him, also: the pain, the blood, and the danger. Whenever a woman lay down in the straw, she faced the possibility that instead of drawing a life out of eternity she would cast herself into it. He stirred inside her, as if he caught her apprehensions. Little worm, little curl of life, little hidden prince.

She was still brooding on all of this when someone slipped into the other side of the confessional, and Thierry Galeran's voice said, "Your Grace. I come. Have you considered, then?"

"Oh, yes," Eleanor said, between her teeth. "I have considered. Hear this, evil thing—I want my freedom from this marriage. You will stop thwarting me, and urge the King to it, at once, or I shall go to Louis and tell him what you said to me in Chatellerault."

He gasped. Beyond the screen he was only a piece of moving darkness. He said nothing, and she went on, "What do you think he will do, when he hears what you have offered me?"

"Your Grace." The voice half strangled, greasy with fear. "I will deny it."

"Bah," she said. "He knows you well enough to recognize one of your hatchings. He knows also I do not lie to him, whatever else happens. And at the very least, he will dismiss you. Louis is honorable. His blood is his greatest treasure. He might even condemn you for treason, for plotting to give the sacred crown of France to a baseborn bastard."

Thierry said nothing, but she could hear him breathing hard, like a windbroken horse.

She said, "Go, Thierry. Go and make ready the council that will set me free. Tell the King I should be able to stay in Poitiers in the meantime. And do not let me see you again, ever."

The door of the confessional banged open. He bolted away. She sat there, her hands in her lap, hot with pleasure. She waited awhile, in case he had set spies around, to see her leave, but she knew she had won. He would do as she commanded. She laid her hand on her belly. Now there was only the problem of bearing the child.

But that would be possible, now, if she could stay in Poitiers. Anything was possible in Poitiers. She shut her eyes, tired, but pleased with herself, gathering the strength to go back to the Maubergeon.

As she went up the steps, she found de Rançun waiting for her. He swung toward her, his eyes sharp, and put out his hand for her to lean on. "Your Grace," he said, "I have news touching on Duke Henry's fortunes, when you would care to listen."

"Ah," she said. "I'll listen now. Tell me."

He walked along beside her; she laid her hand on his arm and leaned on him as they climbed the stairs. He said, "There's a messenger here from England."

She turned her gaze on him. "From King Stephen?"

"Yes. And loose-tongued, and likes his wine." They had reached the landing and they stopped. Several people were coming up and down the stairs, servants with tubs and bowls, and they went off to one side. She stood where she could see around them and looked quizzically at him.

"Then Stephen and Louis are conspiring? He is Normandy's suzerain; can he do this?"

"No, no—the messenger is here to see Thierry."

Her look sharpened with excitement. This was something new. "What is it?"

The fair-headed knight made a face. "The usual dishonorable backdealing. Thierry with his penchant for spying seems to have accumulated quite a web of them in England—ears in every house and hall. Stephen wants those names."

"Huh," she said. "The cheating ball-less bastard." De Rançun was smiling at her, her spy. She thought a list of those names would be of some use perhaps to Duke Henry. At once she saw they would be far more important to the men being spied upon. "Find out . . ." She wondered what she needed to know. "Find out all you can."

"I will," he said.

"Is there anything else? Anything of Normandy himself, for instance?"

His smile slipped a little. "No, Your Grace."

She turned her eyes toward the wall, thinking. There had to be some way to make use of this. She turned suddenly, without talking to him, and went on through the door there, into her room. She felt him linger, and then go away, reliable as always, whom she could trust to do anything.

✦   ✦   ✦

Later, when all the others had gone to bed, Eleanor could not sleep, thinking over what de Rançun had told her. How like Thierry to sell Stephen a list of his worst enemies. If she could get that list somehow to Henry, it could be the turning point of the enterprise of England; she could place herself at the crux of his ambitions, solid as a keystone. She was sitting by the window thinking this over, wishing Petronilla were awake to talk to, when she heard Claire sneak in, well after moonrise.

She thought she knew what the girl was doing, creeping around like this. For a moment, diverted from the bigger worry, she thought about the lute player Thomas. Fine as he was, she should get rid of him, before he ruined one of her favorite women. How to do it was the interesting thing, of course. Then the first matter rose again into her mind, and she saw them both together: the problem and the solution. She looked out the window into the blue and silver moonlight, imagining the ways northward from here.

✦   ✦   ✦

In spite of everything, they did have to leave Poitiers again. They were to spend Christmas in Limoges, and there was no getting out of it. Nor did the King at once announce any council, any certainty of the annulment. Eleanor chafed and paced and snapped at everybody, but two days after she had forced Thierry to his knees, they were packing up to ride off again.

Or at least some would ride. Eleanor herself would trundle along in the wagon, like a barrel of cured meat, like some baggage. Everyone agreed that Petronilla had done so well at being Queen that now she should be Queen again, as long as need be. Eleanor set her teeth together at that, but in her heart, she was relieved.

•   •   •

On the day before they were to leave Poitiers, she sat with Petronilla in the garden, passing a cup of wine back and forth. She had planned out what to do about the lute player, and she said to her sister, "What do you think of our Thomas, now?"

"He has the voice of an angel," Petronilla said, "but Uncle was right, he's a devil for women."

Eleanor held out the cup to her. "Is he clever?"

"What do you mean?" Petronilla drank, and set the cup down by her knee.

"I have a task he is perfect for," Eleanor said. "That requires him to do exactly as I tell him, and not turn me over. Will he do that?"

Petronilla laughed, as much at her sister's bandit talk as at what she said. "What task? You ask not cleverness but honesty; I do not know anyone that well, except for Joffre."

"Joffre cannot do it. We have learned—through good fortune, and some bribes and listening—Louis has entertained a messenger from England, who is going back there, now, as we go on south. He carries a letter it would be of great benefit for the Duke of Normandy to have."

"Hmmm," said Petronilla. "The way to the English throne of course is bought with English nobles."

"Yes, I think so. To get back to England the messenger must go within reach of Duke Henry, and if he is warned in time the Duke can get that letter. I want the troubadour to go with the messenger's train. It's a perfect disguise; there will be many travelers, and he will be welcome enough for what he is. And the troubadour can alert Henry to the opportunity while the King's man is still within his reach."

Petronilla lifted her eyebrows, her eyes considering. "A good plan. If he fails, what's lost? If he succeeds . . . Well plotted, Eleanor. You are master of this."

Eleanor sat back, satisfied. Whatever the appearance, Petronilla still bowed to her. She was still the real Duchess of Aquitaine. At once she laughed inwardly, to think it could be otherwise. She sent a page for the troubadour.

He left the next day, going north with a band of travelers of whom one was the King of England's man, in some disguise. Unfortunately, Claire left with him, which Eleanor had not foreseen.

◆　◆　◆

The Queen and her sister and their train rode out of Poitiers very early in the morning, for once ahead of the King, because the crowds should have been less then. But when the people heard that Eleanor was leaving, although the dawn was just breaking, they flooded into the streets and cheered her all the way to the gate.

Petronilla traveled at the center of it; she battled the frisky Barbary horse, who spooked in the surging tide of bodies, bounced and tossed his head, his ears wigwagging and his breath exploding from his nostrils. All the while she struggled to hold herself high-headed, straight and proud, the way Eleanor did, to greet the tumult gladly, as Eleanor did.

This was becoming somewhat easier. When she could take one hand off the reins, she waved, laughing at the mobbed frantic faces screaming a name that wasn't hers: With some relief, she realized she could do this as well as Eleanor.

In the wagon behind her, her sister rode comfortably, protected, out of all eyes. What could be wrong in that? She knew she was doing the right thing.

Once they left the city behind, she motioned de Rançun on ahead, to keep them to a steady pace so that the King's procession would not catch up. The Barb anyway fussed if she tried to hold him down. Yet she dared not let him step out too freely; she could feel under her in the quick muscular shifting of his body how he would hump his back up if she gave him his head at all, and she knew he wanted more than anything else to throw her into the nearest ditch. He played endlessly with the bit, trying to work it up between his teeth; the reins had worn blisters into her little fingers.

Even out on the high road, she was still Eleanor, as whenever anyone saw her, people came rushing up from all sides, shouting and waving. This grew wearisome after a while. She saw ever more clearly the virtue of being only the younger sister. She felt her life seeping away into this false life. The Barb tossed his head, and she realized she was holding him too tight, and she let the reins slide a little through her fingers. He kicked up his heels as soon as he felt that. She stayed in the saddle; she had him mastered now, and he could not throw her off. She laughed, pleased.

Twenty-two

Thomas had a mule, and somewhere he had found a smaller, gentler one for Claire; they joined a group of people going north that got larger all through the first day. There was a Flemish merchant with his servants and some pack beasts, a tinker with his pots hanging from his belt, three monks, a Jew on a white donkey, a half dozen palmers, a man leading a string of pack mules. As they went along, some market wives joined them, walking up to the next village, one with a goose under her arm. They spent that first night in an open field, scattered apart under the far-flung stars.

Thomas said, quietly, "Are you sorry you came?"

She huddled in her cloak, as near their little fire as she could get without burning; they had brought bread and cheese and there was a little wine left. Across the meadow she could hear the shout of voices at the big fire, where the Flemish merchant and the monks and pilgrims all gathered and were getting drunk.

She said, "I'm sorry I'm so cold. I'm sorry there's nowhere to sleep but the ground." She looked up at him. "I'm not sorry I came."

He smiled at her. He was replacing strings on the lute; the twisted lines of gut were set in pairs, and so he needed to put in two at once. A little jar of oil sat by his knee. He turned the wooden peg with one hand to tighten the string. "Well, I'm glad you came. You surprised me, Clariza. I didn't know you were so brave."

She said nothing. He had not told her why the Queen had sent him north, only that she had. When he said he was leaving, she gave no thought at all to staying behind. She would not give this up, being with him, the music, which was the same thing.

He said, "Here, listen to this," and played a little playful run of notes. Frowning, he twisted the wooden peg again. "I thought of that for the King's song."

She sang it, under her breath; he was still working on his long story about the knight of sorrows, and the queen who loved him. She had heard most of it in several versions. "Is it too merry?"

"Try this." He played it again, this time slower, one note stepped down, so it sounded sad.

"That's better," she said. She wondered if she could make songs, too. It amazed her how he drew meanings and feelings out of a piece of wood and some entrails. "Let's sing," she said. "No one will hear."

He laughed at her. "You are the only musician I have ever met who doesn't want anyone to hear." He picked out the notes of the opening to the knight of sorrow; gladly she lifted her voice to the song.

* * *

Two days later they came into Chatellerault. The Jew at once went to his own people in the city, and the rest of them moved into a dank, stinking inn by the river. There for a lot of money the innkeeper brought them bread and wine. The Flemish merchant and his servants took over the only separate room.

There was only one hearth, and everybody else gathered close around it. Night closed in. Claire bundled her cloak around her;

the smell of burnt garlic, piss, sweat, and filthy clothes made it hard to breathe. She wondered how she would sleep in such a crowd. Thomas put his arm around her. Against her will, she began to think of the Queen's apartments in the Maubergeon, the airy rooms, the quiet, the food and the wine, and her mood gave a little lurch downward. Maybe she had made a mistake. He was pulling her closer; he kissed her forehead. He knew, then, that she wasn't as brave as he thought. As foolish as she acted. A flutter of panic ran over her skin. She stiffened, holding herself away from him, thinking, *I could still go back.*

From the other side of the hearth, someone said, "Sing."

The rest of the group murmured, agreeing. She looked up, surprised, and the man across the way nodded at her. He was the tinker, an older man, his face seamed and lapped with lines. "Sing, the two of you, like the other night."

Claire flushed. She had not known they listened. Thomas straightened and reached for his lute. "You see," he said to her, and his fingers moved deftly over the strings. "Let's sing the Queen's song." He knew it was her favorite.

She licked her lips, trying to gather her rattled attention to the music. They were all watching her, these strangers. She began, and at first her voice wavered. She remembered to straighten, to bring it all the way up from her belly. Then his voice joined hers, and she turned and her gaze met his eyes. The rest of the room faded away, and their voices rose together.

Her fear fled. This was what she loved, what she wanted best to do, no matter where it led her.

A door opened somewhere. They were coming in from the other room to listen. She sat watching him play, and giving forth music, and even in the cold and the dark, her spirit soared up; she thought, *I have done well. I am brave, after all.* She laughed, even as she sang, content.

*   *   *

"What do you want, then?" Thomas asked pleasantly, later, in the dark. "To jump over a broomstick?"

She kept her eyes shut, although they were in the darkest corner of the inn's garret. The innkeeper had brought them up there, with many flourishes, as if he gave away a hidden treasure: this tiny bare room, the narrow pallet. She said, "I want nothing to change."

Her body still sang with triumph. They had won this place, singing half the night in the tavern; her voice was still raw from the hard work of it, her ears still full of the thunderous applause, the cries for more, the calls of desire and longing and tribute.

"Nothing will change," he said, "save I will have a comfortable bed, up there with you, instead of sleeping down on the floor."

She put her hand out, meaning to shut this off. He had been edging toward this since they left Poitiers, but tonight was the first time they had been alone enough. "Good night, Thomas."

His fingertips touched hers. Then, softer than a whisper, he was singing.

She had to strain to hear him, hold her breath, lean a little toward him. He sang in his own tongue, some strange words whose tenderness came even through their strangeness, note by note of sweetness. She shut her eyes, lulled. He was coming closer. His lips brushed her cheek.

She started a little, but he was singing; and the voice smoothed over her, wiped away her fears, and lifted her, expectant. She held her breath to hear him sing. For a moment he only leaned over her, his lips near her face, the soft words crooned into her ear. Then slowly he slid into the bed beside her.

She trembled; she had known this would come. She could say no. She could deny him. Oh, but she could not deny this. She had always wanted this. He took her cheeks between his two hands and sang to her until the tears sprang in her eyes. He stopped singing only to kiss her.

That was a song, too, that deep, sweet kiss, gentle and eager. She parted her lips. Let him stroke the inside of her cheek with his tongue. Uncertainly, she put her tongue into the warmth of his mouth.

He sucked her tongue. She let a moan slip out of her, and somewhere deep down in her body a little spark leaped. He shifted against her, and one hand slipped inside her gown.

"Clariza. My darling one. My wife. Clariza."

She gasped, at his touch, at what he said. Were they married, then? Oh, the warmth of his hand on her breast. His thumb on her nipple, as if he played the strings of his lute. He sang into her ear as he stripped away her clothes. He mouthed her collarbone, pressed his mouth to the pulse in her throat. She ran her fingers through his thick curly hair, her body warm, singing with him. He knew just where to touch her. He whispered her name again. She lifted her knees to him, drunk on the song, and he slid his hands under her backside. Something hard rubbed against her woman's part, fit into it, and then stroked up into her so suddenly she yelled out. She gasped, filled to the brim. She flung her arms around his neck, clutching him, panting, her eyes squeezed shut, amazed. It hurt. Her body throbbed. She groaned, with hurt, with excitement. He held her tight against him, singing.

◆ ◆ ◆

They crossed the river, going north; the Jews left, headed for Troyes, and the palmers scattered. During the day local people came and went, getting some protection for small trips between villages. At the villages, they watered their horses, and people swarmed around them, trying to sell them bread, cheese, wine, even clothes and shoes.

A wool merchant joined them with a string of pack mules, and a couple of rough-looking horsemen who said they were knights. Every night, Thomas and Claire sang, and other people gave them the best meats, wine, and the softest bed.

It was colder as they went north. The wool merchant turned off on another road, and a crowd of black-robed men joined them, chattering in Latin, who said they were from the Studium, going to England, where there was another Studium. That night they stayed at another inn, where she and Thomas managed to find a corner to themselves.

This was behind the kitchen, and warm, and they lay down together. Her mouth was dry. There was enough light to see, but she could not look at him. She wanted to touch him. He kissed her forehead and held her close against him, and shyly she laid her hands on his shoulders.

He pressed against her, full length, his legs moving against hers. She slid her hands down his back, to his hips. She opened her legs a little, to let him in.

But he did nothing, only kissed her. His hand slipped in between her thighs, barely touching her. Her woman's part felt as if it reached for him.

She said, "I'm ready," and flushed, ashamed of having to say it.

"No," he said firmly. "No, I am too big, you are too tender." His fingers stroked the edges of her crease, until she arched her back, pleading with her body, and his kisses made her breath short.

"Thomas—"

"No, no, I don't want to hurt you."

He was laughing. He was playing with her. She gave a yelp. She seized hold of his stalk and drew it in, and they rollicked together in a gasping delicious dance, a new kind of music until the sun came up.

◆　◆　◆

A few days later they stopped at midday at a well by the road; some dozen houses stood around it. She went off by herself, having perfected this now, found a sheltered place in a ditch, and made water. When she went back to where their mules were tied, he was gone.

She started. But before she could even look around, he came up, striding long.

His eyes were intense, as they were when he played the lute. He got her hand and led her a little away from the road, away from the crowd at the well, and from his sleeve he took a bit of paper.

"See this?"

She frowned at it; the edges were dirty. She held her cloak around her with both fists. The chill breeze had turned his cheeks ruddy; she thought he was the most handsome man she had ever seen. She shook her head. "What is it?"

"This the Queen bade me give to Henry of Normandy." He wiggled the paper under her nose.

"Oh." She looked sharper. "What is it? A message."

"I haven't read it. It occurs to me—" His voice fell to a murmur. "I could get better reward for it somewhere else, though. Maybe we should read it."

"What?" Her jaw dropped. The ground seemed to tilt under her. She looked at him as if he had turned into a toad. "You mean—betray her? She would never forgive you." It would be his end. She shook her head at him. Everything she thought of him was suddenly coming loose, flying around her like a dust devil. "No. Who, for one thing? Where? How? Keep honest, Thomas. It's easier."

He laughed. "Good." He stuck the slip of paper away in his sleeve again. "I knew how you would go at that." He slipped his arms around her waist and kissed her.

She sighed, relieved. He had been testing her; it was his way, she realized, joking and gaming, as if he always had to come at truth slantwise. Then he said, "But therefore, what I just heard, by the well, changes everything."

"What?" she said, with some foreboding.

He let go of her, except his hand rested on her hip. "That Duke Henry is in Le Mans, and going south. So if we keep going north, we will miss him."

"Ah," she said. Her gaze went to his sleeve, where the note was, wondering what was in it. If it mattered so much.

"Therefore," he said, "I am going to Le Mans, as fast as I can, faster likely than you can keep up. I want you to go on to Rouen and I will meet you there."

She gaped at him. The suspicion fell over her like a clammy fog. Everything whirled around her again, clattering and coming apart. He was abandoning her. Petronilla had been right all along; he had used her and now he was casting her off. He had turned, looking up the road toward the others, who were making ready to go on. He faced her again. "What?" he said innocently. He looked into her face. "Don't you trust me?"

She composed herself, blinking; she remembered what he had proposed first, betraying Eleanor, which had been a trial, which she had won. Here was another trial. She faced him. "I trust you." Her heart racketed under her ribs.

"Good." He put his hands on her waist and lifted her up onto her mule. "I will meet you in Rouen." He took the purse from his belt and shoved it at her.

"Thomas—"

"And this." He slid the sacked lute off his shoulder and held it out.

She dropped the purse. With both hands she took the lute. Suddenly the upside-down world turned right and settled, still again. He was smiling at her, his eyes merry. By the road, someone called, "We're going, hey, over there." She heard a whip crack. She held the lute in her arms like a child, and Thomas stooped for the purse and tucked it between her thigh and the saddle.

"Watch out for that, it's all we have," he said, and turned away.

She reined her mule around, one arm still wrapped around the lute, and followed the others out the gate. She did not turn to see him go.

She knew he would come back. He would never abandon his lute.

She jogged the mule along to get ahead of the wagons. The Flemish merchant too rode up in front, out of the dust, but she stayed behind him, riding by herself. Ahead the road wound off across the wintry countryside. She thought over what had just happened.

It was like an ordeal, she thought. Like a test of arms. First tempting her, with the Queen's message, then trying her by leaving her. These things came in threes. Here was the second. There would be another one. She felt a little dizzy; abruptly she longed for Poitiers again, for the familiar people there, that easy life. "Yes, Your Grace." Find the comb. Do as she was told. On the other hand, she thought, best to keep her wits about her here, where she was. Her hand fell on the purse, wedged against her thigh, and she took it and stuffed it inside her cloak.

Twenty-three

From Poitiers Eleanor's train rode south through a countryside in the clutch of winter, the wayside reeds standing in hedges of broken black sticks, the sky a wide pale sweep of cloudy blue. By the first evening, when they stopped for the night, a drizzle was falling. She bundled herself up in a cloak, worn to exhaustion, and the horse himself was tired and went meekly along under a slack rein.

They continued on again, the next morning, very early, still moving along ahead of the King with his larger, slower train, and the morning after. So at midday of the third day they came to Limoges.

The rain had changed to wet snow, falling into a keen sweeping wind. Divided in half by its river, the city spread out before them over the valley and up the far hillside, its highest spires barely visible in the heavy gray air. Its river divided it; it was the upper half that mattered. Petronilla thought it beautiful, perched on its hillside, its tiled roofs in steps against the snow.

The Vicomte of Limoges had just girded his city round with a new wall, about which there were some issues of legality, but the gate was open for the King and Queen, and the sentries bowed her procession through into the close passages of the streets. The snow was sticking to the roofs and weighed down the trees and shrubs; the horses walked stiffly on the slippery cobbles.

Petronilla had a sudden feeling of the sky closing relentlessly down on them as if to crush them under the eternal night of winter. She pulled the hood of her cloak full around her face, the fur against her cheeks.

On the road below the castle, in the upper city, she gave a nod to de Rançun to stop their progress and reined the Barb around toward the wagon, and Eleanor.

Her sister was bundled up in the mourning clothes and swathed in veils and looked as big as a cow. Tapping her heel on his girth, Petronilla pressed the snorting Barb to the side of the wagon. With a glance she drove back the curious people around them, who sidled away out of earshot and pretended not to be paying attention.

"How are you?"

Eleanor said, "Very well, actually. Thank you. If this is Raimund, up here, we are in some trouble. He's fairly clever, you know, and I always flirt with him. Can you do that?"

"No." Petronilla chewed her lip. She had met the Vicomte of Limoges once or twice, and he was more than clever, and she certainly could flirt with no one the way Eleanor did. She said, "You must be ill. I shall be very concerned."

"Good," Eleanor said, and lay back, giving out a tragic groan. Petronilla went back up to the head of the train, the reins slippery in her sweating hands.

But only the Vicomtesse, in a crowd of ladies and churchmen, awaited them in the arched gateway of the castle, overflowing with welcomes and explanations. "Your Grace! My lord has gone out to attend the King, but we are very glad to bring you in here, my gracious lady—"

Petronilla leaned down from her saddle to let the woman kiss her hand. "My lady, we are very glad indeed to be here. My sister is suddenly taken very ill, and we must go at once to some quiet place where she can be made comfortable."

The Vicomtesse was a short, round woman, like an apple, with shiny dark eyes like apple seeds. These widened with a sudden expansion of understanding, and Petronilla saw she had heard the rumors and was leaping to her own conclusions about what ailed her sister. "Oh, yes, Your Grace!" She swept out of the way, performing an elegant bow as she did and ushering Petronilla on past her.

They clattered into the courtyard, swept clean of snow, where the castle's servants and guests were gathered all around, their clothes bright as banners against the windy white and gray stone. The wagon rolled in, drawing every eye. Voices rose, chattering, and all craned their necks to see. Petronilla went on across the courtyard, hidden in her cloak, ignored. Ruefully, she realized that, even buried in coarse cloth, veiled out of sight, and traveling under a false name, Eleanor was still the center of attention. She let de Rançun lift her down from her saddle, but even he was twisting to look back at the wagon.

They carried Eleanor off like the Martinmas hog, very dramatically, on a cloak borne by a dozen men. With de Rançun in charge, they took her in through the main hall of the castle and around to a separate set of rooms in the north tower. The stair was narrow and twisting, but with a great deal of shouting and apologies they managed to haul her up to the top room.

Once they were in the bedchamber, Petronilla had no trouble sending away everybody except their own women and throwing the door closed. Eleanor, who had been laid tenderly on the bed, sat up, pulling aside the tangled veil.

"I cannot know how you bear this. It's hot as an oven, all of it." Marie-Jeanne had come to help her, and they peeled off layers of white wool. The Queen of France emerged from the crumpled petals of the widow's gown, her hair a damp red-gold tangle and her eyes shining. "I can be myself, now, as long as I don't have to ride."

Petronilla had sunk down on a stool. Without Claire they were short of help. They would have to bring in pages, sometimes, when they got food, or messages, or visitors, when they sent for an escort so they could go out. Marie-Jeanne dumped the gown on the bed and went to stoke the braziers, and Alys had gotten out cups and was pouring wine. Petronilla faced her sister again. It would make pretending to be Eleanor all the harder if everybody kept seeing the real one on a regular basis. She raked her fingers through her hair, and Marie-Jeanne came at once with a brush.

Petronilla said, "You do not know how you look, Eleanor." The brush dug into her hair; her whole scalp tingled.

"If I am sitting down, I can disguise it still, in my linens." Eleanor's fingers tapped her knee, her rounding belly like a moon from her lap. "Someone has to make the Vicomte take down that wall. You can't allow people to build walls just anywhere they want."

"The wall can wait," Petronilla said. "Alys, show her the looking glass. Even the linen can't hide it now. I think I shall be very ill all the while we're in Limoges." She leaned her head back, enjoying the stroke of the brush through her hair. She watched her sister through narrowed eyes.

Alys held the looking glass before her, and Eleanor leaned toward it. She looked not at her swelling body but at her face, her fingertips touching the skin under her eyes, her lids. Petronilla said, "The Queen's stall in the monastery church is secluded, though. We can go to hear the singing." The singing of the monks of Saint Martial was famous everywhere in Christendom, and she meant to hear it, although that meant going out through the streets in foul weather.

Eleanor turned away from the glass and made no more fuss. She lay back on the bed, and her eyes closed. Her belly mounded up the bedclothes. Petronilla realized with satisfaction that her sister was actually obeying her.

She had become Eleanor even to Eleanor, she thought, and inwardly she laughed at that.

De Rançun came in, with many bows and scrapes, a crust of melting snow on his shoulder. "The King has arrived," he said, talking to them both, his eyes moving back and forth between them. "Everybody here is talking about the lady Petronilla and that she's about to have her baby."

Eleanor sat up; she gave a snort of laughter. She adjusted herself awkwardly on the bed; Alys came to pile pillows and cushions behind her. In spite of the smoking braziers the room was still icy. Marie-Jeanne hung Eleanor's cloak around her again, but the size of her body was evident even through that curtain. "How does my lord the King seem?"

"He looked cold and tired," de Rançun said. He turned slightly toward her to answer. "He paid no heed to any of the talk about the lady Petronilla. He and his lot are in the main tower, overlooking this one; they shall see us coming and going, every step." Dimly through the stone walls, the first peals of church bells rang out.

"Is it still snowing?" Petronilla asked.

"Yes, my lady," he said, glancing back at her over his shoulder.

"Good." She yawned behind her hand. "Then we shall not go out at all this day."

Eleanor said, "Keep watch on them, Joffre. Listen to their gossip. I must know everything."

"I am, Your Grace. I will report." He turned to Petronilla and said, quietly, "Well done, my lady." He went out of the room. Petronilla leaned her head on her hand, enjoying Alys's brushing of her hair, and shut her eyes.

◆   ◆   ◆

In the morning the snow had stopped; Eleanor and Petronilla picked their way through the icy streets and across the river to the monastery, to hear Mass and listen to the monks sing. Petronilla went in Eleanor's clothes, and Eleanor in her white widow's gowns, and then suddenly, in the courtyard of the monastery church, they came face-to-face with the King and his court.

Thierry was among them. Petronilla saw him through a sudden blaze of hatred; she tore her gaze away and drew herself and her train back out of the King's path, bowing as she did. She remembered to give her bow the kind of extravagant flourish Eleanor always presented to the King, a sort of mockery. Louis only paused a moment, his eyes throwing her a swift, shy glance, and then went on. Beside him, the Vicomte was engrossed in the King and paid no heed to her at all. Relieved, she watched them pass. Louis looked sick again, gray around the jowls; the south had always disagreed with him. Behind three monks swinging censers, he paced up the steps toward the yawning church door.

In his train, Thierry lingered a moment, glaring back over his shoulder, and his face twisted suddenly, his lips quivering. Then he was hastening off after his master. Petronilla, her mouth dry, led the women quickly off to the Queen's stall and there sat down on a stool.

The church was old, dark even in the morning. Decked for Advent, its crucifix robed in white, the altar hung with white cloths, the church seemed in a kind of mourning. At the back and to the left, the Queen's stall was high enough that even though the place was filling up with worshippers, Petronilla saw clearly all the way to the altar, where the priests were performing the prayers before the Mass. To her right, on the far side of the church, she could see the King, or where he was, anyway; a carved screen hid him and his court.

As she watched, someone peered around the screen, looking at her, and she sat upright, looking straight ahead, and held her head high and was Eleanor.

Then from the choir there burst out such a blast of song that her whole body rippled with it.

Veni, veni, Emanuel—

Unlike other sacred singing, these voices flowed in separate streams, wove together into webs of notes, and the shimmering sound seemed almost to make her ears drunken. The lush music poured over her, and for a moment she hardly even heard the words in the majesty of the sound.

Captivum solve Israel,
Qui gemit in exsilio
Privatus Dei Filio—

The songs never told of the mother. Petronilla thought of Mary, big like Eleanor, her baby also of a parlous father. Her mind drifted unwillingly to her sister's baby. She had seen traces of blood on the bedclothes, but Eleanor would not discuss it. *God have mercy,* she thought. She could not lose it now. She thought of Mary again, who had endured everything for Jesus' sake, done as she was asked, meek and mild, and been exalted for it. She wondered if Eleanor was somehow defying God.

Something poked her in the back, and she started. She realized that in her gloom she had bent over, curled forward, fallen out of the proud Eleanor into her own smaller, feebler self. It was Eleanor who had prodded her. Stiff with resentment, she straightened and squared herself, raising her head into its queenly curve, looking toward the altar.

Now she listened to the music, and note by note opened up to its glory, climbing around and around itself like a ladder to heaven. In spite of her mood, she began to feel herself lifted, borne upward on the song.

Gaude, gaude, Emanuel
Nascetur pro te, O Israel!

She wished she could make her life as true and perfect as the song, which followed its sure inerrant course through ever-changing curtains of voices, a magic way through the forests of the night. This was a thicket she was in; she could not tell anymore what was true in what she was doing. Who she was, really. Eleanor had surely betrayed Louis, although she had never chosen him, and what did it mean, anyway, a loyalty forced on her? Everybody knew that to be binding, an oath had to be freely given. She remembered the master from the Studium, destroying sin with this one idea. And she, Petronilla, had betrayed no one. All she did was to help her sister.

Yet from one view, she knew, she sinned as much as Eleanor, helping her, abetting her against the King, overturning the order of God.

Still, if she believed she was innocent, did that not matter more? Aristotle had said something: The meaning of an act is in the intent. Even if everybody else believed she was guilty, her intention, to help her sister, was no sin.

That was the danger, she saw, that was how good souls found their way down to hell, by playing with the words and forgetting the meaning. But she didn't know what any of this meant. If she was guilty of something, what was her sin, then, and how did she atone for it? What did she confess?

She had lost the music again, fallen into the jumble of mere noise. She crossed herself. They had set themselves on this course, and they could not change it now. What the end would be she could not make out, if she ever had, really. She felt divided in half: her sister, and her sister's sister. Neither seemed the true Petronilla. She lifted her head, trying to find the way again through the music.

Twenty-four

SOUTH OF LE MANS
DECEMBER 1151

Henry looked up from the ragged slip of paper. He had been coming out the door when this man suddenly approached him; he swept a sharp look around the courtyard again, still wary. Around him were only his own men. He lowered his eyes to the note. It occurred to him he had never seen her written hand before. It could be false. He said to the rough-cut man in front of him, "Where did you get this?"

"In Poitiers, my lord."

"Who gave it to you?"

"The Queen, the lady of Aquitaine." His voice rang with a quick pride. He looked Henry in the eyes and gave him no deference.

"The people you were traveling with—where are they now?"

"Going toward the Boulogne road, when I left."

Henry thought he was telling the truth. Anyhow, he could not take the chance. He wheeled, caught the eye of the page waiting behind him, and sent him for Robert de Courcy. He folded the paper quickly in half. If it was true—if it was true— Impulsively he kissed it. Robert came rushing up to him.

"Get us horses. Ten men, the best."

"Yes, my lord."

Henry swung back toward this odd messenger. "You're going with us."

That startled him, the arrogant bastard. "My lord, my mule won't—"

"Get him a horse." Henry thrust the battered note into the pouch on his belt. If it was false, he would have this man to answer for it. He went on down the steps into the courtyard, then paced up and down a moment. His gaze went again to the messenger. Not Occitan, he thought, not even French; dark, with dark eyes, long ears. Puzzled, he lowered his eyes to the stranger's hands. Soft and slender; not a warrior's hands. But a warrior's pride. The grooms were coming with the horses. He said, "What's your name?"

"Thomas, my lord."

"Thomas," he said, "let's get going."

* * *

At noon, the company of travelers stopped in a good-sized village, and Claire got down from her mount, her bottom aching. She stayed close by the horse, watching the people around her. She had the lute still in her arms, and she looped the strap over her shoulder. Being alone with all these strangers made her edgy. Then someone spoke to her.

She jumped. It was the Flemish merchant, an older man, with long face whiskers and a tuft of beard. He said, "My nightingale. I could not but notice your . . . companion is gone. Let me offer you my table for the midday meal; you will be safe with me and my servants."

Her tongue ran over her lips; it was in her mind to refuse, but then her stomach growled. She said nothing, and he nodded.

"Come into the inn. I will have the board spread." He went away, a little crooked with his age under his expensive fur-trimmed coat. Her heart leaped with gratitude at his kindness.

She went into the inn and sat the board with him and his servants, and they gave her meat and broth and bread and wine. She was glad of this, and for their friendliness also. The merchant sat not far from her and gave her a smile, and she smiled back and thanked him.

"You have given me great joy, you and your fellow singer," he said. "Such music is rare even in the south, where everyone sings." He nodded. "I note he left you with the child."

She jumped, cold, until she realized he meant the lute. It was a joke. He smiled. She made herself laugh. "Oh, yes," she said. "He will be back soon. Maybe by tonight."

The Fleming nodded. "Then I invite you to keep company with us until then. Where are you going?"

"To Rouen," she said.

"Ah, well, then, we will leave you tomorrow afternoon, where the road breaks off to go to Boulogne. But until then I would be honored if you traveled with us."

"Thank you," she said. "But he should be back by tonight."

He was not back. She hardly slept, bundled in her cloak on a pallet in a corner of the common room. The lute in her arms. The child. He had gone, seduced her and left. The Fleming believed that, she thought. He would try to persuade her to go with him. Buy his way into her bed, as he could not sing. She laid her cheek against the lute's fret board, too sad to weep. All this time she had never known him.

She dozed, finally, in the deep of the night, but she dreamed of monsters, and she dreamed she bore a monster child, with dark curly hair and bloody teeth. Then she felt someone draw near and take hold of the lute in her arms.

"No," she cried, and sat up, still half-asleep, struggling, her arms tight around the lute's womb-shaped body.

"Clariza," he whispered, in her ear. "It's me." He laughed. "My darling one. My girl."

She let go of the lute and flung her arms around him, and now, relieved, she did weep. She cried so hard she did not see that the inn was full of men, until they lit a lot more torches, and a harsh voice rang out.

"Stand! By order of the Duke of Normandy!"

She sat up, her heart pounding, the cloak around her and Thomas's arm around her shoulders.

The inn had but the one room, and it was low and filthy; the torches filled it with a hellish yellow light wreathed in smoke. They were at the edge of the flickering circle of light. In the center stood a young man in mail, with spiky red hair and a sword in his hand.

Behind him stood a wall of mailed men. A stab of cold fear struck her. She glanced at Thomas, who looked worn much older from the ride. He said, under his breath, "He never sleeps, this one." And hugged her. "Don't be afraid. He's with me." His head rested on her shoulder, and he yawned.

"What is this?" The Flemish merchant came forward, his voice edged with annoyance. "I have licenses—the Count of Flanders is my—"

A door slammed. Claire, still shaking off sleep, realized that most of the other people in the inn were being thrust out of doors; there were soldiers behind her now, too. The young Duke's voice cracked out.

"I don't need to hear this." He looked past the Fleming to one of his men. "Take his packs apart."

"How dare you do this!" the merchant cried. "Whatever are you looking for—I promise you will not find it. I am an honest man." He thrust his face toward the Duke, but his head turned suddenly, and he looked at Thomas.

Claire laid her hand on Thomas's thigh, beside her, as if she could shield him against that look, like a snake striking. Thomas was leaning on her, half-asleep.

The young Duke walked around in the torchlight. His spurs

clinked. This was the one Eleanor would marry, Claire thought. A trickle ran down her spine. This was the father of the baby. One of the knights came up.

"My lord, we've found nothing. What about the horses?"

Henry's face darkened. His eyes seemed to bulge out of his head, fixed on the merchant, who smirked at him.

"I told you—"

"Strip him down," Henry said. "Strip them all down."

She thought, *He is like a knife blade, cutting through everything to the heart*, and shivered.

The Fleming said, "Now, listen to me."

The Duke's attention sharpened, bright as a torch, and his teeth showed. "Take your clothes off!"

"Look. I'll make a deal."

"Robert—"

"Wait! Wait—" The Fleming reached inside his coat and pulled out a thick packet, sealed. He flung it on the floor.

"I gave it up. Now just let me go on—"

"Shut up," Henry said, mildly.

The merchant pressed his lips together. The young Duke nudged the packet with his foot, and his knight Robert picked it up. He looked at the seal, and grunted.

"L, with lilies, a crown over."

Henry was looking at it, and now his gaze lifted and took in the Fleming again. "There's more," he said, staring at the Fleming. His face shone. His eyes burned like coals. Claire crossed herself. Devils, they were. She had heard that, descended from devils. The sword in his hand gleamed in the torchlight. "There's more. Isn't there?"

"I—" The Fleming put his palms together. "I swear to God, my lord—"

"Strip him down!"

Robert turned, his mouth open with orders. For an instant he was between the Fleming and the terrible Duke, and the merchant spun around. He leaped, not for the door, but for Thomas, his hands outstretched and his mouth snarling.

Claire screamed. Thomas jerked up out of his doze; as the merchant lunged at him, he hurled his body forward, not even rising, going shoulder first into the merchant's knees.

The Fleming tripped over him and fell. Three of the knights had him before he hit the floor. Thomas rolled neatly to his feet, circled them, and sat down again by Claire.

The Duke of Normandy had not moved. His eyes flicked briefly over Thomas, then pinned the Fleming again. They were tearing the clothes off him. His bare chest showed, the hair grizzled. Against his ribs a linen band held a second packet, much plainer.

The knight Robert rose, holding it out to the Duke, who took it and looked at the seal. He stuffed this packet inside his coat. He said, "Truss him, take him to Le Mans, and throw him in the pit; see if anybody wants to ransom him."

"My lord!" The Fleming struggled to sit, his face dripping sweat. He was half naked, and Claire looked away.

The Duke ignored him. He turned to Thomas.

"That's a lute. Is this your wife? You're a trouvère?"

"So I think you northerns call us, yes."

The Duke smiled at him. "That was a nice trick, taking him down. You're coming with me, to Rouen. It's almost Christmas, and my mother likes music."

Twenty-five

Eleanor had changed the whole room around, put Marie-Jeanne and Alys to work, and now, bereft of anything else to do, she sat by the window sprinkling bread crumbs on the ledge for the birds. Petronilla stood across the room, waiting for the kitchen boys to come back with wine and Advent cakes. With a qualm, Eleanor saw something new in her sister's looks; Petronilla stood straighter now than before. She had always seemed such a mouse: round-shouldered, and small, and meek. Now she was beautiful, when every day Eleanor felt uglier.

In spite of her size, she felt herself turning invisible. More and more, the others were attending Petronilla, the real Queen, leaving Eleanor off in her corner, anchored by her lump of baby, overlooked and forgotten. She struggled with an unaccustomed sense of envy— she who had never known a rival. Her legs began to twinge, and she shifted her ungainly weight around on her stool. This had to happen this way, she told herself. Petronilla was saving her much pain and almost certain exposure, and giving up her own good name to ridicule and gossip in the process. But a cold jealousy coiled around her heart like a thorny briar.

The cakes came, spreading their spicy scents into the room; the two pages put everything around on the low table, which was set in the midst of every brazier in the tower. The scent of Eastern spices mingled with the smoke. Eleanor turned back to the birds, crumbling bread in her fingers.

Abruptly they all flew off in a tiny whirring of their wings. A sudden rapid knocking banged on the door, and everybody turned. Petronilla glanced now toward Eleanor, unsure, so at least in Eleanor's presence she did not dare play Queen. Eleanor nodded to her.

"That's de Rançun—let him in." She looked past her sister, toward Alys. "Let him in."

Alys opened the door, and the knight came charging in, his face bright. He went straight past Petronilla and came down on one knee before Eleanor.

"The King has announced the council to declare the annulment of your marriage. For Beaugency, at Eastertide. It's done, Your Grace. Thierry has suddenly withdrawn to his own lands." His smile spread across his handsome, sun-burnished face. "And you and your court are to go back to Poitiers, after Christmas, and wait there, until the council meets. You've won. You are Duchess of Aquitaine, with no one your master. You shall be free to marry whom you wish."

Eleanor let out a whoop, like a country girl at dance. The other women screamed and cheered. In their midst, Petronilla turned and smiled at her sister, and their eyes met. Eleanor's suspicions vanished; she was a fool, after all, making trouble out of nothing. She started up off the stool, her arms out, to embrace Petronilla and their victory.

Then, all through her, a great spasm clenched her, so that she staggered and fell back again upon the stool. She doubled over, her arms across the mound of her belly, and she gave a groan that shook her.

The women all rushed at her, surrounding her; Petronilla cried, "What is it? Is it now? Oh, God—"

Eleanor straightened. The twisting pain subsided a moment.

"Take me—" She shut her eyes. Everything buckled and caved in around her. She felt him lift her up and carry her off, and then she was drowning in a dark, pain-shot sea.

*   *   *

It was too soon, too soon to bear it; the baby could not live, and she, likely, would not live, it was too soon.

Her body ached and cramped and bled. She could feel the wet blood pooling under her now. "Eleanor." That was her sister. "Drink this." She struggled to lift her head. "Here." A wet cloth touched her lips, and she sucked on it and tasted the herbs.

She stiffened herself against the next wracking, crushing pain. She could hear the other women talking around her, but nothing mattered except the pain. They brought her wine, and she threw it up again. They carried her out of the bed to change the linens, and the bedclothes were sodden with wine and with blood.

She moaned, the dark closing in dank and stinking around her. She had kicked up her heels at virtue all her life, and now she would pay, all her sins gathering, debts clamoring to be paid. They bundled around her bed like a crowd of ugly little gnomes, holding out their dirty hands. She trembled at the moment when she would ladle out her life to pay their pestering demands. Her body throbbed and kinked again, and she felt a fresh hot spurt of blood against her thighs.

Someone else was feeding her a foul drink, spoon by spoon. She heard voices around her.

"Has she lost the baby?"

"No. No." A stranger, a dark, southern woman's voice. "The baby is where it belongs. The potion may stop her pangs. She's strong, the baby is strong. God be with her."

She hung on that. God was with her. She was strong. She refused to die. She had dreamed and risked too much to end it all like this.

Marie-Jeanne took hold of her hand and kissed it. Another pain wracked her. Eleanor shut her eyes, hoarding the life in her, gathering it back together in drop by drop of pain.

The strange woman had gone. Marie-Jeanne and Alys brought her food. She did not see Petronilla. She ate some, and this she did not throw back. She drank some wine with more herbs. Slowly she realized she had not felt a throe in long moments.

"Petronilla." She struggled to lift her hand up. To tell Petronilla it was over. "Petra. Where is my sister?"

"My lady—she went to church—it was thought—people would talk—" Alys's hand gently folded hers back under the covers. "Sleep, my dear, good lady."

Petra. She went to be me. She went to take my place again. The old suspicion leaped up through her weariness like a flame in the dead grass.

I could take your place, Petronilla had said, before them all.

Everything rearranged itself around her, what her sister had said, had done, what Eleanor had let her do. She felt herself slipping, falling, leaving a space behind, which Petronilla took as if by right. *No, no, I won't let her have it.* Yet she was gliding into sleep, exhausted, the women murmuring around her.

◆　◆　◆

The church was drab and darkened still; on Christmas every candle would be lit, every statue and vessel and painting unveiled, glorious and golden, to welcome the newborn Christ.

O come, O come, Emmanuel—

Petronilla took comfort in the dark. She had left the others with Eleanor, and so she could be who she was, here, alone. She bent herself in prayer, begging for her sister's life.

Over and over she remembered the moment in the tower room when the news had come of their release, and Eleanor had collapsed. This was a warning, she thought. A message. Eleanor would pay for what she had done, somehow, and if Eleanor, then surely Petronilla.

She dared not think much about what would happen if Eleanor died. Losing her sister would only be the beginning. She would be trapped. She remembered bitterly how much she had loved pretending to be Eleanor. Now she wanted desperately to be able to stop. She prayed for Eleanor, for Eleanor's baby, but she did not pray for herself; she had gotten herself into this.

She thought of her sister: her bright green eyes, her laughter, her face flushed with some excitement, alive, alive, alive. She begged God for her sister's life, unable to think of anything worthy to offer in exchange.

Afterward, with her four knights, she went out onto the pavement in front of the church, and de Rançun lifted her up into the saddle. He would not meet her eyes; he looked downcast and miserable. She gathered the reins. After days in the stable the Barb was eager, and she was fighting with him over the bit and did not see the crowd of strangers pushing toward her until de Rançun shouted.

"Give way! Yield to the Queen!"

She swiveled her head around to look, the horse finally gathered on the reins; Geoffrey d'Anjou on a tall bay stallion blocked her way. A half dozen men in bright red coats packed the narrow gate behind him. De Rançun was still behind her, with the other knights, and she was alone in front of the young Angevin.

She shrank back; Geoffrey d'Anjou's eyes were bright as nailheads, his gaze fixed on her like a beam. She felt that gaze pin her in its unblinking scrutiny, and she thought, *He knows.* Then on his black horse de Rançun rode up beside her and bellowed again at Anjou. "Clear the way!"

Anjou ignored him. He spoke to her, leaning forward a little, beseeching. "You force me to this, Eleanor. You won't see me—you don't answer my notes—" The men behind him were pushing toward him, their eyes on de Rançun and their hands on their swords.

She felt herself recoiling, fear rising into her throat, and a sudden urgency. She could not let them fight; she could not get caught between them. Nor could she let Anjou seize her. But the only way out was past the boy on his tall stallion, and suddenly she realized how Eleanor would take this, and she launched herself forward.

"By God's blood," she cried, furious, as her sister would be furious. "How dare you! Get out of my way, sir! How dare you impede me!"

Anjou's face was high-colored and shining with purpose. "I want you to go with me—just for a little while—let me show you my heart—"

That, she knew, would ruin everything, and the rising panic made her tremble. The Barb began to dance under her, snorting. She flung herself into the drama of Eleanor, her only refuge.

"Get out of my way!" She rode the Barb straight at him, toward the gate; de Rançun followed along beside her, and the rest of her court came hurrying after. Anjou hesitated, and for an instant she thought he would stand, that he would seize her and carry her off, but instead he reined his horse aside and flung one arm to hold his men back. As she passed him, she leaned from her saddle to stare him in the face. "And take this to your heart, sir—I want never to see you again!"

He flushed to the roots of his yellow hair, looking suddenly younger even than he was; she was past him in a moment. In the gateway his men still milled around, but de Rançun spurred ahead of her a stride and called out, "Way for the Queen of France!"

The Angevins crowded back into the courtyard. Petronilla let the Barb trot fast out the gate, into the open bustle of the street; she was sweating under her coif. Her hands hurt. De Rançun slipped past her to lead the way; as he did, he smiled at her, approving.

The knights ranged up alongside them. The court came up around her, and in a comforting swarm of armed and mounted men, she wended her way quickly through mobs of curious eyes, riding over the bridge across the river. On the street beyond, children were sledding along on lumps of ice, and de Rançun and his men rode forward to shoo them out of her way. She let the horse climb the steep slippery cobblestones at his own pace, his head down, his hooves skidding on the icy ground.

Eleanor, she thought. *Eleanor, I am coming.*

In the castle gate she slid down into de Rançun's arms. For an instant their eyes met. She saw the same dread in him she felt in herself. Turning, she went swiftly into the tower, to go up and take her place again beside her sister. She was on the stair when Alys came down, her face glowing.

Petronilla caught her wrists; the woman's joyous face told her before she asked, with a gulp, "My sister?"

"She's getting well. She's kept the baby." Alys threw her arms around her and they hugged. "She's eating. Her eyes are open. She wants wine." She kissed Petronilla and slipped on by her, down the stairs, and Petronilla rushed up to her sister's room.

All the women were clustered around the bed. Petronilla elbowed her way through them, sank down onto the bed beside Eleanor, and put her hand on her sister's hand, and on the pillow the wan face turned toward her.

"Enjoy the music, did you?" A whisper. Eleanor was pale as ash, the shadows under her eyes like coal dust, her voice tired and slack, but she looked better than she had for days.

Petronilla was laughing, helpless, glad. She clutched her sister's hand. "Oh, Eleanor, you are well. Thank God. Thank God. It's a sign, Eleanor—" She was weeping all down her face; she lifted a corner of the bed linen and wiped her eyes.

Eleanor made a skeptical sound in her chest. "It would have been a sign had I died, yes."

Petronilla pressed Eleanor's palm against her face. "It is a sign. God favors us." She straightened, putting out her hands; she saw in her sister's hollow eyes the urge to argue. "No, don't talk. Rest."

Eleanor's mouth kinked. There was more color in her face now than when Petronilla had come in. Her eyes shut and her head moved on the pillow. "Whatever that means."

Petronilla left her, went off across the room, let the women take off her outer clothes. Surely the sign was meant for her, too, she thought. She had prayed, and God had answered her. God favored her, too. She was right to do what she thought right. She felt lighter than she had in a long while, reassured.

◆　◆　◆

"Tell me you are well, my lady."

"Oh," Eleanor said, glancing away. She was sitting in the midst of a ring of braziers; it was the first day she had left the bed since she fell. "I am fine, Joffre." He seemed very serious. She smiled at him, to put him in a better humor. "It was nothing, just a woman's problem. It's over now. What matters is the news you brought me, that day. Are you not happy for me, now that I will be free of Louis?"

He pushed one of the braziers aside and sat down on his heels before her, to be eye level with her. "I am," he said, "most truly and completely happy, as you know, my lady. But also, you know, you must marry again."

She snorted at this obvious point. "Yes. Aquitaine is full of quarrelsome barons; I shall need someone to knock their heads together."

He blurted out, "I want you to marry me."

She began to laugh, astonished. "Oh, very clever. I am going to rule my quarrelsome and jealous nobles by marrying one of them. That's not going to work, my old friend." She stopped; he was turning dark red, and too late, she saw he had meant it differently. She gave another, half-choked laugh. "Joffre." She put her hand on his. "Joffre.

I can't do that. Every lord in Aquitaine would rebel." Then, curtly, to shut him off, she went on, "We shall not speak of this anymore."

He lifted his head; people were coming up the stairs, and he got swiftly to his feet and moved away. She felt his reproachful, angry, jealous, wretched mood, even with his back turned to her, and a little thorn of guilt pierced her heart. She would make it up to him, somehow. But she knew there was no way to make it better, save to give him what he wanted, which she would not do. He turned and went on down the stairs, past Alys and Marie-Jeanne, going away.

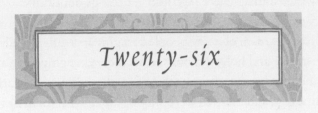

Twenty-six

The Empress Matilda never left the hall of the Duke of Normandy in Rouen, the chief city there. She was old and she enjoyed her comforts. Instead everybody came to her. Everybody needed her, because she ruled the place with her son at war. So she heard news from all over, and that made them need her even more. Just before Christmas she encountered a rumor she intended to find false, and so when she heard her son Duke Henry was north, she sent to him to attend her as soon as he got to Rouen.

⁘ ⁘ ⁘

Henry had been going south to toss his brother out of his last castle when the packet from Louis to Stephen fell into his lap. As soon as he read the letter and the list of Thierry's spies, he knew it meant the end of Stephen's chances. Thierry's net of spies was everybody worth anything in England. No one wanted Stephen to be King.

But to serve his interests, the list had to be shown to the right people and accompanied by the right money. The winter was closing in on them; he had to plan now for what he meant to do in the fighting season next summer. He forgot about his brother and turned at once toward Rouen, where he could get things done.

Two days after he seized the letter, he and his men rode into Rouen past a stream of noisy people bringing in a yule log, all decked with mistletoe and holly. Its boisterous escort, singing rude and holy songs, and tossing wineskins back and forth, reached for nearly half a mile to the city, and his men were singing along with them by the time they reached the gate. Henry joined them, now and again, although he had no voice for it. He liked Christmas; everybody came together, and he could get a lot done.

Inside the gate, he sent his guards to Robert de Courcy's house, off by the river, where he stayed while he was in Rouen. His other choice was the Duke's hall, where his mother lived, and he did not care to have her oversee everything he did. But he had to go there first. He kept the trouvère and his woman with him, to present to his mother for Christmas.

They rode along the main street of the town, full of wagons and donkeys and people going to market. The high-timbered buildings with their wattled fronts looked battered. He reined his horse around the ponds of mud that cluttered in the street. He caught a few dark looks thrown his way, but he ignored them. His father had burned much of Rouen when he overran it some years before in taking Normandy, and they still disliked Angevins here. Nonetheless, he gave them good rule and they obeyed him. He went across the main square, where some peasants were setting up a platform for a Christmas pageant, and turned into the lane by the little old church that led to the Duke's hall, surrounded by its stone and withy fence.

At the gate the sentries saw him and straightened like bolts. He rode in the gate, the two singers at his heels.

Inside was the courtyard, paved with slates. There outside the hall door he came on his mother sitting in the sun, two girls with her to run errands, and a rug over her knees.

Matilda was thin and dry as a twig, a cluster of bones. He knew she put something in her hair to keep it dark. Her skin had a distinct yellow tinge, like old teeth. She was often sick. Now she seemed hale and bright-eyed. Her voice was sharp enough. As soon as she laid eyes on him, she called, "Well, sirrah, I hear you have been misusing your brother."

"He deserves it," Henry said. He dismounted and gave his reins to a groom. With a glance to the trouvère to hold him there, he went across the yard and bowed down to his mother, taking off his hat. He had taken to wearing a piece of broom in it, as his father had. "Is that what you want to talk to me about?"

"What do I hear about you and that wicked Frenchwoman? It's noised about she's got an interest in you. You should have nothing to do with a woman like that; she'll ruin you."

"She isn't French," he said. He glanced around to see who might be hearing—there were dozens of people around. The two girls behind his mother's chair were watching him through the corners of their eyes. In earlier visits he had bedded one of them and tried for the other. He decided this Christmas he would get the other, too.

His mother said, "Avoid that harpy. She would only do to you what she's done to poor Louis. You would never know your children were your own."

He took his gaze slowly from the girls. He wanted his mother off this track. He thought of telling her about the letters, the schemings between Louis and Stephen to cut down the English barons, who would never now let any scion of Stephen's hold the throne. Henry thought he was now King of England in all but the crowning because of that harpy. Behind him, he heard the first low tones of the lute, and he glanced over his shoulder; the trouvère had sat down on the side of the yard not far away and was bent over his lute, his wife behind him, her hand on his shoulder.

Henry turned back to his mother. "I want to call a council in the spring, to plan out another attack on England." He would not tell her about the letter. No reason to tell her any more than she had to know.

The old woman lifted her chin. She thrived on the fight for England. She put out one hand, and the girl on her left, the one he had already had, brought forward a ewer. The other, the quest, came with a cup.

Matilda lifted her cup to her lips, drank, and set it down. The girls retreated to their places behind the chair. "Another council," the Empress said. "Nobody came to the one last fall. Drink."

Henry took the cup. "They'll come to this one. I have to build another fleet." He thought he might have as many as three thousand men, which would be enough. The problem was getting them over to England.

"There is no money." His mother put her fingertips together. "Tell me why you think you will succeed this time, when you've already failed twice."

Her head turned as she spoke, her eyes going toward the trouvère.

Henry snorted at her. She had been scheming for this since he was a baby; she was only dallying with him, which annoyed him. He drank the rest of the wine in the cup. "The first time I was nine years old." He tossed the cup down onto the ground. The intercepted letter would convince her, but he was now certainly going to tell her nothing. "I need money."

His mother shrugged and made a face. Her fingers moved fitfully over the rug on her knees. Her eyes went toward the trouvère again, who was playing something soft and complex, involving many of the songs they had heard in passing from the yule-loggers. The woman began to sing.

"Get me the money," Henry said. She had friends among the Jews. Friends also among the English.

She said, "They will give me not a silver penny until you prove you can get something done."

"What have I been doing since my father died? I hold all of Anjou now except Mirebeau, which I let Geoffrey keep out of love of you." He nodded to her; he wanted some acknowledgment of that. "I've got Normandy subdued. I have an agreement with Louis. He will keep out of an English war and even help me defend the east. If I build a fleet this spring, I could sail this summer." The westward crossing of the narrow water was always hard to figure, the wind contrary and the sea rough. If Louis kept the agreement, he would have all year to wait for the right moment. He did not want to wait a year, not even a month. "Fifty ships." He could be King by next Christmas, he thought.

"We should be thinking of brides for you," she said. "A Danish princess, maybe."

"I'll deal with that, Mother," he said.

"It *is* her, then, isn't it? That Occitan harlot. She is much older than you," his mother said. She fluffed the rug on her lap, her gaze on her knobby fingers. "Of course I was older than your father. But I had some sense of a woman's place. I hated him for twenty years, but I never tried to annul the marriage." Her voice trailed off, her eyes turned toward the music. "Nearly killed him once."

Henry laughed. That he believed; his earliest memories of his parents were of their clawing, kicking fights. "I'm not getting married."

"Oh," the Empress said, her gaze swinging toward him, her voice suddenly lighter. "Good."

"Yet." He laughed again and winked at his new girl.

But now he was thinking about Eleanor. It came to him he did not want to be grateful to Eleanor for his throne. He drew in a deep breath; he wanted to be on top of Eleanor, driving her down, that long red hair wrapped around his wrists.

His mother gave him a sharp, angry look. Maybe she had seen something in his face. But she said only, "Send these musicians closer, that I might hear them better."

"You like them," he said. He himself knew little about music, but he thought they sounded very well.

"I can't know," his mother said, "until I can actually hear them." Her voice was edged with affront, as if he presumed. He had never heard any praise from her, not for him, not for any thing or creature. But her face softened as she turned toward the music, and a wistful look came over her. He turned and beckoned to the trouvère and his wife.

*   *   *

The Duke left, and the Empress ordered Claire and Thomas inside the hall. This was like a barn, drafty and bare except for a few hangings on the walls; Claire thought it had been newly made, or made over, and they had not gotten the chance to fill it up yet. With servants bustling around, Thomas and she sat on a little bench near the end where the Empress's chair was and played. He played a few notes while he was sitting on the bench, then got off and sat on the floor at her feet, cross-legged, the lute in his lap.

First they played the Queen's song, from his long story of the sorrowing knight, and then the song of Tristan. Thomas was having some trouble with his strings, stopping often to tune them; while he fussed over the fret board and pegs, Claire studied the old woman on her chair.

The Empress wore a long, elegant gown, as fine as anything Eleanor had, and far more jewels than Eleanor. Around her neck hung a massive collar of gold and rosy quartz, and in her hair, on her wrists and fingers, at her ears she wore more bobs and bejeweled bits. But her face was lean as a knife, her skin crinkled like dry leaves, her eyes pitiless; Claire saw the small, narrow-lipped mouth, curled always

downward at the ends, and thought she would not be the servant of
such a one.

She thought, with some astonishment, *I am no servant now, at all,
not even Eleanor's,* and a wonderful surge of satisfaction warmed her.

Thomas turned to her. "Let's try something new. You sing the
Queen's song."

Obediently she sat up straighter, lifted her head, and began the
first notes; dreamy and slow, they could be happy or sad. She loved
trying to make them happy and sad at once. The lute played under
her for a handful of notes, and then Thomas began.

But he was singing Tristan's song, now, twining over and around
hers. Two different songs, they still fit together, drifted apart, and
came back with an aching sweetness. She startled and looked down
at him, and found his gaze on her; she sang to him, and he sang to her,
and the song was all different, somehow, rich and deep and tender
and foreboding. He smiled at her. She put her hand on his shoulder.

◆　◆　◆

"Where did you get these people?" the Empress asked.

"I'm glad you like them," Henry said.

"Actually," she said, "I was thinking they need a drum. But they
are above the usual run of the country." One long finger picked at
her nose. "Where did they come from?" Henry was listening to the
singers, who were in fact very good. The woman was pretty, too, and
young, with a fine manner.

He said, "I think the lute player is from Wales, actually, the little
I have seen of him. His wife is French, but . . ." This was curling back
where he did not want to go, and he said, "I have no idea where."

His mother would not let it pass. "How did you come by them?"

He shrugged. "Someone sent them to me. I have much to do,
Mother. I shall see you for dinner. Tomorrow. Take care of my singers, since you like them so much."

"I didn't say—"

He was already backing away; he gave her a deep bow, to make up for this, and went quickly out the door.

*   *   *

Claire and Thomas lived in the Duke's hall and played for the Empress two or three times a day, during which Duke Henry did not appear. The Empress gave them a purse, and then another purse. Claire took charge of these. She found the steward and began talking to him about giving them a place to themselves. Christmas came, with Masses and parades and the great yule log burning in the center of the hall. Still there was no sign of the young Duke, but his mother one day abruptly called Claire into her bower, behind the hall.

She could not deny a command from the Empress, servant or no, and she went into the bower. It was musty, warm from a clutch of braziers, stuffed with an old woman's gatherings: fluffy bedclothes, shawls and furniture, a faint smell of dog. The Empress sat in the middle, and Claire bowed down to her.

"Your name is Claire, I'm told?"

"Yes, Madame." And at the sharp look, hastily: "Your Majesty."

"Tell me." One bony hand rose to the old woman's lips. "It was the Queen of the French who sent you to my son, was it not?"

She stiffened, but she should have known. *Honest*, she thought, in an instant. A lie got her in all sorts of trouble. She said, "Yes, your Majesty. But it was not me she sent. I only came with my husband."

"This outlandish lute player is your husband? But you are gently born. It shows in your manner, in your speech."

"Thomas is my husband, Your Majesty. I have no other family." Which was certainly true now. Even if her father knew or cared where she was, he would not take her back after this.

The Empress's eyes were like beads. "But you came from Poitiers."

"We were in Poitiers, your Majesty, before Advent." Claire held herself straight, as she did when she sang; she knew something was coming. The third test, she thought.

"Did you see the French Queen there?"

"Yes, Your Majesty. And the King. My husband played for them there."

"Yes. Not a good word for him that they let him go. They say, for all her sins, she has a fine ear for a musician. Tell me—" The Empress leaned toward her, fingertips to her chin. "They say she is very brazen and unwomanly, a harlot, and a hussy, who will spread her legs for any man. What did you think of her?"

Claire blinked, and her eyes slid away from the Empress's. It came to her that she had what the old woman dearly wanted to know, the perfect reason why her son should not marry Eleanor.

She had carried this secret all this while, unthinking, until now, when it rose in her mind like a dragon from a dark cave: treasure in its wake.

And now, to her surprise, she had no interest in it. She had everything she wanted now: Thomas, and the songs, and a life of her own. Smoothing her face, she faced the Empress again.

She said, "I know nothing of her, Your Majesty, save that she is beautiful and clever and rich."

"Nothing?" The old woman jerked her head back, frowning. "How long were you there?"

"I know nothing, Your Majesty."

"Did you see her at court? In her chamber?"

"Only at court, Your Majesty."

"Did you ever see my son with her?"

"In Poitiers? No, Your Majesty."

"But elsewhere?" Matilda leaped on the words.

"In Paris, Your Majesty. Long ago."

"Then you were with the Queen there."

"Your Majesty, I am Thomas's wife, no more."

"I do not believe you."

"Your Majesty."

The old woman grunted, her purpose crossed. She glared at Claire. "You're a dull thing, after all," she said. "Go on, I have no use for you." Claire rose, and bowed, and went away out of the bower, a light skip in her walk.

She had passed the third trial. She had won, although she knew not what. Up there on the snowy pavement, Thomas stood, smiling at her. She ran to him, happy.

• • •

She said later, "I want to go back to Poitiers."

"Why? What did she say to you?"

"Nothing. Nothing much. I just miss Poitiers. I loved it there."

"Then we'll go. But not now. It's bad traveling weather now. In the spring. And there are a few places I'd like to see first."

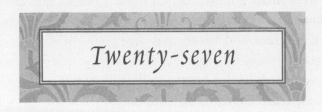

Twenty-seven

The charters went out at last, summoning the great churchmen of France to the council to decide the issue of the King's marriage, all to meet at Beaugency in the week before Palm Sunday. Meanwhile Eleanor spent Christmas as if it were ordinary. Petronilla went off to the church, to the glorious blaze of thousands of candles and the glitter of unveiled gold, to light and beauty newborn after the long dark waiting, while Eleanor sat behind a curtain, listening to a boring priest stumble through his Latin.

She grew stronger, day by day. She had stopped bleeding entirely, and she had not lost the baby. He still kicked and rolled in her belly, sometimes making a visible lump through her skin. She slung her arm around him, glad for him, who was as strong as his mother.

They had no Christmas feast, save a few scraps they ate together in their chamber; at least Petronilla did not attend the Vicomte's great feast in the hall, from which the laughter and uproar and music and excitement wafted up to them all the whole dreary day. Eleanor could not read, or even sit still, and yet the great burden of her body wearied her. She was constantly tired even though she could not sleep. She dreamed of monsters.

The days plodded by. She stayed restless, bad-tempered, burning all of them with her temper, here and there, as she paced endlessly around the room.

Then came Twelfth Night. All that day the women purred and fussed around her in an excess of solicitation, but as the darkness fell and the revels began in the hall, one by one they slipped away. Even Marie-Jeanne, smiling and simpering, after putting Eleanor to bed with most tender care and kindness, made off to join the Feast of Misrule, when the lowest was highest, and every pleasure was permitted.

Eleanor sat alone in her bed, massive as a boulder. She had always loved this night, and it seemed hard and cruel that she should not be able to enjoy it. She wished Thomas were still here; she could call him in to play for her. Likely he would not come, though, willful as he was, as if his music set him out beyond even a duchess. And in any case, he was not here.

Slowly she began to imagine that she could, somehow, still take part in the revel. She would disguise herself in drab clothes, and it came to her that if anybody saw her, they would take her for Petronilla. She could go down and join the crowd, and kick up her heels as best she could.

She pried herself out of the bed. She, who never had to dress herself, struggled into an old gown, pulling and tugging at the skirt to get it over the mound of her belly. She wrapped a coif around her hair and knotted it like a peasant woman, and found a pair of wooden shoes. With a cloak around her against the bitter cold of the stair, she went out the door, where even the guards had gone away to gambol.

She started down the stair, one hand on the cold wall to keep her balance. Somewhere, down there, someone would be willing to make merry with even such a great lump as she was. She could hear them as she went down, the shrieks and laughter, the flurries of music, and the rhythmic thud of dancing feet.

In her belly, the child turned, as if it danced also.

She paused, her feet taking up the cold of the stair even through the shoes. If she went on, if in fact she found someone to toy with in the dark, the child would be tumbled with her.

She licked her lips. For an instant, her old rebel heart rose up, thinking, *No one shall stand in my way, still less a little worm I never asked for.* Her hand fell to her belly. Hers, no matter that she could not ever be his mother, yet he was hers, her charge, her baby. Suddenly a wave of love for him passed through her. She thought, *He did not ask to be. I made him, however much I didn't think to do it. He should not suffer for my thoughtless fault.*

Then below her, around the bend in the stairway, she heard the voices of children, whispering and giggling. Her hand on the wall still to help her keep her feet, she moved down through the dark; the glow of a torch shone around the curve in the stair. She went around onto the landing and found a crowd of children huddled there, peering down the last few steps into the hall.

They were the youngest pages and little girls in waiting, five and six years old, drawn to the heated excitement but afraid to go closer. When they saw her, they pressed themselves back against the wall; they would have run off, she saw, scattered like elves, if there had been a path, but she blocked the stairs upward, and the dark, uproarious hall below daunted them. She smiled at them and came down into their midst.

"Now, don't be afraid. I've come to see, also—what's going on out there?" She turned to peer out through the last tunnel of stairway, where a lone torch burned on the wall, into the shadowy dancing and laughing and merry tumult of Twelfth Night.

Only a few candles glowed in the cavernous darkness beyond, and those were at the far end of the great room, so at first all she saw was the churning mass of bodies, the arms upflung, heads bobbing, the spinning of a dance. Music played, somewhere, wild and a little off-tune and out of rhythm. She drew nearer the top of the stairs, trying to make out faces among the dark mob.

They were dancing in a great rope of bodies, each with her hands on the shoulders or waist of him before, twisting and turning their course through the hall. The candlelight shone for an instant on an upturned face, broad with laughter and red with drink. A foot kicked out, a skirt flew up. The whole wild jigging of bodies seemed one vast creature making love with itself.

She sank down on the step to watch, seeing out there the Vicomte himself, in jongleur's costume, strenuously leaping with a servant girl. Another girl ran shrieking through the crowd, pushing between dancers, her hair streaming and her bodice half off, one breast bouncing naked. Eleanor gathered her skirts around her knees; she realized, startled, that the children had nestled in around her to watch, one tousled head against her left arm, a small hand on her right knee.

What a strange little revel, she thought, delighted. She spread her cloak out around them to keep them warm, like a mother hen with her chicks.

"Look!" she said, and pointed toward the great hearth, where someone stood tossing buns from a basket into the crowd. People leaped up to catch them, climbing over each other in a wild tangle, knocking each other around. Down the hall a half dozen men came, mock fighting with staves; de Rançun was among them. As she watched, he leaped onto the table, parried the others a moment, and then jumped off over them and smacked the nearest on the backside.

Closer, against the wall, she saw two upright bodies working energetically together, and she drew the children's gaze in the opposite direction.

"See the King of Misrule! Who is that—do any of you know?"

"'Tis Joques, the cook's boy!" The children's laughter chimed around her. "Look at him, the big silly! Cook will make him scour pots tomorrow!" Out there people were singing, and the long rope of the dancers began to sway in time. A leather jug came sailing over the heads of the crowd to strike the wall and fall to the floor, obviously empty. A long young man in a woman's houppelande, with enormous sleeves like wings, rushed through the crowd with three girls in pursuit; when they had gotten him out of the dense pack of people, they caught him and began to spin him around in their midst, shrieking with laughter.

"Dance, Reynaldo, dance!"

"Lady." One of the children plucked at Eleanor's sleeve. "Is that the Queen?"

Eleanor startled, apprehensive. She looked where the little girl pointed.

It was the Queen, or Petronilla, anyway, gliding through the crowd. As she passed, in spite of the leveling spirit of Twelfth Night, the people all bowed down, so it was as if she made a progress through them. She paid no heed to anybody, Petronilla, but minced along with a high-headed pride that set Eleanor's teeth on edge. She said, "Yes, the Queen."

She tucked her arm around her enormous belly. The excitement and fun of watching the revels had turned to ashes in her mouth. She thought, *This is mad. There can't be two of us.*

The little girl was looking up at her, wide-eyed. "She isn't as pretty as you, my lady."

"Ahh." Her amusement was gone, and she could not bring it back. The children around her were giggling, daring each other to run out into the wild dance. Gently she disentangled herself from their midst, got her clumsy self up onto her feet. One hand on the wall to keep her balance on the slippery stair, she made her way back up to the dark empty bed.

◆ ◆ ◆

Petronilla wore a half mask, and a hood over her coif, but they all thought they knew who she was, anyway. Twelfth Night, she thought, was the perfect time for her, the false Queen disguised, two deceptions making a fool of someone, herself for one. The crowd bowed deep as she passed through the crowded, boisterous hall, and she smiled and waved, Queen of Misrule.

Only a few lights burned here and there, so that there would be comfortable darkness in which to make merry. On the long tables the piles of bean cake and jugs of wine were rapidly diminishing. Up at the head of the table, the cook's scullion, King for the evening, was already rapturously drunk on his throne, a paper crown on his head, bellowing half-coherent orders nobody bothered to fulfill. A line of dancers passed by her, hands on each other's hips, kicking out and laughing. Petronilla strolled among them, head high, and a ripple of adoring comment went after her.

She glided through the room, accepting bows with a queenly, condescending smile. The people around her shouted and danced and sent up gales of laughter. A man in a hat tipped with bells leaped up out of the crowd, bent in an extravagant bow to her, and led her in a quick little dance down past the hearth. A cup came by, from hand to hand, and she took a sip of it. Someone gave her a bean cake, although there was no bean.

Near the door, someone touched her arm; she wheeled, startled, toward a strange little page, snow freckling the shoulders of his coat. He bowed double, put his finger to his lips, and beckoned.

She hesitated. She wondered at the effrontery of such a summons. She wondered whose page he was—the Vicomte was a famous lover. Her curiosity warmed her. This was the Night of Misrule, a time only to be merry in the dark. She wanted suddenly to be wanted, to be courted at least, if not necessarily won.

The page led her out through a side door, across the snowy darkened courtyard to the gatehouse, and in through a narrow door. In
the bare little room beyond, a single candle burned. As soon as she
went in, a man embraced her from behind.

"Eleanor." He turned her toward him, pulled her mask away, and
kissed her. "I had to come. I had to see you again." His mouth pressed
again on hers, eager, and his hands groped over her breast, her backside. She looked into eyes as gray, as hard and sharp as flint. It was
Henry of Anjou.

Her first wild impulse was to kiss him back. She sank into the
fierce embrace, excited, the strong arms around her, the powerful
chest beneath her hands. It had been a long time since anyone had
kissed her like this. A rutting bull, she thought, who would carry off
whomever he willed, Eleanor or anyone else. She remembered his
brother's voice, saying, *He never sleeps alone.*

That memory pierced her like an arrow. A cold veil fell over her.
She could not yield. She could not submit to him, or she would vanish into his lust, his ambition, just another conquest.

She put her hands on his chest and shoved him back. He did not
let go easily, but he drew his face away, frowning. He said, "You were
more eager when last I saw you."

No doubt, she thought, but she tossed her head at him and glared
him in the face.

"Then I had not heard you had taken another into your bed, sir.
Your brother told me. You have torn what was between us." She slid
out of his arms and backed away, crossing her arms over her chest
and pinning him with her stare, making herself into Eleanor.

"I have helped you with your cause," she said. "I have kept faith
with you. But you have betrayed me, and I am not sure anymore what
there is between us, Henry."

His jaw dropped. She glanced over his shoulder at the door,
which was shut; they were alone in the little room. She turned to face

him—the hard gray piercing eyes, the harsh face not so handsome as his father and his brother. Stronger, fiercer. The muscles working at the corners of his jaw. He was getting up a temper. She smiled at him, indifferent to his heat. She said, "You will not treat me thus, sir. No. Not ever."

He gabbled out something, caught between his anger and his guilty surprise, and she laughed, all scorn. He had thought her secured to him already, his property, like Anjou, and Normandy. His face reddened. The high color made him look much younger. His mouth closed, and his lips moved in and out, and his brows curled over his nose. His eyes softened; she saw he was hunting for excuses.

He said, low, "What you did for me—that was, I hope, for both of us, for our kingdom. As for the other—" His hands muddled the space between them. He said, "It was just—I don't care about them."

She laughed again. "Them!" She thought, *Does he not hear what his own voice says?*

She turned toward the door, and he stepped in the way, barring her. A chill of fear went over her skin. She dared not let him see that; she faced him with a thunderous frown.

"I shall go now, my lord. I will not be here with you, alone like this."

"Eleanor." He put out his hands as if he would seize her again. She gathered herself to fight him, to scream.

This he saw. His face was open as a mirror; she saw all the thoughts behind it. She saw him decide against attacking her, saw him think of something else. He drew his arms back, and he went down on one knee.

"Forgive me," he said. "You are right, and I was wrong. You alone have my heart—I swear it. Please. Forgive me."

This sudden submission startled her. She swayed, as if she had been leaning against his force. She looked into his hard gray eyes, wondering if he was true, and she knew, she knew as if he spoke this aloud, that he was saying only what would get him what he wanted. But he would do anything for Aquitaine. She laughed again. He was deceitful, wily, not just strong, and they could never trust him, but he was a marvel. She said, "You are too clever, sir. Let me by."

He stood up where he was, but his voice fell, wheedling. "I should not have come. I am very busy in the north; I am trying to summon a council, and I have to raise some money. What you sent me has all but given me the throne. But I thought—the Twelfth Night feast— it's like a night out of time, anyway. A few days' gallop." He shrugged. "Then this is the welcome I get."

"This," she said, "is the welcome you deserve."

She started toward the door again, and he reached out and gripped her arm. But his gaze met hers; he did not try to overpower her, and he let go of her at once. He said, "The annulment is to happen."

"Yes," she said. "At Eastertide." She lifted her hand, and he let go of her. Then, impulsively, she tipped forward and kissed his mouth.

This began chastely enough, and he did not try to seize her, but the soft hairs of his beard caressed her cheek, and her lips parted, and their tongues touched. A wave of desire nearly overwhelmed her. But she dared not. She pushed herself out of his arms again and fled out the door.

In the dark and snowy courtyard the cold air burned on her cheeks. She went around toward the tower, and in the arch at the door, under the torchlight, she stopped and straightened her dress. Her heart was pounding madly under her ribs. She lifted her fingers to her mouth. She had wanted to go on kissing him. She had wanted to go much further.

He had not suspected—not for an instant; he had taken her for Eleanor without question.

She thought, *He does not love her. He wants only Aquitaine.* She remembered the power in him, which drew her as it drew her sister, and she wondered if Eleanor could master him, or if he would not break her like a wild mare.

When she looked again the gatehouse door was open, the yellow candle glow weakly gleaming out, and he was gone. A little later, she came upon Alys, a little drunken, sitting by the stair up to the tower.

"Has there been any word of a—a stranger come here? A northerner?"

Alys looked up at her, her eyes large and dark, smudged. "My lady," she said, and laughed. "My lady." Laughing, as if this were the hugest of jokes, she put out her hand. Petronilla gave up trying and sat down beside her.

•   •   •

Outside Limoges, Henry tossed aside the pilgrim's hat he had used to get inside the city, retrieved his horse from a shelter near the road, and went out toward the highway. At least the snow had stopped. He thought he had come a long ride for just a kiss. His mouth still tasted the kiss. He wanted her more than ever; she was even more beautiful than he remembered, her pride around her like a golden glow. When they were married, he would lay her down whenever he wanted. Make that lush red mouth moan.

He remembered the lithe, vigorous body in his arms. The world called her a harlot, a well-used woman, but she seemed almost like a maiden to him, fresh and wild, full of her own worth.

He rode on toward the main road that ran north past Poitiers. As he passed he saw the country around him, more hilly than Anjou or Normandy, the tidy villages tucked within their walls, the castles on the peaks. Their castles were bigger than in the north, and better placed. He thought also he would not have let the Vicomte of

Limoges build that wall. Ahead, the road ran out onto a broad plain, and the river valley opened up before him.

All of this would be his, soon. His. And the most beautiful woman he had ever seen. He drove his horse steadily northward, back where his work was, but he kept thinking of Aquitaine.

Twenty-eight

In the dream, Eleanor found herself standing alone in a long hall, with the light coming in through windows. Behind her, above her, somewhere, a voice was speaking the same words over and over. It was Bernard, she realized, the old abbot's thunderous profound voice seeming to come from heaven.

He was saying, "Trust no one. Trust no one. Trust no one."

In the dream, there was a table, along the wall below the windows, like an altar, covered with white, and on it a row of daggers. She went along the table picking up the daggers one by one, weighing them, and putting them back. Each one seemed wrong to her. One was too short, another too heavy. Was she choosing one? What was she looking for? One was ugly, one dull, one broken. She reached for the last, a long shining silver blade, and her hand closed on the grip, and the knife turned to a snake in her hand.

She recoiled, still clutching the hilt, and the snake doubled around to bite her, a patterned, wedge-shaped head, jaws yawning; she saw the curved fangs dripping green with venom. Then she woke up.

She knew what the dream meant. Now, after Twelfth Night, she even thought she knew who was the snake.

◆ ◆ ◆

With Christmas over, and the summonses sent out, they all left Limoges. The King departed first, going back to Paris. A day later, the women struck out for Poitiers.

Petronilla rode in her disguise, Duchess of Aquitaine, for a few months still Queen of France, the gray Barb dancing between her legs. By habit she kept herself straight and her head high, but inwardly she felt herself torn in pieces.

Since Twelfth Night and the meeting with Henry of Normandy, she had spent every morning long at her prayers, begging God to tell her what to do and how to act. God gave her no answers. She had always had Eleanor, before, to talk things out with, and now there was no one. Henry of Normandy crowded into her mind: the rough harsh voice, his arrogance, pushing into her embrace as if he owned her. Eleanor meant to marry this man. She dared not tell Eleanor even that she had met him, much less what else she had done.

And he had lied to her, to gain his purpose. He had no honor, for all his high birth and noble name. He was the more dangerous for that. Young as he was, he had a devil's wit. He had known how to wiggle inside her outrage, how to blunt her fury, that humble kneeling bow. He would not keep faith. He would follow only what he saw as his interest.

This was the man that her sister meant to bring to Aquitaine, to rule in Aquitaine.

But also, he could be King of England. He had taken Normandy and Anjou, in the short space since they had seen him in Paris. Eleanor had said the letters she sent him would sweep away King Stephen's last support. Her whole body remembered his embrace; she wondered if she was imagining that he had been so warm, a fire in her arms.

She glanced at de Rançun, riding beside her, and then over her shoulder, to see who was riding within earshot: only the standard-bearer, half asleep in his saddle, and some soldiers. "Joffre," she said. "What do you know of Duke Henry?"

He shot her a sharp look and nudged his horse closer, so they rode stirrup against stirrup. He said, "I think he is an Angevin, my lady, coarse and cruel and ambitious." His voice was pitched to reach her ears only.

"But he is a warrior." Saying that, she felt suddenly the phantom impact of his kiss.

"Yes. He's a great soldier, I'll give him that."

"My sister means to marry him, once she is free," she said.

He twitched away, as if at a shower of sparks into his face. He said, "I know that. And it will be the ruin of us all. I tried to talk to her, but she would not hear me."

As they walked along, the Barb was reaching out to nip at his horse, which tossed its head. Petronilla drew the reins tighter. She thought, *The ruin of us*. Or the making of something greater. Joffre, she thought, saw his own will here, and made it Aquitaine's. "He is young—much younger than her. And he will grow. She might teach him."

De Rançun was staring straight ahead, his body rigid as a stone. "I should not have spoken. I have no place in this."

"That you did, loyal as you are to her, is a sign of the truth in what you tell me," she said.

"My lady," he said, looking away, "please, talk of it no more. I fear what else I might say."

"No more, then," she said. She thought he had said far more in fact than he intended. Behind her, in the wagon, her sister traveled, carrying a child she dared not keep, leaving a husband who loved her distractedly, preparing to take another who would be much harder to deal with. Headstrong, passionate as she was, he might lead her more than she led him.

Petronilla wondered what her place was in this, and whether she had done well with any of it. She thought, again, and with the help-less knowledge that she would not do it, that she should tell her sister what had happened between her and Henry. It would probably do no good and certainly cause a lot of trouble. She could think of nothing else she could have done save what she had. She rode along in the wintry sunshine, and a sick little fear grew in her belly that anything she did would probably make things worse.

◆　◆　◆

They wended a slow way home, for Eleanor's sake, stopping often. The snowy fields lay all around them. Crowds of people came out to see them go by. Day in and out Eleanor lay in the wagon under piles of furs, cradling her vast belly in her arms. Everything in her now was turning toward the baby. She dreamed of him, and imagined him, nurturing him in her mind as her body fashioned him in its cauldron; the understanding that she would have to give him up made her heart ache. Yet she saw no other course for them. She promised him she would care for him. She would see that he was rich, and honored; surely he would be handsome enough.

If she bore him soon, she might be able to go to Beaugency herself. She could receive the annulment herself; before the world she would again step back into the place of Duchess of Aquitaine, the issue with Petronilla firmly settled. If the baby came not soon enough for that—if this strange deception had to go on . . .

Rattling along in the wagon she saw her sister riding up ahead, drawing all the cheers, all the looks, the homage, while she herself lay like a lump. She saw how Petronilla struggled sometimes with the Barbary horse, and with a certain glee she realized that her sister was afraid of him. She began to will the stallion to shy, to leap, to toss her into the ditch.

As soon as she felt that, she thought, *What a small woman I am, after all, everything brought down to a baby no bigger than a cat, and wishing ill to my sister.* She should be grateful to Petronilla for doing all this, sacrificing her good name for the sake of Aquitaine. Gratitude was an empty purse, nothing but wind. Love was a failing reed. Her power, her name, her very face and form were passing away, might never be hers again. Lying cushioned and wrapped in the wagon, with only the sky visible overhead, she dozed most of the time, in and out of sleep. The wagon jounced slowly along; she cradled her arm around her belly and fell to thinking about this child, imagining his face, his voice, as if dreaming about him brought him more into being. What else was there? she thought drowsily, with some bafflement.

◆ ◆ ◆

They went into Poitiers late in the night, to avoid any crowd, and with a minimum of display took over the Maubergeon. Eleanor climbed into the top story of the outer tower, what she thought of as the Green Tower, and looked out over her city, and willed the baby to be born.

She and Petronilla were hardly speaking. They slept in separate rooms—in the two opposite towers of the Maubergeon. There seemed some great chasm between them, something unbridgeable, something broken. During the day her sister went in and out of the hall, never staying long, never looking at Eleanor. She had moved her own court into the other tower, with its blue chambers, and she was there more and more often as the days wore on. With Petronilla out of sight, Eleanor began to brood on the suspicion of her sister's treachery. If she was not Queen of France, Duchess of Aquitaine, she was no one.

Petronilla would not even look at her, and Eleanor knew she held something secret from her. She went around the city, and the crowds followed her, and she went to church and gave out alms in the name of the Duchess of Aquitaine. She did not hold a court, with the holy days over, and Lent approaching, and her sister allegedly sick. She went everywhere else as the Duchess.

Alys said, wryly, "I did not know Petronilla would be as pleased with this as she is. She has embraced this, I think."

"She would as lief I had died, that time," Eleanor said, half asleep. Sitting by the fire, she was letting the other women bathe her, stroke her with a warm cloth, and dry her skin to a ruddy glow. Marie-Jeanne got a fresh towel. Eleanor watched her dry her enormous belly, laced with pale seams, her navel poking straight out. Something moved, pressing momentarily against her side and shifting toward the middle, and then it all went smooth again. "It would have made things much easier."

Marie-Jeanne gasped. Alys said, "My lady, that's not so. She loves you. She just loves being you also." She put her hand to her mouth. "She means no harm."

Eleanor shut her eyes. Alys wanted this to be so, as she said it; but the more Eleanor thought of it, the harder her suspicions grew. Between her and Petronilla now there was only silence, and with every day that passed, one day closer to Beaugency, one day more without the baby's birth, the silence deepened and grew thorns.

Lent began. She climbed the stairs every day, up and down, several times; she had always heard climbing stairs would bring on labor. The baby remained stubbornly where he was, growing bigger and heavier. She dreamed he had two heads, one for each of her breasts. She dreamed she bore a litter of kittens. She dreamed, over and over, of the blade that turned into a snake in her hand. She began to sleep with a silver dagger under her pillow.

Stories flew about Henry of Normandy, who had made himself

master of Normandy and Anjou and called a council for the spring, to begin the attack on England. The first council, six months before, had interested no one at all, and rumors flew that King Stephen was paying the Norman barons to refuse this one, too.

One day Alys came to Eleanor, her forehead rumpled, and said, "Your Grace, did you know that Henry of Normandy was in Limoges on Twelfth Night?"

She started up—she had been lying in her bed, the only place she was comfortable anymore—and said, "Oh, no. I didn't. He was there? God's breath. Thank God he did not see me." She remembered that moment on the stair, when some impulse saved her; she remembered sitting with the children watching all the unruly crowd.

Then horribly the understanding shone in on her, like a blast of fire, and she flung the coverlet away.

"But he did, didn't he?" An irresistible rage swelled within her, hot and furious, something long held pent. She slid her feet down to the floor. "Or thought he did, perhaps. Send for my sister."

De Rançun stood by the door. He thrust out his hand. "Please—be careful—" He shot a narrow look at Alys. "What have you done?"

"Bring her here," Eleanor shouted. "If you must drag her by the hair, bring her before me!"

Her face white, Alys scuttled by him out the door; he looked over his shoulder after her. Eleanor flung her cloak around her. Not even her temper could keep her warm. She paced across the room, her teeth clenched, and then back again, as de Rançun and Marie-Jeanne shrank against the walls, and then, in the door, Petronilla came.

Her sister wore a queenly gown, one of Alys's finest fashionings, her hair done in red-gold braids on her head. She was wearing no coif, but a jewel glittering on her breast. She was beautiful, Eleanor knew, as beautiful as a star, and she—she—

All her festering suspicions burst into a boiling rage. She shouted, "Did you lie with him? Did you?"

Petronilla's eyes popped open, and her lips parted. For a moment the old Petronilla surfaced, her shoulders rounded, meek, and she said, "My lady, I don't know what—"

"You know!" Eleanor rushed at her, furious at this dissembling, convinced now that Petronilla was the snake; she almost struck her across the face, but instead roared at her, nose to nose. "Did you lie with him? The truth, false-hearted, evil woman! I want the truth!"

"No," Petronilla cried, and shrank away. But her face altered; she did not submit at once to Eleanor's furious glare, as she would have before. She reared back, her face white, but unafraid, and her eyes piercing.

"No. I did not." Her voice rang with certainty. She turned back to her sister, and she bared her teeth in something not a smile. "He would have, thinking I was you, and knowing you for a she-wolf in heat—"

Eleanor shouted, and this time she did swing her hand at Petronilla, but her sister reached up and caught her wrist and held her arm away.

"I forced him to his knees," Petronilla cried, triumphant. "I made him apologize for his faithlessness." She thrust Eleanor's arm aside. Her eyes were brilliant, steady, unblinking. This was the new Petronilla, her rival, her equal. "I did what was right, Eleanor! You dare not come at me like this."

"I dare do anything I wish," Eleanor cried. "You saw him—and he kissed you, did he not?"

Petronilla yielded nothing, her face blazing with anger. "Are you jealous? Yes, I kissed him. You should make a study of this—he doesn't love you—he doesn't even know the difference between me and you. Not even in a kiss. All he wants is Aquitaine."

Eleanor let out a howl. She whirled away from the knowledge, flung herself across the room, her fists beating on her thighs. "Bernard's curse was real—even those I trusted—Ah, God, I am undone! He—even he—And you! You!"

Abruptly, exhausted, she was gushing tears, and she sank down on the floor and wept into her hands. "Go away. All of you. Get out of my sight." The baby heaved and kicked inside her, as if he would flee too from this madwoman, his mother.

Behind her, Petronilla said, "Everything does not turn around you, Eleanor. There is more to all of this than you would let it be." She went out. The door slammed. Around the room, fearful as mice, the others began to move, their murmuring voices like the rustling of mice. Sobbing, Eleanor crept back toward her bed and buried herself in the covers.

Twenty-nine

The black winter shut them down. The Empress kept a very harsh Lent. She had maneuvered Claire into her waiting women, without much asking, but Claire was glad of something to do. The old woman needed constant attendance, and the girls were always coming and going. Thomas being in a very dark mood, she was glad anyway to have somewhere else to be. The Empress made them all go to Mass often, which made no one any happier.

Being so much with the other women, Claire shared their gossip. They chattered about people she did not know, found out she had been in Poitiers and Paris, and rained names on her from those courts.

She said, "Paris is not so much," and this made them all very pleased, but then she said, "Poitiers, though, is the prettiest place in the world, and I wish I were there," and they scowled at her, and began to sneer at her and talked behind her back.

They were asp-tongued. They told tales of her to the Empress, who seemed not to care. One woman, younger than she was, sidled up to her at the wardrobe and smirked. "He's a handsome fellow, your husband. You must keep close watch on him, I think." The other girls laughed. After that, she could not help it; she watched Thomas with a narrow eye.

Henry suddenly reappeared soon after the pancakes. Claire thought he looked a little harried. When she saw him come into the hall, she was bringing a robe for the Empress, who was out of bed for the first time in a while and sitting up, surrounded by braziers. As soon as she saw him, the old woman called out to him.

"Well, my boy, and where did you get off to?"

Henry came up the long room to her. His cloak was filthy and he threw it off one way and tossed his cap in the other; pages ran to pick them up. Claire drew back out toward the wall. Most of the girls quietly battled to get into his sight, which reminded her of Thomas.

The reminder of Thomas vexed her. The winter seemed to have laid a heavy hand on him. He had gotten very silent and gloomy since the Empress declared that her prohibitions for Lent included music. Even before Shrove began, he was sneaking away by himself to play, as if he would punish the court, which thought his passion sinful.

Claire had gone with him a few times; the Empress's edict worked in all of Rouen, so they had to walk beyond the city. In a farmer's shed, they sang together, and he struggled with a new part of the Tristan story. Then his melancholy seemed to lift, and he even smiled at her. But it was cold, and she had much to do; without his playing to keep them at court, someone had to be useful. But he went out a lot, by himself, every day, sometimes several times a day. She wondered if he had another woman. She began watching the other girls in the court, to see if one was always gone when he was gone.

Henry was saying, "I still need more money."

"God's body, you are a bog for soaking up metal," his mother said. Although the room was not cold, she was bundled in the fur, her thinning hair tucked under a fur cap, her hands hidden in the laps of the pelt. "I have no more money to draw on, sirrah, understand that."

"Get it from the priests," he said. Claire twitched, startled.

His mother said, slowly, "Well, there is always the Crusade."

"Yes," he said. "Get the money they've been squirreling away for the Crusade."

His mother drew herself up, affronted. "You blaspheme. You are more like your father every day."

"I want that money."

"The Church—"

"Has money," he said, and smiled, as if this made perfect sense to him. When he smiled, the tips of his teeth showed. Claire thought, *Eleanor and he are a good match.*

His mother turned away, her hand up. "I'm not going to talk about this with you."

He circled around her, making her look at him, his head thrust forward like a fighting dog's. "They'll do it. Go to them, demand they make me a gift. All the Crusade money."

She twisted the other way. "Leave me. I'm tired." Her eyes lit on the girl off to the side. "Claire, fetch me some warm cider."

Claire went off. Henry was still nagging at his mother; Claire thought he enjoyed harassing her just to see her try to elude him. It was an old game with them. She thought again of Thomas, going behind her back, the dark suspicions mounting. When she brought the cider in a wooden cup, the Duke was still there, but standing aside, looking pleased. His mother had agreed, although likely only to get rid of him. She turned to Claire, her scrawny old hands reaching for the cup.

Claire held it out to her. As she did, on an impulse, the girl turned and looked at Duke Henry.

He caught her eye; she had seen him watch her before, interested, and now his interest quickened. She lowered her eyes. Then, knowing what she did, she raised them again, and looked at him through her lashes.

His eyes popped wide; he understood. The old woman said, garrulous, "That's too hot." Claire jerked her gaze down again to the task she was doing; suddenly she was rough with embarrassment. She wished she had kept her eyes off him; she wondered what she had let out of the bottle. She swallowed.

"I'll bring you another, Your Majesty."

"No, no," Matilda said wearily. "I'll just hold it. It will keep me warm." She put her hands around the cup and looked off down the hall.

Claire glanced through the side of her eyes at the young Duke, standing there, watching her. Waiting. She turned and rushed away through the side door.

◆   ◆   ◆

She could not find Thomas. He was in none of the usual places, their corner in the hall, or by the hearth, and she was going toward the door when he came in from the outside, his lute sacked on his shoulder.

She ran to him, so glad to see him she was crying. "It's the cold," she said, at once, burrowing into his arms. "It's the cold."

In her heart, she thought, *I'm sorry, I'm sorry, I will never doubt you again.*

They moved inside to be where it was warmer. He put his arms around her. "What's the matter? What happened?" He held her against him; he slid one hand quickly down over her belly, and then pretended to be pulling her gown straight. She leaned her head against him, amazed. She had not thought he had noticed what was happening with her; she hardly even knew it herself yet. He kissed her forehead.

She thought, *I nearly lost all, for nothing, for a suspicion; I would have given myself to the Duke.* She shut her eyes. The evil she had seen in him she had let sprout in herself.

She said, "Let's go back to Poitiers. We don't have to wait for spring, do we?"

"Poitiers," he said. His voice rose, eager. "That's good enough. I want to get out of here; I cannot bear this cold, and the style of Lent here is very sore."

Duke Henry with a crowd of his men was going by them, out the door. The young Duke's head turned, his gaze flicking toward her and Thomas. She shut her eyes and longed to be somewhere else. She would never do it again. She leaned on Thomas, crying again, and he took her off toward the fire.

♦   ♦   ♦

The Empress was not happy that they were going, and she raged at Thomas when he went to tell her. "Gently born," she cried, over and over. "You cannot drag her through the snow." The more she argued, the more determined he was to leave, and eventually she realized that, stopped shouting, and stared at him for some moments. He stared back.

At last she said, "God's body. The arrogance of you songmen is beyond understanding. What is it but noise and gibberish? Go, then. I have heard enough of your filthy music anyway." She tossed her hand in the air, as if she threw him aside.

He worked quickly to get them ready. In this he had another good reason to be glad of Claire, because while he spent whatever he could find, she had saved every coin she could; and when other gifts came, she had turned them into coin, too. Therefore she had a good purse, which he took to buy them each a horse for the trip south, with half the money left over. They were only waiting for a company to travel with, few enough in the deep of winter, especially in Lent. Finally they heard of some Jews from the Rouen Yeshiva going south, and they agreed to join them, at least as far as Blois.

• • •

Thomas hooked the lute to his saddle by the strap of the sack and stooped to check the girths; Claire was standing by her own horse. Duke Henry came up to him.

"Lute player. You are leaving here. I'm sad to hear this." His gaze stabbed over Thomas's shoulder toward Claire.

"I have light feet," Thomas said. "I don't like to be anywhere very long."

"Yet—" Henry's eyes met his, sharp. "I've heard you are going back to Poitiers."

Thomas thought he was looking at Claire. He said, "Yes, my lord, eventually. There are a few places I would go first, but my wife wants to go back there."

"Your wife." Henry looked past him again, and this time Thomas knew he looked at Claire. Thomas frowned; he remembered how she had clung to him that day. Henry shortened his gaze to him again.

"You are a clever man; you could be of use to me. While you are there, whatever you see of the Duchess, take note of it. I will make this worth your trouble."

Thomas put his head to one side. This was going the other way now. He said, "What will you give me?"

"What do you want?" Henry said. His mouth kinked, half smiling. "Tell me what you see." He nodded toward Claire, behind him, and went away.

Thomas went up to her, thinking with some excitement about what the Duke had said. It was the game, more than the money, that tempted him. His wife said, "What did he want?"

He could not tell her; he pretended, instead, to be jealous, and said, "Don't look at him like that." At that she blushed and turned away, and he was sorry he had played with her. He turned to his horse and mounted, and they went off to join the rest of the company.

Thirty

In Poitiers the days were dull. The winter had turned, and the sun rode higher in the sky, its light stronger, and on the slopes below the Maubergeon the first green buds appeared on the trees. Lent was almost over.

Eleanor toiled up and down the stairs, trying to bring the baby on, but even he betrayed her; he would not come in time to rescue her.

One day she met Petronilla, coming down the stairs, and they stopped and faced each other.

Her sister wore a splendid green gown. She stared at Eleanor, and Eleanor stared back, expecting some apology, some gesture of contrition, some opening through the barrier between them. Petronilla met her eyes and said nothing. Finally Eleanor trudged on by her. That night she wept for hours.

He cannot tell the difference, she thought, over and over. *He cannot tell the difference.*

The day was soon when she should go to Beaugency. In her own room, anchored to her bed by her belly, she waited to be told that her own women, once again, with her own clothes, and her own crown, were transforming her sister into Duchess of Aquitaine, the Queen of France. She wept, thinking of it, and cursed between her teeth, and in her great belly the baby turned.

*   *   *

Petronilla sat like a doll on the stool while Alys fussed over her, a dab of paint upon her cheeks, a swish of a brush over her throat.

"Is she well? My sister."

She should say, *The Queen.* But it was not the Queen Petronilla fretted for, but the sister. She herself was becoming Queen, under the touches and devices of the women, but she could not paint and brush herself another sister.

Since Eleanor had shrieked at her, she had been arguing the justice of it over and over in her mind; she had not sought out Henry d'Anjou, she had done only what she had to do. She had put him in his place, as he deserved—as Eleanor herself should have done. She felt Eleanor's rage like a wound in her heart. She bundled off the memory of that last, passionate kiss.

The thing between her and her sister was hard as cooling iron, was turning rank, would poison them both. She knew Eleanor would never bend her neck, would never admit to being wrong.

It was Petronilla's duty to ask forgiveness, even if she had done nothing. Once Petronilla had almost yielded, on the stairs, and done what she knew Eleanor expected, bowed to her, and let her have her way. She resisted that. A lie would not heal the wound; a lie would only deepen it.

Alys held the Byzantine looking glass before her, and Petronilla inspected the face reflected in the oval of gold and jewels. She was beautiful. More beautiful now than Eleanor was. Yet her heart ached for the sister whose face she saw in the mirror, the sister she had lost.

"How does Eleanor fare? Is her time upon her yet?"

"No," Alys said. "She lies abed, very sad, and cries much, and the baby is still high up under her belt."

Petronilla said, with a pang, "I would see her, if I could."

Alys said, "Lady, it were wiser perhaps not to. She is in such a state."

Petronilla turned her eyes away. *In such a state*, she knew, meant Eleanor still hated her. To see her, anyway, was not enough; to make things whole between them she would have to betray herself, accept the blame, and let Eleanor keep her false pride.

That, she knew, would be her own destruction. She would never be happy again.

Now she had to go off to Beaugency, alone. She gathered herself up. The long ordeal was not yet over, but soon. Then, perhaps, when they were free, they could find their common ground again. She promised herself she would go to her sister then, when they were free, and whatever happened between them would seal it, one way or the other.

◆   ◆   ◆

Eleanor lay abed, and de Rançun came to her, his hat in his hand.

"My lady." He knelt by the bed. "The Lady Petronilla is going to Beaugency."

"You are going with her."

"If you bid me, I will not," he said. "But she is supposed to be you, and I have never left you. Someone will surely mark it if I don't go with her."

Eleanor struggled herself up. A black rage burned in her; she had lain so long, waiting, that her temper had swelled like a boil, full of evil. She reached under the pillow of the bed and drew out the silver dagger.

"Joffre," she said. "You must attend her. For that reason, and for another. There cannot be two of us. If he cannot tell the difference, when he comes, there must be only one. She must not return to Poitiers." She held the dagger out to him. It trembled in her hand. Her voice trembled. "If you love me, you will do this."

He understood; she saw it in his eyes. He straightened up, his mouth open, his eyes on her. All the color went out of his face, and his throat worked. His gaze slid away from hers. Then he took the dagger, and in silence he went out. She lay back on the pillow and shut her eyes.

◆　◆　◆

Later, when the pains began, she thought bitterly about Duke Henry, for whom she did all this. He had brought this on her. He had never loved her. He wanted her only for Aquitaine. She lay in the bed and heaved and screamed. He wanted her only for Aquitaine, for Aquitaine.

Then, as if these thoughts were a looking glass, she saw herself revealed. She wanted him only because of England, Normandy, Anjou. She had never loved him. She had done all this as evilly as he had.

In a terrible slow understanding, she thought that she had never loved anybody.

She had loved her sister. She howled, caught in the grip of the convulsions of the birth. Marie-Jeanne came to her, and she gripped the old woman's worn, wrinkled hand that had rocked her cradle, dressed her in her first gowns, prepared her for her wedding, traveled with her to Paris and to Antioch, and was now here, constant and true. The door into eternity was opening; she lay like an altar on the threshold. Across her belly, the two hands of the life force fastened on her and began to twist. She held the old woman's hand, and the tower echoed with her shrieks, but she knew not why she screamed: for the pain, or for the order she had given de Rançun, for her sister.

. . .

Beaugency stood on the north bank of the Loire, on the southern edge of the kingdom of France, a long day's ride upstream of Blois where the old bridge crossed the river. Petronilla reached it four days before Palm Sunday. With the year turning, the dark and cold of winter was now surely in flight, every day more mild and sunny, grass growing golden green between the cracks of the stones, and the first tender spring breezes blowing up the river from the sea. Behind her, Eleanor was just a tiny memory, locked in a tower room.

The next day, several of the most powerful prelates and nobles of France met together in a stately formal council and declared that the marriage between the King and Queen was annulled, as if it had never been, because they were cousins within the forbidden degree.

It was a classic bit of church work, saying everything necessary and nothing really true. An earlier pope had already declared them to be married, which was set aside. The little princesses, Marie and Alix, would remain with their father and were to be considered legitimate, however much this contradicted the essence of the decree. Eleanor received back her patrimony of Aquitaine, where she had always been Duchess in her own right. Both the King and his never-had-been Queen were free to marry, although Eleanor, as Louis's vassal, was supposed to seek his permission first.

Petronilla witnessed this, sitting in the back of the church among a crowd of attendants, all but Alys being women of the local nobility who hardly knew her. She kept at a good distance from anyone who really did. But then she moved out onto the porch of the church, into the open and the sunlight, and the spokesmen of the council came before her to announce the decision to her, face-to-face, and one of them was the Archbishop of Bordeaux, who had known her all her life.

Arrayed in a magnificent new gown of green and gold, with sleeves embroidered cuff to shoulder in gold and pearls, her coif also of tissue of gold, and her head aching from the burden of the crown, she awaited them on the open porch, wondering what to do. What he would do, if he guessed. He would say something. He would have to. It was all nothing, if she was not Eleanor. He could not be party to a fraud.

Her head throbbed unbearably and she could not think. She put her hands to her head, lifted the crown off, and threw it down on the floor at her feet. Let some other woman be Queen of France.

Her mind flew to Eleanor, in Poitiers; had she borne the baby, had that changed her temper, as it sometimes did? Did she know already that they were free? That Petronilla had set them free? Abruptly her eyes flooded with tears, as if all this rising feeling pressed out and overflowed. Now Bordeaux was coming, and she was all in tears, falling apart.

At once she realized this could save her with him. As the little band of churchmen advanced across the porch, she put her hands up to her face and let herself weep uncontrollably.

He bowed before her, with the other grave-faced prelates lined up behind him; she raised her eyes for an instant, glimpsed their startled faces, and went back to sobbing into her hands. Bordeaux fumbled a moment, saying, "Eleanor, my dear, Eleanor," and then read the decision hastily through.

Done, he bent over her, his hand on her shoulder, and whispered, "My dear, now, too late for regrets, isn't it?" He made a motion with one hand, and a page scooped up the discarded crown. They all shuffled off across the porch, their robes swishing.

Out from under his scrutiny, she straightened up, pressed her hands to her eyes, raw from the weeping, her mind scoured and empty. A moment later, she realized she had won.

She lowered her hands to her lap, startled; she had won, they had

given her the annulment and opened the shackles of the awful marriage that bound both her and Eleanor to the cold heart of France.
A swell of pleasure took her spirit soaring upward like a leaf on a gust
of wind. She crossed herself. Whatever Eleanor thought of her, she
had gotten them both through this. She had won them this, their
chance at new lives. Now all she had to do was face her sister again.

And that, she thought, might be the hardest thing of all.

Thirty-one

The day after the Queen of France went by on her way to Beaugency, Claire and Thomas came into Blois, the ancient city on the Loire, and there they stayed. They took a room in a tavern by the river, and for almost a week Thomas played there only for them, teaching her new songs and working on his old ones. When the money ran out he played in the public room, for which the tavern-keeper gladly gave them their keep.

Blois was filling up with people come in for Holy Week and the Easter festivals, and the tavern was always crowded, and besides what the tavern-keeper gave Thomas, other people pressed money on them, flowers and rings and cups of wine, invitations to other houses, pleas for other music. He saw that they could do very well here.

But he saw that Claire was less than happy with this arrangement. One morning he came upon her standing in the doorway and looking out, not into the street, but beyond toward the river, and the bridge, which was just visible from the threshold. The road over the bridge led south to Poitiers, and the sight of it alone made Thomas uneasy.

He stood behind her, slid his arms around her, and kissed her shoulder.

"Let's go up and practice," he said. He wanted her not to be looking toward the south.

"When are we going on?" she said.

His hands lay over the soft swelling of her belly, growing more every day. This moved him more than he had ever imagined. He was already making songs for the baby.

He said, "What's wrong with here? We have everything we need."

He was afraid that if she went south, back to the court of Aquitaine, she would remember who she was and how she had lived before, and he would not be good enough for her. Her hands closed over his, and she leaned her head against his shoulder. She said, "I want to go back to Poitiers. I dream of it every night. I want the baby born there. When will we go?"

He said nothing for a moment. Along the street a steady rumble of wagons passed, and a pack of horsemen in fancy silver coats with red bands on them, wearing swords at their hips. Those, he knew, were the Count's men. At last, he found the right answer; he said, "When we have been married."

"Married." She turned toward him, her eyes gleaming with sudden humor. "We have been saying all along we were married." She kissed him.

He held her tight. "Yes, but—your father has never assented."

That brought a gust of broad laughter from her. "Well," she said, "what lies between me and thee, I think, does away with the need for his assent." Her eyes searched his face, the smile lingering on her lips; he thought she looked more beautiful every time he saw her, as if she ripened with his seed.

She said, "Very well, then, we shall be married. When?"

"Oh," he said, "when I can find a priest."

"Then find a priest today," she said. "Or as this goes on we shall be having him dip the child at the same time he puts our hands together."

"Well, it's not that soon," he said, but he kissed her again and went off to find a priest. The idea made him a little giddy, but more and more eager.

◆   ◆   ◆

He found a priest; they would be married during Holy Week, a time of good luck for such things. As soon as the tavern-keeper's wife and girls found out, they would not leave Claire alone, but bustled her around to find ribbons and a gown, new shoes, an embroidered coif. They were to be married on the porch of the church on Holy Thursday, and the day before that, they got her naked into a tub in the kitchen and poured buckets of hot water over her, and scrubbed her until her skin glowed red and washed her hair with rosewater.

They gossiped, too, telling over their little local scandals, but also about the Queen of France, who had gone to Beaugency to lose her crown. Claire ducked her head under the water and lifted it, dripping, to hear the oldest girl say, "They say she wept and wept. What a terrible thing, your husband casting you off like that."

Claire said nothing. She wondered which of the sisters was at Beaugency—if Eleanor had borne her baby yet. Her heart ached to go back to Poitiers. She laid her arms on the sides of the tub and suffered the girls to drag a comb through her hair.

"Your husband will never do such a thing, sweet lady," one said, and patted her shoulder. "Tomorrow you will be married!" They all sighed.

"And none too soon, either," said the tavern-keeper's wife, acidly, and they all laughed, even Claire.

"He is a troubadour," she said. "He lives by his own law."

Again they all sighed. "I have never heard such music. I hope you stay forever."

Claire was silent. The comb tugged at her hair. She felt as clean and warm as the sunlight, surrounded by the scent of roses. *He is my troubadour*, she thought; she knew why he wanted to marry, and it amused her that he thought she might ever leave him, for anything. But the idea of actually being married made her happy; she felt as if they were passing through an invisible door together.

"We'll have another marriage soon, if the man in the castle has his way," said the tavern-keeper's oldest daughter. She had brought a cup of wine, mixed with herbs and honey, and sipped from it and held it out to Claire.

"Ssssh," said her mother. "Such things are never certain. Don't speak of it until it's done."

Claire passed the cup on. The warm sweet wine made her head whirl. She thought of Thomas's hands, on the lute, on her body, soon to be holding the baby, to be putting the ring on her hand. She stretched the fingers of her left hand; it was a wonder how so small a thing now began to seem so excellent.

"She'll have to come back this way, won't she?" another of the girls said. "The Queen. And then we can see her."

"Not the Queen anymore," another said. The daughter opened her mouth, and her mother dug her elbow into her ribs to quiet her.

"Oh, she'll be here," the mother said.

"Maybe longer than she thinks," said the daughter.

Claire was studying her hand still, but what the women had said rose uppermost into her mind. She said, "The Duchess will pass by this way, to go to Poitiers?"

"It is the quickest way," the mother said.

"Then we can see her," they all chimed, "and see how unhappy she is." And again the mother jammed her elbow into her daughter's side, and they exchanged a glance and laughed.

Claire reached for the cup again. It was like music, she thought. Given half the notes, you could sometimes make out the whole. She lifted the cup to her lips, thinking this over.

• • •

That evening, before they went to play, she said, "We have to put the marriage off a day or so."

He jerked his head up. "What?"

"I must go away for a while." She tore a bit of bread in half, and laid one piece on the table before him. "I'll be back quick enough, and we'll marry right away, I promise."

He said, "I don't want you to go."

She said, "Remember, on the road north, how I trusted you then?"

His head turned slightly, so he eyed her from the side. He said, "I remember you were afraid. And you're with child. Where are you going?"

"Not far," she said. "Half a day's walk, likely. But I have to do this." If she told him, it would only make things more complicated.

"Then you'll come straight back?" He picked up the bit of bread, his gaze still on her, suspicious.

She said, "Put off the wedding to the day after Easter, and I will be back to marry you. Then we can even do it in the church."

"I'll come with you."

She said, "If you want. If you don't trust me. But this is my purpose, not yours."

He chewed the bread, studying her. She smiled at him, and leaned forward and kissed him. And in the end, she went alone.

• • •

On Holy Saturday Petronilla rode out of Beaugency, on the road home.

The highway led along the north bank of the Loire, rising with the spring flood. Outside Beaugency they passed along the skirt of the river, below the smiling little hills patterned with trees and fields and vineyards. Every few miles, the highway became the street of a village, a path that wound among scattered houses of stone and wood, already hung with carpets and tapestries and bunches of reeds in anticipation of the Easter week processions. Between the villages the fields climbed in strips over the rising slope, the deep soil opened up in long furrows to the sun, between patches still overgrown with the winter's brambles and the dried leavings of the previous year. In spite of the approach of Holy Week, people were working in their fields, bending and stooping and straightening in their endless toil.

She saw them sometimes through a screen of wildflowers; the ditches of the road were full of stalky green growth, the white and yellow buds just beginning to open. *Solomon in all his glory*, she thought dutifully, but her gaze went by them to the toilers in the fields.

She always wondered at that parable: Let the wildflowers go, she thought, and the world would be little the worse; without the toilers and spinners, everything fell to ruin.

God, of course, made the wildflowers; Solomon's glory, however splendid, was only made by men. More likely, women. She crossed herself, a little irked at God's whims.

The Barbary horse was eager to move out, mouthing the bit and tossing his head. He had a new groom, who had braided his mane with red rosettes and polished all the silver on his harness; the bells on his saddle skirts jingled like music. She held him down, both hands on the reins, and sulkily he obeyed her.

It struck her how odd it would look to the people in the fields, this little gaudy train parading by. After her de Rançun was coming along on his black horse, carrying the sparrow hawk on his wrist, and then the wagon followed with Alys and some other new ladies, who sat chattering away together and eating cakes. Their coifs fluttered; the brisk wind reddened their cheeks, and when they tossed their hands and laughed, it was like the wildflowers dancing in the wind.

De Rançun was keeping silent, hardly even looking at her. She wondered at his distracted mood and guessed he worried about

Eleanor, in Poitiers. She wondered if he had ever been so far from her. Behind the women and the several servants walking along beside and after the wagon came four knights in mail, wearing red surcoats with Eleanor's pacing lion emblem across front and back, and their horses all in red leather bridles. Most of the knights were downy boys, younger sons of younger sons, their swords bright as new-minted money. De Rançun had spent much of the ride north yelling at them to keep order. Still they cavorted on their horses, whistling and making mock charges at each other, eluding his discipline.

The train of her baggage rolled after, led by the steward with his rod of office in his hand, and then a loose crowd of more servants and hangers-on. Many wore Eleanor's colors, and they went along talking and singing; some walked, some rode, all straggled off along the way for what looked half a mile.

Wildflowers on a progress. As they went along, the people in the fields propped themselves on their hoes and turned to watch. Their faces were as brown as their fields. A little child in ragged smock and bare feet ran along on the edge of the ditch, laughing and excited. Someone began to cheer Eleanor's name. As they approached, some people moved in from the fields; women in dirty aprons and men with their smocks down around their waists clustered along the edge of the road. She waved to them, wondering what drew them to her— not Eleanor, obviously, since any Eleanor would do. Something they made of her, perhaps, themselves enlarged in her. She should be then as grand and beautiful as possible. She smiled and waved to them, drinking up their cheers, glad of their welcome.

She thought, *What of this is me anymore? Who am I anymore?* The miserable castoff wife of a few months ago seemed as strange to her as this splendid outward duchess. Maybe that was why the world seemed so fresh to her as she rode along, seeing it with new eyes. Maybe she really was a different person now.

The forest closed down around the ancient road; they left the plowed and planted fields behind. Steadily they rode on toward Blois, with the river running green and calm along the foot of the little slope. The water was still high from a recent rain, and little trees stood knee-deep in the shallows. Since it was Holy Week, there were few other travelers, and those that did appear leaped out of the way and stood gaping to watch the Duchess of Aquitaine ride by. At noontide the little company stopped and ate their dinner of bread and cheese sitting on the side of the road, like common folk.

They did not reach Blois that day. Late in the afternoon, they stopped at the convent of Saint Casilda, on the bank of the Loire, to spend the night there. Wild roses covered the walls of the convent, in tribute to the saint, who had carried them in her skirt in some old fable. The winter-blackened vines were just coming into new leaf, like lace against the gray stone wall.

Inside, the nuns were busy readying themselves and their relic, Casilda's fingerbone, for the Holy Week procession, and Petronilla and her train were much in the way. Packed with her women into the two dormitory rooms kept for high-born travelers, Petronilla ate a supper of bread and sour wine; and when the sun was just going down, she climbed into the bed with Alys and two of the other women, wondering if she would be able to sleep.

Her mind turned again and again to Eleanor's fury, and to what she had said, what it all meant, now that she and Eleanor had escaped the hateful marriage and the dismal court of France. She could not see how they could be friends again. Yet she had to return to Poitiers. She had nowhere else to go. She wanted to go back to her home, but she had no true home. She stared into the darkness, and all she saw before her was nothing.

◆   ◆   ◆

She did sleep. When the voice spoke, she startled awake out of a roiling dark dream and sat bolt upright in the bed.

"Who is it?"

"Lady," de Rançun said, just outside the curtain. "Come quickly, you must hear this."

The other women were stirring; Alys sat up behind her.

"Are there men in the room?"

Petronilla said, "I'm opening the curtain," and swung the heavy hanging back and slid off the bed; she wore only a light shift and she held the edge of the curtain up over her. Two candles still burned in the dark, so it was not very late in the night—short of midnight. De Rançun was standing there, trying to look everywhere else than at her, and she pointed and said, "Bring me that cloak. What is it?"

He held out the cloak and she swung it around herself, letting the curtain go, careless of the moment between. He turned, and barefoot, she followed him across the crowded little room to the door.

Just outside, in the arcade, Claire stood, with one of the young knights right behind her.

Petronilla stopped, amazed to see her. The girl looked older somehow. She wore a long dark gown, a heavy cloak over it. She had been talking to the young knight, over her shoulder, and now turned toward Petronilla, her gaze direct.

"Oh," she said. She swept down in a low bow. "It is you, my lady."

Petronilla said, "I should hope so," her voice sharp, warning. Claire had known her at once for Petronilla, which did not surprise her. She glanced at the young knight, who did not seem much interested in the girl's odd words of welcome. "I'm very glad to see you, though. I thought never to see you again. Where have you come from? We all thought you had gone away forever with the lute player."

Claire straightened. There was a new pride in her bearing. She said, "I did. I am about to marry him. And we were coming down to Aquitaine again, but—you know Thomas, how he is—he wanted to stop in Blois. So we have been in that city for a while, enough to hear the gossip, and I have come here to warn you that there is trouble for you, ahead, in Blois. You must not go there."

Petronilla put one hand out to the young woman before her. "God's blessing on you, then. But what, tell me, is there for me to fear in Blois?"

Claire gripped her hand. "The place is suddenly full of men in mail, knights and sergeants, all armed, even in the city. I have seen them myself, and—I overheard folk talking about something that awaits you." She reddened, but her eyes were direct. "It was some secret, but it was about you, and I think perhaps someone there means to carry you off to marry you by force."

Petronilla twitched, clutching the heavy cloak around her with her other fist. She thought, *I should have guessed that something would happen. This is not over even now.* "Who?"

"I know little more than that—and what I know is all around corners. But I think the lord there, anyway, it's his men who are everywhere around there."

"It would be crowded anyway for Easter," Petronilla said. "But to bring in all his men-at-arms—are you sure? How do you know they are all his?"

"They all wear his blazoning," Claire said. "Silver, bands crosswise red, each with three disks."

"Henry of Champagne," de Rançun said at once.

Petronilla shook her head. "Not him, the band makes a difference. It's the younger brother, Theobald. He is Count of Blois." Her heart was pounding like a mallet in her chest. She faced Claire again, meeting the girl's direct gaze, their hands still linked. She squeezed the strong, capable white hand.

"Thank you, Claire. You have saved us, as you know—come to Aquitaine, that we can thank you."

Claire smiled at her, her head to one side, eyes gleaming. "My lady, you have done as much for me, although you know it not. I am loyal to the Lady of Aquitaine." Her grip tightened briefly and let go, and she was backing away into the dark.

"Wait," Petronilla said, but the girl was gone. Back to Thomas; back to the life she had somehow made for herself, where she should have been only a lady-in-waiting, attendant on someone else, until she was shoveled into a convenient marriage.

De Rançun came before her, his eyebrows cocked, and she knew he needed orders. She dragged her thoughts again to what Claire had said. Her hands were cold and she slid them under her cloak, her mind going to the trap ahead of her.

If anyone seized her now and took her to his bed, it meant he married her. One of her own aunts had suffered this indignity, before Petronilla was born, when her barons carried her off by force to keep her from marrying someone they didn't like. The man who raped her became her husband instead. That could happen to her, and that she was not really Eleanor made it all the worse. She turned to the knight.

"At least Claire has given us a chance," de Rançun said. "We can circle around Blois. Make for Tours."

"No," she said. "They would anticipate that. Or catch wind of it, very quickly. Such a train as we are cannot move fast enough to out-run armed men." Her mind leaped forward, past this first threat, to all that might lie ahead. There could be others lying in wait, between here and Poitiers, following the same course, the same evil design, marriage by capture, as old as the ring. One other, especially; she remembered Geoffrey of Anjou, in Limoges, trying once before to carry her off. "What about—" She was trying to imagine this as a game of tables: getting her counters past a clog of opponents. "What about boats? On the river."

De Rançun glanced over his shoulder at the young knight behind him, who went swiftly off into the dark. Petronilla turned her head, looking into the chamber behind her; the women were all gathered there, listening. De Rançun faced her again.

"That's good," he said. "If we can get across the Loire, we can go straight south, through the wild country, direct to Poitiers."

Wide-eyed, her hair tangled, Alys had come to the door of the chamber. She said, "Should we pack?"

Petronilla's mind was hurrying through this, imagining the boats floating across the river, and then picking a way through the cave-riddled hills and forests south; she turned to de Rançun again. "What do you think?"

He nodded. "As you do, my lady. We can take very few people across at a time, and no baggage."

She turned to the woman behind her. "Wait here. I think you may be going on tomorrow the usual way." It came to her they could go on as if she were still among them, and disguise her flight.

"But—"

Petronilla gave her a sharp look, and the older woman was silent. Up through the darkness of the arcade the young knight came striding into the torchlight.

"My lord," he said to de Rançun, "the convent has two barges, both rigged, down on the riverbank."

"Very good," Petronilla said. To de Rançun, she said, "I command you, then, go arrange all this. See how many horses we can take on each barge. Find out what's across the river."

De Rançun said, "It's all swamp, I think; it would make for very slow going. We should go down the river farther, maybe even past Blois."

"Well, then." She imagined that, sailing straight past the ambush, escaping right under her ambushers' noses, and her blood heated. "Good. However many horses, that's how many people shall go."

"Yes, my lady. I'll find out where we can make a crossing." He went off, and she turned back to Alys and the other women in the doorway.

"You and the others—you are safe enough; they will not harm you. You can come to Poitiers by the usual way."

"No," Alys said. "I won't let you go alone." The other women murmured agreement with her, pushing up into the doorway.

Petronilla laughed, borne up by their stout loyalty to her; she moved into the closed, filled space, into the warmth of their gentle womanly love. "How I love you all for this. But you must do as I say. There will be room for three or four horses at the most." She did not say that their progress would make it seem she herself kept to the road. "Go on to Poitiers, and I will meet you there." As long as she had de Rançun with her, she thought, she could do this.

Alys said, "We shall, then, my lady. We shall get to Poitiers, as best we can." Her hand lay on Petronilla's arm. "Take care."

Petronilla laid her hand on Alys's, grateful for the other woman and her devotion. She thought, *We take all these people's faith without even thinking of it, but if they fail, we are lost.* She bent and kissed Alys's hand on her arm, and the woman murmured in surprise. Petronilla said, "Come, now, I have to have better clothes than this. And shoes." She went into the room, to make ready to escape.

Thirty-two

The moon was just past full, a gauzy lopsided egg riding high in a starless sky. The nuns had intended to use the barges to get to Blois for the Holy Week processions there, and so they were ready at the quay, like the kind of boats that children made, two great flat chunks of wood, each with a tall sweep at the back. De Rançun roused the boatmen from their shanty, and when they protested and wanted to go for the Abbess, he drew his sword and forced them onto the boats. The chief of them, whom he brought to Petronilla, was a bent lanky man, groaning and pulling his forelock, ready with answers.

The boats were sound enough, he said. He thought each might carry three horses, but more likely two. Across the river the land was swamp and wilderness and there was no road.

She had long since given up the idea that they would simply ferry the whole of her little court by twos and threes across to the other side, when she had seen the benefits of dividing. But now she realized that across the river, there would be nothing to eat, no comfort, and a hard ride through enemies.

They would have to go downriver, as she and de Rançun had

already realized, and she designed her questions of the boatman with that intent. How could they pass by the bridge at Blois? She had ridden across it, and she struggled to remember it in detail. The boatman thought the barges would float beneath through the arches, if the river wasn't too high and nothing had gotten snagged against the bridge in the flood. He said they would reach Blois if they left soon, in the deep of the night, when she could see nothing at all.

Beyond Blois, he thought there might be places where they could put into the Loire's left bank, depending on the flood. The boatman shrugged, though, and shook his head a little. That place was very wild, and he himself had never gone there. Who knew what was on the other side? Nobody went there. Petronilla took all this in, trying to make one big idea of all these small things, trying to see her way home.

Eleanor, she knew, would make her mind up right away. And she could trust de Rançun. She thought again of the power of those who served her.

They would be at the mercy of the flood-swollen river, and the plan got more vague as it went on; yet she knew she could not stay here. She looked around her for de Rançun.

He was standing behind the boatman, his young knights gathered at his side. She said, "Put the horses on the barges, the Barb for me and your black horse for you on one, and on the other as many of the knights' as you can. Get us bread and wine and water and whatever else we need." She guessed he had already thought of all of this, but she had to command him; this was her decision and she would make it. She reached out her hand to him. "Hurry," she said.

Giving orders settled her. She began to see it better: If she could pass by Blois during the night and then land on the far bank, she could get well ahead of anybody and reach home in a few days. If they could pass the bridge, if they could find a place to land on the left bank. The uncertainty in all this made her knees quiver, but to be caught, to be captured, would be much worse.

Everything then would come undone. The annulment was sealed and witnessed, but if she was caught and her identity revealed, would that not be thrown aside? And she and Eleanor would both be dashed down. But in the meantime, what humiliations she would suffer, when the truth was found out—and how—froze her like an iron hand. For both their sakes, she had to escape.

The groom was already leading down the Barbary horse, saddled and bridled, his mane still knotted with red rosettes. Getting him onto the first barge took three men and several ropes; once he was on, he half-reared, neighing, his hooves booming on the wooden barge. The men hung on him, trying to calm him. The noise of all this raised the attention of many people. The Abbess came down in the middle of it and accosted Petronilla.

"I must protest this, my lady. This is Holy Week. You are no longer Queen of France."

Petronilla peeled the woman's hand from her arm. She was wound tight, her blood racing, and she restrained herself with effort from slapping the Abbess's face. "Go tell Theobald of Champagne about Holy Week."

"But you are stealing our barges!"

Out at the end of the quay they had now gotten de Rançun's stout black horse on beside the gray Barb. Petronilla said, "Are you not brides of Christ? Think of it as giving to the needy." She went to join de Rançun and the horses, and the boatmen with their poles pushed them off into the current of the river.

The great lumbering slab of wood slid along through the dark water, hardly seeming to move. Yet the torch-lit quay dropped back into the dark and was soon only two flickering spots of light behind them, the intervening water dotted with reflections. In the center of the barge, the Barb stood braced on widespread legs. Petronilla paced up to the front, too edgy to try to sit; there was no place to sit anyway. The water glittered in the moonlight, its expanse fringed on the distant left bank and on the nearer right side by drowned trees and stands of reeds.

De Rançun came up beside her. She moved a little closer to his steady warmth. She needed him. She wanted to lean on him, to rest her worries and her fears on him. The Barb had settled down finally, and his head drooped; he looked mild as milk, dozing. Out behind them on the river, the second barge floated after, a dark blob of horses and men; beyond that, the tiny flecks of light that marked the nuns' quay were almost too small to see.

She said, "What happens if they catch us?"

"I don't know," he said. His voice was harsh. "You should make them know right away that you're not Eleanor."

Her gut tightened. It was hard to see what might be worse, if they knew—whoever took her—or not. Thinking her Eleanor, he would force her, and at once, so there would be no doubt that he possessed her, no refusing the marriage. But knowing her to be someone else, he might still rape her, out of revenge, or pique, or mere lust, and then throw her aside.

A sudden new rush of terror filled her, to be thrown aside again, to be made nothing of again. She fought that down. She conquered that fear with a surge of righteous anger.

She said, "I hate him. All of them. Am I a castle, to be seized and occupied?"

He said, "They won't take you from me, that I promise. Not while I live."

At that a sudden grateful sweetness toward him enveloped her; she lowered her head a little, cherishing this. She knew he meant what he said because of his own honor, not of her. His love for Eleanor. Yet his honor and his love bound him to her. She could depend on him like the sun rising. She said nothing for a while. They were floating along the right bank of the river, through velvety darkness; the water chuckled along the side of the boat, and the moonlight turned the water's surface to a sheet of silver. *Beautiful*, she thought, and shivered in the cold.

"You should get back out of the wind," he said. He was not looking at her. She wondered again why he avoided looking at her.

"No," she said. "But bring my cloak, if you would, please."

He went back past the horses. She stood watching the river ahead for the first sign of the city, of the bridge. Once the boat bumped, and shuddered a little, and she guessed they had run up against something below. A voice behind her called out, the barge gave a sudden sharp unfluid jog, something scraped past, and then they were floating smoothly on again. De Rançun came back again, settling the cloak around her.

He said, "I just talked to the boatmen. I think they are going to be trouble—they are used to going only as far as Blois, and then coming back with horses towing the barges along the bank, and they want to stop in Blois, on this bank."

She gave a start. "Well, that's no good. We have to cross to the other side of the river, at the least." She remembered the long well-traveled stretch of road below Blois, where her pursuers could have laid any number of traps. "We should get as far west as we can, don't you think? See how far west they will take us. Find out what they must have to do it—there will be some price, and I will pay it." She made a face in the dark. "Do we have any money?"

"I got the purse from Matthieu before we left."

"That was clever," she said, relieved. "Go buy them."

He went back up the length of the boat, and she turned her eyes into the darkness ahead. The barge hardly seemed to move, creeping along the moon-drenched river. The sound of the water gurgling along the front edge was like laughter; then it changed slightly, faster, like arguing or warning, and the barge moved leftward, and in the silvery haze of the moonlight she saw before them and toward the bank a gaunt black shape rising from the water like a claw. Swags of weed flapped from its rigid process. A huge branch, she thought, brought down in the flood and lodged somehow on the bottom. They ghosted by it; the barge touched something, again, on the side toward the snag.

They were rounding a shallow curve; the water curled white ahead of them along the inside edge, and ahead, on the black strip of the bank, a dim red light showed. Some torch or lantern. As she watched, another appeared, and then more lights, behind the first, higher up. They were approaching Blois.

She glanced back toward the rear of the barge, wondering if the boatmen would quit here, push into the near bank and refuse to go farther, leaving her in the middle of her enemies. If that happened, she would have to force them off the barges, make her knights do the work, which she knew they would not do, not well enough, men of swords and hawks and horses, not rivermen. The Loire was flooded; there might be treacherous currents, submerged rocks and trees like the one she had just passed. Snakes, she thought. Underwater monsters. Dragons. She tried to think of some alternative, if they were forced ashore here. The barge drifted steadily on, and ahead, like a wall, the narrow black band of the bridge stretched across the gleaming river.

Her back prickled up. They were not stopping. The barges glided past the outthrust quays along the right bank, the thick dark clots of buildings standing inland of that, some here and there pecked with faint lights. On its hill the black column of the castle stood, the torches at its peak fluttering like pennants against the night sky. She heard voices behind her on the barge, sharp, giving orders.

De Rançun's voice, somebody else's, a boatman. Too fast, heavy, unstoppable, the wooden float swept on toward the wall of the bridge, now rising sheer up before them like a cliff. She thought of the Barb and twisted around; de Rançun himself was there at the horse's head. Swinging forward again, she began to make out that the span of the bridge opened, underneath, into the loops of archways. They seemed impossibly low, too narrow to fit through, bottomless, endless, caves down into the abyss. The barge was heading straight into one arch, sliding as if down a slope into it, and there was a sudden darkness, a roar in her ears, dank stone passing overhead; the barge shook under her, and they rushed out again into the silvery light. She gasped as if she were coming to the surface. The barge gave a sudden sharp buck and she caught her balance. Behind her was a drumming of hooves on the barge and de Rançun swearing. Off to her right the last lumpy dark shapes of the city passed by, studded with faint lights. The barge floated calmly along. The river muttered under her, benign.

De Rançun came back from dealing with the boatmen. "I gave them some wine," he said. "And promised them money. One of them has a cousin down the river at a place called Amboise and says we should get off there."

"Good," she said. She was glad to have him there; she thought without him she would be helpless. "We should stay away from the main road, though, going to Poitiers."

At that, she thought about what lay ahead in Poitiers, and she blurted out, "I hope Eleanor is well."

He crossed himself. "I pray God so, my lady." But again he turned his face away from her, as if he hid something.

"God keep her," she said. "She must have had the baby by now." She hesitated a moment, unsure whether to talk of this, but she had to talk of it. "I love her still, but what lies between us is as if she cut out my heart. I did everything she asked of me; I have done what had to be done, for her and my sake, both. And she doesn't care. You know she said such things to me that I can't even bear to remember."

He said, "Well, yes, I heard." His voice went a little ragged. "But she—you have to take her for what she is—Eleanor. She is who she is; she won't change. Her will is all that matters to her."

She sank down into the warmth of the cloak, looking down the river. She realized that he still, always, forever loved Eleanor. He did all of this for Eleanor, not for her.

This hurt. She wondered why she had let herself care so much for him and his opinions, and thought, *I need him*. Yet it seemed she could not reach him; he saw only Eleanor.

She thought, suddenly, *I love him. And he hardly sees me*. She stood staring off down the river, thinking she had always been in love with Joffre de Rançun.

He stood there silent in the dark beside her, an impossible space between them. She said, "I have changed."

At that he gave a start and turned toward her. She saw the gleam of his eyes in the dark. Then abruptly he turned and walked away from her, as far from her as he could get. She wondered what she had said to have driven him off. She felt the thrill of warning. But he was faithful, Joffre, and honorable. She realized she had always admired him. And she had always stood aside for Eleanor, who took him all for granted. It made no difference, she thought, to admit it. A long road lay before them, and all they did was for Eleanor's sake, and she had to trust him.

Whatever he thought, he kept to himself. That chilled her. She was tired down to the bone, and she wished he would comfort her, but he stayed off on his corner of the barge and stared out at the river. She could think of nothing to say to him, to cross whatever cold barrier suddenly lay between them, and he said nothing to her.

In the corner of her eye, she saw something move, and turned and saw him draw his arm back. He had thrown something into the river. There was a splash, far off. She jerked her head around, looking the other way.

The night flowed on, until ahead the deep sky was fading to a paler purple. The wind rose, light on her face, blowing westward. The purple turned slowly pink, and pinkish orange, reflecting sleek on the water ahead of her like a path of gold. Behind her the edge of the sun blazed over the horizon, flinging out ahead of it a pure, fiery light that climbed across the sky and out over the river and the land until the very air glowed with a bloody radiance, and the river was a lapping gilded tide. Was this a promise, or an omen? She took in a deep breath, gathering herself, ready, and let the coming day engulf her.

Thirty-three

The rumors flew as fast as horses galloped, along all the roads and paths of France, and so in Aquitaine and farther, within a few days of the announcement in Beaugency, they knew what lay ahead for Eleanor.

They read the proclamation in every church in France, and in all the churches of the French King's vassals, too. All across the whole of Christendom they knew that Eleanor was unmarried. In Normandy, in Rouen, the Duke heard it, standing impassively beside his mother in the church. In Mirebeau, in the south of Anjou, in the last castle his brother allowed to him, Geoffrey of Anjou heard it in his chapel. They heard it in Paris, too, in Troyes, in Toulouse. And they heard it in Poitiers, but in a different color.

Hard behind this came the second flood of rumor. It was spoken in the street, and all over the markets, and in the halls of the court, that certain traps had been laid for her. Men seeking to capture her, to abduct her, to use the old law on everybody's lips: *raptus*, bride theft. Take her for a night and make himself rich for a lifetime as Duke of Aquitaine.

In the Green Tower, Eleanor herself, who to everybody else was Petronilla, lay in her bed and heard the excited stories, and prayed that nobody caught her sister.

De Rançun would know well not to let Petronilla be taken—that it would all come apart if she was taken. But the other thing—she had commanded that of him, and he had always obeyed her. No matter what Eleanor had done, he had obeyed her order. There was no way to stop that. He would use the dagger.

She told herself she had not meant it the way it seemed. Just keep her away. But she had given the knife into his hand.

She considered also the sainted Bernard, who had foreseen how, once freed of the royal marriage, she was prey to any bold and well-armed and conscienceless man. Bernard had not thought himself of the wiles of women. He had thought too contemptuously of the sins and weaknesses of women to understand how a woman could outdo a man. He had not seen, either, how a woman's own wiles could cut her to the bone. For Henry's sake, she would slay her own sister. Everyone had betrayed her; finally, ruinously, she had betrayed herself. The price was unbearable. Maybe she would die out of grief and guilt. More likely just live in grief and guilt for all her years. She lay in the bed, her hand in Marie-Jeanne's. The old woman gave her sops of bread soaked in wine. Sometimes, far away, she heard a baby's lusty cry.

A son. Well grown and lusty, her son, whom she had never seen. Would never see. If she saw him, touched him, even once, smelled his lovely baby skin, noticed any resemblance at all to anybody else, she might never let him go. She was too weak to speak. Almost too weak to decide this. She would have more children. She had already given up two, and now this one, but ever after she would keep her children by her, and love them, love them with all the heart she could not give this child. Love them, with a heart schooled from loving her sister. She swore this. She slept.

• • •

On the river, nothing happened for a while. All that day and the following night the two barges floated down the Loire. Petronilla finally
slept, curled up on the back deck. They had nothing to eat but bread
and cheese and some bad wine, most of which was going to the boatmen anyway. They stopped twice on grassy banks to try to gather
food for the horses, but the little hay they cut was gone almost at
once. The horses stamped their feet and neighed all through the second night, so that the barge rocked under her. In the early morning,
the barges drifted into the swampy left bank of the river, grating and
scraping through stands of stalky reeds, and they staggered off the
heaving decks onto the land again.

They had come to ground on a swampy meadowland, where the
horses sank into the black muck to their fetlocks and a swarm of
ducks went up squawking into the air. The smoke and haze of a little
village showed just down the river. The three young knights took the
horses to find grass and de Rançun went to look for the village, leaving the boatmen to manage the barges. They poled off at once into
the river, struggling to find an eddy going upstream again.

Petronilla walked down the river a little, found a stand of old
trees out of sight of the men where she could do the usual morning
things, and afterward went down to the river and washed her face
and hands.

Hunkered down by the river, her hands red and stinging from
the cold water, she thought of Poitiers and it seemed as distant as
golden Cathay. Her coif had come almost off, and she pulled it down,
gathering the pins as she did, and smoothed the white cloth over her
knees. She had no idea how to put it on again. Since she was a little
girl, someone had always been there to dress her. Before she left the
convent, Alys had thrust a bag into her hands, with a comb, some
ribbons and cloths, and a pomander, and she used the comb on her

hair for a while. Her hair felt matted together like some rude fleece. Finally she gathered it at her nape, wrapped the coif around it once or twice and knotted it, and let the ends trail down her back.

She had to get to Poitiers. But in Poitiers, there was Eleanor. And Eleanor hated her now. She had no home, really, and once she had shed the disguise of being Eleanor, not even much of a name anymore.

She sat staring blindly out across the river, thinking of the ancient city, the palace and the garden, and of herself and Eleanor in the garden when they were little girls, making dolls out of the flowers. Eleanor had always used the red flowers for her dresses, and Petronilla the pink ones, or white, the pale ones. Eleanor had made crowns for her dolls out of daisies, but never Petronilla.

She saw that all her life she had known she would be overlooked. She had accepted this, all her life. Grimly she got up and went back toward the men.

Just before noon de Rançun came back from the village with a local man, leaning on a walking stick, who knew a way south through the forest. The knights brought in the horses again, and they all sat around and divided up the last of their bread and wine. Mounting the horses, they rode off after this new guide. She picked off the red rosettes on the Barb's mane and stuffed them in the saddle pouch.

They soon left the lowland behind, the path rising in steps and benches through oak woods, trees as stooped and gnarled as gnomes, half buckling under the weight of their vast heavy heads of branches. The sunlight reached down in long shafts to the ground. Everything was fresh and green with the first tiny perfect leaves. Mushrooms like broad round hats sprouted around the knobbed roots of the trees, and flocks of birds clamored incessantly in the branches, lifting up wild trills intermingled with screeches. It was Holy Week, she remembered, here even in the wild country; the whole world brought to life by the love of God. She said morning prayers to herself, fretting again over Eleanor, and how she did, and how the baby did, and how she, Petronilla, fit into it all, and still, she saw no place for herself anywhere.

The guide led them over a ridge, where yellow rocks burst up through the ground, rough as old bones. At the foot of the next slope was a little river, and they rode along a way until they found a place to ford it. In a village of three little huts, after haggling and pleading and giving up several gold coins, they each got a handful of unleavened honey cakes, so coarse they cracked and snapped when she chewed them.

The cakes cheered her stomach like the finest feast. The thin cider she drank with it was as heady as wine. Carefully she kept back three of the cakes, although she was still hungry, and saved them in her cloak.

De Rançun set the young knights out to hunt, but Petronilla knew, without dogs or hawks, they would likely catch nothing. Whenever they stopped, she looked around for fruit, for berries, although in this young time of the year everything she found was green and small and hard as rocks. All around her the earth was bursting alive and she was starving. She sucked on a strand of grass, surprised at the wild flavor.

That night no one else had saved any of their food, and she ended up sharing her three honey cakes with the others, so nobody got more than a bite. They slept on the ground, in the crisp cool of a clear night, the stars blazing above them. The bit of the cake had not dulled her hunger much and she could not sleep. Instead she lay thinking how she was outcast in her own country. She felt cut off, isolated, insubstantial as a ghost; she thought, *I am free now, but for what? To do what?*

At dawn they rode on; the guide took them down the river to a ford, where some people lived. There they found more bread, this time in thick, sweet loaves, and crossed over the river.

There also their guide left them, with some vague gestures south and east. He watched de Rançun count the gold into his hand and said, "The River Creuse is there, at the end of that path. Go south a little, and you can cross at the old bridge at Port-de-Piles." Then he was walking back the way they had come, swinging his long stick; he waded down into the ford and splashed across toward the far side, never looking back.

◆　◆　◆

The next day, they came out of the forest down to the bank of the River Creuse, just a little west of the arched stone bridge that crossed it. The sky had been full of ominous gray clouds all day, but now it seemed to be clearing. On the far side of the bridge they could see only a few dark rooftops of the village stretched along the road behind the trees.

One of the young men behind her said, "Well, at least there will be something to eat tonight." Petronilla let go her reins a little, so that the Barb could graze. As usual she had saved some of her bread, but the boys had not; if it turned out there was no food ahead, she thought meanly, it would have served her better to have eaten it all at once.

She ached all over from the long riding, and she felt cramped and crooked with hunger, but the close quarters of the bridge up there made her wary. By now, everybody would know she had eluded Theobald, and everybody knew where she was going. How hard would it be to conclude she must cross this river here?

De Rançun sat his big black horse next to her. He said, low, not looking at her, "My lady, you think what I am thinking."

She smiled at him. "Yes. Send someone in, look around, come tell me what you find."

"I'll go myself."

"No," she said quickly, holding her hand out to him. "Everybody knows you—send one of them. Two of them. Have them take their surcoats off." She nodded at the young knights behind her.

At that they all three pushed forward, eager, their voices in a bad chorus. She turned toward the town again, looking for people in the streets. The place seemed oddly deserted, at this distance, but it was Holy Week, after all; people could be at their prayers. De Rançun sent off all three of the young men, stripped to their mail, who trotted off along the road to the bridge, with orders also to buy bread if they saw any.

"At least it isn't raining," she said. "Help me." He dismounted his horse, and she swung her leg forward, over the saddle pommel, and slid down the side of the horse into his arms. She kept her eyes down; she did not want to see him trying not to look at her. He set her gently on her feet and turned at once to adjust the Barb's girth, while the horse began to crop at the grass along the road.

"We are almost there," de Rançun said. His voice was stiff. He straightened, running the reins back and forth through his fingers. "Once we're on the far side of the Creuse, we can reach Poitiers in a few days." He stared away toward the bridge.

She let out her breath in a sigh; abruptly she did not want to be back in Poitiers so soon, even if it meant a full belly. In Poitiers she would have to make another choice. As much as she tried, she could not think how to come face-to-face with Eleanor again. She tried not to think about that, to watch the horses grazing, enjoy not being in the saddle.

"Joffre," she said, "you are so quiet."

He cleared his throat. His gaze was aimed steadily away. It seemed to her that the nearer they came to Poitiers, the more he turned away from her. As if reaching Poitiers were the worst thing that could happen.

He said, finally, "We can find something to eat down there." Putting aimless words into the hollow air between them.

"I hope so." She turned, looking down at the bridge, and said, "No. Look."

The three young knights had ridden at a walk down to the bridge and across, but now suddenly they were galloping back. Something was wrong. She wheeled around to the Barb, who snorted, and jerked his head up, his ears pricked. De Rançun said something under his breath and turned and boosted her up into the saddle before she even said a word, and she gathered the reins into her hands.

The three young knights clattered along the road toward her; back on the bridge, another band of men was coming after them. A faint shout rose, like a hunting cry. Petronilla's heart jumped into her throat, and the Barb caught her mood and began to twitch and dance. The three knights reached her at a gallop.

The first of them was calling out before his horse stopped. "Geoffrey d'Anjou's men. Waiting, just over the bridge. They knew us as soon as they saw us, they knew it was us."

"Come on," de Rançun said.

"Where?" Petronilla looked back up the road to the north, the way they had come, and then to the west, where the trees grew thick along the riverbank. On her left hand, eastward, the river curled away past a broad stretch of farmed land, cleared and half-plowed, bunched with trees, more trees in the distance. She turned the Barb that way and set him at a canter, and they followed after her.

Behind them, by the bridge, a shout rang out, unintelligible. A horn blew. Every hair on Petronilla's head stood on end; this was how the hind felt, she thought, when the hunt was up. With the knights tightly gathered around her, she galloped straight across the grassy meadowland.

Even as she clutched the Barb's reins, she twisted to look back and saw the pursuit coming after her, thirty men at least. She and her escort had ridden all day, and for days before; those chasing them were fresh and eager, and they were gaining with every stride.

Leading them was a hatless man whose tawny hair stood out ragged as a mane: Geoffrey d'Anjou himself. When he knew how she had fooled him, he would not treat her well. She dared not fall into his power.

But he was catching up to her. Ahead, the river curved slightly, pinching off the long sweep of the meadow against a low rise, a stand of trees. By then, she thought, if he were a hawk, and she were a rabbit, she would be fast in his claws.

Her own men were falling back a little; the three boys of her guard ranged themselves in a rank that screened him slightly from her. De Rançun galloped along at her stirrup, his black horse's neck already scummy with sweat. She turned toward him, clutching the reins with both hands, and shouted, "What should we do?"

He waved his arm at her—at her horse. "Let him run! We'll fight—give you some head start—run!" He looked back at the charge coming after them and faced her once more, for only an instant. "Run, Petra!" Sitting back in the saddle, he reined his horse in and around.

For an instant, afraid, she began to take the Barb back also, to stay with him. The horse fought her, bounding against her hold, tossing his head at the reins, pulling her up out of the saddle. She felt the power in him, and she opened her hands and let the reins fly.

The horse bolted. Even after the hard riding, he was eager and ready to run and he leaned into each stride, his head thrust out. His mane lashed her. She clung to the pommel of the saddle with both hands; standing in the stirrups, she felt the giant flex and stretch of his body between her legs and gave a startled yell, half exaltation and half terror. The wind blasted her in the face hard enough to raise tears, and the ground flew by in a green blur. At every stride she knew she was about to fly off through the air and hit something hard. He would stumble, he would throw her; she had no way to stop him. Yet the power of him made her shout again, giddy. The trees ahead hurtled toward her. Something large stretched across the edge of them, a wall of broken trunks and stumps and branches raked up out of the field here. She glanced quickly over her shoulder.

The others had dropped far behind her. De Rançun had rallied his three men and turned and lined up in Anjou's way, and even out-numbered they were still holding her pursuers almost to a standstill. They would not catch her now, unless she fell.

She swung forward again, gripping the saddle pommel. The trees loomed over her, and at the border of the woods stretched the wall of cleared brush and trees. Panic seized her; there was no way through, no gap, and the great horse was not slowing down. She let go with her right hand, trying to catch the reins where they hung on his neck. They thundered down on the wall of brush and under her the surging body steadied itself, shortened up, and then sprang out into the air.

She screamed, jarred out of the saddle. The horse flew over the barrier as if it were a stick on the ground and he knew exactly what lay beyond it. She sailed along well out of the saddle, traveling through the empty air above him. They came down together, Petronilla slam-ming down hard into the saddle again, and the Barb dropping knee-deep into a tangle of briars and saplings just behind the brush wall.

While the Barb lunged and clawed his way free, she got hold of the reins. But when he galloped away down a narrow path under the trees, she let him have his head again.

The trees pressed in on either side, their branches low overhead, and to avoid them she pressed herself as flat as she could, leaning around the high saddle pommel and laying her head alongside his neck. The overhang raked her back, clawed at her cloak, lashing her shoulders. She saw his hooves pounding the ground beneath her; he leaped over another tree, swerved hard to the right, then hard again to the left, following the old path.

After a while he slowed his pace to a jog, then a walk. In the woods the darkness was coming early and she could see nothing but a confusion of shadowy trunks and leaves. She heard no sounds either of anyone coming after her. She wondered what had become of de Rançun, who had given himself up for her, and some swift, tender ache opened in the center of her chest. He was better than either her or Eleanor; he had no thought for himself. The horse carried her on, following a thread of a trail; twice he stopped, snorting, where the way divided, and each time she let him decide which turn to take and he went swiftly on.

At last in the ruddy light of sundown she rode out onto another meadow, slanting off to her right. They had come far away from the river, which had to run in the lower land down to the south somewhere. She let the reins loose and the horse began to graze. Looking all around, listening to everything, she saw nothing but the trees and the grass and the river, and heard nothing except the wind and some birds.

She had the piece of bread she had saved, and she fished the bits from her purse and chewed them up. Even when they were gone, she was hungry, and really tired now, and lost, and alone.

She wasn't afraid, which surprised her. She would find the river, and after she crossed over, Poitiers was only a day or so away. She would not starve in a day. And being alone would help her think things out, perhaps.

First she had to find the river. She let the horse graze, but she nudged him along toward the south, down the meadowland.

Thirty-four

When she woke up, in the next dawn, the horse was gone.

She sat straight up, alarmed. Without him she was much more lost than before. She looked around her at the copse of saplings where she had slept; she had come here in the dark, seeing nothing save that it was quiet and open and she could not go another step. She stood up, looking around her for the Barb.

In among the spindly trees it was still dark, but just beyond, the first sun lit up a stretch of green meadow, and she walked out onto the grass into its sudden warmth. She had taken off her shoes, and the dew soaked quickly into her hose. The new sunlight glittered on every blade of grass, twinkling and shimmering, as if the stars had fallen overnight and were struggling to get back up into the sky.

Only a few yards away the Barb was munching grass. In his long rippled mane one last red rosette clung just behind his forelock. She had pulled off the saddle when they stopped and slipped the bit out of his mouth, but left the bridle hanging around his neck and tied the reins to a branch. He had torn the branch off its tree and was dragging it after him as he moved. She watched him as she went up toward him, and saw his ear twitch toward her, and she went up to his head and patted him.

He raised his head from the damp grass and snorted at her. He had huge dark prominent eyes, full of knowing. The skin of his nostrils was velvet soft. He rubbed his head against her, and she untied the reins from the branch and led him back into the copse of saplings. Her belly hurt with hunger.

She had wrapped herself in her cloak and the saddle blankets and slept curled up against the saddle, and now, awkwardly, she began to put it all back on the horse. She got the blanket on easily enough, but the bulky saddle, dangling stirrups and girths, was heavier than she expected, and when she first tried to heave it up onto his back, the hangings hit him and he leaped sideways and eluded her, and the whole thing fell into the dirt.

She remembered seeing the groom swing the stirrup up over the saddle seat to get it out of the way. The horse was standing still, his ears up, but unmoving, watching her. She went up to him and patted him, murmuring sweetness to him, and pulled the blanket straight again, smoothing the hide under it with her hand. Carefully she looped all the stirrups and girths across the seat of the saddle, and on aching arms lifted it up high and lowered it gently onto his back. He snorted, but he stood still. She struggled getting the girths tight enough; the saddle seemed very loose.

She went off across the stretch of grass, leading the horse, looking for something to stand on so that she could get up onto his back. It felt good to be walking. She felt thin and bright with hunger, but her spirits rose, in the sunlight, with the horse walking docilely beside her. For once in her life, she was doing things for herself, by herself. To her surprise she liked being alone, with no one else to care about, or measure up to, for a while, at least. Little white and yellow flowers spangled the grass, and she picked some and threaded them into the Barb's mane. He ate steadily, tearing at the new green shoots.

When she thought about being alone forever, the sunlit meadow seemed like a cave closing down on her. She would not think about that, not now. First she had to reach Poitiers, and Eleanor. She had to come face-to-face with Eleanor, she thought, and settle this.

For the first time, she realized she could overcome Eleanor. That was where all this led her: that she would triumph, that she would come into her own kind of kingdom. She would never be the mousy little sister again.

Birds flushed ahead of her as she came near the edge of the trees, chattering angrily from the high branches. They found food here, where she could not. She led the horse on down a path as worn as a street, no wider than her foot, beneath the dense overhanging branches of the trees. Such a path had to lead somewhere, and she followed it on down a narrow bank and around the edge of a swampy place, the whole ringing with birdsong, and through some dead stalks of reeds and came upon the river.

The water rushed along brown as dirt, flooding up over the edges of its banks; a tree branch floated briskly by, one arm flung up into the air. She could not cross here. She began to work her way up the bank, which was overgrown with brambles and stands of reeds and pockets of sagging black flooded marsh. The horse followed her, grazing as he went.

Around midday, she came to a place where an outcrop of yellow rock bent the river sharply around. On the outside of this curve, on the far side of the river from her, masses of driftwood had collected, thickets of entwined branches wedged against a half-buried stump. Above that the stony river bottom looked only a few feet deep. On this opposite side, the bank had fallen in, and there was a steep slide down into the current, but the space between the two sides, where the river ran, was hardly more than the horse's length. She could see, on the moist earth of the slide, some prints of deer; obviously deer crossed here.

She had seen no better place anywhere else. Standing up on the bank with the horse drawn alongside, she eased herself over into the saddle; he stood well for that, to her relief. She patted his neck and told him he was wonderful, and then reined him around and set him down along the steep sandy ramp to the water.

The ground was soft under his feet, and he began to sit back, resisting, his ears switching around. He snorted. "Go," she cried, and nudged him with her heels, but he did not move. The ground was shifting under him, and he began to slide with it, his head bowed and his ears pricked. She grabbed hold of the saddle pommel, and then in a rush they plowed down the ramp and off into the deep, swirling current.

The river slammed into them like a fist, knocking the horse sideways; they sank down into the icy dark water until only his head showed and she was in to her waist, her skirts billowing around her, her body floating up out of the saddle. She kept herself attached to him with both hands on the square pommel. He swam strongly but the river was thrusting them downstream, away from the shallow bank. For an instant she thought of leaping off, of scrambling through the water by herself, but she held on to the saddle and prayed.

The current swung them around again, and the horse clawed for his footing on the bottom. His hooves struck solid ground. At once he charged, head down and quarters pumping, heading upstream, up through the shallow water in a blinding splash, and caught unawares, she nearly went off. She lost her stirrups; she hung alongside him for a dizzy moment, clutching the saddle with one hand and his mane with the other, and then grappled her way back up onto his back. He was clambering up a steep, short yellow bank into the sun. She was soaked to the skin, but they were across the river.

She was wet and cold, and she found a grassy place for the horse to graze and dismounted. Peeling off all her clothes but her shift, she spread them out on the ground to dry in the sun, and wrung as much water as she could out of her woolen cloak and wrapped herself in that. Somewhere ahead she would find some sign of people, a village, a hall, something, certainly; the whole of Poitou was not desolate. There she could beg something to eat. She raked her hair with her fingers, trying to untangle the knots. She probably looked like a beggarwoman; her hands were dirty and her face was probably dirty as well. She began to think of a thick slice of bread, some creamy cheese, apples, a glass of good wine. The horse munched away at the grass nearby her. She watched him work methodically through the new growth, wishing she could make a meal of weeds.

Then suddenly he lifted his head, his ears pricked, and his curled nostrils opened wide. She leaped up, looking where he was looking, her hand out toward the bridle, in case she had to run.

Up the way they had come from the river, leading his black horse, walking with his head down as if he read the ground, was Joffre de Rançun.

She let out a joyous cry. He wheeled around, saw her, and shouted. The black horse lifted its head, and the Barb, behind Petronilla, gave a soft nicker. De Rançun dropped his reins, took two steps toward her, and swept her up in his arms.

"Petra. My God, I thought you must have gone down in the river there." He held her tight against him, his hand on her hair. She felt his lips graze her temple. She flung her arms around him. She realized she was wearing only her shift—that between her body and his was only the sheerest of linen. Through the linen the iron ridges of his mail. She stepped back, letting him go, and crossing her arms over herself.

"Joffre. Thank you." She could think of nothing else to say. Her eyes were hot with tears. "Thank you."

He smiled down at her. His face shone. "You're alive. That's my thanks. You were in my charge, and I failed you, and you won through anyway. You are such a woman, Petra." He glanced down at her body, all but naked in the shift, and then calmly turned his gaze away from her. His voice went on, light and quick. "You'd better get dressed. We should go on."

She said, "I'll get my clothes," and hurried around gathering them up. He stood there, his back to her, defending her modesty. The coldness in him was gone. He had found her, and they were friends again. She sat down to put on her hose, now stiff and ill-fitting. Rising, she fought her way into her stained underdress and the gown.

"I'm—you can turn around now."

"What are you going to do?" he asked, facing her.

She came up to him, winding her coif around her matted hair. "I have never wished so much for Alys and Marie-Jeanne. I suppose I have to go to Poitiers. What else would I do? Do you know how to get there?"

He reached out and plucked wisps of grass from her sleeve and her coif, his smile crinkling his eyes, but now his face clouded over again. He said, "Poitiers is only a day away by now. You came a long way south, you know." He tucked a curl of her hair behind her ear; his fingers grazed her cheek. She thought he was about to try to kiss her. "Half a day on, or so, I think, we'll meet the main road south, and there's a village; we can find something to eat there. Maybe some better clothes. Another half day, a little more. But—"

He seemed to gather himself. The kiss was gone. "Maybe you should not go to Poitiers."

At that some chill went through her, as if she touched cold stone, and she said, "Why not?"

He gave a little shake of his head, and his mouth twisted, tasting something bad. His eyes turned away from her. He said, "Well, there's Eleanor."

She frowned at him. "I need to get things out with Eleanor. And where else can I go? Poitiers is my home, and she is my sister, after all."

He opened his mouth, closed it, licked his lips, and twisted away from her, walked a few steps off. He spoke in a gust of words. "Your sister. What she—I can't—" His hands rose, casting something up. "How can I tell you, what I could not even imagine doing? She gave me a dagger, when we left Poitiers. And some instructions. That night on the barge, when you said you'd changed—I knew I could not follow them. I realized I wanted Eleanor to be more like you, that it was you I loved. So I threw the dagger into the river."

"What is this?" she cried. "What are you telling me?"

He lifted his hands, helpless. "I don't think she meant it anyway."

She gave a yell of fury. "She ordered you to murder me?"

"God help me, Petra, believe me, please believe me, I could never have done it." He put his hands on her arms, bending toward her, intense. "I have always obeyed her, but what you said on the barge—I could not." He let go of her, backed away a step, his eyes downcast. "Anyhow, I don't think she meant it."

"Then why are you telling me not to go back to Poitiers?" She tramped past him toward the horses. "I think this is all the more reason to go."

Then what he had told her came together, and she turned. She said, "Joffre. You saved my life." Against Eleanor's will, he who never failed her, he had defended Petronilla. She stretched out her arms to him.

He came full into her embrace, his arms around her, and his body hard against hers. He kissed her forehead and then her mouth, soft on her mouth, caressing. He cradled her head with his hand. He said, "I love you, Petra. I couldn't have hurt you." Then he was stepping back, red-faced. "I do love you," he said.

Her arms dropped to her sides. The kiss on her mouth like a lingering honey. The space between them awkward. She saw what this meant for him and said, "Joffre. What will you do now?"

"I can't go back to her service. I've broken faith with her. That's how she'll see it, anyway."

"Then she does mean evil to me," Petronilla cried, and turned toward the horses. "I shall go to her, Joffre—take me there or not, I shall stand against her over this."

He came up beside her. "Petronilla, we could go to my castle at Taillebourg. It's just a few days south of here."

She faced him again, resolute. "I am going to Poitiers, Joffre. Whatever happens." She put her fingers to his cheek. "What you did—thank you. Thank you." It was on her tongue to say: *I love you, too.*

He said, "I'm going with you. I won't let you face her alone." He turned to the Barb and slung the stirrup over the seat so he could reach the girth to tighten it. This little echo of what she had done pleased her, affirming her somehow. She looked down at his belt, and for the first time marked that the small sheath behind his sword was empty. A chill passed through her. She looked away, toward the river, wondering what she might find in Poitiers.

◆   ◆   ◆

The rumors ran in the streets, up the hill, in the stairways of the palace. The voices buzzed in the courtyards, in the kitchens, excited, eager. In Poitiers, the woman in the Green Tower heard it at once.

Somewhere on the road between Beaugency and Blois, the Duchess of Aquitaine had disappeared. When Count Theobald's trap closed in Blois, it caught only her servants. She had been seen somewhere near the Creuse but lost again. Nobody knew where she was now.

In the Green Tower, the woman in the great bed lay alone, and slept, and she dreamed, over and over, that de Rançun with the silver dagger came in through the door, and plunged the blade into her heart.

Thirty-five

Just as the sun went down they came to the village, where they got meat and cheese and bread, and slept the night under a haymow. She rolled herself in her cloak, which was still damp in places; although she heaped up the hay to lie on, the ground was hard. De Rançun stripped off his mail and his sword, lay beside her, and spread his cloak over them both. She put her head on her arm. In the dark she saw only his shape.

"What are you thinking of?"

He said, "All my life, I've done everything to serve her, and now I have to do something else. I've got my own lands. My brothers have been mishandling them long enough. But it seems strange."

She began to cry, exhausted. "I can't believe—I can't believe—"

He murmured to her and drew her into his arms, kissed her, let her cry. He smelled like horses and hay and sweat. He did this, she thought, perversely, unwilling to be happy, because of Eleanor, still, in defiance rather than obedience, but still. Her head rested on his shoulder; his fingertips grazed her face. He said her name.

She said, "I'm not Eleanor, you know."

"That's why I love you," he said.

She was afraid to believe this. She was falling asleep, safe in his arms, and for a moment, too drowsy to resist, she yielded, and knew she was beloved.

◆   ◆   ◆

By noon the next day they reached the high road, busy with travelers on their own journeys. No one looked at them much, although she noticed a couple of men eyeing her horse. They passed some pilgrims singing on their way south, and a train of wagons full of goods. On the side of the road, beggars in rags cried out for alms, their hands cupped, as if they caught invisible rain.

Late in the afternoon they were riding up over the bridge into Poitiers. The gate stood wide open, letting through farmers driving their wagons, traders and their packs and donkeys, merchants and local people, palmers with their staffs and belled hats, nameless wanderers. No one marked two more ragged travelers on foot with weary ungroomed horses. They had nothing to pay a toll for and went on into the city.

Petronilla went along looking all around her. The city's white walls and red roofs, its lively smells and noises closed around her in a welcoming embrace. All the flowers were beginning to bloom. She rode through a heavy aroma of roses, the air almost edible. The narrow cobbled streets, crowded with shops, loud with people all speaking Occitan, even the steep familiar hillside gladdened her heart. It seemed warmer here. The light breeze smelled of fresh green leaves. Little brown birds flew around the eaves of the tiled roofs, like mice going in and out a wall. In an upper-story window a woman sat singing, and on the street just below a man stood singing along with her. She had been here before, but it was all different now. She was free now, to choose what life she wanted. She just didn't know what that was.

De Rançun rode beside her. Both of their horses were tired, and without having to talk they dismounted to walk in the sloping street, a horse on either side. She wanted to reach for his hand. A moment later he took hold of hers.

At the top of the hill they came to the palace. In the great dark mass of the main gate, the ordinary door was open, and de Rançun led the way inside. The porter came up and saw him, turned, and recognized her at once.

Or he recognized who she was supposed to be. He dropped to his knees, his hands clasped. "God be thanked," he said. "God be praised for your deliverance, Your Grace."

He was half drunk, like most porters, and he bumped his head up and down, his eyes blinking wide with bleary recognition. In the courtyard, de Rançun called sharply for grooms for the horses. He gave her a meaningful look, and she went ahead of him into the Maubergeon.

She climbed the front steps and in the door to the Green Tower at a quick walk. On the stair she began to run. He was behind her, close enough, but letting her lead him. At the door into the upper-most room, the sentry was leaning on the window looking out, and did not even turn around until they were past him. She burst into the chamber beyond.

The sun was going down and the red gilded light spilled in through the windows, so the whole room glowed. She looked quickly around, saw no cradle, saw Marie-Jeanne staring at her open-mouthed and round-eyed by the wardrobe, and then, by the bed, Eleanor, standing alone.

Her sister turned, and they faced each other. Petronilla gave a low cry, trembling; she swayed on her feet, but she held her ground, her head back.

"He could not do it," Eleanor said. The words shook. She came forward into the middle of the room. "Bernard was right. Everybody I have ever trusted has betrayed me." Her cheeks were pale, with a fierce red blush on each cheekbone, and there was a giddy thread of relief in her voice.

Petronilla was hot with anger; she could hold back no more. "You tried to murder me!" She took two steps forward and swung her open hand full at Eleanor's face.

Her sister gasped, and dodged her, raising her arms between them for a shield, and Petronilla struck her with the other hand. Eleanor caught hold of her coif and a hank of the hair underneath and pulled, and Petronilla shoved her. For a moment they struggled together, pushing and wrenching at each other, entangled. Then Petronilla struck Eleanor full in the face with her palm.

Eleanor sat down hard on the floor, taking a long strip of Petronilla's coif with her. Petronilla stepped back, her blood singing, her head high.

She said, "You deserve that, Eleanor, for turning on me, after all I did for you. You deserve worse."

Panting, Eleanor said, "I knew he wouldn't do it." She got to her feet and went unsteadily over by the table. She wiped her face with her hand. Her gaze went to de Rançun, standing in the doorway, his face intensely not smiling.

"I knew you could not do it. I knew you loved her more than me. You betrayed me, even you—I never want to see your face again."

He turned on his heel and left. Eleanor turned her harsh look on Petronilla.

"As for you, sister." Eleanor's eyes burned. "What will you do now? Weren't you plotting, all along, to take my place?" She snatched up a paper from the table. "Here is the proposal to Henry, all signed, who does not know the difference! Isn't that what you want? To be Duchess, send for him, and rule with him? And do what with me then?"

Petronilla gave a startled laugh; at once she remembered praying for her sister's life in the church at Limoges, for fear she would be trapped as Duchess.

Eleanor said, "Now might you do it—get me out of the way—seize a blade, and run me through—will you?" She stiffened herself, her eyes blazing.

Petronilla shook her head. "That's what you would do, Eleanor." She nodded at the paper with her hand. "Go on, then. Marry your little King. Rule the world, if you want. But I am Petronilla again, now, and I am so glad of that; I never want to be anyone else." She stepped back, her hands at her sides, and her head back, and her eyes aimed at Eleanor. "I have seen that love does, also, and I will choose love over power. You began this; you bear it."

Her sister's lips parted. Under the pallor of her skin the blush rose in a ruddy wave. Petronilla turned toward the door; she thought, *I could still catch him. If he waited.*

"Stand," Eleanor said. "Stop—Petra—stay right where you are. You can't go."

"I'll do as I please," Petronilla said. She faced her sister again. "I'm free now, too, after this. Everything's changed, as he said. You broke faith with me. And I know who I am and what I want."

She went out the door and swiftly down the long steps. The sun had gone down. The pavement outside was dark, all but empty, a few ragged folk by the hall door, waiting for alms. He was not there. She went to the gate and looked into the city. Surely he would be waiting for her. Her heart pounded, uneven; she wondered if she had mistaken him. It was true, it was Eleanor, always, he obeyed. She went out into Poitiers and went around the streets until the moon rose, but she could not find de Rançun.

◆　◆　◆

She had nowhere to go except back to the Maubergeon. No one stopped her. No one seemed to notice her, much. She went to her old room in the tower. It was empty, as she had left it: the hearth cold, the stool in the middle of the room, the bed tossed as she had gotten up those weeks before, the wardrobe door ajar. The window was wide open and the cold air swept in. She went into the room and stood there, strange in her own mind, wondering what she was to do now.

She wondered where he had gone. Back to Taillebourg, his family's great castle on the Charente. She remembered waking that morning, wrapped in his arms, to a moment of perfect happiness, and thinking, *This is all I ever get.*

She went and sat on the bed, weary. After a little while, there was a knock on the door.

She opened it to find a short, squat young woman, a village girl, standing there with something in her arms, wrapped in a blanket. The woman bobbed a little bow. Petronilla frowned at her, puzzled, and then looked at the blanket.

A low cry escaped her. A wash of warmth flooded her. She lifted the little bundle out of the little woman's arms, and with one hand spread apart the blanket. Inside layers of wool the baby's face was a perfect flower, pink, with tiny lips, and closed eyes like curves of gleaming shell.

Then the dark blue eyes opened, and their shining look wrung her to the heels.

"Yes," she said, breathless. "Yes." She turned to the wet nurse. "Come in. I will keep it with me." She lowered her head and kissed the baby's forehead. "This is mine, now."

She laid the baby on the bed, and opened the blanket, and then unwound the swaddling bands; the wet nurse murmured something, and Petronilla gave her a sharp look and the girl smiled apologetically and was quiet. Petronilla turned back to the baby.

It was a boy, with a square chest, great red balls, a little hooded hose. She crowed at this; a son, at last. He was big, a strapping boy, his broad shoulders lightly fuzzed with hair, and long legs, a wide forehead, a strong jaw. She laughed to see him; she was in love at once. She thought, I took him for my own, back at the beginning, in Paris. I won him, in this ordeal. This is my prize.

His thick hair was dark, but she thought she saw a red tinge in it. For a while he lay there, his eyes open, and his arms and legs waggling aimlessly, while she stroked him and talked to him and counted his fingers and toes, inspected the black stump coming out of his navel, and let him curl his hand around her thumb. He was the most beautiful boy she had ever seen. She told him so several times. He turned toward her voice, his eyes vague.

She lifted him into her arms; he seemed to weigh nothing. He nuzzled at her, and began to mewl. At first she stiffened, frightened, with nothing to give him, helpless before his demands. Then she began to sway him back and forth, and sing. That quieted him, and he lay in her arms, his eyes open, looking up at her face.

She said, "I need to name you. Nothing that means anything, you see, no Williams, or Ranulphs, or Fulks. Or—heaven help us— Henry. Else everybody will know, and you are my secret boy." She laid him down on the bed again, licked her thumb, and made the sign of the cross on his forehead. "I name you Philip. And may you love horses, and everybody else love you."

The wet nurse emitted another disapproving squeak. The baby began to quest around with his lips, and presently wailed, and Petronilla drew back and nodded to let the nurse take him.

She sent for firewood and had them lay a good fire in the hearth. Some women she had never seen before came in and made her bed for her. They bowed to her when they left, their eyes never looking at her. One murmured, "My lady Petronilla," before they left. The name was like a draught of wine. She was Petronilla again forever.

But she dragged along Petronilla's fate; she was left behind again. She thought of de Rançun, probably well gone now toward his own castle, and shut down the memory before it hurt too much.

The wet nurse took the baby off to wherever she slept, probably next door. She might hear the baby cry in the night. She wondered if she could have him and the wet nurse sleep in her room. Her breasts felt taut, useless. She wished she had milk to give him; it seemed the most tender thing in the world.

She stood alone in the room, suddenly feeling all the space around her. Empty. She had thought herself coming into her own kingdom, and maybe this was all there was, this loneliness, this uselessness, someone else's child she could not even nourish.

She lit a candle and stood by the fire, taking off her coif; Eleanor had ripped it, and she cast it to the floor. She shook her hair loose. Tomorrow she would find someone to brush it. Now it reached down in a tangled mass to her waist. She would need women of her own, a court of her own. A house, perhaps, of her own. Gracelessly she fought her way out of the filthy gown.

"Petra."

She whirled, every hair on end.

"Petra," he said, again, standing there, and she rushed into his arms.

"I looked for you—" She was near weeping. She pressed her mouth to his, her arms around his neck.

"Did you think I could leave you?" He hugged her tight against him. "I could not leave you here." He laughed and drew back, to look her in the face. "I thought to protect you from her, but it was Eleanor who needed protecting!" He kissed her again. "The way you flew at her—she was afraid of you. You have the soul of a hero, my darling, in a woman's body."

His hands pressed against her back, covered only by the underdress and the shift. His lips tickled her ear. His finger slipped over the crevice at the top of her buttocks. "Which I am forever finding you unclothing."

She kissed him again, her arms around his neck, and felt his embrace tighten around her. She never wanted to stop kissing him. His tongue grazed her underlip, the inside of her cheek. She blazed with a long-pent, pure desire; she had been waiting long, long for this, and she would wait no more.

He said, "Shall I help you take off the rest?" His fingers tugged lightly on the underdress, gathering it up.

She leaned back, his arms still around her waist, and put her hands on his coat. "How do you get this off?" She reached down to his belt and unbuckled it. He gave a startled, amused yelp, and caught the belt and the scabbarded sword before they hit the ground, one arm still around her waist. He tossed the sword to one side with a clatter and bent so she could see his shoulder.

"Undo the clasp." He went back to pulling her dress up; he got the skirts around her waist, and his hand slid down over her bare buttock. She shuddered in a rush of feeling. She found the brooch on his shoulder and pulled the pin out, and his coat fell away. Lifting her arms, she let him lift the dress and the shift up over her head.

He dropped them on the floor, let her go briefly to strip off his tunic, and stood with his hands on her arms, looking at her body, his eyes wide. She put her hands on his bare chest.

"I've never seen you naked before," she said, and her fingertip ran down a long white scar through the curly blond hair on his chest.

"Nor I you," he said. "We're new to each other now; we need to learn everything new." He bent and kissed her mouth, tender and sweet. "Everything starts now, all new." She wrapped her arms around his neck, her body tingling with desire, and he scooped her up in his arms and carried her to the bed.

. . .

She woke beside him, in the first dawn of Easter Sunday, when everything was redeemed. He still slept. Her gaze trailed slowly along him, his mass of fair curly hair, his sun-browned cheekbone. The square jaw stubbled with light blond beard, which had rasped along her thighs the night before, tickled her in hidden places. He had shown her ways to love she had never known before, more intimate, more thrilling than anything she had ever known before. With his mind sunk away in sleep, his body was like an offering to her: the broad chest with its fair hair, muscled like armor, the belly sunken a little below the ribs, and beneath, the soft curl of his penis. She wanted to touch him there. She wanted to inspect him all over, as she had the baby, hers, now, hers alone.

He stirred. His eyes opened, bright blue. He said, "I have to go soon." He reached for her hand and held it, and kissed it. "Come with me to Taillebourg. I beg you. I'd not dishonor you, sneaking like this." His smile bloomed, turning his eyes brighter. "Although there's too much love between us for a marriage, I think."

She said, "You have made your honor into a shield for me; you cannot dim it for me now, whatever you do. But I have to stay here, Joffre. There's still something between me and my sister."

"What?" He put her hand on his shoulder, pulling her closer; his penis was stiffening, fierce.

"I don't know," she said. She wanted him again, and she never wanted him gone again. She said, "Stay with me. Please. Stay." She gave him her mouth, her lips parted.

He rolled her onto her back and kissed her, long and deep, a kiss that pinioned her fast. "For a while," he said. "Not forever. You'll have to choose sometime, Petronilla."

She gulped; she spread her knees for him. *I have chosen*, she thought. The sudden thrust of his body filled her, connected her, made them one being. She cried out, her head thrown back under the power of it, possessed.

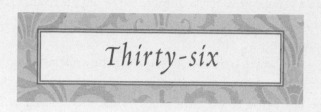

Thirty-six

NORMANDY

MAY 1152

The Empress Matilda had ailed all winter, as she sometimes did, getting even thinner and paler, but she would not stay in her own bower. Her sharp voice was always edged with temper. She complained that the trouvère had left, and had more lute players and singers brought to her, in a constant stream, but all of those she cast aside. She sat on her bed, and her servants carried the whole bed around, and she cursed the servants and ordered everybody around, even Henry, when she could find him, although Henry seldom did what she wanted.

Now, some days after Easter, she had her servants carry her, bed and all, to attend the council at Lisieux that would proclaim the Duke of Normandy's new campaign against England.

The council was in the great hall, and as she came to the door, her son came there also. She paused to admire him, although she would never admit this. He was strong and square and high-headed, and even in his youth he gave off a glitter of power. She thought, *I have done well with him.*

He gave her a proper bow, as she had taught him to do as a child, whipping him soundly when he forgot. He approached her, her strapping son, in a fine coat carelessly worn. The little sprig of yellow broom in his cap was an emblem he had taken from his father. In his hand there was a paper, maybe something to tell the council. His eyes shone. He said, "Arundel has come, and Leicester is here. Did you get the money?"

She said, "There is money enough, in the coffers, if you are not profligate." She plucked the paper from his hand. "What is this?"

"One last castle to take," he said. "This one yielding of its own will."

He watched her eyes turn to the fine slanted writing. Leaving the letter in her hands, he went off toward the hall, where the barons were gathered.

Months before he had come here to an empty room. This time from the door he looked out over a pack of bodies from wall to wall. All waiting on him now, a bow, a smile, a "Yes, my lord, of course, my lord." He felt his chest swell under his coat. He saw, out there, in a circle of retainers, the Earl of Leicester himself, come from England just for this, tall, white-haired, a bright feather in his cap.

Henry had everything all prepared, a plan in detail for attacking England, and he did not need every one of these men—only some— but having all would bring the some along with them. In fact, he suspected that with the support of some, Leicester, for instance, and the letter he had intercepted from King Louis, he could make an arrangement to win England without a blow struck. Stephen had betrayed them all—and somehow the fool had put it down in writing. But always best to have a mailed fist and a sword ready, in case.

Now he would have another matter to put before them, not that they had any say in it; he would marry where he wanted. It was possible that getting married could delay the invasion. Louis for one would have some objections. Behind him he heard his mother cry out in despair. At last she had felt her way through Eleanor's letter to the part that mattered. He stood looking into the hall, seeing the men who only a few months ago hadn't bothered even to answer his summons, who had closed their castle gates against him, until he forced them open. When they saw him they would bow, acknowledging their master. He went down quickly among them, to take them by surprise.

Thirty-seven

POITIERS

MAY 1152

Eleanor had sent out the letter to Henry soon after the battle with Petronilla. She was Eleanor again, and all knew it. Petronilla kept to her tower. Henry of Normandy kept to the north.

Only a few days after Petronilla reached Poitiers, the wagons bearing Alys and the other women rolled up through the gates. Eleanor met them in the courtyard of the palace. Alys flung herself from the wagon and rushed to her, remembered abruptly to bow, and then came into her embrace.

"Ah, we're back, we're back—" Into Eleanor's ear, she whispered, "Did Petronilla come?"

Eleanor hugged her. "We are all back," she said, in a voice to reach all those around them, "where we belong. Petronilla's in her tower, and I am in mine." She met Alys's eyes, and Alys gave a little nod. Her smile widened, triumphant, and her forehead smoothed, clear as a child's.

She said, "Your Grace, wait until you hear our tale." The other women and the grooms were emptying the wagons; of them only Alys was the Duchess's real friend, and the two of them went up the steps into the Maubergeon.

In the hall, Eleanor looked her kinswoman over, head to foot, smiling. "I have missed you much. But you seem to have borne it well."

"Oh, Your Grace." Alys turned to her; around them the servants bustled with boxes and baskets, a rising chatter of voices, and the other women fluttering and laughing. Eleanor led Alys toward the stairs.

"When we rode into Blois," Alys said, "it was as we had been warned; a host of men fell on us. We had told each other to scream and fuss and try to hide, to make it that much harder for them to realize they had been duped." She laughed. "How they looked, when they began to suspect—it was all I could do to keep a long face."

They climbed the stairs toward Eleanor's own chamber. Eleanor wound her arm through Alys's. "I wish I had seen it, the beast. And here is Marie-Jeanne."

The other woman rushed down the top few steps to Alys and hugged her. They all went into the Duchess's chamber. Alys was still bubbling with the excitement of the wild flight, although Eleanor suspected it was more exciting now that it was safely done.

She wondered if she would ever hear the rest, how Petronilla had raced away alone into the wild, how Petronilla had escaped.

"Finally," Alys said, "the Count himself came, who knows you by sight—please sit down, Your Grace—Marie-Jeanne, bring me the brush—and he looked at each of us in turn."

Eleanor smiled to imagine this; even Marie-Jeanne chuckled. Alys said, "He turned the color of a raw beefsteak, and made us all get out, and searched the wagons, all the while giving off oaths—I dare not repeat them to you, they were so awful—especially not what he said when he finally admitted you weren't there."

The brush dug into Eleanor's hair. She said, "What a rude boy. Did he at least give you feasting and safe haven overnight?"

Alys crowed. "Oh, they didn't care about us. He was so angry, my lady, I wanted only to be far away—but you were long gone by then."

She stooped and kissed Eleanor's shoulder. She said, "You made all women great with this, Your Grace. We are all greater for you."

Eleanor murmured something. Alys's memory had flowed back smoothly into its prescribed course, wiping out the traces of what had really happened, maybe even in her own mind. The other women were coming in, leading pages and grooms with crates of clothes. Each of them as she arrived came and knelt down at Eleanor's feet and blessed her happily; their eyes shining. Alys was right; what she had done enlarged them. What they thought she had done. Her mind went unwillingly to Petronilla. But if they saw any difference between this Eleanor and the one they had seen last on the banks of the Loire, no one spoke.

She said, "Some ladies of good birth must be found to attend my sister, if you will all stay with me."

Alys was stroking the brush through her hair. "Let me see to it, Your Grace." Her voice was smooth. Eleanor felt a ripple of unease in her belly. She thought, *You do not know. What lies between me and Petronilla still seethes. You think it is all over.* She put her hand up, and Alys took hold of her fingers, reassuring.

◆   ◆   ◆

With Petronilla back, Eleanor could step forth in her own name. She began at once to shape her court. Several people still clung to office who were relics of King Louis's rule, and she sent them home. She named Matthieu, her long-faithful steward, to manage her household, but she still needed pages, attendants, knights, all of the highest families.

A few families sent younger sons to be pages, but she could tell, by the ones who did not, that they were still waiting to see how she fared here, ruling alone. She got some women from the city up; mannerless as they were, they were apt enough, and their talk lively. She already had the knights who had gone with her sister to Beaugency and back, and a few more came, younger sons, wanderers. Without de Rançun, there was no one to command them.

The greater lords sent not their children, but heralds, greeting her, rejoicing in her escape from the traps laid for her, promising her whatever they thought would get them some advantage. She received them in the great hall, all hung now with tapestry and gold cloth, crowded with as many of her new court as she could get in there, loud with trumpets and drums, a great show. Bordeaux's herald was especially fine, with a scarlet tabard trimmed all in fox, and a hat with a long Spanish plume, and his speech went on upward of an hour.

There also, in the great hall, she held her court. She had a single throne put on the dais in the center of the cold, echoing room, and heard everyone who came to her with a grievance: the jilted bride wanting her dowry back, the shepherds with a quarrel about marks on rocks, the merchants fighting over street stalls and gate tolls, wanting favors, wanting privileges. She gave no one privileges. When a rich man of Bordeaux offered her a bribe, she threw him into the stocks and hung his purse from his nose.

She settled every argument according to the justice of it, as keenly as she could see it; she knew that was all that stood between her and robbery.

She sent off the palace cooks and got new ones, and made the grooms wear coats all of the same red. She found women to sew bold red coats for her pages and bargained for more cloth from the east. Every morning and every evening her kitchen gave out whole-baked loaves to the poor. She invited the local merchants to bring her their goods to see, so that every day, in the hall, there was a display of fine things. Every day she went to a different church in the city and lit candles.

When she went out into the street, the crowds cheered her; they called her name from the rooftops and followed her all the way home. Still, there was no sign of Duke Henry.

She summoned a council of the local lords—she knew the great barons would not answer: Talmond, Angouleme and Limoges, Chatellerault, Lusignan, and, now, de Rançun. The local men were more dependent on her and could not ignore her. At the council, to reward them, she named them all to high offices, seneschal and marshal and constable, which they were glad to have, preening themselves. She laid heavy taxes on them, then, which they liked less, but could not deny her. So she had money coming.

Through this council she commanded the Vicomte de Limoges that he should remove his unpermitted wall. She also commanded her cousin, the Vicomte of Chatellerault, to bring her men-at-arms to go against Limoges. She sent forth generally a command that the French law no longer held in Aquitaine, and that she would give law here, and no other.

No word came from Limoges. From the Vicomte de Chatellerault a written message arrived that he would bring an army to her when she consented to marry him.

She had the money now to buy an army; all she needed was a commander. She had never needed one before, but she had botched that. Still, she thought, maybe she could do this alone.

That was less than she wanted. She stood on the top of the tower, looking north, wanting more. Wanting everything.

♦   ♦   ♦

One morning while she was hearing two people argue about ownership of a stream, she looked up and saw a dark curly head she knew coming in the doorway.

Behind him, wrapped in a gray cloak, was Claire. Her heart jumped like a lovelorn girl's, and she shifted impatiently in her throne. The weary arguments of the two Poitevins who had been fighting over this waterway for generations could drone for hours, and she cut them off with a wave of her hand. She told them to come back later, when she had thought it out, and as they left, she sent a page for Thomas the lute player.

"God keep you, lady," he said, with a bow.

"You are very welcome here," she said. "That I bade you do, in Normandy, how did that go?"

"I gave the message to the Duke himself, my lady," he said. "He was very glad to get it, I think. He acted on it right away."

"Good. He kept you at his court?"

"Until Lent, my lady, and then we went off again."

"Then tell me—how does my lord Normandy?" She stopped, ashamed to look overeager. Her gaze went by him to Claire, who was smiling and bent her knee in a quick dip.

Thomas said, "He was well enough, when I saw him. But we left Rouen a while ago, my lady; I know nothing of him now." He bobbed his head again, as much as he ever gave anybody of a bow. "My lady, we need your permission, Claire and I—" He reached his hand out behind him, and she came forward, smiling. "We have married," he said, "which may not sit well with her family."

Eleanor laughed. "No, I suppose not. It sits with me." Her smile widened, and she looked on Claire with a new pride. "God bless you both. Welcome to my court." To him, she said, "Play."

But she wished he had some news for her of Henry. Her skin felt cold; he was not coming. His mother, or something he had learned, or his barons kept him north.

Thomas had sat down below the dais, and the first soft tones of the lute reached her ears. She turned to call a page and announce that the court was over, so she could go somewhere quieter and closer, to lose herself in the music.

·   ·   ·

Claire went off as soon as she could and climbed the stair to the blue tower. The door at the top of the stairs was open, and she could hear Alys's voice; she went to the threshold and looked in.

What she saw gladdened her. Alys was helping Petronilla dress, the gown slipped on over her head, her arms raised to find the sleeves.

In the corner, a baby suckled noisily, his nurse wrapped around him like a piece of furniture. Claire slipped into the room, and Petronilla, poking her head up through the gown, saw her and said, "There you are!"

She pulled out of Alys's arms and went to Claire and hugged her. She held Claire's hand, and smiled at her, and turned to Alys.

"Remember? She saved us."

"Sssh, my lady," Alys said. "But I am glad to see you, Claire."

Petronilla said, "Come see the baby. Alys, tell her what happened after—in Blois." She straightened her gown and stepped into her own shoes. To Claire, she said, "We do not live such quiet lives, after all."

Alys picked up the nightdress and shook it out. She began a story that sounded as if she had told it several times before, which still got Petronilla laughing. Claire laughed, thinking of the balked fury of the would-be abductors. Petronilla had lifted the baby away from the nurse, and danced around the room with it, which beguiled her more. She went across the room to watch her, laughing at the right places in Alys's story. Petronilla stopped long enough to show her the child's face.

"Philip," she said. "He's a boy." She danced off again.

Claire smiled to see this; she thought everything had worked out well. She stood by the bed, which was still unmade. Alys was coming to the peak of her tale, her arms waving, describing the knights' desperate searches. Claire smoothed the bedclothes, meaning to put the bed together when the story ended.

She saw, then, that the pillows were hollowed out as if two heads had slept there, side by side. She glanced at Alys, who with wild arms and tossing head was demonstrating the Count of Blois's complete dismay. Alys might not have noticed. Quickly Claire plumped the pillows up and drew the covers higher. A curly fair hair flew from one linen flounce into the sunlight. She glanced at Petronilla again, amazed.

Petronilla had stopped dancing, had seen Claire do all this, and stood staring at her, a challenge on her face. The baby in her arms waved a little fist.

Claire said, "I'm glad he didn't hurt you," to Alys. She stood in front of the bed.

Alys said, "Oh, he wouldn't dare."

Claire turned to making the bed up. "I think you were very brave, nonetheless."

Petronilla said, "Alys, you should go—my sister needs you."

Alys said, "I can—"

"Come back later," Petronilla said, and the tall waiting woman left. Petronilla fixed her eyes on Claire.

"What are you thinking?"

Claire said, "That a lot has happened. You and the Queen—the Duchess—you are where you belong." She nodded at the baby. "He is a beautiful baby."

Petronilla's face settled, and she took the baby to the young nurse and shooed them both out. When she came back, her face was grim. She sat down next to Claire on the bed.

She said, "We are not where we belong. We are at odds, Eleanor and I, and like to be forever. She tried to have me killed. If he were a lesser man, I would be killed."

Claire started. She turned her gaze back toward the pillow, thinking of the curly fair hair. She realized then she had not seen him, who had always before been close around the Duchess. She said, "God bless him, then. But I cannot believe—"

"I can. She saw some danger in me, in spite of all I had done, and her use for me was over." Petronilla's hand was furiously pulling at the bedcover. "Except that I should take her baby, which I gladly do."

Claire said, "You will not forgive her."

"I can never forgive her. I am not a sister to her, or even a friend, just a tool she can use. If she ever loved me—"

She broke off. Bright tears trembled on the lashes of her eyes. She said, "I'm glad you're back, Claire. You at least I can talk to." She slid off the bed. "Help me make this bed. That was careless of me; thank you."

◆　◆　◆

He stretched out on the bed, his arms over his head, the candlelight glinting on the golden hair on his chest. "She won't tell anybody?"

"No," Petronilla said. "She has changed, too, you can see it; she is a woman now. She hid what she saw from Alys. She knows Alys loves to gossip."

He caught her hand and kissed it. "I worry about you. What Eleanor might do."

She laughed. "More worry what I might do to her."

The baby stirred in the corner; she lifted her head, but he settled again. The wet nurse was downstairs, and Petronilla would send a page for her when the baby woke hungry.

De Rançun said, "I can't stay much longer. Someone will see me. She has sent for Henry. I have not spent the last year studying him for no reason. I know what he will do. As soon as he gets here, she will set him on Limoges and that wall. I need to be behind my own walls before whatever happens there happens."

Petronilla wondered where he went during the day; he appeared here only after dark. She said, "If he comes."

He made a noise in his throat. "Of course he will come. Would he decline the doubling of his lands, his power? If she were a pocky hag, he would come."

"She's hardly a pocky hag."

"The more hastily he will come."

Petronilla said, slowly, "Then, if he comes, if he makes the right choice . . ."

"Which is?"

She put her head down, saying nothing. She laid her hand on his chest; he was watching her, sharp, the light shining clear in his eyes. He turned and blew the candle out, and did not ask her again.

◆   ◆   ◆

Some days later, when Claire was in the hall with Thomas, a page came to bid her up to the Duchess's chamber. No one was there but Eleanor, standing by the hearth, and she sent the page swiftly off. Claire made a bow to the Duchess. She had spent the morning helping Petronilla with the baby, and she imagined she still smelled of spoiled milk. The mother of the baby faced her, exactly as Claire remembered her: the gold circlet of her coronet on the thick coppery braids of her hair, the red slippers peeping out below the hem of her gown.

Eleanor said, "I am glad to have you back, Claire. You need not fear your father."

"Thank you, Your Grace." Claire folded her hands in front of her; she was joyous to be back in Poitiers, and to have the Duchess so kind to her. This loosened her tongue, and she blurted, "In truth I wondered which of you I would find here, Your Grace." At that she put her hand to her mouth, amazed at what had come out of her.

Eleanor's face widened with her smile. "Well, are you disappointed?"

"Your Grace, you are both here, I can hope for no better. And you have always been Aquitaine." She shook her head. "No one ever else could be the Duchess of Aquitaine save you."

To her relief, she saw that pleased Eleanor, or amused her. She seemed much loftier, as if before the King had dragged her down. Muffled her. Her eyes now met Claire's, direct.

"You went with your husband to the Duke of Normandy?"

"Yes, Your Grace. He wasn't my husband then."

The smile grew impish. "I remember how he was. God give you the strength for him. Did you see the Duke of Normandy at all?"

"Oh, not much, Your Grace. He took us to his mother's court, in Rouen."

The wide green eyes flashed, brilliant. "His mother. The Empress. What sort of woman is she? I have never met her."

Claire said, "She is lean and dry as a stick, Your Grace. She looks sickly to me, as if something eats her inside out, but she still wants to put her hands on everything." She drew a breath and told Eleanor what she had to know.

"She does not want her son to marry you. They are stodgy in the north; I see not how they have children." *Except*, she thought, *they all be by Duke Henry.*

Eleanor gave a southern whoop of laughter. Claire smiled wide; their eyes met. Claire said, "The Duke Henry pays her very little heed. He is a hard one, Your Grace."

"He has other women," Eleanor said.

"I saw that not, but I heard it, Your Grace."

"You spoke to him."

"No, Your Grace. Not once. Thomas did."

"You spoke to his mother."

"She heard nothing interesting from me, Your Grace; she said I was dull."

Eleanor understood that; her eyes widened, and her chin lifted. "You kept my secrets, Claire. For this I am obliged to you."

"Lady," she said, "for what I have had of you, I am more obliged."

The Duchess nodded. "What lies ahead of us we cannot know. What went before we soon forget. You have seen my sister."

"Yes, Your Grace."

"You know she and I are out with each other."

"Yes, Your Grace, she told me."

Eleanor gave a shake of her head. "Then she told you why." She waited a moment, but Claire said nothing. Eleanor said, wistfully, "Is she well?"

Claire said, "She is, Your Grace. She is herself again. I think this is all she ever wanted."

The woman before her made a sudden movement, her hands rising. She turned away, and her fingers intertwined. "Ah, that's a torment. Then I can remember her as she truly is. Yet I cannot be in her company that so delighted me. This is cold." She walked around the room, rubbing her hands together.

Finally, she faced Claire again. "You are to go again to Petronilla."

Claire said, "Yes, she has asked me."

"Tell her—" The green eyes blazed. "Tell her I want my sister back."

"Your Grace—" Claire shifted uneasily, her hands rising uncertainly before her. "You must talk to her, not I."

"I can't." Eleanor turned away. "I fear too much what she would say. I would throw myself into a fire before I could hear what she might say. Do as I bid you; no harm shall come to you, whatever happens."

"Yes, Your Grace," Claire said, and she bowed and went away.

◆ ◆ ◆

Claire went down to the common hall again, full as always with the Duchess's people. Thomas sat by the hearth playing. She thought of what the Duchess had said, and Petronilla, and tried to fathom what had come between them, when they had always been so close.

She thought, Duke Henry. Yet surely that was not the redheaded Henry's hair on Petronilla's pillow. She went up and sat next to Thomas, who glanced at her and went back to playing some line of notes, over and over, humming to himself.

She laid her hand over her belly; she thought about what was happening down there. For that they needed a sure place here. That required the favor of the Duchess, which meant there could be no double-dealing. She waited until Thomas had stopped a moment and taken a drink of wine.

She said, "When we left Rouen, I remember, you went aside with the Duke a moment, didn't you?"

"Unh. I don't remember. Oh, he gave me a purse." He twiddled the quill in his fingers, his face bland.

"You are such a bad liar." She swatted him. "I should lie to you about how he caught me in the corner, one time, and tried to kiss me."

His face flew into a furious scowl. "Did he? I'll kill him."

"Or do I lie? Tell me what he said to you, that time in Rouen." She cupped her hands together in her lap.

"Oh, nothing much." His eyes narrowed. "I remember that time—how you looked, afterward—frightened. Was it then?"

She stared him in the eyes. She said, "So, one lie or another, what does it matter?"

He frowned at her a moment. At last, he put the lute down. He said, "I take your point. The Duke bade me heed everything that happens here, and report it to him, and he would reward me well."

She had thought this was likely so. She thought, ruefully, she knew too much of courts. "What did you say?"

"That I would—I did not say yes. But you can't say no to a man like that."

She gave a low growl in her throat. "Are you a musician or a spy?"

His frown deepened a moment, and then went away. His eyes glinted. He leaned forward and kissed her mouth. "You are my soul, my dear one."

She said, "I have been a spy. I would rather be a musician." She thought at least whatever happened between Eleanor and Duke Henry and Petronilla would not fall at her and Thomas's feet. She put her head down on Thomas's shoulder, her hand on her belly, content.

* * *

Petronilla could hear the noisy excitement of the court, and she could not keep herself from going to see it. She went down to the side door, at the foot of the stairs to her tower, and stood there.

Before her was the court of Aquitaine, a dance of color and faces. Thick as bees at a hive, men in splendid coats and women in ornately twisted coifs were gathered, talking, and watching each other watching them. They moved constantly, a shifting of interest, allegiance, opportunity. Over by the hearth, Thomas the lute player sat beside another man with a lute, maybe teaching him something; Claire stood beyond him, with three other women, their mouths open wide and their chests pumping. They were singing, but the uproar in the great hall was so much, few could have heard them. A swarm of knaves came in with a great load of wood, which they began to pitch into the pit of the hearth.

The people around Petronilla saw her and dropped into elegant bows. A man swept the floor with his cap. Up there she saw that the great table was empty. Her sister had not come down yet. Around her all were murmuring, bowing. She wore no finery, but, she thought, she needed none. She went out among these people, glad of the noise and laughter.

She waved her hand to Claire, who sang as if her chest were bursting, her voice inaudible in the general racket. Behind her, someone said, "'Tis the Lady Petronilla!"

She almost turned and smiled at him. A scattered cheer went up, and she raised her hand again, and more cheered. In the back door came the cook, leading the way for four scullions bearing aloft a huge platter with a whole boar, the head still on, the eyes bulging black plums, shiny with sauce and lying on a thicket of green boughs.

A trumpet blew. The whole crowd turned, suddenly, toward the main door, and their voices rose in a roar of excitement. Petronilla stood, the hackles on her neck rising; then she saw her sister coming in.

Eleanor wore a gown of green stitched with gold, bands of gold along the front and on the deep cuffs. She wore no coif, her red hair done high on her head in coils of braids. The gold circle around it seemed a decoration to the real crown. Petronilla turned and went, swiftly. Everybody else surged the other way, crying out Eleanor's name, trying to get closer to her radiance.

◆   ◆   ◆

The trumpets were still blaring out their flourishes. The Duchess of Aquitaine went to the great table and stood behind her chair, and before her the whole room bobbed down in a grand obeisance. She stood straight, her chin up, their ruler. Far across the room, she saw the one whom she really wanted to see rush out another door, gone.

She lowered her eyes to her subjects. They swayed and dipped before her, a sea of patchy colors: gold and red, green and silver, dark blue, Tyrian purple. They loved her. They were not enough. She let the steward draw back her chair and sat down.

◆   ◆   ◆

A few days later, she sat in her privy chamber, before her a dozen men from Bordeaux. She had already discussed this with the Archbishop, who was their lord, but she knew she had to get these men, the city men, the merchants, to agree to this to make it work.

She sat with her hands on her knees, square to them, and looked each one in the face as she spoke. She said, "Lately enough ships have come in and out of Bordeaux to cause problems. You've told me this, blaming each other. What will help is this. I saw this in Antioch, where my uncle was prince, and where ships have used the harbor since Jesus' time and before." She stopped and stared at them, her eyebrows arched, until they fumbled and mumbled and bowed.

"Yes, Your Grace."

"First, let each ship in and out in order. This means you must keep good records of their arrivals and departures. Second, gather a company of your own pilots, train them, and let only them handle ships. Third, you are to stop bribery, and instead collect regular fees. Of which I shall have a certain part. And four times a year my steward will come in to see how your records look, to make sure this is all as it should be."

That struck them as if she had spat at them; they stared at her a moment, stunned, and then they all babbled at once, their voices piling over each other as the women's voices did in a round. She picked out certain phrases.

". . . families who have been pilots for generations—"

"There are no bribes."

"Satan's work, it is. Number is the mark of the Beast."

She said, "You will do this or my uncle Bordeaux will have you under an interdict and you will get nothing."

"It won't work." Through tight lips like a squeezed purse.

"Oh, it will work. And there's more, once we have these simple rules in place. And you will heed me, because I am your Duchess, and all you do is by my will."

That silenced them. She sat back, drank some wine, and let them fret awhile. Then she gave them some gifts, absolving them of certain taxes and duties, which made them much happier.

Just as she was beginning to dismiss them, Alys burst in.

"Your Grace. He's here. He's here, Your Grace—"

Eleanor gasped. She knew at once what she meant. She was not ready. She drove the burghers of Bordeaux out and turned to Alys.

"Send him up. Him alone." She shook out her gown, not her best, but a good color.

Alys flew out. Eleanor's heart was hammering in her chest. She reached up to her coif, pulled it off, and let her hair tumble down all around her shoulders. With her fingers she picked out the braids. She would come to this like a maiden, a new woman. She shook her head to toss her hair around her, and slapped her cheeks to make them rosy.

* * *

Henry went up the steps, outpacing the pages; the guard shrank back from the door. He walked into a beautiful room, all green and gold, and in the center of it, Eleanor with her blazing red hair.

She said, "Welcome, my lord."

His heart was beating fast from the run. He felt light-headed. He said what he had planned, coming down, "You're even more beautiful than I remembered." But she was. He had not remembered how green her eyes were. She came to him and kissed him, and he put his arms around her, his body pulsing. She smelled like roses. Behind him, the door opened again, and closed.

Eleanor was facing that way, and she gave a start. Breaking out of his arms, she moved a step away from him. He turned, and saw another Eleanor.

This one held a swaddled baby in her arms. She said, "Eleanor. Will you tell him the truth, or shall I?"

Eleanor was moving. She went straight toward this other woman, like a hawk stooping to the kill. The woman with the baby stiffened, as if to meet an attack.

But reaching her, Eleanor slid her arm around her waist and, side by side with her, turned to face him. Her voice rang out. "My lord. Behold, our son."

He took a step backward. His jaw dropped. His mind was a jumble; he remembered all the rumors, the puzzles of the last year. She had tricked him. Lied to him, at Saint Pierre. Brought him someone's bastard. Then at Limoges—that had not been her. They had both tricked him.

When he realized that, the red temper surged in him. No woman had ever mocked him so. The two facing him had made a fool of him. Of him, of Louis, of all of Christendom. Their faces were bright with defiance, they knew they had done evil. They never looked at each other, but they clung to each other. His first feeling was a rush of shame. Words sizzled in his throat, to curse her, the whore, both of them, to disengage himself.

He choked that back. He steadied his mind. He had not worked all this while to turn now from the triumph. Anyway, as his temper waned, his ardor rose.

He could not take his eyes from the two women. He remembered she had a sister; this was Petronilla, then. They were so alike, and yet unalike. Each more beautiful than the other. The lush mouths, the high sloped cheekbones, the skin like cream. He recognized the one he had tumbled in Paris and in Saint Pierre, and the one who had made him kneel in Limoges. Eleanor was a hair taller. The sister was slighter, her hair a shade lighter. They gave off some allure, some aura, like a golden glow around them. He wanted them both, whatever they had done. The more, because of what they had done, like wild mares that would not be tamed, that he longed to bridle and ride.

He went to the real Eleanor. He said, "My lady Aquitaine. I knew I loved you from the first I saw you. I did not know how much, until now. You were born to share a crown with me. This boy, untimely come as he is, let him be the harbinger of the princes and princesses who will crowd our court. I want you; be my wife."

She gave a low cry, and came into his arms and kissed him. Her gold-spangled eyes were suddenly huge with tears. So she had not known what he would do. She had risked it all, for the sake of her sister, who stood there smiling wide at them, the baby in her arms.

Eleanor said, "Then we marry tomorrow. Are you ready?" She spun on his fingertips, glittering, within reach now, the sun in a woman's body. Aquitaine. He heard a door shut quietly. Petronilla had gone. He put his hands on Eleanor and drew her into his arms.

◆ ◆ ◆

It was a hasty wedding, without much decoration. All through the ceremony, not caring to be noticed, Petronilla stayed in the dark of the little palace chapel, in the back. Afterward, she went out by a side door to the churchyard, to where a great crowd waited, merry as a maying. The day was bright and lovely, with a few little clouds scudding through the sky, and the smell of new-turned earth in the breeze. She climbed up the wall to the rampart by the arch, out of the way, and watched Eleanor and Henry come out of the church.

With whoops and cheers, her followers and his surrounded them, laughing and throwing flowers. Alys and Marie-Jeanne hugged each other. Eleanor had worn her long hair down, loose; certainly her life was beginning over. They made a new marriage, here, and a great new kingdom.

Only Eleanor, she thought, only Eleanor could have done this, defied the men's order and the women's bargain, seen that this thing was possible and then done it. Leaped outside the old cramped shell of womanhood and doing so, shattered it, maybe forever, and made the whole world wait on her.

The long red hair swung like a shawl around the Duchess of Aquitaine. Out on the pavement before the chapel, her new Duke caught her hands and kissed her. She flung her head back and laughed, her face high-colored. Flowers dappled her hair, her gown. Henry clutched her against him, kissed her throat, her ear. Petronilla guessed they had not waited on the ceremony to start the true work of the marriage.

Her lover came up behind her and slid his arm around her. She put her hands on his where it rested on her belt and leaned back against his chest.

"Was that the right choice?"

"For Eleanor, it was," she said. "For him, well, he's brought it on himself."

When she carried the baby into the Green Tower, she had seen in Henry's face how close he was to backing away from all this. But he had not. He deserved Eleanor.

"For you?" he said. "Are you friends again?"

"Yes," she said. "She stood with me against him. And we were always sisters."

In the courtyard, Eleanor and Henry held hands, turning around each other, laughing, her hair streaming like a silken flag, his face shining dark with mirth. He was trying to get her to go one way and she was pulling the other, laughing, still, laughing about it now, but this would be more a combat than a marriage.

She looked up at de Rançun, beside her. "Do you miss her?"

"I have you," he said. He kissed her hair. "Come along."

She followed him to the stairs down the outside wall. At the foot of the stairs, by the gate, his black horse and the gray Barb waited, their reins in the hands of a groom. The Barb's mane was studded with red rosettes, and he tossed his head, eager. She went down to him, and de Rançun came after her, to lift her into the saddle.

Afterword

This is perhaps a novel interpretation of the scraps and pieces we know about the great Queen Eleanor of Aquitaine. Nothing herein contradicts those few known facts.

Medieval politics were family politics, and Eleanor of Aquitaine was the matriarch of the greatest family of them all. Her time could be called the Age of Eleanor. She became Queen of France at age fifteen, when her father died suddenly on pilgrimage. Her younger sister, Petronilla, her constant companion in those early days, went with her to Paris. Eleanor dominated her young husband, Louis VII; engaged in notorious flirtations under his nose; and gave him reckless political advice. When he went on Crusade, she rode side by side with him all the way to the Holy Land, where they disagreed so violently that they returned on separate ships.

The Pope engineered a brief reconciliation, but in the summer of 1151, when she was thirty, Eleanor met the young Duke of Normandy, Henry of Anjou, apparently for the first time. Over the next several months, she wrangled an annulment of her marriage out of Louis. This was announced on Palm Sunday at Beaugency on the

Loire in 1152. Some ambitious young French noblemen conspired to capture her and her duchy on her way home, but she escaped back to her great city of Poitiers in Aquitaine, a rich, ancient land of poetry, song, and combustible nobles. There she sent a proposal to Henry. A few weeks later they were married, and in the next fourteen years they produced the most celebrated brood of children in the Middle Ages.

Eleanor was Queen of England from 1154 to 1189 and lived another fifteen years after that as Dowager, Regent, and Duchess. Two of her sons became kings of England, and her daughters and grandchildren ruled half the kingdoms of Christendom into the next century. She was a great patron of the arts as well as a capable ruler, holding court and dictating policy, bringing a dozen new styles and ways of thinking to work and play in the High Middle Ages. Above all, she raised the prestige of women to a new height.

Her marriage to Henry II was even more tumultuous than her marriage to Louis VII. Henry was only nineteen when they married, a hard hand and ambitious, already known for his volatile temper, unflagging energy, and impulsive amorous adventures. Shortly after they married, Henry fought, wheedled, and connived his way to the throne of England, so that between him and Eleanor they ruled a great swath of western Christendom that dwarfed the kingdom of France. Within only a few years they were battling each other for control. Henry had mistresses, and he hoarded all power to himself like a dragon on a pile of gold. They argued about their children and about their officers and their policies. Eleanor hated Thomas à Becket when he was Henry's intimate and then hated how Henry got him killed. After the birth of John, her last child, she left the King and went to live alone at her splendid court in Poitiers. As soon as her boys were old enough, she began encouraging them to attack their father. Henry retaliated by locking her up for fifteen years.

Nonetheless, when she got out, his life was over and hers was still in high gear. While her son Richard was on Crusade, she ruled as regent, and in Aquitaine she was always lord suo jure, even if she was a woman. At age eighty she rode across the Pyrenees to collect a bride for the heir to the French throne, choosing a woman who would become almost as powerful as she was, Blanche of Castile, mother of Saint Louis.

She set a new standard for what a woman could do then and now and followed her own will all her long life, dying in 1204 at age eighty-two. She is buried at Fontevraud, the great abbey on the Loire that her family patronized, and where her effigy still lies on top of her casket, although her bones are long scattered.

Petronilla of Aquitaine, who never remarried after the caddish Count of Vermandois divorced her, faded from view soon after her sister's annulment and possibly died the next year. She also was buried at Fontevraud. Joffre de Rançun went on to a long career as the most indefatigable of the many Poitevin rebels against Henry II and later his son Richard the Lionheart. Louis VII of France married twice more, and late in life at last produced a son, Philip Augustus, who reigned after him, wily and successful. The French Princess Marie, Eleanor's daughter by Louis, became Countess of Champagne, presiding over a renaissance of music and literature at Troyes, patronizing Chrétien de Troyes, among others, one of a generation of women who owed their prestige and their grasp of power to Eleanor of Aquitaine.

Finally, there is an old text, now vanished, that claimed Eleanor and Henry did have a son named Philip, who disappeared in infancy. When in the steady stream of Eleanor's children he was born, what happened to him, and how he came by the odd, un-Angevin name, no one now knows.

READERS GUIDE

*The Secret
Eleanor*

DISCUSSION QUESTIONS

1. Early in the novel, Eleanor doesn't pray at church about her complicated situation with Henry because "God was a man, anyway, and would not understand" (page 29). In the context of the book, Eleanor seemed to defy this mentality and behaved contrary to the typical male-centric way of thinking in the twelfth century. Discuss whether or not Eleanor would have spoken this same phrase by the end of the book.

2. Although Eleanor lived a life of luxury and power, she seemed to want more freedom and less complication, as when she first acted as Petronilla, riding her mare and "in her heart she laughed and danced for her freedom like a bacchant" (page 38). Do you think Eleanor did ever yearn for a simpler life, especially later on in the course of the novel?

3. Do you think most women in the twelfth century desired more opportunity and freedom to choose their own lives?

4. When Eleanor and Louis are discussing her lack of bearing a son, Eleanor states, "'I know this is God's judgment. . . . I shall never come to you again as a wife'" (page 91). Do you think this is simply an easy excuse to get out of her marriage, or does she really believe this?

5. Do you think Eleanor was a dishonest woman? Discuss why or why not. During this time period, would any woman of her stature have acted similarly, or was it her idiosyncratic personality?

6. Eleanor's ladies-in-waiting are involved in every aspect of her life. Do you think this bond helped or hurt women during this time period? Do you think women of lesser stature had similar bonds with other women? Cite examples when social standing is ignored and real friendship is shown amongst the women.

7. When Henry's father dies suddenly, the three remaining sons battle each other for his throne. Discuss the lack of loyalty among these brothers, and how it affected the shifts of power during the Middle Ages.

8. At one point, Eleanor claims Henry "had what was better than love; as he had proven again, now he had the gift of power" (page 146). Is this really what's most important to her with regard to him? Did your opinion shift by the end of the book?

9. Claire disbelieved Petronilla after meeting Thomas the lute player for the first time, when Petronilla tells her men only care about one thing. Why do you think Claire doesn't believe her at first? Was Claire right to resist him initially?

10. When Petronilla finally takes over as the Queen on their progress, it's enlightening to her. Discuss how the opportunity to play Queen changed Petronilla for better or worse.

11. Petronilla grapples with the sin of lying but Eleanor seems to have no qualm in this respect. Do you think it's because Eleanor is trying to get ahead in a man's world? Petronilla also believes that the intention to help her sister was no sin, even if the deed itself was. Discuss whether or not you agree with her, and how this might pose a different problem in modern society.

12. After Eleanor almost loses the baby, Petronilla says, "It is a sign. God favors us.'" But Eleanor retorts with, "'Whatever that means'" (page 233). Discuss the sisters' differing viewpoints at this moment and what it might mean for their faith and the future of Aquitaine.

13. No one in a position of power is to be trusted in the book—they are all plotting one way or another. Cite examples from the book of jealousy getting the best of the characters, especially Henry, Eleanor, and Claire.

14. Do you believe that Henry's love was for Eleanor or the crown, and vice versa?

15. After Petronilla learns of Eleanor's plot to kill her, she feels she has "no true home" (page 283). Discuss this within the context of the book—is "home" a castle, a family, a homeland? With shifting loyalties and borders, is this concept ever really possible?